Praise for
The Reli

This is a novel about a bridge burning, a trial, and a hanging. But it is also situated in Civil War Tennessee, which means that none of those events will occur according to any expectations of normal. The characters—from the Unionist Harrison Self to the dramatic Parson Brownlow—are all historical enough. But Susan Lohafer has given them a special edge, as they seek to make sense of a world that is breaking into pieces around them, where friends are foes and one wrong glance may be worth your life. It is a fast book, it is an unnerving book, it is a polished, shining book—all right then, it is a great book.

—Allen C. Guelzo, author,
Fateful Lightning: A New History of the Civil War and
Reconstruction and Gettysburg: The Last Invasion

An exquisitely written love letter to America. Based on a true story, Lohafer gives us a moving account of the life of Harrison Self, a Tennessee farmer who, in an effort to save his child's life, is unwittingly dragged into the American Civil War. This is the amazing story of a reluctant patriot in desperate times as he endures the horrors of prison life, and, in one gruesome episode, the brutal death by hanging of an innocent boy.

Set during the Civil War in East Tennessee, this story is about the countless sacrifices made by ordinary people attempting to create a fairer society. In a novel full of compassion and humanity, we witness the occasion when black people, in fear of their lives, arrive to cast their votes for the first time, and the extraordinary show of solidarity from their white compatriots who act as human shields for their fellow men as they escort them safely to the polling station.

In elegant and clear-sighted prose that brilliantly captures the speech of its time, this is a novel that is epic in its scope and local in its experience, making it a story of universal proportion. Accompanied by endnotes that expertly explain background and context, this is a book everyone should read, not only for its outstanding portrayal of life during America's Civil War, but to better understand the complex issue of race in America today. More than anything, it is an essential reminder of something that is often not talked about—how decent Americans have always struggled to do the right thing and often at great personal cost.

—Martin Roper, author of *Gone*

Susan Lohafer's historical novel about the notorious bridge-burning incident of 1861 in East Tennessee is an engaging and poignantly written story about the disruptive effects of war on a close-knit community. Scholarly accounts depict the episode as a relatively minor one in the larger panorama of the Civil War. Lohafer, however, expounds the event's importance, presenting the bridge burnings as a pivotal moment for those directly involved, when the comforting routine of traditional farm life was abruptly and cruelly turned upside down. She centers her narrative on the real-life family of Harrison Self, a proud, pro-Union farmer who was implicated by Confederate authorities in the bridge burnings. In doing so, Lohafer crafts an eminently plausible tale of angst and heartbreak. Self, along with a host of other colorfully drawn characters, discovers that personal decisions made under wartime duress bring unintended consequences, which in turn call into question long cherished values. Harrison Self personifies this unfolding chaos as he loses control over his farm, his family, his very life. Readers will enjoy how Lohafer writes with an empathy that reveals both her understanding of the period and her respect for human complexity. Moreover, her novel shows that even seemingly insignificant events and people are every bit as integral to the Civil War saga as such great battles as Gettysburg or such great leaders as Lincoln. *The Reluctant Patriot* offers rich, literary insight into the minds of those Civil War-era Americans whose lives are otherwise left out of the pages of academic history.

—Ben H. Severance, Professor of History,
Auburn University at Montgomery

The Reluctant Patriot

A novel based on a true story of the Civil War in Tennessee

SUSAN LOHAFER

Aubade Publishing
Ashburn, VA

Edited by Joe Puckett

Cover design and book layout by Cosette Puckett

Cover illustration and portraits by Susan Lohafer

Illustrations by Cosette Puckett

Library of Congress Control Number: 2020939147

ISBN: 978-1-951547-10-3

Published by Aubade Publishing, Ashburn, VA

Printed in the United States of America

For
Michael,
first and always,

*and for the
East Tennessee
Unionists of 1861*

Contents

PROLOGUE

A S HE WAS PUSHED THROUGH THE DOOR, Harry struck his chin against the skull of the man in front of him, who was about a head shorter. "Forgive me," he murmured, but the words were jarred from his lips as he was butted from behind. Once he was inside the room, a big cavern of a place it seemed, he was still bumping shoulders with the men around him. And then the smell hit him.

Harry was a farmer. His nose was accustomed to the ammonia of cow dung and horse manure. But this was different. Soon enough, he'd know why, but there were other things to learn first. Like everyone, he was scanning the faces he could see, hoping, yet not hoping, to find a friend, or at least an acquaintance. He was mortally sure that some of his Greeneville neighbors were prisoners like him, and perhaps Alex and Jake were here, too, and maybe Henry and Tom. There were, he guessed, upwards of one hundred twenty, thirty, maybe fifty people sharing the fetid air, but for almost an hour, his world was ten or twelve persons wide.

There were no chairs, no benches, and so they fell into approximations of comfort. The lucky ones leaned against a roughly plastered wall. Others squatted, frog-like. Who thought of it, he didn't know, but suddenly, there were pairs of men who pasted their spines together and sank down to the floor, sitting back to back, with their arms around their knees. Harry wasn't that tired. He didn't relish the vulnerability of those bookend pairs, stapled to the floor, bruised unintentionally by the feet of others. Coated with filth. He'd stand.

1

For a while yet.

The next lesson had to do with sustenance. Word spread that there was a bucket near the window closest to the door, with a tin dipper. If you squeezed your way there, and if you were lucky, there was liquid inside. Harry had arrived late in the day, riding with bound hands the more than sixty miles from Greeneville to Knoxville. "If you hadn't burned the bridge, you'd be riding on the railroad," the guard had jibed, apparently forgetting that if the bridge hadn't been burned, Harry would be home now. But it had, with no help or advice from him, and here he was, and he was hungry.

The light was already fading when the door opened, a barrel was shoved through, followed by two guards, one carrying a knobby sack. Like leaves finding the current of a stream, the men began to move, blindly at first, until a queue emerged at the center of a milling crowd. Harry was reluctant at first to use his elbows, but soon he had no choice. To keep his feet under him, he pushed and jostled until the flow delivered him to the door through which, only an hour, a lifetime, ago, he'd entered this hellhole. He learned that plates were shards of broken pottery or rough hemispheres of wood. He was taught that food was a lump of something dark, heaved up from the barrel and dumped into his bowl. Behind him, somebody said, "And where is mine host today?" The joke, gleaned from other comments, was that the man who ran the jail was an innkeeper. Once a day, he carted over to the prison the slop barrel from behind his flea-ridden hotel.

Grass. Tender, fresh blades of grass. That was the difference. In the intestines of animals, grass becomes something just as natural, something with a warm and earthy tang that blends with the smell of hay. What passed for food here, plopped in cracked bowls, smeared on slats of wood, had the greenish iridescence of decay, the slime of liquefaction. Even in the dim light, Harry could see the black specks moving in the broken chunks of bread the second guard, with a flourish, whipped from his sack and deposited on top of the . . . other things. In the bowels of dirty, coughing, weeping men, fear worked on these scraps, turning them into something hard as pellets or runny as snot, as putrid as gangrene.

When night arrived, it brought a simple problem in arithmetic. On a floor of x number of square feet, how many men—ranging in height from five to six feet, and in breadth from twenty to thirty inches—can lie, head to foot, side by side, in the bed of their clothes? Answer: only about half of them. The room wasn't big enough for everyone to recline, so some of the men stood while the rest of them slept. In the small hours, with groans and curses, the prone were hauled to their feet and the upright took their place. Harry had been one of the ones standing, too shocked by his environment to close his eyes. Now he watched in dismay, heard thudding bodies, and sank to the floor, too. He stretched out his legs carefully. Behind his head, he rolled his collar for support. The hardness of the wood assaulted him, but he flowed into it. The snoring began again. If you are weary enough . . . you can sleep . . . anywhere. . . .

That was the last lesson of the first day.

Harrison Self

Chapter 1

The Conspiracy

A S HE STEPPED CAREFULLY AMONG THE SADDLED HORSES, Harry could hear them moving their hobbled weight in the gloom. Their warm breath clouded the November chill. Here and there, he stroked a muscled neck, lifting the nap of coarse hair. In the dark, he was wary of their stamping hooves. "Pay me no mind," he whispered. Time was short, and yet he slowed in their midst, feeling their inner heat, their careless strength, their indifference to the road they traveled. They were as tolerant of him as if he'd once had four legs.

Peering up into the heavens, he lost his gaze in the liquid dark, hoping to catch God's eye. All he saw was the paleness above the tree line. All he knew was what he'd learned in half a century. *Must be about nine*, he judged, as if he'd heard nature's clock chime. Then the pain flooded back, gushing through his veins and pooling in his stomach. How much simpler it would be if his toes were mashed to pulp. His heart on a spit wouldn't satisfy Corniah if he failed to bring their son back.

Harry crossed the patch of swept earth and mounted the single stair. He leaned into the solid wood he'd helped Jake saw and plane and settle into place on hinges strong enough to stop a bull. The planks gave an inch, then resisted, heaving with the crowd on the other side.

Harrison Self firmed his jaw. This was his brother-in-law's house, where, on any other day, he could enter without knocking. From his own front door, it was only a mile's walk, though tonight he'd forced

5

Castor to a gallop that surprised them both. Nor had he expected what followed. To be standing on this doorstep, fighting to gain a toehold, was like milking a wooden cow. If you had sense, you lost interest.

But he couldn't give up. They had his son in there, he was sure of it, and there was no going home without Hugh. When an opening appeared, he lodged his foot in the crack. They would not keep him out, no, they would not, though earlier in the day he'd refused to be one of them, said it was none of his affair. "Only a fool lights a match in his own barn," he'd said, thinking he had clinched the argument. Yet his son had trailed after them, so here was Harry, come to pull the child back, lest he burn himself.

No one's fault, then, but Hugh's, that his father looked ridiculous as he fought with the stubborn door, though no one saw him but the waiting horses. It was a sizable herd, and he reckoned most of the able-bodied men of Greeneville must be visiting the Harmons.

One thing he knew: their dirty boots would be breaking his sister's heart, fouling the boards she scrubbed every day, in case the Deity dropped by. Sometimes he smiled at her housewifely care, but tonight he shared her outrage. They'd be making a mess in there, words pouring out regardless of consequences. He'd have kept his distance, but here he was, pounding on the door. How his fingers ached for Hugh's collar. Let him but get a hand on the boy. First he'd hold the truant close—a foretaste of the moment pierced him—then he'd grab Hugh by the belt, hoist him in a circled arm, and haul him back to sanity.

Once again, he aimed his right shoulder, muscled from a lifetime behind the plow, at the door to Jake's house. It gave way, throwing him off balance, but he sidled through the opening. Bare heads fenced him in. That's all he could see, pressed as he was behind a wall of broad backs. What reached him were the smells. Damp wool that stank of sheep, the bitter tang of tobacco, the sour flatulence of churning guts. Harry craned his neck to reconnoiter. These were his neighbors and fellow townsmen, and they'd come in from the fields or ridden over from the village, carrying with them the sweat of their day's work, their chins darkening with stubble. Malinda's home had been breached. Friend or foe, she wouldn't care, she'd want them gone. She had a feud with hobnail boots, his own included, and he vowed to honor it someday.

Chapter 1: The Conspiracy

The crowd was shifting, and Harry rose on tiptoe. In a pool of light cast by a single candle, the men were forming a rough circle around the Harmon family dinner table. When he could see them, the faces were known to him—Haun there, looking dazed, and Matt and Henry, their mouths gaping holes. And wasn't that Seth Gordon over there, the schoolteacher who taught boys how to argue with their fathers? In the flickering light, they were creatures in a dream, with noses too long or eyes gone to slits, no longer themselves, but who else could they be? He'd known them all his life.

Driven though he was to find his son, Harry felt his head turn, without having willed it. That, then, must be Captain Fry, the tall black silhouette with broad shoulders, right arm raised toward the ceiling, and—as Harry glimpsed through a sudden gap—left hand clutching to his chest the starry end of a giant flag. Rusted red, dirty white, the dim stripes flowed over the table's edge. Men were swarming in now, eager to grab their handful of cloth, their fistful of patriotism. But where was Hugh?

Harry searched for the broad forehead under a fringe of brown hair. The boy's eyes would be round as cartwheels. Shorter than his elders, he'd be somewhere in the rear, jumping up and down to get a look.

Even the half-grown boys, and Harry had noticed many, could see Fry's arm reaching higher now. The shouting died down, like the hush before a storm. Harry felt the silence on his skin, like a passing shadow. In its wake came the ragged breaths and shifting feet of men used to hearing speeches. Fry's voice, when it came, was low but clear. He'd been appointed, he said, "by our own Reverend Carter, whose idea this was," who had been up to Camp Dicky in Kentuck and had the word from Sherman and McClellan, and, yes, Old Abe himself.

Eyes met eyes and grins flashed at the name. Inwardly, Harry groaned. Against the allure of adventure, he might prevail, and, yes, perhaps, even against the glamour of a real-life Union soldier, like that black-bearded rabble-rouser up there. But against the image of Father Abraham, what hope for a mere parent?

The rumors were true, assured Fry. Up and down the valleys, on this very night, men, good men, men just like them were meeting, in secret, preparing for the mission. Here in Greeneville, it was he himself—"you know me, boys," he reminded them—who'd been chosen to bring the word. If they were willing (are you willing, boys?), he would lead them over to Lick Creek Bridge, and, by God, they'd make a bonfire those Rebs would see all the way to Knoxville, no, by God, all the way to Nashville. They'd raise a shout that would be heard by the Federal Army that's just waiting, boys, for our signal. General Thomas is hunkered down up there, just over the border. He'll finish what we start, boys, but we have to light the match.

Every word had dropped to the pit of Harry's stomach. Had he been close enough to be seen and heard, he'd have raised a hand and bent each finger in turn. *One:* the bridge is guarded, by men whose faces ye know—men whose children ye know. *Two:* how long will it take for the bridge to be rebuilt? Have ye thought of that? *Three:* an army in Kentucky is an army beyond the mountains. *Four:* winter is coming. *Five:* what if the generals change their minds and leave you hanging by your necks?

But he did not shout above the noise. He did not fight his way into the lighted circle. He didn't even try. Reason had no purchase in this room. He'd not moved, but not—no, he really thought not—because his neighbors would think him cowardly. The why of it was simply this: he was not his brother's keeper, or, in this case, his brother-in-law's. Nor was he responsible for his neighbors. They were freemen, just like him. They'd have to live with their decisions, or, he trembled to think of it, die for them. No, he was here to retrieve his sixteen-year-old son. That was all.

Still, he had not seen the boy. Fry was in full voice. He was explaining the plan, devised by their own Reverend Carter. At the same time as the men in this room marched on Lick Creek, others, up and down the line, would attack other bridges along the rivers and streams of East Tennessee, from Bristol to Chattanooga. Nine of them! With the railroad crippled and the telegraph wires cut, well, we'll just see how Jeff Davis can manage without those cotton-heads from the South and those supplies that come by rail. "We'll show 'em whose land this is, won't we, boys!" The deafening response made the walls shake. Harry, picturing his small but tidy farm, whispered to himself, *I know whose land it is.* Not Davis's, no, but not Thomas's, either. Not even Uncle Abe's. *Mine.*

Fry then cried out. "Wait!" It was a moment before he could be heard again. He said there was more required of them than just a brave

spirit, though he was glad to see he hadn't been wrong. He'd said to the generals, "You can rely on the men I grew up with." Because, yes, he'd been whelped under Bays Mountain like the rest of them. Cheers again. Harry was sure he'd heard that claim from every circuit-riding office-seeker who'd ever canvassed in Greeneville.

"Men," said Fry more solemnly. The "boys" had aged quickly. Harry would have smiled, had not the hairs on his body pricked up. "Understand what this means. This is an act of war against the Confederacy, and ye may be taken or questioned afterwards." The silence that followed was like the ring in the air after iron has been struck.

"And so," Fry went on, his words as clear and strong as hammer-blows, "ye are, for this one night, no longer citizens of Greeneville, but soldiers in the Federal Army. Take ahold of the flag, men, those who are close enough. Inasmuch as the rest of ye are here, ye are holding a piece of it, too. Say it now, 'I swear to . . .' " And so the oath was administered.

In the blink of an eye, Jake's sixty-odd neighbors, most of whom had never, to Harry's knowledge, touched another man's property, were transformed into Company F, Second Tennessee Volunteer Infantry, sworn to march on a local bridge and tear it limb from limb. For just a second, it was like a tableau, a restaging of a scene from history, the sort of parlor entertainment designed by bookish women. Then the heroes came to life, bumping each other's sides and stepping on neighbors' toes.

While the oath was being taken, Harry's lips did not move, but his eyes darted everywhere. From a rope among the rafters hung a few white shirts Malinda must have washed and left to dry. Ghostly yet intimate, they stretched down their arms. He wondered if his sister remembered that her laundry was on view. He was too distracted to form a thought, but, for a fleeting second, he felt the light, alien, admonishing touch of the female world so roughly displaced this night. But no one else was looking upward, and he lost the brief sensation. Once again, he scanned from head to head, face to face, looking for the shape that would fill him with relief, catching his breath at a half-seen possibility, all but moaning as some other child, some other father's son, gazed back at him.

Fry was still speaking, telling the men to get going now, to string themselves out so as not to announce their coming, and to tie their horses a quarter mile from the bridge, by the old oak split by lightening, and to wait for him there. The crowd began to stir, funneling toward the door through which Harry had forced his entrance. The place to be, he decided, was just outside, where he could watch for Hugh to poke his head through the opening, and then catch the boy as he tumbled through.

As the men scraped over the threshold, as Harry dismissed every bearded jaw, every brawny arm, his heart sank and then soared. Was it possible Hugh *hadn't* disobeyed him? What if, ordered to stay at home, the boy had wandered off to sulk, and was already back in bed? If that were true, if Harry had spent the last hour making a fool of himself, while all the time Hugh . . . He worked his fist spasmodically.

The last one out of the house was Haun, pausing on the step to raise a slender hand to his chin, stroking it absently. From that gesture alone, Harry would have known him. "Alex," he'd once said to the master potter, long before the women clamored for his bowls and pitchers, "have ye a clay chin, that ye keep fingering it? Ye cannot change the face ye were born with." But Alex's face *had* changed at those words, closing up with embarrassment. The playful nudge had drawn blood. Ever since, and even now, there'd been a penitential care in Harry's tone when he addressed the man.

"Alex." Harry bent close, touching his friend's arm with a finger. "Did ye happen to notice . . . was Hugh inside? Did ye see him?"

"Hugh?" Haun's eyes focused on him, turning urgent, as if he had a question of his own to ask. Then he said, "Oh, Hugh. Yes, I think I saw him. And Jake's two boys. Tom. And Henry."

"But I didn't see him come out." Harry seized another hope. "Could he have stayed inside, d'ye think?"

"Let's look. Maybe he . . ." Haun, as if glad of the errand, turned around and reentered the house.

Harry followed. Apparently deserted now, with only the guttering candle for light, the room felt cavernous, but signs of the recent meeting were everywhere. Chairs were overturned, and the flag, in a mockery of its solemn role just a few moments ago, had folded itself into a heap on the floor. Now the most human thing in the room was the laundry. In the breeze from the open door, the pale linen shirts swayed like shrouds.

Chapter 1: The Conspiracy

A sound made Harry's heart leap—but it wasn't Hugh. The tall, angular figure of his sister gathered solidity, detaching itself from a curtained alcove. Despite his own need, he was stilled by her remoteness. Then he stepped toward her, warily, as if she might fly into a fury or shatter into pieces the moment she saw him. "Malinda?"

Getting no answer, he tilted his head and moved into her line of sight. "Malinda, ye have to tell me. Was our Hugh here? Did ye see him?"

She turned a face to him that gradually fell into grieving disbelief. "They're gone. Jake took the children. I was not asked."

"The children?"

"Tom and Henry," she listed her sons, "and Hugh and Sarah's boy, too—the one that lost a finger last year. . . . Will God take the young ones? He will not, will He, Harry." Her eyes burned, and she nodded emphatically. "He will take that Captain, the one that started it all, making a mess on my table."

"I'll send Corniah to help you"—he waved at the disarray— "tomorrow. She'll come tomorrow. They'll all be home by then." He laid the flat of his palm on her shoulder, patting twice. Then he hurried away, barely noticing that Haun trailed behind him, almost stepping on his heels, as if afraid to lose him in the dark.

EARLIER THAT DAY:

Glancing from habit toward the eastern window, Harry knew there was time yet till cock-crow. Beside him, Corniah puffed rhythmically and softly, as she would probably do on the morning of Judgment Day. His skin was aware of the animal warmth of her full limbs, the odors of stale linen and moist skin, the tang of her sex, as familiar to him as the shape of the bed, as the clothes he had stripped from his body the night before.

There was a deeper awareness, too. When a man wakes, he feels the world centered on his breastbone, and Harry was accustomed to that early-morning consciousness, radiating from this room, embracing the scattered children in their beds, extending to the barn he had inherited, the fields he had tilled at his father's side. All was well in his domain. Why, then, did he feel a pinprick of anxiety?

In a few moments, he'd hear Lizzie stirring into her clothes to do the milking. Instead, he swung his restless legs to the floor and dressed quickly, carrying his shoes out into the hall and descending the plank stairs in his wool stockings, prancing to avoid snagging his feet on splinters. He would do the milking for her, just to prove she was wrong. He was *not* too proud to do women's work—though an unmarried daughter of twenty-four must earn her keep. And, by the way, the bucket *was* still usable, cracks notwithstanding.

As he scuffed his way to the barn, his neck chilled by the November air, he hoped he was proving something about the vigor of middle age, about the freedom to choose, on a given day, to milk Sadie in his daughter's place. And yet, in his bones, he knew himself to be a creature of habit, enslaved to the seasons, to the udder and the plow. That he had willed it so himself, that he had lived by his decision through hail and drought, wasn't that autonomy enough—maybe even courage enough—for any man's lifetime?

Certainly, at breakfast, he got no thanks from his daughter, who might as well be sitting in another county. His son, too, ignored him, but that was because he was trying to spoon porridge into his mouth while reading a folded newspaper. The effort failed, and Hugh began scraping a wet lump off Mr. Brownlow's editorial. It was the same essay, undoubtedly, that he'd read aloud to them the night before, when he'd spilled molasses on the floor.

Hugh, it seemed, could not hold two things at one time. Harry had wondered how this son would ever build a hayrick or birth a calf, but Corniah had come to the boy's defense. "Cannot you remember when you were that age? Your head was in one place, your hands in another. Try to be a little patient." So Harry sighed now and kept silent. He had no wish to hear more of Brownlow. Like most boys, Hugh probably read him for the name-calling. To the editor of the *Whig*, Rebs were "gassy Union-destroyers" or "irresponsible vagabonds" or—a favorite of Hugh's—"unprincipled dastards."

The man could stir a crowd, that was true, but if you had heard him preach—as Harry had in the days when Brownlow was a circuit-riding pastor—you knew that the invective against the Rebels was remarkably similar to the diatribes against Satan. Harry could appreciate the efficiency: here was a man who recycled his venom. He concluded, however, that both evils—the Devil and the Confederacy—had been magnified by Brownlow in his role as God's champion. Had

Chapter 1: The Conspiracy

Harry thought he would one day meet the editor in person, he might have been kinder—and fairer—in his judgment. For now, though, Brownlow was just a voice competing for Hugh's attention.

Lizzie had been watching Hugh scrape at the page. Suddenly, with her own pewter weapon, she scooped up the blob, then reached over her brother's arm toward his bowl. "Git *off*," he muttered, striking upward so sharply that the spoon and its contents went flying into the air and landed in her lap. Instantly, Lizzie was on her feet, swiping at her skirt convulsively. "*Look* what you've done!"

"She . . . !" Hugh began to protest, with all the righteous dismay of the criminal innocent of the present crime. Harry brought his fist down on the table, causing his own spoon to dance on the wood. "Elizabeth, be seated," he ordered. "But . . . ," she claimed. "*Sit . . . down.*" She did. He rubbed his hand. "Are ye infants, the two of ye! I'll have peace at my own table."

Corniah, her eyes drifting past them toward the window, said, "Malinda was here yesterday, helping Lizzie turn that very dress. She says . . . I remember hearing about it . . . that Mrs. Lincoln . . . she oughtn't to wear those capes . . . took her children to the Jersey coast in August. D'ye suppose it was warm enough? Her shoulders look wide as a barn, and he so thin. He would not let them go to the ocean, d'ye think? If things are really so . . . if this war is really so . . ."

Harry shrugged. He'd had enough of the topic, but Lizzie stirred argumentatively. "Folks like that go where they please. She's quality, Ma, or thinks she is. *He* would think so, but he is only a backwoodsman."

The "only" was a baited hook, but Harry swam around it. "I will hear no more of this," he said flatly. At his own table, under his own roof, he would have no insurrection, not again. In the silence that followed, each would be thinking of the previous evening, when the talk had turned to someone named Fry, and Hugh had dropped the pitcher of molasses on the floor, and Corniah had spilt as many tears for the jug with the C handle Haun had made for her, and . . .

Lizzie had defended that cockscomb Peter, and Hugh had asked what a Black Republican was, no doubt thinking it was a congressman in blackface. After Harry had explained that Lincoln was not really against slavery, just the spread of it, up piped Lizzie with "So says Papa Tory," causing Corniah to send her to the kitchen for the pie,

after which Hugh asked why Mr. Lincoln was called a rail-splitter.
If only he could erase the memory of his answer. "Because he
was born in Illinois, on a farm, just like you," he'd replied. "Oh, no,
Pa," Lizzie had sung. "He was born in Kentucky, just like Jeff Davis."
And what had he done, but throw tallow on the fire. "You're
mighty sure of yourself, an't ye?" he'd growled, wishing Lincoln
in hell. He'd meant his words as a concession, but his daughter had
perched aggressively in her chair, eyeing him levelly.
"We can ask Peter," she'd said. "*He* will know."
Harry groaned to himself. Peter! That swaggering, self-
centered . . . "That Popinjay!"
"You don't like him because he's Secesh!"
"He can vote for Jeff Davis or the Devil, for all I care," he'd shot
back. "I saw his Ma in the field last summer. She plants her own
'taters, with no help from her son." The indecency had angered him,
but served a purpose now, discrediting that . . . wordmonger.
"Anybody can grow 'taters," had been the lofty reply. "He's
studying the law, to help the new country."
"Ha! There is no 'new' country, my girl. There is only the one we
have, and if we don't know how to keep it, we ought to have stayed
in England." There! Well, yes, that had been pompous. Irrelevant, too.
So be it, if he'd silenced her.
"*Why?* Why can't there be another Revolution? Just because you
say so?" Lizzie, flushed, had thrown his own stubbornness back at him,
and his own hurt, too. Fury had risen in him, and he had longed, God
forgive him, to smite that impudence from her face, but when he'd
found his hand aloft, he'd passed it through his hair before lowering
it. What he'd really wanted was someone else to be sitting in her
chair. He had wanted the daughter who believed him without question,
whose eyes followed him everywhere.
"Yes!" he'd flared in response. "Because I say so!"
Today, as he looked at her in the morning light, he knew that
what he'd felt the evening before hadn't been just annoyance. He
still couldn't put words to it, but it was as if she'd been withdrawing
something, taking something away that he'd thought was his for
eternity. Unable to retrieve it, he'd blindly demanded it. *Because I
say so.* That she needed a better reason should have pleased him, for
he delighted in her intelligence; instead, he'd been wounded in a place

he couldn't find.

The sense of betrayal returned now, a sour aftertaste from the night before. "Papa Tory," indeed! The very same bully who had milked Sadie for her that morning, or hadn't she noticed? Her ingratitude eased his stirrings of guilt. If he'd been unreasonable, if he'd been harsh, it was because she had goaded him. When she behaved herself, he would gladly explain why there could be no second Revolution. Not because he said so, no, but *because the men who made the nation a century ago provided for the orderly shifting of power among competing interests.* You did not need a new country, if the one you had was endlessly renewable, like a well-managed field with rotating crops.

Corniah was sending him looks of pained suggestion, willing him to soften. She'd always had a kind word for Peter. The whelp called her "Miss Corniah" instead of "Mistress Self." Well, if her breakfast was spoilt, let her teach Lizzie better manners. The room smelled of cooling grease and curdled thoughts.

Standing up quickly, Harry said, "I'm in the east field today." Hugh was on his feet immediately, giving his sister a sidelong look before saying, with filial eagerness, "I'll help ye with the corn, Pa."

His son's motives were transparent, but Harry didn't mind. "Well, come on, then, lad," he smiled, throwing his arm around the boy's shoulders as they left the women at the table.

During all of the preparations—hitching up Castor, the fifteen-year-old gelding, working the stiff gloves to make them limber, maneuvering the wagon into the field—Harry ignored Hugh's frequent, stock-taking glances. He knew the boy was gauging when to speak, and he offered no encouragement. Instead, when they had reached the combed rows of brown corn, he set Hugh to following along in the wagon, and he bent himself to the task of gripping the stalks and twisting off the corn, not even breaking stride or turning his head to see where the wagon was as he threw the dried ears in its direction.

He remembered them in their green summer coat, proud and erect on the stalks, their splayed tassels aloft, and their silky topknots golden in the sun, soft as a woman's nether hair. Now the corn was brown, drooping among the rustling leaves. Quickly, he found his rhythm, moving down the row with arms and hands and feet moving in mindless coordination, as the ears flew from his fingers into the bed of the wagon, with not a single kernel lost. He took into his lungs the light and fragrant air, wondering if God, too, enjoyed it. Though he'd never admit it, Harry sometimes thought of God as a farmer—a bit scatterbrained about wives and weather, but smart enough to invent a pig.

Alex Lowe and John McDaniels would also be at work, or at least he hoped his tenant, Lowe, was doing his share in the field closer to the road. For now, though, Harry was glad to be out of hailing range. He wanted no jocularity today, no gossip, no arguments.

In truth, more often than not, he preferred his own company. There were days when he could work for hours in a waking sleep. Grasp, twist, toss. Occasionally, he'd replay, over and over, some dispute with a tradesman, second-guessing himself, until all of a sudden he'd flip the memory away like a moldy piece of bread. Other scenes he held close, never tired of reliving them. When Lizzie had been a child, Corniah had told her about Cain and Abel, Joshua and his coat, but he had told her stories from another ancient book that had come from the old country, tales of kings and daughters, and there was one time when, seeing fear in the widened eyes as she turned in his lap, he'd seized the reins from the dramatist and changed the ending, watching the glow of joy, caused by him, offered to him, as she'd settled against his chest, murmuring, "I *knew* Cordelia wouldn't die!"

He'd been master of the story then. When, exactly, had he lost the power to create his daughter's world? This was the pain of every father, he knew that, and yet the eternal sorrow merged with new bitterness and galled him afresh.

"Pa?"

"What is it."

"Is Captain Fry really from Greeneville?"

Harry frowned. Was Hugh baiting him? As of yesterday, birthplaces were a sore topic, but no, there was something else in the boy's voice. Calculation.

"Yes, he was born here." Grasping an ear of corn, he twisted hard. "He went away into the Army. Fought in Mexico, so I hear. But we are civilians here . . . keep up with the wagon . . . not soldiers. He will bring trouble to his friends and relatives, and to anyone who listens to him." Toss. He'd heard the rumors. There was a plot afoot, and Fry was buttonholing men on the street corners, drawing them into alleys.

Harry's arms suddenly stopped moving.

Hastily, the boy went on. "I heard him talking to Uncle Jake the other day by the train station. I wasn't eavesdropping. I was there to get the paper. Ma said I could."

"Your uncle, eh? Was Henry there? Was Tom?" He inquired casually. Hugh had always followed where his cousins led.

"N-no."

"They obeyed their father, then," said Harry, meaningfully.

"But Uncle Jake told them all about it."

In silence, Harry cursed the amiable man who would chat with the hangman about the length of the rope.

"We're for the Union, too, Pa, aren't we? You always say it's what they fought for at King's Mountain."

Having arrived at a full stop now, Harry bent forward, then rose tall and leaned back, arching his spine to relieve a twinge. "Here's what they fought for"—he waved his gloved hand in a sweeping gesture that included the stalk in front of him, the field, the tree line at its edge, and beyond that, the blue ridge of mountains. "Because the land belonged to them, and they would not be told how to live on it. I will not be told how to live on mine, not even by your Mr. Fry."

Even as he brandished these sentiments, he knew they were as quaint as an old blunderbuss. These days, you didn't say "my land." You spoke of "property." Of acres and slaves. You talked of "interests." Of cotton or iron. He had neither plantation nor investment, just his small stake in everything—cows, pigs, chickens, corn, wheat, flax, beans—everything you needed for getting through the year without bowing to anyone.

"*Captain* Fry."

"What?"

"He's a captain, Pa. In the Volunteer Infantry." Harry did not have to look to see the glow in his son's eyes.

"Hmmph." Harry dusted his hands against his thighs. "Y'think he's here to save the Union, do ye?"

"But he is, Pa!"

Harry coughed out a short laugh. Lizzie with that Rebel, Pete—and now Hugh with his Lincolnite. When it came to spoiling his morning, there wasn't much difference between a silver-tongued Confederate and a rabble-rousing Unionist. A plague upon them both!

The sun was already halfway up the sky, and Castor was lipping a shredded ear of corn. "We'll speak of it later," he said, resuming his path down the row.

That there even was a war had surprised him. Before the fall of Sumter, he'd have said his countrymen had more sense. Even when Governor Harris had defied Lincoln, refusing to send troops to quash the stirrings of rebellion, Harry had just sighed at the braying of politicians. Yes, he'd cast his ballot in the June 8, 1861 referendum to decide between presidents—Lincoln or Jeff Davis. And, like most of the men he knew, he'd sided with the Union. It was in the genealogy of the region. What he hadn't fully realized was the character of the middle and western counties, which thought of themselves as Southern. Tennessee as a whole had voted to join the Confederacy.

What an uproar there had been nine days later, when the Knoxville Unionists, those who had convened so hopefully before the referendum, came together again, this time in Greeneville, to rebel against the Rebels. Harry had listened to the speeches, wondering at the vehemence of men like Temple and Brownlow. Some had proposed that East Tennessee form a state of its own, as—rumor had it—West Virginia hoped to do. The idea was an old one, though, and familiar to local residents, whose ancestors had created a short-lived "State of Franklin." Periodically, the mountain people turned their backs on their fellow Tennesseans.

Harry would have been delighted to secede from Nashville, as he would have taken pleasure in flying through the air, but neither was going to happen. Gusty passions would have their day, and it was best to lie low. Here in Greene County, storms either failed to cross the ridges, or gullied down the valleys until they blew themselves out. You waited and repaired the damage, no matter who was president. He'd thought to do the same after the coming gale subsided.

And, for a while, his hope had been justified. In the swelter of August, General Felix Zollicoffer, the first man in charge of the newly formed Confederate Department of the Eastern District, had kept a cool head. Reasonable, even generous, he was. Unionists could go about their business in peace, he'd said—so long as they carried no arms and kept their opinions to themselves. Harry's response had been to nod in relief. *Didn't I tell you?* his look had said. *This storm will pass.*

Chapter 1: The Conspiracy

And, according to Harry, Greeneville was a good place to wait it out. He was, through and through, a local man. Even when he thought of the nation's history, it wasn't General Washington who came to mind, though he'd have bowed to that one man alone in all of Christendom. For Harry, country had begun earlier, and not too far away, on the banks of the Watauga River. The earliest settlers, taking a moment off from clearing land and raising cabins, had nailed together a social order in the wilderness. The rules had been made by the men who enforced them, as unyielding in their course as the progress of the seasons.

Harry's children knew the old stories. Hugh had grimaced happily at tales (no doubt apocryphal) of debtors flayed alive. But when Harry had tried to explain to a very young Lizzie that Robertson had *paid* for the land he'd borrowed from the Cherokee, she'd asked—to his amused discomfort—"Didn't the Indians want it back?" What those white men had done was to ensure their own survival, wasn't it? It was a form of husbandry Harry could understand. Of course he could. He sometimes shuddered at his ancestors, but he accepted what they'd left to him, and was grateful for it.

Badgered at times by his family, but sure of his duty to provide for them, Harry kept up his trade with both Rebels and Unionists, in the language they shared, of bushels and stone weights. The neighbors were still his friends. His farm was still his home, where there were battles enough with drought and infestation, and small enough victories, but year after year, the green shoots arose.

Despite the coolness of the November air, sweat stung his eyes as he wiped his face around noon. They'd reached the end of a row and were seated on a pile of leaves beneath a maple that still clung to a few shreds of gold. Castor, unhitched, was nuzzling the dry grass, knowing his meal would come later.

Hugh was listless, munching a heel of bread as if it grew larger, not smaller, in his mouth. No doubt he regretted his show of dutifulness. Moved suddenly by the overwhelming ordinariness and familiarity of the barely fuzzed cheeks moving in their mindless rhythm, Harry tapped his son's arm.

"You must listen to me," he said, trying to hide his urgency. "What we are *for*," he began, searching for words he rarely used aloud, "what we want to save, is the country that started right here, in these mountains, and grew into the Union. That's the country we understand, the country that understands *us*."

He looked harder at his son, willing his words to create a protective shield around the young head. "But the Confederates, you see, they naturally want a country that *they* understand, that believes in *them*. Maybe they will start over. I reckon this war will end one way or the other, Hugh, but nothing will change for us if we go on as we have before." Was he pleading with the boy?

Had he been talking to Lizzie, she would have gathered herself into a coiled spring, but Hugh just twitched slightly, as if waiting for a buzz to stop. As Harry ended with "as we have before," Hugh's face came alive, pressing words on his father, as he'd once brought odd stones or bright leaves to show proudly. "Master Gordon says the Union started in Philadelphia. He says that if the South can break away, then the territories can, and the mill states up north. He says then we would be like Europe. He says we would be many little countries without a bigger purpose. He says we would fail the test."

Pummeled by so many "says," Harry stammered, "The test?"

"Ma said she would need me this afternoon," replied Hugh, and it was clear to Harry that Corniah had replaced him as the usable parent, the excuse for escape.

"Get on with you, then," he said curtly, but regretted his tone instantly. Hugh mustn't think Master Gordon had won. With a wink, he quoted his son's favorite author—"you 'irresponsible vagabond!' " The boy, grinning, scrambled to his feet and scampered off, turning once to shout, "Back later, Pa." It was a promise Hugh would forget before he was halfway to the house.

By five o'clock, the shadows were lengthening. Harry rubbed his arms. The temperature was dropping, or perhaps the cold came from inside. "Time to go," he said to Castor. When he moved closer, the animal lowered his huge head, swinging it around and nudging him in the shoulder. Harry smoothed his hand over the warm hide. Under the rough autumn coat, he could almost hear the churning blood. Then he raised his left arm up the far side of Castor's neck and leaned his face against the muscular jowl that rippled slowly with every chew. He stood still, leaning into the familiar body, letting the animal's faithful heart keep the chill away a moment longer.

By six, Harry was back at the barn, tending to Castor and his barn-mate Pollux, wondering where Alex Lowe was. As Harry's tenant, Lowe was cheap labor—when, that is, he could be found. Harry would have to check the hens and the pigs himself. As he was hanging up the pail at the hogpen, a voice greeted him from behind.

"Harry?" It was Lowe.

When Harry did not turn, the other man took a step closer and lowered his voice. "Did Jacob Harmon find you?"

"I have not seen my brother-in-law today," answered Harry, speaking normally and, he hoped, with finality. Lowe fancied himself a Cavalier, in exile as a farmhand. "The off hog there has caught a stone, or mayhap a thistle blew in."

Lowe bent his curly head even closer, and facing him, Harry could see, even in the deepening dusk, that the young man was bursting with self-importance. He sighed. "Very well. Speak."

"Harmon has been riding to all the farms today. John and I were down near the road, and he saw us. We did finish the whole lower field. . . ."

"What did Jake want?" Harry hated himself for asking.

"He says, if you're a Union man, bring a horse and a gun to his house tonight. Captain Fry will be there. I do not know if you have a gun—"

"Do *you?*"

"What?"

"Have a gun?"

"My wife is ill, so this is not a choice I have, but I told Harmon I would bring you the message." Lowe's voice almost broke with excitement. "He says the railroad bridge at Lick Creek is to be burned tonight. Fry will lead the party, and others will strike at bridges all over East Tennessee. I cannot say I approve. What do you think? Will you go?"

"I think it is a bad thing," said Harry.

"You are right, of course," said Lowe hastily. "We are Southerners, after all, not firebrands."

Coming from a man like this, aimed at a man like Jake, the smugness was irritating. "Oh, I may go," he said. "I have not decided. Perhaps the meeting has another purpose."

Lowe raised his chin. "I have told you exactly what Harmon said."

"Well, if the bridges are burned, our homes will be next." Yes, there was a gun in the house, and Harry had used it—for killing foxes and scaring poachers—but only a fool strikes a match in his own hayloft. "No," he said. "I have no mind to destroy another man's property. You tell me the Federals are in Kentucky." Alex blinked *Not I!*, but Harry raised a finger. "And *I* tell you the Rebels are in Knoxville. What will be gained, d'ye think? I have better things to do at harvesttime. No. *It is a bad thing.*"

Dinner was silent that evening, with Hugh stirring his cabbage round and round on his plate, and Lizzie with her lips pursed up tight. Harry, looking pointedly at his son, had remarked only, "There may be some deviltry tonight while we are in our beds, and I am sorry to say that Jake may be involved, but it has nothing to do with us." That was, he hoped, the last word he would ever have to say about Fry's escapade.

An hour or so later, returning from his last visit to the barn, Harry shot the bolt on the kitchen door and gave the handle a parting tug. Crane-like, he stood first on one leg, then the other, to peel off the heavy boots. With a hand braced on the wall, he worked each foot into a leather slipper, soft with age. Then he planted his heels, straightened to his full height, and squared his shoulders. But her seat by the fire was empty.

His own chair called to him, offering its dented cushion, its nearness to hearth and pipe. Twisting his lips, he turned toward the unlit rooms and found her standing by the parlor window, gazing at her face in the darkened glass.

"Well?" he asked impatiently. "Out with it." When she ignored him, he imagined himself back in the other room. His feet were raised to the low stool; his knees were covered by the old swaddling blanket. Closing his eyes, he smelled the tobacco she was keeping him from tamping, just so, into the resin bowl. . . . Kindness, he reckoned, was the shortest route to his waiting pipe.

"Corniah, my dear—"

"You will drive him to *them!* He will do it to spite you and they will catch him and I *won't* forgive you."

In vehemence, in total disregard for common sense, this outburst was only slightly more anguished than many others in the past. She still blamed him for pulling Hugh out from behind her skirts and placing the tearful child on Castor's broad back, so he might learn to hold the reins. What Harry had said then, he might have said now: *He'll be the safer for being crossed by me.*

"Come," he said more gently, knowing argument was useless. "Come sit with me." He reached a hand toward her plump shoulder, but she twitched herself away. He thought of leaving her alone in the chilled room. The fire beckoned, and he was tired. The longer he stood watching her, the more foolish he began to feel, and the more irritated he became.

There'd been a time when he'd have closed the distance in a stride, caught her shoulders in both hands, and forced the logic of his reasoning on her eyes, her breast, her belly. Some ghost of that younger self awoke in him. It hovered by her neck and brushed a curl behind her ear. Hugh had fallen from Castor that day, and Harry's heart had bled with terror and remorse. A year's life—no, two or three—that's what he'd have given for her forgiveness. Did it matter that, among Hugh's few accomplishments, was now an ease around horses? It would have been something to be thankful for, a soothing touch on his cheek, granting him his pain.

Maybe, in her way, she meant to give it now when she rubbed her forearms briskly and stepped around him to the door. "Don't stand there in the dark," she said. Following her to the hearth, he took the poker from her hand and stirred the embers back to life.

It was after nine o'clock when his arm was shaken. He pulled back instinctively, half asleep. The pipe had fallen from his hand, leaving a trail of ash across his chest. Gradually the words he was hearing coalesced in his brain, startling him awake and ending his peace forever. "Harry. Har-r-r-y! Hugh's gone."

Chapter 2

Lick Creek Bridge

THE MOONLIGHT WAS DIM, BUT THE ROAD WAS FAMILIAR. With Haun riding close behind him, Harry turned a weary Castor in the direction of Lick Creek, hoping to catch up with Hugh before it was too late. Images of the boy shot by Rebel guards came and went in his mind, but the face he saw was Corniah's, not weeping, not pleading, but searing him with the knowledge of her reliance on him. More impossible to fail her than to walk through any fire.

The distance was only a couple of miles, but the ground was marshy, and it was necessary to keep to the edge of the fields. At last, up ahead, he saw the snaking line of trees that marked the streambed. He could hear the sounds of dismounting, of men drawing closer to the underbrush by the water.

When his own feet touched the ground, he tossed the reins to Haun without asking and wormed his way between the other men. "Hugh!" he called, in a hoarse whisper.

"He's not here, Harry." It was Jake's voice. Solid, amiable, reliable Jake, who played host to saboteurs.

"How d'ye know?" Harry croaked back. "T's black as tar in these trees."

Jake was whispering to someone, then he answered, "Ay, but Tom here says—"

Another voice broke in, excited, younger than its twenty-three years. "I saw him, Uncle Harry! He said you didn't know, but . . ."

Tom's loyalty, even to a cousin, faltered in the confusion of the moment. Henry, Tom's younger brother, was probably around somewhere, too. Harry remembered Malinda's crazed face. He agreed: Jake shouldn't have brought his boys along. But at least they were together. A father and son escapade. A story to tell after the war was over in a few months.

There was a faint, brittle crunching sound. At this time of year, the gray leaves curled like dead fingers and snapped underfoot. Captain Fry had returned. His voice, low and throaty with command, said, "Kin y'hear me in the back? There be seven guards, two at each end o' the bridge, the rest near the tent on our side o' the water. Same as last night. You boys know Isaac Hacker. He's in charge. After midnight he walks to the other side and back, and then there's just one guard awake at each end. We'll wait'll just before two."

"Won't they hear us coming? So many of us?" Who had asked? Harry could hear, and very dimly see, bodies moving among the trees, men drawing up through the grass, forty, fifty, more? Men with land and families, huddling in the weeds by the side of the creek.

"They won't know what we've come for till it's too late," explained Fry.

"Why not sneak down there. . . ." Harry had nearly said the same thing, but then he'd realized: sixty men couldn't sneak anywhere. That kind of sound would panic the guards more than horses on the road. Fry had reached the same conclusion. "No, we are too many for that. A few of us will ride down the road making God's own racket, while the rest of ye leave the horses in the trees and come the rest of the way quietly."

Someone joked about taking scalps, but the laughter drained into the murmur of water sucking on stones. Then Harry had another thought, and this time he spoke aloud. "You live in Greene County, and so do they. Even if you cover your faces—"

"We're not bandits, by God! We swore an oath to serve the Union." The whites of his eyes flashed.

Jake spoke up in his brother-in-law's defense. "He's not here for the bridge, Dave. He just came to find his son."

True, but willy-nilly, Harry belonged to Fry's raiders for now, and he must ply that assumption: "Should we tie up the guards and leave them to be found? If so, they'll report us to Colonel Wood, and we'll

GREENEVILLE, TENNESSEE
NOVEMBER 8–EARLY DECEMBER, 1861

hang before the Federals can get to us. We can't lock 'em up in a barn somewhere. Somebody's likely to be killed, one way or another. Reckon you've thought of that?"

There were grunts and twitches from the men squatting in the dark. They were here to burn a bridge, but not this other thing, no, not *that*. Murder a fellow Tennessean? The biggest creature most of them had ever killed was a cow. Fry was speaking again, trying to sound as if he'd never been interrupted. *If* he could be allowed to continue, his tone said, he would explain what he had intended to say all along. "We'll bind them and give them a choice. If they'll swear not to reveal our names, we'll honor their parole."

Harry sighed. Wasn't one of those fellows Isaac Hacker? When it came to promises, Hack was the most generous man in Greeneville. Always giving, never keeping. He was jostled as the others shifted away, feeling for their horses. Shadows came unglued, then converged, growing tall as they mounted. He strained his eyes. "Hugh? Answer me, boy!"

"*Shhhhhhhh.*"

"I saw him a minute ago, Harry."

Harry spun around, heart in throat. "Where?"

"Over by the crick. Or it could have been Tom." The rise and fall of hope was sawing across his nerves, but Harry steadied himself and prepared to follow the other men. He would not be like this gang, hurtling themselves blindly forward. He would think ahead, testing likelihoods. The best place to find Hugh would be in the clearing by the bridge.

Alex Haun had appeared beside him, leading their two horses. "We're soldiers now, an't we?" he'd whispered to Harry, in disbelief. Harry put his foot in the stirrup and heaved himself up. Castor, old as he was, tossed his mane, on fire to be going. Slackening the reins, Harry let himself move with the group.

Several minutes later, a commotion up ahead told Harry that the flanking men had arrived at the encampment. Shouts lapped each other in waves. Soon he could hear Fry again, giving orders. And then Harry, too, was in the clearing where the railroad met the bridge that loomed above them. A canvas tent was pitched on one side. The prisoners were already inside, and Fry had placed a guard at the entrance. The rest of the men were waving pistols or squirrel guns or fence poles. Some were grinning as if they'd found what they'd come for—a carnival.

Men he could no longer recognize threw burning brands onto the trestle, leaping and hallooing with every lick of the flames. Heat dried Harry's face, while his back remained clammy. Sweat cooled on his chest, itching beneath his shirt, and the acrid smell of burning creosote stung his nose. His eyes watered. Hugh was to blame, and for a second he felt aggrieved. Corniah, too, had willed him into trouble.

Then he was himself again. He should circle the crowd. Before he could move, there came a lull in the noise, like the pausing of the wind before the heavens break apart. A quiet sentence filled the void: "Where is Henry Harmon's gun?" Harry froze. A voice answered: "I've got it." Pray God nobody said Hugh's name aloud, or his own, for that matter.

In the torchlight, he could see what they meant to destroy. Beams crisscrossed each other in two rows to support the narrow bridge. Down its center, like an endless spine, ran the tracks of the East Tennessee and Virginia Railroad. The logs that rimmed the outer edge seemed to move and dissolve, and yet were still there, with a row of cloudy snakes curling up and around them.

A cheer split the air when the kindling on the ties began to glow. Having no luck with the stanchions underneath, men were poking their torches into the lattice above. Then, with a whoosh, came a spray of cracking noises, like many branches snapping under snow. Then it was more like a peppering of grapeshot. The braces were swallowed by a billowing orange cloud that opened like a wound. At its center burned a flame of molten gold. Even Harry—who hated vandalism of any kind—stopped, turned, and could not look away.

Eager as he was to find his son, he was fused to the spectacle, tingling with the enchanted terror of all creatures at the sight of fire. Everywhere, the blaze was turning wood to quilted charcoal. Heat slapped him again, and again, across the face, whipping him like a flag. A dry leaf twirled lazily toward the ground. Then another. If one of those cinders, dancing like fireflies . . . Then he saw him.

Hugh was standing still, brushed and bumped by the men around him, as if he were a sapling in the way. Paralyzed by relief, Harry stared. No one, thank God, had given the boy a torch. He'd have dropped it on the leaves. Instead, the boy stood rooted to the spot, his face in a trance, painted orange by the light. A cry punched the sky, forcing Harry's head around. One of the trestles had splintered, and now the ties swung down with a series of groans. Slowly, like a skeleton lying down, the bridge collapsed.

Glancing at his son again, Harry watched as the glazed look fell apart, the eyes widened, the mouth gaped in wonder. Or was it savagery. Some of the men waved pieces of charred wood as if they were tomahawks. With a twinge of shame, Harry hung back a moment, not knowing if it was Hugh or himself he shrank from confronting. And then, as suddenly as the boy had appeared, he was gone. Groaning with frustration, Harry forced his way toward the now vacant space and swung his eyes in every direction. The boy had gone up in smoke.

Cursing himself, Harry bent over, hands on knees. When he slowly straightened up, he noticed a shift in the crowd's attention. The bridge had been decommissioned, but the show wasn't over. Fry had rousted the guards from the tent, and they stood in front of the canvas, bound hand to hand, and to each other, by hempen cords. Their faces were greasy in the firelight. Some were masked with soot, as if painted to look like Negroes.

Of course, no one had thought to bring hoods for them. Fry stood with his hip akimbo, and put the choice to them reasonably. They could swear, on their honor as free men, never to bear arms against the Union and never to reveal the identity of anyone they recognized—or they could die. The decision was unanimous. They gave their parole.

Already, some of the audience was turning away, thinking of anxious wives, early-morning chores, or maybe a trip north. The countryside would be swarming with Rebel soldiers as soon as the news reached Knoxville. Daylight would bring sobriety and second thoughts. Harry guessed that many of the younger men, and even some of those with families, would hide in the mountains or run off to join the Federals in Kentucky. What if they had been recognized? What if the guards talked after all?

The crowd was thinning around him, saddle leather was creaking, and Harry was beginning to think he had only imagined the boy's image in the firelight, when he looked straight into Hugh's panicked eyes. Exhaling with relief, he jerked forward, wanting nothing but to whisk the child out of sight. He put out a hand—and heard, loudly and clearly behind him in another man's voice—"Hugh! Hugh Self! Is that *you*!"

As the sky above the mountains turned from gray to rosy pink to pale blue, Harry stood in his open doorway, looking out at the rolling fields that had taken a generation to free of stumps and vines. His eyes traveled to the barn, nestled in a fold of land, and then followed the seam in the earth all the way to the tree line. Nothing moved. All was quiet. The clamor was inside him. He scanned the horizon again, then turned and entered the house, closing the door behind him.

At breakfast, the porridge was tasteless. She'd forgotten the salt, barely remembered the spoons. "We must decide," Harry said to the three downcast faces around the table. "He could hide out in the mountains for a while. Many were talking of it . . . last night. Mayhap his name was not heard, but—"

"Why, he's just a boy!" Corniah made this claim as if she had just noticed her son's age. "Surely, no one—"

"The guards may not talk, but—"

"But you think they might." Lizzie's voice sounded dull, but she'd asked a real question. Unlike her mother, she was considering the problem that sat before them, hunched over, head hanging. Hugh had said almost nothing since Harry had marched him into the house, answering the boy's closed, taut, shaken expression with yes, of course he was angry, but they would talk about it in the morning, which was only a few hours away by then, though no one would sleep. And this, too, Hugh had done—stolen their rest, their food, their good name.

That was it. Harry suddenly understood what it was that had shifted within him, estranging him from himself. He was no longer a model citizen, a fellow to be trusted. He had slipped below the rim of the unimpeachable. He was now the kind of person who debated routes of escape, ways of hiding from the authorities. Hugh had sabotaged him, and the thought of it went somewhere beyond anger, somewhere so dark he couldn't face it.

"Pa," said Lizzie, and then again, more sharply, "Pa!" Her eyes were expectant, hopeful.

Getting hold of himself, he said, "Likely the Rebs have more worries now than chasing after Hugh, but we'll not take the chance."

"It's awfully cold, isn't it, in the hills?" On the surface, Corniah's voice was mildly disapproving, as if the only issue before them were the time of year. Underneath, Harry knew, was the tremor of hysteria. Turning to Lizzie, he spoke of Hugh as if the boy were not sitting there. "Hugh needs to sleep first. Then he should go over to Hinshaw's place. I think Matt is headed into the mountains, and he can take Hugh along." A strange sound came from Corniah, causing Harry to add hastily, "For a few weeks."

"I'll pack some clothes," murmured Lizzie, slipping off the bench and hurrying away.

"The plates . . . ," said Corniah weakly. Then she rose unsteadily, walked behind her son, bending over him to wrap her arms around his shoulders and lay her head upon his hair. As she straightened, she helped him rise, and together, supporting each other, they left Harry alone at the table.

Within an hour, he was in the barn, feeling Castor's leg. Swollen, is it, old boy? he mouthed silently, his mind elsewhere. He had told everyone to carry on as usual. Ma had set out the pans for the Saturday baking, including many she wouldn't use, and Lizzie, quietly removing them, helped without complaining, a sure sign the world was out of joint.

Before the sun had cleared the trees, Alex Lowe rode into the clearing, where Harry joined him. Standing in the brisk November air, they talked of early snows and winter hay and never once did the words "burn" or "bridge" cross their lips. Perhaps Lowe really did not know what had happened. And so the day lurched and crept through its cycle.

After nightfall, Hugh, looking like a tinker under his huge pack, trudged into the back pasture and disappeared. The lost look on his face, which he turned back toward them every few steps, almost, but not quite, made Harry change his mind. The boy *was* safer in the hills, but Harry's soul pinched him. Because of Hugh, he'd lost his good standing, and, yes, the loss rankled. Was he punishing Hugh for listening to Fry? Nursing his own hurt? He started forward, but the boy was out of sight.

Behind him, his wife sobbed. Harry turned to her, but she faced him, eyes under water. "You *wanted* him to go . . . !" He tried to explain that it was for the best, that the Rebels would have no mercy, that it was the pru—the blow was a glancing one, for there had been no force behind her hand, only a blind, wide-swinging refusal when he'd tried to wrap her in his arms. "Corniah!" he begged, but she shook her head and stumbled away.

How unjust it all was. Briefly, the unfairness soothed him, as he crossed his arms over his breast, his breath coming in quick, shallow puffs. If God saw fit to turn the world upside down, to make good men into criminals, then who was innocent, who was guilty, who . . . His arms relaxed and his chest rose and sank more slowly, calmed by a deep, familiar resonance. Sadie was lowing in the barn.

Then habit spoke to him. There could be no excuse, in God's universe or his own, for not checking, as he did every night, on the water level in the buckets in the horses' stalls. Then he would consider other things, and what was to be done about them. The likelihood of rain tomorrow. That hog's puzzling limp. The chance that Rebels would come to take him away.

The next morning, and many times during that second day, Harry roofed his hand over his eyes, scanning the tree line that stitched the landscape to the horizon. The corn needed pulling, and so he went into the field, while Lizzie, donning an old pair of Hugh's trousers and hiding her long hair, drove the wagon. Steady she was, far better at the job than her brother, and yet, angry as Harry still was with Hugh, he missed his son's antics. And it was he, Harry, who had sent the boy away. Many of the ears he tossed missed the wagon entirely.

THE BEGINNING OF THE END:

Rail and telegraph lines having been cut, it was men on horses who brought the word from Knoxville. Only five bridges had been burned, but attempts had been made on four others. Who knew how far the conspiracy had reached! Hundreds had left their homes that night and were hiding in the hills, or escaping, like Unionists before them, into Federal camps in Kentucky.

The Confederate authorities had been shocked, but they were scared, too, and furious. They saw now that their earlier tolerance had been a mistake. The eastern counties, far from keeping their loyalties to themselves, had been plotting treason all along, and must be dealt with accordingly. So martial law was declared, and its agents moved quickly.

Late on the second day, Jake Harmon, his two sons Tom and

Henry, and Alex Haun were captured by a fast-moving troop of soldiers under Colonel Wood. By the time Harry learned of it, the Harmons and Haun were on their way to prison in Knoxville. And they were the fortunate ones.

The Confederate secretary of war immediately dispatched Colonel Danville Leadbetter to the region, with orders to hang every bridge burner he could find, as a warning to the Lincolnites. By late November, several other "insurgents" had been picked up in the northern part of Greene Country. Among them was another man named Henry, but also Matt Hinshaw and a teenaged boy. Brought before Leadbetter, they had apparently confessed their crime and named their coconspirators. Or, perhaps, simply bragged about them. In spite of their cooperation, the men were to hang within hours. The boy . . .

The boy was not with them now. That much Harry knew, though he was not in the audience on November 30. Many of the other Unionists stayed away, too, or perhaps another civil war would have happened near the edge of the woods a few hundred yards west of the train station. Henry and Matt, marched up Depot Street by a squad of Rebel soldiers, called over their heads to weeping friends in the crowd. The doomed men assured everyone that they had indeed burned a bridge, and would burn more if they had the chance, as if apologizing for an interruption due to hanging. Loyalists cried broken words of encouragement, and Rebels shouted insults, for which they were often cuffed in return, as the citizenry flowed toward the large oak draped with two ropes.

That it had come to this! Two neighbors executed—by men in uniform! Bewildered and enraged, more of the local men drifted into the hills at night, promising to return with an avenging Federal Army. Harry did not learn until later that Hugh had, indeed, been arrested with Matt and Henry; he knew only that a boy of that age had been questioned by Leadbetter and was presumably in captivity. To Corniah and Lizzie he said Hugh must be alive somewhere, and he tried to believe it. He needed them to believe it, too, if he was ever to meet their eyes without flinching.

The worst times were at the table, where the empty place beside Lizzie made raw contact with their hearts. He tried only once for a salve, joking that Hugh was likely playing with the coons and squirrels instead of eating them for dinner. Lizzie and Corniah just stared at him, as if he were that creature Leadbetter. He sighed, but with a different sorrow. At some point, he had put his foot wrong, but where? He couldn't say.

In the first days of December, he saw what he had been watching for—movement on the edge of his property. It was almost a relief. If there was pain in store, let it come, so he could deal with it. Telling the women to stay in the house, and not, for any reason, to show themselves if strangers happened by, he said he had it in mind that morning to repair the harness for the plow.

As he walked to the barn, his shirt stuck to him, despite the cold air. Tufts of grass were fawn colored in places, leaf brown in others. Winter was on its way. Inside the old building, the air smelled reassuringly of sweet hay and fresh manure. Seating himself on a barrel, he began rubbing oil into the long traces, looking for weak spots, pretending he would be home for the planting season.

With every pass of the old rag, he was hoping his eyes had been tricked by fear. It wasn't the thought of capture that unmanned him in the days after the hangings. It was the possibility that Hugh had betrayed not just his father—for his name alone would have done that—but others, too. Had the boy been misled, or had he acted willfully? To form that question was to die a little death.

The man who found him wasn't from Greeneville, nor even, from the sound of him, from Tennessee.

"Git on up t' the house!" was all he said.

"Good morning," said Harry, tightening the lid on the tin of oil. "Where d'ye hail from?"

"I an't speakin' to a damn Yankee lover," said the man as he waved Harry toward the house with an eloquent pistol. A small band of soldiers lounged in their saddles near the front door. Harry's guess would later be confirmed: they belonged to General William H. Carroll, the man who had replaced Colonel Wood at headquarters in Knoxville.

When he was brought into the yard, Corniah came down the stoop so quickly, she caught her heel, and stumbled forward. *Go back inside,* he commanded fiercely with his eyes, but she was joined at that moment by Lizzie, who pulled her back into the arch of the doorway. *We will not,* said his daughter's face, quivering but defiant.

34

Chapter 2: Lick Creek Bridge

One of the men dismounted and unwound a rope from behind his saddle. He fastened Harry's wrists, pulling his shoulders back, until Harry's arms forked behind him like the breastbone of a chicken. "You," said the leader to the man who had rounded up Harry, "where's the horse?" Swearing, the fellow trotted back down the path to the barn. In the dead time that followed, the soldiers rubbed their necks, adjusted their belts, and looked everywhere but at the two women who stood frozen on the doorstep. Finding his voice at last, Harry said in an undertone aimed at Lizzie, "Go inside. I won't be gone long." Barks of laughter came from the men who overheard him.

Then, suddenly, Lizzie moved. If she had darted forward, or if she had sauntered brazenly, no doubt they would have stopped her, but she walked with the awkward lope of a girl just learning to use her limbs. When she reached him, she placed her hands on his waist, shaking him almost roughly, and then her arms slid around his chest and her fingers locked behind his back. She rested her head on his shoulder. His eyes filled and he pulled against the rope until his wrists flamed.

He heard Pollux before he saw him, saddled and bridled and whinnying at some indignity. There was going to be a fuss when the men realized Harry couldn't mount with his arms tied behind him. They would have to undo their own knots, then order him into the saddle. But Lizzie tightened her arms first, and he felt her hands move. Helplessly, he watched some white specks drift onto her hair and disappear. It might have been snow, or ash from their own chimney.

"Pa," was all she said, but the word flooded him. Against the tender bulge of her head, he moved his lips in her hair, letting the strands catch in his mouth. "Put a splint on Castor's leg—he's old but he's strong. You may"—his throat went dry—"need him. My good girl." He forced himself to go on. "Take care of Ma, and—Lizzie?—you tell that feller Pete I an't fond of him, but if he stands by you now . . . I might change my mind."

She was pried away, and he mounted Pollux. They bound his hands to the pommel, so he didn't find out until later that she'd slipped him his pipe. A lead rope, held by a soldier up ahead, jerked the animal into motion. With his torso wrenched painfully around, Harry watched his daughter and his farm until they fused with the landscape. All that was left was the Harry inside, who faced forward now, toward the new world he was entering.

Elizabeth A. Self

Chapter 3

On the Farm:

Or, the Diary of Elizabeth A. Self

Harrison Self's Farm
November 2–8, 1861

Saturday, Nov'r. 2. There was frost in the shade this morning. Miss
Sadie kept lifting her feet. I think she feels the cold as much as I
do in spite of her thick coat. Took my wool kape out of the box for
the first time this year and saw one or two holes. Sadie bawled at
me and kicked the old bucket which is already cracked. Pa says
it is good for another year but I am the one who uses it. I lost at
least a cup of milk (covered it with straw). I asked Pa once why
it was always the women in the family who milked the cows, and
he said it was because we are milk-producers too. Sometimes I
cannot tell if he means me to laugh. I was much younger then, and
could not write what I said in reply, but will do so now: Do men
pull corn because they grow beards like tassels? He did laugh, and
heartily, at that, and patted me on the head—as he never does now
that I am grown and such a trouble to him.
Why must cows be milked before sunrise? I am sure that was Pa's
idea not Sadie's. On my farm there will be a stove a mashine to
milk cows. Uncle Jake says there is a mashine now that washes
clothes in a drum you turn like a grinder. He says we have to step
lively and keep up with the times. Pa says the times are rushing
headlong over a clif—along with the lively steppers.
Since the war started next door in Carolina, Pa is always saying unkind
things about people, as if he could make the trouble go away by
pretending it is just another exampl of human foolishness. I know

37

he is really worried, even more than the time we lost the wheat crop. I wish he would tell me what he is thinking. When I ask he tells me his shirt needs mending or the corn needs shelling or the harrow needs sharpening for next spring. I need sharpening too. I am dull with all this milking and washing and sewing and baking.

On my way back from the barn I saw the sun on the ridge of the hill like a flaming egg in a nest. I saw a dozen turkeys move across the edge of the field. When they are close, you can see the big muscles in their upper legs and their necks are long and scaly like a snake's, but in the distance they are just huge beetles with their noses in the stubble of the hayfield. One got left behind and then chased after the others flapping and lurching like a child that runs after its mother. They are quiet in the morning, but at dusk they do their gobbling and their wings sound like leather when they fly straight up to the tops of the trees for the night. I suppose they feel safe there. Up among the leaves they are big brown sacks hanging in the rafters of the forest. While I was watching them this morning I thought I saw the trees on the ridge shake off the mist and step forward. I thought it was the Yankees coming. I ran into the house to get warm.

This afternoon I picked out three panels of my old blue muslin dress for turning. I am always too impatient and broke the thread at least three times, but most of it was saved. Ma says she would give three years of her life for a Grover & Baker. I asked would she think so 20 years from now when she is 69. Besides, you need very fine thread from the store for a sewing mashine and there is none in town but some that is very high. We have taken to spinning our own like those old settlers Pa talks about so much.

There is little more to write today. Sarah Ogilvie has lent me her copy of ALONZO AND MELISSA and I shall have a quiet hour to get acquainted with the heroine. As she sent the book by way of her brother, who is riding to Mosheim to sell a horse, there was a letter from her tucked inside the cover. Her sister is with child and fearful that the war will call her husband away. The family has been saddened by something very unexpected: Ella has asked to be freed. Sarah says all are deeply hurt, as Ella has lived with them so long and been so very well treated. They will send her to the Ogilvies of Alabama, for of course they cannot keep her at

home. Will they sell Hiram too? It must have been Hiram who made Ella so disloyal. Still, it seems so very cruel to separate them, and it cannot be true that they suffer less than we do. I have not seen Ella for several months, but I remember her kind hands, and the way she always ~~gives~~ gave me the news about her sisters and brothers. I am sad too but it is Sarah who troubles me I know not why.

MONDAY, NOV'R. 4. I could not see the tree-tops this morning for the low-lying clouds and high-rising mist. It was not so cold that my breath turned white in the air, but I saw footsteps in the frost. We still set out the barrel for washing but had many more trips to fill and refill it with water from the kettle.

The sun broke through by the time I went down to the barn to churn butter. I wore my heavy jacket but soon removed it as the exercise warmed me. As I was entertaining myself with thoughts of Melissa, about to be sacrificed at the hymeneal alter, a shadow fell upon the churn and a hand touched my shoulder. A cry escaped my lips—but it was neither Beaumont nor Alonzo. It was only Cousin Tom.

—Are you not enraptured by the auroral splendor of the sky, I inquired. Tom looked so frightened that I told him to sit down on a bale of hay and take a turn at the paddle to give my arms a rest. He worked so poorly at the task that I retrieved the churn and asked him why he was not at the kilns.

When satisfied that Pa was not nearby, he asked me in very worried tones if I knew why his father might be going on a journey.

—Why don't you ask him? said I.

—He says nothing or always the same thing: the times are uncertain, replied Tom. He told me Uncle Jake was often away from the farm in the last few days and once Tom had seen him talking with a stranger down by the railroad tracks. Tom is easily made anxious, and I remember that in games we played as children he could often be found crying, abandoned by the stronger boys. I noticed today how slender and pale he looked, although he is a grown man of three-and-twenty years. He kept running his fingers through his hair and twisting his face until I thought he had the Saint Vitus dance. I would have patted him on the shoulder if my hands had been free.

Tom, I said as kindly as I could, have you spoken to Henry?

—Henry! said Tom in the most dispairing voice.

—Lost! I cried, imagining every disaster. In just the last month, I had heard of a child kicked by a horse, a man fallen beneath his plow, and a woman struck by lightning while her husband, untouched, walked beside her. Henry! Sweet Henry, two years younger than Tom, but twice his age in all the graces of manhood. My arms dropped to my side and tears started to my eyes.

—Ay, he's worse than Cousin Hugh. There is nothing for it but the Federals must come and save us from the Rebels, with Henry in the lead, waving the Stars and Stripes.

I wanted very much to shake Tom for scaring me but one cannot be angry with a willow for bending in every breeze. I comforted him as best I could. If there is some mischief afoot, some dangerous enterprise, I am very much afraid Tom will be caught in the wake of it without knowing why.

After he left, I sat for a long time with the churn idle in my hands. I thought of Pa in the fields and Ma in the kitchen, and wondered very selfishly why our life should be ruined by quarrels we had no stake in. I do not see that Mr. Lincoln or Mr. Davis has more claim to my loyalty than Pa. He says the war is not between the two presidents, or between slaveholders and abolitionists, but between the cotton-growers and the manufacturers. He says Greeneville is in the middle, as we are farmers and artisans and tradesmen. But I do not relish being in the middle between two bullocks.

TUESDAY, NOV'R. 5 At breakfast Hugh said he was going in to town today because the papers would be coming over from Knoxville on the cars. No, said Pa, the hog-pen needs fixing, and Lowe and I need your help. (I do not like Alex Lowe. He thinks I ignore him because he is only a tenant farmer but it is because he is less kind to his wife than the Ogilvies are were to Ella.)

—But Pa, said Hugh, there might be news about the Federals.

—And what about the Federals, Pa said, as if he didn't know the rumor everyone is talking about! Then Ma asked will they take all our pigs and cows as the Rebels say they will and Pa said Corniah! in his tired voice and everybody ate bacon for five minutes.

Pa is worried that Hugh will listen to the wild talk that is going around, about Lincoln's army marching down from Kentucky and putting the Seceders in their place. Hugh told me he wants to join that Army when it comes. I am the only person he has told (so he says) except for our cousins Tom and Henry who are just as eager to wave the flag as he is. But people will be waving guns not flags.

People are wondering what will happen since that big fight over at Manassas in the summer. Pete says the Yankees are yellow cowards who run away when they see a Southern man with a hickory stick. The last time Pete was here I asked Pa if we were Southerners and he said we were Wataugans. Pa is always trying to find a topic he knows more about than Pete, who has been to college at Tusculum.

Pete asked if he meant those stiff-necked old land-grabbers who snubbed their noses at the British, and Pa said he meant those first settlers who framed the first government, and behind Pa's back I shook my head at Pete, trying to get him to stop, but he could not any more than I can when my blood is up. Pa said he hadn't any bondsmen to do his work for him, so he needed to get into the field, and that was how it ended.

I spent most of the morning helping Ma with the baking. There was just enough powdered yeast for today and tomorrow. While the dough was rising I had a meeting with the feather duster in the parlor. I found spiders in the window casement as usual and brushed them outside. Pa has not touched his books for a long time so the dust made me sneeze. I took the heavy blue one down and opened it with closed eyes before looking. It was the one about the prince who comes home to find his country and his family taken over by his father's brother.

My favorite is the one about a father betrayed by all his daughters except the one who made him angry by telling him the truth. When Pa told me that story I was five or six and perched on his knee, but I remember that he put his hand on my head after he was done and lookt at me so kindly. Many years later I discovered that he had changed the end of the story. When I asked him why, he stroked my hair and said he liked Cordelia too much to let her go. ~~I wish he~~

Ma says it is wrong to feel sorry for yourself. You must accept whatever God gives you to do or to bear. But if someone slaps me on the cheek, I slap that person right back on both cheeks, in words if not blows. Ma says that is why I am nobody's wife so far, and now that I am 25 no one will ask me except maybe a widower. Even that is not likely. If the war does not end soon, there will be more widows than widowers but married or not I can milk cows and bake bread so I shall be of use to Ma and Pa when they are old.

Picked out three more panels on the blue muslin.

Heard the geese flying overhead and went outside to watch them cut across the sky. How easy it is for them, flying south for the winter. How hard it is for our men, sneaking north through the mountains to Kentucky. They go at night by hidden trails to join the Federals.

Right overhead, the sky is a very dark blue some days in November but lighter in the middle distance and pale at the horizon. Pete did not visit today.

WEDNESDAY, NOV'R. 6. The almanac says that the sun rose this morning at two minutes before 7 o'clock but I did not see it. The fog was so heavy above the ridge. Hugh got his trip in to town when Ma sent him to fetch more yeast. She wrote down for him Andrews Excelsior Yeast Powder because he cannot remember any words that are not about the war. He can quote long paragraphs from the Knoxville WHIG. Pa and Alex Lowe were pulling corn in the field behind the ridge and did not see him ride off on Pollux. I was glad everybody was away (I do not count Ma). In the middle of the afternoon while I was sitting on the back step cooling off from the kitchen Pete rode up. Whatever else may be said of him he does sit a horse well (!)

—How are you today Miss Lizzie, he remarked without getting down, just leaning forward with his arms crossed on the pommel. I am become a Miss since he went to college. He held a pair of gloves with those broad cuffs I saw in the picture of the cavalry officer in Harper's Weekly. These even had fringe and were mighty handsom for a law apprentice in Greeneville. He kept slapping them against the sleeve of his father's old greatcoat.

—Those are mighty fine work gloves, said I. Did you come to help Pa and Alex?

Chapter 3: On the Farm

—Laugh if you wish, Miss Lizzie, he said, and put a leg up over the horse's neck and slid to the ground in one swoop. Then he draped his arm back on the saddle as if it was the mantle in the parlor. There never was anyone like Pete for making himself at home. Before he could ask for one, I went inside to get him a biscuit with gooseberry jam. That is the difference between being one's own mistress and being sent on an errand! When I came back he was sitting right in the middle of the stoop, so I went over to the mounting block and made a throne of it.

—I've come to say good-bye. He put on such a look of melancholy and nobility that I suppose the girls in Greeneville are impressed, but I have known Pete since he could barely reach the door handle.

—Where are you going?

—Knoxville, he said, looking as sad as a person can while enjoying one of Ma's biscuits.

—Why? (I reelly did want to know. I have never been to Knoxville. I have heard it is all stores and taverns and train depots.) I asked him are you going to be a soldier?

—I am leaving tomorrow, he said, to serve my country. He reminded me that he has been studying law with Mr. Ogilvie. He said that if I had read the Constitution of Tennessee I would know that it says just what the Federals said in the Declaration of Independence. He stopped and squinted his eyes as if he reading these words on the air in front of him. He said the people have At All Times, An Inalenable And Indefeesible Right To Alter, Reform, Or Abolish The Government In Such Manner As They May Think Proper. He repeated it several times to make sure I had learned my lesson. Then he said it is right to abolish a government that would take away our liberties.

—Which liberties? I asked.

—The South cannot let its honor be trampled in the dust. Then he stood up and he did look reely very stiff and determined and I think a uniform will become him. Then he asked if he could beg a favor of me.

—Whose rights? I asked. He said even some of the Union lawyers in Knoxville like the famous John Baxter were helping the Confederacy now. The North is full of greedy scowndrels who have no regard for the natural order. They would deny us our

43

property (I did not ask What property). Pete said that he and Mr. Baxter had no choice as Southern gentlemen but to resent such treatment, even if it meant exchanging the pen for the sword. In case he did not come back he would take it kindly if I would give him a kiss to keep while he was obeying the call of duty.

—I would rather not, I said because I knew he would lose it among the others he collected.

—Oh, damnation, Lizzie, said he, forgetting his dignity as a future colonel of the Confederacy. Then he said, Soldiers always get kissed when they go off to war.

—I pointed out two facts to him, counting them on my fingers as Pa always does: One: you an't a soldier yet. Two: there is jam on your face. Then I marched past him into the house. He could have stopped me, as I was walking slowly enough to let him, but he did not. I watched him ride away and felt very strange. We have started looking at all the young men in a different way. It is hard not to think of them lying on the ground somewhere, turning into something to be buried and never seen again. Pete is full of other people's words but it hurts my heart to think of him wounded or killed.

Of course he will come back. I have known him since he was just big enough to hold one of the wooden stick-swords Pa makes for all the little boys this side of Lick Creek. I will pray for him at least once every day until the end of the war or until he comes home. I must see him again before he leaves tomorrow because I was not kind to him and I am truly sorry for that now.

Late today the swallows were darting in circles behind the barn. They never tire. When they flipt over on the turns the sun shon white on their bellies.

THURSDAY, NOV'R. 7. Fifty years ago today the Indians under Takumsah were defeated by ~~John~~ Wm. Harrison at the Battle of Tippeekanu. History it seems to me is a string of battles. I did not think I could write down what happened today. There is not an Ayer's pill for the mind or I would take one to purge my sour thoughts. I would be free of this ake.

There has been more talk of the Federals coming to our rescue and Hugh says the men in town have gathered in small groups and are whispering together. He was pushed away when he tried to get close but heard the word BRIDGE.

This morning Aunt Malinda came to help me with turning my dress. We sat in the kitchen with a small fire to keep away the chill but I could still feel the cold on my ankels. Aunt M. is generally more cheerful than Pa because (he says) she does not have the running of a farm but only the managing of a house. Yet I think their skulls have the same bump labeled Contrariness. She calls him a scoffer and he thinks her softheaded. I cannot help thinking of Hugh and me. Do all siblings have their North and their South?

The muslin was very worn near the bottom and faded in strips where the tucks had been at the waist. We turned the panels inside out and upside down and began to sew a new line of tucks. I think we will have to narrow the sleeves at the elbows where the cloth is worn through. It will do for wear in the house. Who said The Wider the Sleeves the Smaller the Waist? It was someone who has a maid or a slave to do her work.

The word stares at me from the page: slave. Pete says that Africans have a place in the natural order, just as all of God's creatures do, and that it is our duty to care for them just as it is their duty to serve us. I had heard very similar words in a sermon one Sunday, except that the dutiful caregivers were husbands and the dutiful servers were wives. I am not sure that Pa agreed with the preacher, for I remember that he laughed afterwards and said that he raised hogs and planted corn to keep his wife in bonnets, so he rather thought he was the bondservant and she the mistress.

I did not see a slave until I first went into town with Pa to visit the Ogilvies. I was perhaps five or six years old. The woman who opened the door frightened me, and I hid behind Pa's greatcoat. When we were alone in the parlor, I asked him why she was painted all over black and why her nose was so wide. He said he would answer me, but first I must tell him why I was painted all over white and why my nose was so thin. I protested that my flesh was the real color of skin, but he asked me then what was the real color of feathers or of flowers. Then he called for the strange woman, told me her name was Ella, and asked her to sit with me while he went to retrieve a forgotten packet from his saddlebag. He said that when he returned, I must be able to tell him how many sisters and brothers Ella had, and what their names were, and where they lived. I wonder now if she did not feel more like a slave at that moment than at any other. When I think of her being sent away to the cotton fields something catches in my stomach.

What I wrote this afternoon seems very long ago. Sleep will not come. I did not think to add any more today, but it is less painful to write than to lie abed remembering.

Pa came in from the field when the sun was already very low. As always he stopped by the barn to wash the dust from his face and arms and pick the leaves and ticks from his clothing. His eyes were tired and in spite of the washing there was yellow dust in the wrinkles on his cheek. Hugh should not have spoken to him but he did.

—Captain Fry is in town, he said. We had a mess of potatoes and onions tonight and some salt pork. Hugh put so much molasses on his bread that it ran over on his fingers.

—That is enough, said Pa and pulled on the jug but Hugh had his thumb in the handle and it slipped and fell on the floor where it cracked and fell apart in the syrup. Ma cried out because it is her favorite jug, the pretty one that Alex Haun made for her. No one lacks for earthenware in Pottertown but Ma always prized this one. The handle was a letter "C" for her name. Hugh scraped together the pieces and said he would mend the jug but all he could do was scrub the stain on the floor. It was not very large, most of the molasses having gone down his gullet in advance.

—Finish your meal, said Pa. I'll hear no talk of Captain Fry nor any other gossip if you please.

—But it is not gossip if it is true. In town they say he came directly from Washington.

—Did he, indeed. I heard he is come from Kentucky, said Pa. Hugh looked sheepish for one moment but then he said that he wished he could go to Washington to see the president.

—He has two arms and two legs like any other man, said Pa. But then he looked thoughtful and said, No, he is not like the others. He was a poor man who schooled himself and is as ready with his tongue as any politician.

Hugh almost knocked over his bowl in his excitement and said Mr. Lincoln was going to do more than write speeches. He was going to thrash all the Rebels before Christmas.

—Like Mr. Ogilvie and George Wellmont? said Pa, naming two people we sat with on Sundays, though everyone knew they talked Secesh in their homes.

I was sorry to see the brightness fade from Hugh's face, but thought Pa was about to tell us of the bear and the stag again, who each have their good and bad points. I hoped to please him in what I said next: Why should not Mr. Davis have as much right to a revolution as Mr. Washington?

—So says that coxcomb Peter I suppose, said Pa, as if I had quoted Satan. There is no point in writing this down if I am not honest in these pages, but I do not know which made me angrier: the unfairness to Pete, who is very silly but also brave, or the charge that I must have stolen words from someone else because I have none of my own. I have read more books than anyone else in this house and can speak as well as Pa, when he lets me. But the truth is that Pete did say those very words last week and it was I who was unkind to him today. I had not yet made amends for that, but could at least speak up for him.

—Many people think the Black Republicans go too far and must be stopped.

Ma broke in at this point, giving me a very stern look. But there is something that drives me when I am once started and I cannot stop, not even when I see the warning sign in Pa's face. He is so even tempered with others, but when I cross him, there is a patch below each eye that turns white and begins to pulse. He frightens me then, but I cannot turn back.

I had said too much and my throat was very dry. Hugh said, She's wrong an't she Pa? He hoped to hear the last of the spilt syrup. He asked who are the Black Republicans and would they be coming down from Kentucky with the Federals?

Pa laughed but it was not from good spirits and I did not know what to expect. He explained to Hugh that the party of Mr. Lincoln was thought to be hell-bent on ending slavery in the Southern states, but it was only the spread of the institution that he was against. What he wants said Pa is to prove that a federation of states can remain a country, despite the evidence of history. Hugh was disappointed, as he did not hear the sound of battle in those words.

—So says Papa Tory, I remarked, not sure what I meant. I know that Pa believes in the Union, and I have heard him say that slavery in our time is even worse than slavery in the land of pharaohs, because Christ was closer to God than Moses was, and gave us a better law, but I heard in his voice a dismissal of all laws but his own, and was that not a kind of tyranny, too? Ma pointed at the empty dishes and at me.

When I had carried the plates a little way from the table she whispered to me to be silent. I was not to cause a civil war in her house but to carry in the pie and give my brother and father each a large portion to keep their mouths full. I did as she asked but I was hotter inside than the dish in my hands.

Hugh asked why Mr. Lincoln is called a Rail-splitter in the papers and Pa said that he had been born very poor in Illinois and grown up on a farm just like Hugh. There was no help for it. I said, Oh no, Pa. He was born in Kentucky, like Jeff Davis.

—You're mighty sure of yourself, an't you? said he.

—We can ask Peter, I said. *He* will know.

—That popinjay! declared Pa.

—He's Secesh now, Pa, but you have known him since he was a boy. You always say that people are more important than politics.

—He can vote for God or the Devil for all I care. His Ma plants her own 'taters, with no help from her son.

I felt obliged to defend him. Anybody can grow 'taters, I said. Pete says he has a higher duty now, helping the new country.

Pa blew out his lips, fffff! There is no new country, my girl (as he calls me when he is angry). There is only the one we have, and if we lose it, we ought to have stayed in England.

I knew that to be true and yet I could not abide his mocking tone. What rose within me was the same burning resistance those early settlers must have felt when they saw the British riding across their fields. I lifted my chin and said, Why can't there be another Revolution? Because you say so?

Pa raised the hand nearest me and then lowered it. There was a look on his face that I had never seen before. YES, BECAUSE I SAY SO he said, and would not speak to me again. When I write those words here they seem very simple and not harsh at all, yet

I cannot bear to look at them. ~~They were~~ His face was very cold, as if he did not recognize me. I wanted to argue in my usual way, or to look nobly aggrieved, as Melissa would have done, but I sat like a whipped child. Even now my face burns to think of it. I ~~hate~~ He then reached for the cracked china cup in which he likes to drink Miss Sadie's milk and took a long draught of it and told Hugh that he would like to hear again what Mr. Brownlow said on the occasion of his newspaper being shut down by the Rebels.

Hugh grinned with delight and reached into his pocket for the folded paper we all knew he kept there. I can remember most of it now, having heard it before, although I was too unhappy to listen while it was being read tonight. I asked Hugh if I might borrow the page and now reproduce the more spirited lines:

> This issue of the Whig must necessarily be the last for some time to come: I am unable to say how long. The Confederate authorities have determined upon my arrest . . . I can doubtless be allowed my personal liberty, by entering into bonds to keep the peace and to demean myself toward the leaders of Secession in Knoxville, who have been seeking to have me assassinated all summer and fall. . . . Although I could give a bond for my good behavior, . . . I shall obstinately refuse to do even that; and if such a bond be drawn up and signed by others, I will render it null and void by refusing to sign it. In default of both, I expect to go to jail, and I am ready to start upon one moment's warning. . . . Stimulated by a consciousness of innocent uprightness, I will submit to imprisonment for life, or die at the end of a rope, before I will make any humiliating concession to any power on earth!

When first I heard these words, I thought them the posturing of a man whose country was no bigger than his own swollen head. Although opposite in allegence, his speech seemed no different from Pete's high-sounding talk of Southern duty and honor. Tonight however I hear someone staking his claim to his own soul. I hear only a settled defiance, and something in me rises to meet it.

The news is that Mr. Brownlow has escaped from Knoxville and is waiting in the mountains like so many of our men.

Whether they are patriots or traitors, heroes or cowards I cannot say. I think it is not a question of who is right, or of South against North, or of agriculture against industry, as Pa says. I think it is a question of which is more dear to you, liberty or power. There are some men, like Pa, who are very glad of how little they need from anyone else, but Pete is always telling me what is due to himself as a servant of humanity.

I cannot tell how men should live their lives, but it is very sad that so many die of the argument. I have heard that many women are worse than the men in their eagerness for battle, but I cannot agree with Aunt Malinda, who says that Mr. Lincoln and Mr. Davis should settle their differences between themselves and leave the rest of us in peace. Something is pending for us, too, but I do not find it in all the talking on both sides. I pray I will know before the war comes to Greeneville.

I hear Pa's step. He will see the light below the door and scold me for burning a candle so late. ———— He has passed without stopping. He did not call to me, as he always does, and say that my eyes will be red in the morning.

I have no heart tonight for the adventures of Melissa, because there is not the slightest doubt that all the dangers she survives will bring her back to Alonzo without a scratch on her white skin. She weeps *crystalline droplets*, so her eyes never burn.

FRIDAY, NOV'R. 8. When I wakened this morning I knew at once that something was amiss. The light was different. I had slept beyond my usual hour, and no one had roused me. The house was very quiet as if all had started the day without me. I found Ma in the kitchen and told her I must go to Miss Sadie but she said that Pa had done the milking this morning. I should have welcomed this kindness as a sign that he had forgiven my rebel talk but instead I felt a strange foreboding. At table, we made friends with our plates, saying nothing to each other, until Hugh made a mess as usual, ruining the dress I had worked on with Aunt M. He thought to escape punishment by helping Pa in the field.

It has been cold today. By noon the clouds were brushed across the sky like carded wool and the wind blew off many of the orange and gold leaves on the trees. Their bare branches have turned the hills gray. I helped Ma with the mending and baking as she is calmest when her hands are full.

After midday, I set out to take some bread and cheese to the men pulling corn. At this time of year, they will be working until it is too dark to see the stalks in front of them. As I was coming around the side of the barn, I could see the lower field where it borders on the public road. I saw two men on horseback stopped there to talk with Alex Lowe and John McDaniels. Pa was nowhere in sight. Even from that distance I knew that one of the horsemen was Uncle Jake, although he rode off very quickly before I was close enough to hail him.

John then walked away and I might have turned back for I would not like his companion to think I had come especially to see him, but my curiosity was stronger than my reluctance. We exchanged greetings and then, pretending uncertainty, I asked if that had perhaps been my Uncle Jake Harmon in the road. Lowe narrowed his eyes at me and hesitated but then said he hoped I would know my own uncle if I saw him.

—I was too faraway, I said. Was it my Uncle Harmon?

—Have a care, Elizabeth, said he. You will soon need glasses for those pretty eyes. The man who spoke to me was a passer-by inquiring the road to Tusculum. We spoke of the weather and the corn.

I could think of no reason why Uncle Jake's presence should be kept from me, so I determined to press Lowe further. I remembered Tom's fear that his father was preparing for a journey.

—Ma thought she heard horsemen last night, I said.

To keep him talking I offered him a round of bread and a slice of the cheese I had brought as a peace-offering for Pa. I told Lowe that Ma was worried about strangers passing through, and asked if the man he had been talking to was a Rebel.

—I am sure he was a Southern gentleman, as I hope I may be accounted when the time comes.

It is no secret that Lowe wants to rise in the world. But whether he was speaking of his political allegiance or of his social advancement, I could not tell. No doubt they are the same to him. He does not argue with Pa, but I have heard him say that no true Southerner can trust Lincoln after the Fremont Proclamation freed more slaves in Missouri, and that if he ever draws a sword, it will be for the Confederacy.

—I am glad to hear it, I said. Something is stirring among our boys, and I should be sorry to hear of your being shot.

He looked as startled as if he had indeed been shot, and turned the subject at once to the bread, which he swore was the best in Greene County. I suggested he not tell his wife so, and asked if she felt better today. She has suffered from the catarrh, but he said she is altogether herself again and will be in church on Sunday. I think each of us was pleased to part with the other. Knowing Pa would be alone, as Hugh was already home, I turned back to the house, my courage failing me.

I had not been long returned when Ma sent me for some onions in the root cellar and there was Lowe down by the hog-pen, talking with Pa. I know it is wrong to eevesdrop but one must be devious when one is prevented from knowing what concerns one, as Melissa would say. I heard very little, but was chilled by the words. Lowe asked Pa if he had heard about a plan to burn the bridges and Pa said he had, but that he thought it a bad thing. I gripped my jacket around me, frightened by what I was hearing but even more afraid to move.

They spoke about a meeting at Uncle Jake's house, and Pa said he did not know if he would go. He thought the raid would cause little harm to the Confederacy but much harm to us at home. Lowe said he could not go himself, as he could not leave his wife, who was very ill. On hearing this false excuse I had a strong desire to jump from my hiding place, but did not.

Dinner was very quiet. Ma was still worried that our chickens might be stolen, and Hugh kept raising his spoon to his mouth and lowering it still laden. Pa stared at the table with a heavy brow and I fancied that only I knew what was troubling him. If Uncle Jake is helping the radical Unionists, what will become of him if he is caught? What will happen to Aunt Malinda? To Henry and Tom? Each name is an icicle through my heart.

Pa was asleep before the fire when I retired to my room. I have laid a rug against the bottom of the door to block the candle's light. Several times I have heard rustling in the hallway. Once from the window I thought I saw a light in the barn. We often hear the sound of horses in the night, but I am listening very hard now and hear nothing but the hoot of an owl and the creak of wood cooling in the night. I ~~wish~~

William G. Brownlow

CHAPTER 4
IN THE WILDERNESS

KNOXVILLE, TENNESSEE; SMOKY MOUNTAINS
NOVEMBER 4–DECEMBER 6, 1861

T HE TIME TO KILL A BEAR IS JUST BEFORE HE HIBERNATES. His limbs are heavy and slow-moving. His meat is richly veined with fat, his fur is lustrous and long, and his tallow burns as bright as any wax. All this, Brownlow knew. How? Because his cradle had been rough-hewn, neither gilded nor carved. Because, after his parents died, he worked like a slave for the relatives who took him in out of charity. Because he learned the trade of house carpentry, not the graces of the parlor. Because his pennies earned him a certificate as a Methodist Travelling Minister, not a diploma from Yale or Harvard. Because he had been a circuit preacher before becoming an editor, and more than once had slept under the naked heavens wrapped in a horse blanket with a rag for a nightcap. Because he had eaten bear meat before.

Eaten, but not killed. He knew the tenderest meat was next to the spine, but not that it must be hung for several days to lose some of its moisture and toughness. Here's how he learned more about bear meat. It all started on Monday, November 4, 1861. This was soon after the management of the East Tennessee District passed from General Felix Zollicoffer, a tolerant if wrong-headed man, to Reverend Colonel W. B. Wood, a native of Alabama, a Methodist (!) preacher and, in Brownlow's eyes, a full-time "hypocrite" and "unmitigated villain." On that Monday, William Gannaway Brownlow, often called "the Parson," became a fugitive.

Why so? Because Wood had allowed bands of excited Rebel soldiers to congregate outside the editorial office of the *Whig*, hurling insults, brandishing weapons, and casting aspersions and rotten fruit in the direction of the last Union newspaper in the South, founded, edited, and published by W. G. B. A stray bullet, cunningly aimed, was likely the next missile.

His instinct and desire was to present as broad a target as possible, while at the same time launching a hail of verbal Minie balls at his enemies and the enemies of the Union (one and the same). But his friends reminded him that his wife, his daughter Susan, his son John Bell, and others who were his kindred or known affiliates, might be caught in the cross fire. Rumors of a pending indictment in Nashville, refusals to distribute his paper by the usual conveyances, and threats to his well-being if he did not write to the dictation of the Secessionists, all were like so many ropes tying his arms to his side.

The better part of valor, urged by his friends and his common sense, was a strategic trip to the neighboring counties to collect fees for advertisements in his newspaper. And so, late in the afternoon of November 4th, he packed two shirts and a woolen shift, a gap-toothed comb for his shock of dark hair, and some notes for a sermon or two he expected to be begged, on the spur of the moment, to give in a local church here or there. He stowed four apples from his cellar, a small flask of honey for his raw throat, and a packet of salt pork to carry him through to the first home where he would be welcomed and, if need be, hidden (he was, after all, a famous man, the Cicero of Federalism). Finally, he swept up the large, soft-brimmed hat—the one Susan called his "Spanish galleon hat"—pursed his lips as he gave a last glance around the room, and strode down the hall.

At the door, his wife peered out, and seeing the usual gathering of interested citizens—vultures, she called them—she ducked back inside. Her bonnet was not, in her estimation, ready for public view. Brownlow gave her a quick embrace, his mind already on the road. Susan straightened her shoulders and her jacket, before stepping out into the yard. As he bent to kiss her forehead, he noticed something that brought the moment into focus. Above her left breast, she had sewn, with a delicacy that surprised and impressed him, a small replica of the United States flag.

He met her eyes quickly, pinching his brow, as if to say, Yes, I see, and I am proud of your courage and ingenuity. They remind me of me, by the way. But must you really draw the attention of our enemies, when I won't be here to kick them out? Then, seeing his tentativeness reflected in her eyes, he relaxed into affection. Left on her own, she could stare down a general. Or so fathers must hope in these perilous times. With that thought, he settled the crown of his hat, mounted his horse, and trotted toward his rendezvous with the Rev. James Cumming. Together, they slipped out of Knoxville under cover of darkness.

On Sunday, November 10, Brownlow stood before hundreds filling and overflowing from the church in Sevierville, and, husbanding his voice as best he could until the end, raised up a mighty prayer to God to *give the common people grace to perceive the right path, which Thou knowest, leads from the camps of Southern madcaps and Northern fanatics, and enable them steadfastly to walk within.* Having heard by then of the bridge burnings, and knowing he would be charged with complicity despite his having been nowhere near any of the bridges in the predawn hours of the previous day, he pointed his horse's head toward the distant outline of the Smoky Mountains.

The evening chill was settling upon him and his companion by the time they reached the small settlement in Wear's Cove at the base of the foothills. They weren't the only newcomers. In the twilight, men passed between cabins carrying long rifles, checking on tethered pack animals, and greeting each other in hushed tones of instant fellowship. Among them were surely some of the bridge burners, along with others who feared the noose because they had raised the stars and stripes on a pole in their yard, or spoken too freely of their devotion to the Union.

Wear's Cove sheltered a small contingent of Home Guards loyal to the Union, and these men and their families joined the gathering that formed like the pooling of rivulets in a pond. In the home of Valentine Mattox, a log cabin smoothed on the inside with chalky pipe clay, now water stained and smoke dulled, Brownlow proceeded to the front of the room, and took the chair that was quickly vacated for him. He listened, sunk behind the furrows of his dark face. Then he said, "I agree." Those in most danger, those whose clothes literally or figuratively smelled of fire, would retreat further into the mountain gorges for the time being, with the promise that food and news would be supplied by their friends below.

The men stood, expectantly, and, as always, Brownlow rose to the occasion. "Friends," he said, glancing from one bearded face to the next, "I am saddened by the rending of our peaceful lives, less than two months before Christmas. Herod's devils are in the land. I am not the most patient of men"—teeth gleamed here and there—"but I fear that recent actions . . ." He shook his head. "Let us not be like the boy who would rid himself of a buzzing bee by kicking at the beehive.

"There are plenty of scamps and fools who are profiting by Secession, who are using a false sense of injury as an excuse for lying and stealing. But there is a better sort of man who did once believe, as we do, in the Union, but has been swayed by false reasoning. General Carroll may be such a man, and I am not without hope that he will rein in the hellions unleashed by that Sunday Methodist and Monday devil, 'Parson' Colonel Wood. But for now, we must disappear. We must nestle in the bosom of these mountains until it is safe to walk the streets again. May the Almighty God of our fathers keep us safe, and may he bless these brave and honest friends who help us on our way."

In his days as an itinerant preacher, Brownlow had slept on many a cornhusk pallet offered by quondam parishioners, but where he was going now, there would be only leaf meal for a bed. Along with the other fugitives, he climbed paths where no horse had ever gone, deeper and higher into the gorges and ravines of the Smokies.

In a small clearing at the edge of the eastern branch of the Little River, the new mountaineers cleared away thickets and set up camp. It did not take them long to find two straight branches, the width of a hand, that were forked at the height of a man's head. These were trimmed and sunk into the earth five or six feet apart. A third pole was laid across the forks, and against this beam other branches were leaned in a sloping roof thatched with brushwood from the riverbank. Under this canopy they sheltered their belongings and made pallets for the older men.

Parson Brownlow, a sturdy man of fifty-seven, did his share of the work, noting aloud the parallel with Christ's retreat into the wilderness, and reflecting on the difference between Judean deserts and American woodland. His final sally—"Well, fellows, let's hope we're not here for forty days!"—was met by a few friendly grunts and the offer of "my old woman's pone." Brownlow promptly shared his flask of honey to sweeten the dry lumps of cornmeal baked in ashes. The verdict on all sides was "damned good," while Brownlow, whose principles forbade swearing, declared it "manna from heaven." In his evening prayer, spoken aloud to the gathered men, Brownlow evoked the earliest days of the territory, before statehood was imaginable, when their forbears had tracked deer and bear through virgin wilderness. They were sons of Daniel Boone. Dreaming of flintlocks and powder horns, they slept that first night on boughs of fragrant pine, within sound of rushing water.

Morning brought the men aching backs, itchy skin, and somewhat less enthusiasm for their heritage. Brushing ants and leaves from their clothes, they splashed water on their faces, wandered behind laurel bushes to relieve themselves, and rubbed their hands over a small cooking fire. The first order of business was to collect firewood. Two of the men had axes, and the rest gathered pine twigs for kindling or hauled and stacked the cut branches. Fearful that the smoke might be seen from a distance, they kept their fires small, under a canopy of laced branches in the trees above, and did most of their cooking in the early dusk of autumn.

Brownlow, finding a mossy hummock with an oak for a backrest, leaned a small notebook (he was never without one) against his raised knees and hunted similes, using a stubby charcoal pencil in lieu of a pen. Like most of his companions, he believed that a man of the New World should be on familiar terms with the wilderness, as strong as a bear and as quick as a fox, as free as a bird, as bold as a lynx. He told himself that he had lived too long under the roofs of Knoxville, that he was glad to test his sinews in the woods again. Then he rubbed his stiff neck thoughtfully and wondered how much longer the trial would last.

The next day brought word that a company of Rebels had been seen at Maryville, heading toward the mountains. It was no secret that Loyalists were hiding there, but the little band of refugees hoped they were well hidden. The camp was tucked into a small opening, the size of a train carriage, on the left bank of the stream, with only a ribbon of sky between steep hills on either side. Armed with pistols and rifles, this handful of men could roust a brigade. But it was not an army they feared. Far more dangerous would be one or two scouts who knew the trails and the vantage points as well as their own homes. The mountain men of North Carolina and Eastern Tennessee were famously pro-Union, but if two or three of them should be Confederates at heart, or in service to Colonel Wood, they could steal down the hills like cougars in the night.

At first, every day was a novelty for Brownlow. While he carried a pistol, he was not much of a hand with a rifle, and so the hunting was left to others. The biggest game that first week was a large-breasted turkey. Its scaly neck and fierce claws removed, it roasted on an improvised spit. Brownlow took three of the largest feathers, ran his finger down the soft outer edge, and tucked them into his pack. He looked curiously at the trees with smooth green trunks flaked with thin slices of peeling bark, and at curiously shaped leaves he couldn't identify. But soon he began to feel restless. Trees had no ears and no tongues.

Every morning, Brownlow composed, aloud, his daily editorial, but all his attempts at conversation were met with polite nods from men who economized on speech. And so, picking the burrs from his coat, he grasped the walking stick that gave him the air, he thought, of Bunyan's Pilgrim, and set off to explore the upper reaches of the stream. The path, winding close to the purling water, was only a scar in the underbrush. Ferns brushed his ankles, and stones he could not see made the going precarious. More than once, his foot rolled over a spiny chestnut, further cracking its carapace. Lifting his eyes, he saw birds and squirrels in the barren branches, but he looked in vain for a mourning dove that kept him company for half an hour, with its soft, cooing call.

He wished now that he had his old copy of Emerson's *Essays: Second Series*, given to him by his wife for his fortieth birthday, and carried for months in his pocket. The idea of Nature as a language, as *the* language in which God talked to Man, had appealed to him in middle age. No longer an itinerant preacher, but often on the road as a man whose words were in demand, he had taught himself to parse the landscape, until one day, finding himself in Maryville when he had set out for Loudon, he had decided to read maps instead. Now, however, he was a man without appointments, a naturalist on holiday. He might just find himself writing a line or two worthy of the Sage of Concord.

Snapping branches cracked the air. Up ahead, something moved through the woods, a slow-moving rumble that shook the leaves in the distance like the heat waves of summer. Brownlow's feet had grown roots. A blackness rose before him, human in its height, but alien in its shape, with growling coughs, doglike jaw, tiny ears, and mammoth paws. The bear had stopped, too, not ten feet away. Brownlow and bruin eyed each other warily.

Whatever Nature meant to say to him through this messenger, the Parson heard only "meat." With a growl, the bear lunged forward. Yanking his pistol from his belt, Brownlow swung its muzzle toward the bear, and fired the weapon straight ahead. As he did so, he heard a roaring echo of the sound, much louder than its pop, and felt a numbness by his ear. Stunned, he watched the bear rear back, turn, toss its head as if tortured by a swarm of bees, and come crashing to the ground, where it thrashed like a dragon's tail, and finally jerked still.

Brownlow had barely moved by the time he heard shouts from behind him, "Parson, are ye hurt?" "What's happened?" and the clap of hands on his shoulders. Several men from camp crowded past him, staring at the huge animal, and then back at the pistol, admiring its eloquence. They stood aside as he stepped closer. It was his prey to examine, but he could hardly believe he had killed so great a vital force with so small a metal object. He almost gasped, as it seemed the jaws moved, but on closer inspection, he saw that the muzzle of the bear was crawling with tiny mites. What riveted him was the eye, or, rather, the place where the eye had been, for the socket had been ravaged, the jelly seared away, so that nothing remained except raw strings of flesh in a spreading pool of blood. Had his tiny bullet strayed so far from its target, yet done its work so well?

Unsure of why he did so, Brownlow reached out a finger to the bear's upper chest. The hair was matted in many places, but he felt rather than saw a sticky patch where he remembered he had aimed. Now, using both hands, he pried into the pelt, as if forcing a way through tall grass. Then he saw it, nestled in the skin but still visible. A pistol ball, not much larger than a kernel of corn. Had the bear even felt it? As Brownlow continued to gaze down in confusion, a drop of bright red blood fell on the knuckle of his left hand.

What a fuss everyone made, as if he were the one with the blasted eye. Quickly enough, it was discovered that the top of his ear had been nicked, and only one drop was spilt. Never one for a mystery he couldn't solve, Brownlow rehearsed the last few moments, starting with that persistent sound of the mourning dove that had followed him from tree to tree. Then the trembling of the earth as the bear . . .

Then the raising of his . . . Then the . . . Slowly he turned around in the path and looked behind him.

He saw the tangle of underbrush and the crowded trunks of pine, chestnut, and oak, and then the limb of a tree elongated itself and swung to the ground, bending upright with a spring. A figure as tall as Brownlow, but as thin as a rail, stood in the path, leaning easily on the stalk of a rifle and regarding him with a twinkling eye. "Howdy, fellers," said this branch of humanity, with a pleasant lilt that sailed his words toward them.

Brownlow was striding toward the man before he knew he had moved. As soon as he was within reach, he grasped the muzzle end of the rifle, felt its warmth, and, as if cradling a burnt hand, crossed his arms on his chest. Clearing his throat, and aware of the men who had followed at his back, he lifted his chin and spoke. "Am I to conclude, sir, that you fired that rifle in my direction?"

"You could say that, Parson. But from where I was sittin', I had the bear in my sights, and he was lookin' at you cross-eyed." He swooped a clawlike hand up at the tree, clearly enough indicating that he had been perched in that nest and had fired from that vantage point. Brownlow paused, not entirely surprised that a stranger had recognized him, but feeling a snag in the conversation. Then he realized why. This man had nearly murdered him, but where was the apology? Significantly, the Parson fingered the rough spot on his ear: "Are you aware that you could have killed me?"

After appearing to give the idea some thought, the hunter replied, "I *could* have, that's true. But I don't much hanker for parson meat, and I do like a bear steak now and then. So I decided t' kill the critter."

Brownlow stared at the man, but saw no insolence in his deeply lined face. On the contrary, he saw only friendliness. The creased eyes were untroubled. Their clear and candid gaze reminded him of the folks who'd shared a tale and a fire with him in his circuit-riding days. That memory released others, and for a moment he was again the orphaned boy who lived by quick wits and good humor. "Parson meat." Indeed! One corner of his mouth twitched. The two men held each other's eyes for a long moment, and then Brownlow began to chuckle behind a slowly widening smile.

"You chose the right target," he said. "I'm told my head is so hard, even bullets can't dent it." Hearing an appreciative laugh behind him,

he added benignly, "Tell me your name, friend, so I'll know who saved my life."

"Why, that's Andy Slocum," said Ed Manning behind him. Others chimed in. "How're ye, Andy?" "Seen any Rebs in the foothills?" "Andy can take out a squirrel's eye at half a mile, cain't ya, Andy?" "Where y' been, Slocum? My datter's been moony for a month."

Slocum, ducking away from thanks and jibes alike, drew a large knife from his belt and marched over to the bear. Brownlow guessed the men would skin the animal and hang its meat in a tree for several days, but he did not see that operation. Ed and his brother-in-law Seth offered, not with the best of grace, to accompany him back to camp. "Nonsense," said Brownlow, to their delight. "I got myself here and I can get myself back." He set off quickly, but not before he heard the excited whistles and guffaws behind him. It came and went in a flash, the regret that he hadn't been asked to join them. He'd have been useless there, a mere hanger-on. With their country courtesy, they'd have pretended otherwise, but he'd have spoiled their enjoyment. Brownlow tested his ear again. No fresh blood. Already a scab. This fellow was the very devil of a shot. The Confederacy is a raging beast, but let him bellow and rampage in his fury, it takes but one keen eye, one true hand . . . it takes but one true shot from one loyal heart . . . it takes but a steady aim along the barrel of the Constitution. . . . Before he knew it, Brownlow was back in camp.

That evening, the men were cheerful, reliving their adventure, correcting each other's memories. Those incisors were two inches long. No, three. C'mon, now, fellers, I saw 'em, too; they was only as long as yer hound dog's. Although the bear meat wasn't drained yet, there was venison for the fire. Andy had brought a haunch with him for dinner. He told them he had caves scattered throughout the mountains, hidden from Rebel eyes, where he stored food, clothing, matches, and ammunition.

"Try this," he said, handing over a few chunks of dry bark. "From last year's dead trees." He said it would burn clean, and it did. There was hardly any smoke to betray their whereabouts. But Brownlow was sure that if a human being were anywhere within miles, he'd make a beeline for the camp. The Parson closed his eyes and sniffed the air. The rich, vinegary scent of the meat made his saliva tingle. When at last he bit into a crusty chunk, it was tough as a hoof, but he believed he was in heaven.

When there was nothing to do but groan, release belts, and find a mossy couch, Slocum drew a clay pipe from a fold in his leather shirt. Despite the tree-swinging antics of its owner that day, the pipe was intact. Using a bent thumb with a nail as thick as a tortoise shell, Andy tamped down the tobacco—a gift, he said, from a farmer whose hog he'd saved from a Rebel poacher—and lit it with a rush from the dying fire.

"Heer'd you took along some fellers thinkin' of stampedin'," stated someone Brownlow couldn't quite place in the dusk. "Did y' git 'em to Kentuck'?"

"Got 'em as far as Carter County. Dan Ellis piloted 'em from there. He says there's snow in the mountains now. On the last trip he made, they ran from a troop o' Rebs and lost their shoes crossing a river. They stamped and hopped for hours to keep their feet from freezing off."

All eyes were fixed on Andy. "And did they get to the Federals?" asked Brownlow, from the opposite side of the embers. Their pulsing glow was the only light, catching the whites of eyes now swiveling toward the editor. "Ay," said Andy. "Our boys'll do anything to give the slip to those devils." The darkness breathed with murmurs of agreement. These were men with homes and wives, children and crops, but if they must hang by the neck or be conscripted by the Rebels, they would rather die in the wilderness. That was one page of Nature Mr. Emerson had never read.

Clearing his throat, Brownlow signaled the end of the discussion by bowing his head and calling upon their Creator. As he had done each evening, he asked for His protection on all those forced into hiding by the minions of the Confederacy. He thanked God for providing fresh water and good hunting, "and for giving Mr. Slocum the steadiest hand in Tennessee."

The first to stand guard that night was Ed Manning. There were many instructions. "Give us a call if ye hear anything." "Keep the fire low, and keep an eye out for cougars." "Cougars?" "Ay. Last week, five of 'em crept into camp, and climbed over the lean-to." "Wanted the warmth, I reckon." "Wanted me for dinner."

The sounds of the night were familiar to Brownlow now. What kept him half-awake, or half-dreaming, were the moving pictures on the curtain of his eyelids. He saw himself being ushered to a chair in General Carroll's office, where the troubled general admitted his confusion and asked the reinstated editor for private counsel. The plaster walls gave way to marble columns and gilded cornices, as a senator, who very much resembled himself, cast a vote against pillows with iron spikes in them.

"Whaaa . . . ?" he cried, pushing away the hand on his shoulder and sitting up. He had been sound asleep. Disoriented and dazed, he now rubbed his head where a branch had poked his skull. "What is it?" he demanded.

"Shhhhh!" came the response. "Come with me, Parson." He could see that the quickly retreating figure was Andy, and he planted his feet and cantilevered himself upright and did not swear. At some distance from the stretched-out forms of the other men, Brownlow saw someone standing under the shadow of the trees. His clothes and face were blacker than the night, which was just growing pale around the edges. Brownlow guessed that dawn would be breaking soon.

"This here's Isaiah," said Andy, in a whisper Brownlow could barely hear. "He has news from below."

Brownlow nodded and extended his hand. The cloaked figure hesitated, and then responded. To Brownlow's surprise, the fingers that met his were coal black. "Tell us, Ike," said Andy. "You can trust him." Meaning me, thought Brownlow, which was a third surprise before the sun had reached the treetops.

"Dey's a passel o' Rebs come by de house, and ask Massa George if he seen de Parson anywheres around hyah."

Brownlow looked inquiringly at Andy. He'd understood the words but not the message. Andy explained, "Ike belongs to George Hastings, down closer to Tuckaluchee Cove. The Rebel soldiers often stop there, and Ike keeps his eyes and ears open. When he can, he slips away at night, to warn me. But he has to go back now." Turning to Ike, Andy touched his arm and the two men exchanged some words that Brownlow couldn't hear. When the informer had merged into the larger blackness of the ravine, Andy turned back with a sigh. "Ike thinks they'd rather shoot you than capture you," he said. Brownlow would always be grateful he hadn't asked at that moment, *Can we trust him?*

Quickly, they roused the other men, and held a council as

everyone rubbed his arms and hunched his shoulders in the cold. Brownlow, insisting that he was now a danger to the group, said he would leave that very morning. It was Andy who pointed out that the Rebels were sure to know that Brownlow was not alone in this retreat, and so it was best to abandon the camp altogether. Two by two, the men would descend the mountain, and then go their separate ways. The Rebels might stop two men on the road, but they would murder a band of twenty.

Brownlow and the Reverend W. T. Dowell set off down the trail, picking their way carefully, long before the sunlight could penetrate the forest. Brownlow had said good-bye to Andy with a strange mixture of regret and relief. He saw in the man the habits of independence, the natural ease in the wilderness, the sturdy loyalties and native wit he associated with the earliest settlers in what he would later describe as the American Switzerland, the green mountains and lush valleys of East Tennessee. But he saw in him also a man whom circumstance couldn't sway, and there was something in the impassiveness of the hunter that cast a cool light of indifference over so many of the concerns that agitated Brownlow. The mountains belonged to Andy, but the town belonged to Brownlow. He knew he must return to it. Yet in the end, unexpectedly, he found his opinion of himself enhanced—something he usually managed without anybody's help—by Andy's last words: "Glad to know ye, Parson. You've a steady hand, too."

By midmorning, they were back in Wear's Cove. Ed Manning's wife gave them packets of dried meat and fresh bread. She bundled their hats and coats into a roll, which they could strap behind their saddles, and gave them worn caps and patched jerkins that smelled of the pigsty. Then she handed each of them a sack of children's apparel, so they could say they were couriers for their wives, delivering cast-off clothes to their relatives. Even the Confederacy would respect two grandfathers on such an errand.

For her kindness, Brownlow pretended to accept the ruse, but once on the road, he gave his bundle to Dowell, saying he could not hide behind a sock. He rode silently, his mind busy with alternatives. By the time he reached his destination, he knew what he must do. His decision pleased him so much that he retrieved both bundles from Dowell and, sighting a negro child playing outside a rotting cabin in the woods, called out to her "Early Christmas!" and made a gift after all.

Having heard rumors that Brownlow had been captured, John Williams was very glad to see him. In Blount County, through which Brownlow had passed just a short month ago, he had many friends and supporters. What a delight it was to feel a desk beneath his elbow again, to hold a real pen in his hand, to dip it in the inkwell and leave a raven tracing on the page. On November 22, he wrote the letter he had composed in his head while riding across the valley. He had learned that General W. H. Carroll would be replacing Zollicoffer as commander of the Eastern District of Tennessee, and so he addressed his letter to the new man in charge. After roundly accusing Colonel Wood of the villainy that had forced good men into hiding, Brownlow came to the first of his main points:

> As it regards the bridge-burning, I never had any intimation of any such purpose, from any quarter. I condemn the act, and regard it as an ill-timed measure, calculated to bring no good to any one or any party, but much harm to innocent men and the public.

Then, with a flourish of righteousness, he added:

> I am ready and willing at any time to stand a trial upon these or other points before any civil tribunal. . . .

Unfortunately, he did not receive Carroll's reply until December 1. On the surface, it was a conciliatory response. Carroll promised Brownlow that no harm would come to him if he returned home. Further, he stated that,

> If you can establish what you say in your letter . . . , *you shall have every opportunity to do so before the civil tribunal, if it is necessary,* —PROVIDED YOU HAVE COMMITTED NO ACT THAT WILL MAKE IT NECESSARY FOR THE MILITARY LAW TO TAKE COGNIZANCE.

Carroll ended by saying he would protect "every loyal citizen, regardless of former political opinions." Could anyone wish for more considerate treatment? Carroll clearly thought not. Brownlow wasn't so sure. The next day, taking with him the two reverend old men who had shared his exile, W. T. Dowell and James Cumming, he visited Soloman Farmer, a justice of the peace for Blount County, and prepared a statement to be witnessed by his two friends and notarized by Farmer. In this statement, he declared, once again, his innocence of any involvement in, or prior knowledge of, the bridge burnings. This sworn testimony he then inserted into a new letter to General Carroll dated December 4.

It was a masterpiece. Referring to Carroll's promise to protect "loyal citizens," Brownlow dismissed the hidden message of allegiance to the Confederacy, asserting:

> I am loyal to the Government of the United States, and that is the only Government I consider as having an existence in this country.

Then he crafted his finest gesture. It would, he believed, be all the more effective because he genuinely believed in the better man within Carroll. Softening his tone, he spoke to that fellow human being:

> I am not in arms against your Confederacy. I have not encouraged rebellion on the part of Union men, but the reverse, and I am quietly awaiting the result of the contest going on. In this *neutral* condition I feel that I ought to be let alone, and left to the quiet enjoyment of opinions I honestly entertain and cannot conscientiously surrender. *You*, but a few months ago, entertained the same opinions I do, and acted with me in opposition to Secession. Toward me, personally, I think you would entertain none but kind feelings, were you not associated with the men you are.

Wiping his pen on a piece of cloth, Brownlow reread what he had written and found it good. That no sane person would consider him "neutral" never occurred to him. He believed he had never been more honest or reasonable.

In this spirit, he returned to his house, where he was reunited with his family. What Brownlow did not know, was that thirteen days earlier, on November 20, the Confederate Secretary of War, Judah Benjamin, had been pressured to intervene. The Parson's friend, the once-Union, now-Confederate attorney John Baxter, having been present in Richmond at the time, had urged leniency toward the editor.

Reluctantly, Benjamin had given the following command to Major General Crittenden:

> I have been asked to grant a passport for Brownlow. . . . I cannot give him a formal passport, though I would greatly prefer seeing him on the other side of our lines, *as an avowed enemy.* I wish, however, to say that I would be glad to learn that he has left Tennessee; and I have no objection to interpose to his leaving, if you are willing to let him pass.

In obedience to this directive, Acting Adjutant General A. S. Cunningham wrote to Brownlow on December 4, offering the most generous terms the Parson would ever receive from his enemies:

> The Major-General commanding directs me to say that upon calling at his headquarters, within twenty-four hours, you can get a passport to go into Kentucky, accompanied by a military escort, the route to be designated by General Crittenden.

In the light of this good news, his heart expanded with relief. From Kentucky, he would have the North as his audience. From Kentucky, he could send for his family. He recalled Andy's stories of the stampeders, the local men who braved icy rivers and tall mountains and starvation just to fade out of Tennessee into the light of Kentucky, where loyalty to the Union was no crime. He, on the other hand, would make the journey in state, with a military escort to protect him from the renegade Confederates who killed Loyalists on sight. Savoring this thought, he poked his head out of his door to wave at the two or three people who had gathered in the road, having heard he was at home again.

On Thursday, December 5, accompanied by the newly returned John Baxter, he presented himself to General Crittenden. The welcome he received was cool and brief, as if the general wished him gone. He did not mind. It was enough to know that his pen had, once again, carved a path for him. The general informed him that, on Saturday, December 7, he would be escorted to Kentucky by Captain Gillespie.

On the morning of the sixth, his bedroom was still shuttered. Eliza was shifting a large trunk into the center of the floor. "Let me do that," he said, coming up behind his wife. He had not been certain how much baggage he could take with him. She opened the lid, turned from him, and began drawing shirts from the chest below the window and laying them flat in the bottom of the trunk. As she did so, she kept the brim of her cap between his eyes and her face. At last he interfered, taking her by the upper arms as the shirts dangled in her limp hands.

"Think of it as just another one of my trips into the counties," he urged. "In another few months, I can send for you, or the war will be over." She shook her head, bit her lip, and sniffled. He tried again. "You'll have Susan and John with you. I think you really like having the house to yourself. No ink stains on the table."

She still wouldn't look at him, and he began to wish he'd let her get the packing done and the crying spent before offering his help. He bent his head to look under the frill. "What is it, 'Liza?" he asked, with an edge of impatience. "I'm really not upset. I'm sad to lose the office, yes, but I can write from Kentucky. What's troubling you?"

"Sally," she blurted. The Parson was confused. "S-sally?" he repeated.

"Sally Foster. She was my age."

"I don't . . . What are you talking about?" Time was passing.

"We swam in the creek together that day. We grew up together."

"What day?"

"Sh-she passed me in the street yesterday."

"Well, you must have been glad to see her." He tried for kindly warmth, removing his hands and rearranging the clothing in the trunk. "She isn't a close friend, is she? You can write to her." He wondered if he were talking of sunrise to someone thinking of sunset. "Don't fret, m'dear. We have a great deal to do."

"She called me a Yankee whore." And the tears came, relentless, unreachable, unforgiving, leaving Brownlow wordless. After she had run from the room, he remained standing there, not at rest but immobile. While he could not fathom why, at this particular moment, she had decided to feel aggrieved, he understood that he was the cause of it, and that he could do nothing to remove or ease her pain, but would only add to it, by being who he was.

In the still-darkened room, he knew his daughter was now standing where her mother had been, looking at him with shining but clear eyes. He sighed heavily, and bowed his head as she came closer. He could feel her thumbs wiping moisture from his face, hear her murmuring, "It's the war's fault, Papa, not yours," and sense the bracing of her strong young body as he leaned his forehead on her shoulder.

Later that day, William Gannaway Brownlow was arrested at the door of his home in Knoxville, Tennessee.

A marshal, sent to conduct him to prison, allowed him a final return to his desk. There he wrote an urgent plea to General Crittenden:

> I am now under an arrest, upon a warrant issued by Commissioner Reynolds, at the instance of J. Crozier Ramsey [the District Attorney for East Tennessee], upon a charge of treason, founded upon sundry articles published in the Knoxville Whig since the 10th of June last. [Later he would prove that the cited articles had, in fact, been written on May 25, *before* the state seceded.]
>
> I am here, as you will recollect, upon your invitation and the instructions of your Secretary of War to give me passports into the old Government. Claiming your protection, as I do, I shall await your early response.

At first, he insisted on being hopeful. Partly, this was for the sake of his family, but there was another reason, too. He trusted the written word. By now, he knew of Benjamin's guarantee. He had Crittenden's offer of protection. These assurances came from men who believed their cause was honorable. How could they, then, in all conscience, act dishonorably? As the author of fiery editorials, Brownlow had been lashed in return. He was no stranger to vitriol and vituperation. It was the atmosphere he lived in. And yet there was something in him that could not accept a failure of communication, when he, himself, had written in good faith.

There would be a reply to his appeal, but it would come not from Crittenden himself, but from his aide. Brownlow would already be in jail by the time he read these words:

> SIR: —Your note, stating that you were under an arrest upon a warrant upon a charge of treason, &c., has been handed to General Crittenden.
>
> He desires me to say, in reply, that in view of all of the facts of the case, (which need not be recapitulated here, for you are familiar with them,) HE DOES NOT CONSIDER THAT YOU ARE HERE UPON HIS INVITATION IN SUCH MANNER AS TO CLAIM HIS

PROTECTION FROM AN INVESTIGATION BY THE CIVIL AUTHORITIES OF THE CHARGES AGAINST YOU, which he clearly understood from yourself and your friends you would not seek to avoid.

Even before he held this letter in his drooping hand, long before it fell to the prison floor, Brownlow knew he had been betrayed. There would never be a civil trial. It would be far too easy for him to prove the falsification of dates in the charges brought against him. He was at the mercy now of the Confederate Army, of men like Carroll and Crittenden. Soon he would meet, too, the infamous Leadbetter, who had hanged two bridge burners in Greeneville. And Ramsey, that lying son of an embezzler, would gloat over his downfall like the fiend he truly was.

After the first shock, Brownlow had absorbed these truths as he prepared to leave his home again. He felt almost calm, as if, after all, he was more comfortable with indignation than escape. Wasn't he the "Fighting Parson"? He would have a new pulpit, and he would learn how to use it. When he kissed his wife good-bye, he told her his imprisonment would be his greatest editorial.

Noticing the crowd that had gathered to see him off, and ignoring the many jeers among the shouts, Brownlow signaled to his captor, *a moment, please*, and mounted the horse block by the door. "I go to prison a free man!" he declaimed, waving his Spanish hat, adorned, it was later said, with a cockade of turkey feathers.

And yet, as he was marched through the streets of Knoxville, his mind was somewhere else entirely. He was picturing himself in the camp by the river, laughing at the puny bullet he thought had killed a bear, gnawing the bones of freshly killed venison, and clasping the hands of men like Andy and Ike.

Joshua

Chapter 5
Our Own Lil' Zouave

*L*ATER, HE WOULD TELL ABOUT IT, *but first he had to live it.* . . .
The floorboards hit his elbow, jarring him awake. Pale light
skimmed the planks, an inch from his nose. A spider went high-
stepping by. Joshua rolled to his knees on the pallet, catching the
heavy coat that had covered him. He shook it out before hanging it
over the corner of the open door. Then he gave himself a full stretch
(fifteen hands! the Colonel had said) under the low roof.

The bedding rustled as he leaned over and scooped it into the
corner. He did not fold it, as he'd been taught to do, because there is
a difference between a mother in front of you and a mother far away.
Instead, he hunched his shoulders and rubbed his upper arms in the
chilled air. Way up north, they said, water turned solid if you left it
outside. You could scrape it, or chip it, or splinter it like wood. Mam's
brother had seen it with his very own eyes, before they caught him
and sent him back.

Giddy from standing up so fast, Joshua sat down on the rough
floor of the attic, lifting his knees to his chin. He listened hard. There
it was—the faint vibration of a deep, wet snore, as rhythmic as the
cooing of the doves on the roof. Down below, the Colonel was asleep.
Every morning, at precisely the same time, he opened his eyes and
wrinkled his nose. Just then, and no sooner, the coffee must be brought
to him. Joshua had plenty of time before Mary set the water on.

Pulling the coat down onto his lap, he sat on the broad windowsill with his back to the morning. The peppery smell of the raw wood and cotton sacking and dried husks made him sleepy as he rubbed and rubbed, first on the three stars, then on the buttons that were left. Old Joe's voice drifted in with the sunlight, "So-o-o-PHEEE-a-a-a-a!"

Hustled up by Mam, the three of them—Joshua, Obie, and Bushrod—were standing in front of Miss Delphine in her bedroom last summer. Old Joe gripped their shoulders, nudging them from side to side until the spaces between them were equal. Joshua shook off the gnarled hand, and Bushrod flicked an eye at him. *Missus look like a cloud*, because it was morning, and she wore her puffy white dressing gown. Joshua had seen Mam ironing the rows of lace, wiping her face so the sweat wouldn't drip. Missus cocked her head and went *hmmmph*.

"Stan' up, boys. Obadiah, you taller than yestiddy?"

"No, Miss'," Obie grinned. How Mam had cried, when she heard about the measurings. *Nev' gon' see yuh agin.* "Now don't you cry, Sophie," Miss Delphine had told her. "The Colonel's just testin' his 'quipment." Joshua had been the tallest.

Mas' was over by the desk, where the boys couldn't see him. Missus raised her chin: "Dan? Come stan' here, so I can see 'em beside you." Joshua turned his head, because he liked to watch the Colonel in his uniform, tall and stiff "as a Georgia pine," Miss Delphine liked to say. She'd been to At-lan-ta. Joe tapped him on the cheek, making him face front, but he still saw the Colonel looming up. High white forehead. Long straight nose. Mouth level as the measuring stick—*go fetch me the ruler in the box there.* Fringe of brown hair, ear to ear, tucked beneath his chin like a bib. He was different from the men who came to the house sometimes, talking in small voices in the parlor. Sharper corners. Faster starts. Quicker stops.

Mam had taught the children to look at white people's faces the way you look at the sky. Crinkles at the eyes meant sunshine; creases in the forehead meant drizzle; tightness around the mouth, well, then you better move fast, or hunker down and hide. That morning, the Colonel was cloudy, with a promise of blue. "I don't have *time*, Delphine—any one of them will do. All I need is a boy to make the fire and clean the boots. I've told you, dear. Richmond is civilized, and when I'm in the field . . ."

She frowned quickly, then swung him around by the waist and placed him in front of her. Next she made Obie, tan as wheat, and then Bushrod, brown as coffee, and then Joshua, black as coal, stand next to him. Each time, she took a step back, as if studying a picture. "We're goin' make you a li'l less *Maine*, and a li'l mo' *Dixie*."

It was Joshua who was standing next to the Colonel when she said that. His laugh barked overhead. "*You*'ve done that, my dear. You've just about threshed the Yankee out of me. You, and *this*"—he waved his free hand at the curtains blowing at the windows, letting in the light but keeping out the flies. Or maybe he meant the other things he always talked about when he said *I'm not a Northerner anymore*. The stately columns. *The ocean of white cotton, bobbing with dark heads.* This lovely woman. Delphine. The South. *Beleaguered and beautiful.* That demon spawn, Lincoln. *He can't understand us.*

Peter, the only one in Mam's cabin who could read and write, said that the master was lucky, because marrying Miss Delphine meant he was a Confederate now. He wasn't just a man who built forts for the army, but also a Southern gentleman, and the mistress was lucky because he wasn't enough of a gentleman to make tan babies like Obie. There wasn't much that Peter didn't know.

He was the one who had taught Joshua how to make the drawing—J O S H U A—that was his name, and an outline in the dirt that was Alabama. He'd shown him the notches in the wall that were the months and the days, and explained how *that* worked. It took a while, and at the end of every lesson, he'd repeat: "So's y' know *who* you is in God's eye, an' *where* you is in God's country, and *when* you is in His plan." Then he would look around to make sure nobody could hear, and he'd whisper, "Savior comin', inna crown like a stovepipe." Joshua wasn't too sure about God or Moses, but he believed in Peter.

Suddenly, Miss Delphine gave a jump. "I know jus' the thing, Dan!" She pounced on the table beside her bed, flung open a drawer, and pulled out a soft red ball that opened into a stocking . . . no, a cap! She pulled it over Joshua's head, laughed when it covered his eyes, and pushed it back on his forehead. "There! Our own lil' Zouave."

The Colonel gave Joshua's shoulder a gentle squeeze and then a push. "Tell Sophie to get this one ready," he said.

There'd be no reason to let Mam come with them to the train, so she and Joshua and Obie and Bushrod and Peter and Sarah and Sally did their hugging and crying beforehand, in the cabin. Mam rocked him in her arms, big as he was, like a baby: "Nev' gon' see yuh agin." But nuh-uh. It wasn't winter. It was summer. Nobody changed hands then. He spoke from the deep part of his throat, wanting no argument, but he was old enough to know that white truth was only half-true. Then he thought of a gray and perfect truth. The Colonel was coming back to Miss Delphine, so Joshua was coming back, too. All he had to do was stay close to Mas'.

He felt their warm, salty faces pressed against him, but part of him was already in the crowd at the station, staring up at the wooden rooms on wheels, holding tight to the Colonel's valise. Someone was shouting, and the black folks were being herded down the line, but Mas' took Joshua by the arm and said to the shouter, "He'll sit with the bags, but he stays in my sight." The man frowned at the North in the Colonel's voice, then bowed to his coat. Still, Joshua could feel the man thinking. *Ten-or-twelve-year-old male. Five feet, give or take. Scar on chin.* That's how they found you later on, if you got lost, like Mam's brother.

The blast of the steam made him jump, and he yelped under his breath when the cabin jerked and swayed and began moving with him inside. At first, he kept his eyes on the top of the Colonel's head, but the glint of moving things outside the box—clouds, rooftops—made him look. Bracing himself against the leather bags, he stretched his neck so he could see more through the windows. Like magic, trees and buildings and fields were yanked behind him, until—he didn't know when it happened—Alabama was gone. Mam was gone. Miss Delphine was gone. There was only the Colonel, the box on wheels, and the darkening sky.

Many of the soldiers left them at a place called Knoxville, some joined them at Bristol, and finally they were at Richmond, where Mr. Davis lived. It was only later that he learned he'd been carried all the way across Alabama and Tennessee to Virginia.

The Colonel was called something different now: "Chief Engineer for the Confederate States of America." Once, he took Joshua with him to Yorktown, where there was water again, stretching through a narrow place and then out into the wide ocean. Were these the same waves he'd seen, in the old days, in the Gulf? If so, they must be sorry to be in Yorktown. Allowed now to carry the Colonel's instrument case, Joshua walked with him over the muddy flats where the soldiers were cutting logs and women were washing laundry in round tubs on wooden trestles.

He'd heard Mas' say that nobody could slouch like a nigra. It was Joshua's opinion that nobody could stand, or sit, or lie down with arms and legs more lazily crossed, than soldiers at rest. There were lots of them. The only thing there was more of was iron balls, stacked in rows, big as melons but harder (he'd tapped one) than a turtle's shell. While the Colonel was talking to a man with an axe, Joshua had put his hand under one of the iron weights. So heavy! They'd crush a foot, or a man, if they started rolling. Once, he'd seen a tower of oranges become a floor of moving balls. Couldn't that happen here? Joshua smiled inwardly. Then his face cracked open. It would almost be worth seeing! It would sound like thunder. But the cannon balls were stuck, just part of the dirt, like the crooked nails and the splinters of wood. Nobody raked *this* yard, he could tell.

And then, one peaceful morning back in Richmond, the world did come tumbling down, and nobody smiled. It was the tenth day of the eleventh month in the year of our Lord 1861. Joshua was sitting on a stool in the passageway to the outbuildings, dreamily rubbing a torn piece of cloth, a remnant from an old homespun shirt, over the Colonel's magic tool, called a "transit." He'd stared at it so often, the Colonel had finally let him touch it, and now it was his duty, and his joy, to clean off the sandy grit, and wipe off the beads of water that miraculously appeared when the metal came indoors.

Joshua loved the brass tube fixed on braces over a piece of round glass. Watching the Colonel, he'd seen the tube raised and lowered by a wheel (he'd turned it one time, by the little knob with ridges that hurt your fingers). The smooth strokes had made him sleepy, and he'd almost closed his eyes when he felt the ground tremble. A knocking shook the house before somebody rushed into the room where the Colonel spread his papers. "Joshua!" The Colonel's voice flew to his ears, loud but calm. "Come here." It was like a hand on his collar, pulling him upright before his legs could work.

At the Colonel's door, he was almost knocked aside, almost lost his grip on the transit—still somehow in his arms—when the dusty smell of sweat came rushing by. It was the messenger leaving, stuffing papers in a saddlebag. There was the green glow of a storm in the Colonel's lowered face, and Joshua wished he could slink away. "Pack," said the Colonel. "Everything. Now."

But he couldn't move. The air twirled him, like a screw, into the floor. Then the Colonel looked up, and his hands stopped moving on the desk. Seeing the transit, he said, "This isn't that kind of job." Joshua hugged the metal even closer. "All right. Yes, we may need it. We're going to build bridges—and gallows, too, I think." Then, as if remembering it was only Joshua in the room, he added: "Pack your cap, boy. We're going to war."

They were near Elizabethton later in November, where the Colonel left on a horse and came back with many people under guard, and more men were taken near a place called Doe River. Next, the Colonel was in Jonesborough for several days, and then traveled on to Greeneville, with a bigger room and a bigger desk. Joshua was often told to sit outside the door, to be within call if somebody needed water, or a jacket sleeve mended. So he heard what was said.

On Friday last, bridges had been destroyed by men banding together at night, maybe hundreds of them, thousands more gathering perhaps. They were mountain and valley men, renegades without a conscience, hankering after that devil, Mr. Lincoln, even though— hadn't they heard?—Tennessee had voted out. The whole state belonged to the South now, even East Tennessee, and it was the duty of every citizen to accept that decision, whether he liked it or not. But these hooligans were waiting for Uncle Abe to fly down and rescue them. Any day now, Federal troops, like a plague of locusts, would come swarming in from Kentucky. Would they?

"I've been advised," announced the Colonel to the listening men, "as have Zollicoffer and Carroll. We're under orders from the secretary of war"—papers rustled—"as follows: 'First: All such as can be identified as having been engaged in bridge burning are to be tried summarily by drumhead court-martial and if found guilty executed on the spot by hanging. It would be well to leave their bodies hanging in the vicinity of the burned bridges.' " Joshua heard breathing, nothing else. Then the Colonel said. "Colonel Wood has caught six of the conspirators"—a quick half cheer—"We will start with the ringleader, 'Fry' I believe his name is, and we will proceed in pairs. It is neither practical nor effective to hang more than two at a time."

Four nights later, on the twenty-ninth of the eleventh month, the last of the day's foot scraping and door closing left the rooms empty with the buzz of silence. Barely loud enough for Joshua to hear, the Colonel called for the combination ruler, the smoothly jointed sticks that opened and closed and had a tiny bubble in a glass window on one side. He took the instrument from Joshua's hand and laid it flat on the paper before him, passing a leaded pencil along its edge. He didn't look up when he dropped the pencil, but squeezed the corners of his eyes a few times, as if trying to see better. Joshua had watched the Colonel make maps, but they didn't have straight lines, so this must be different.

The next day, there were many people coming and going, including the ones who had visited the Colonel the day before. They took his hand, and said happy, loud things through their whiskers. Did you hear how the passengers got off the train, so they could say they poked the hanged bodies? Maybe the news had traveled north, how the Confederacy dealt with pests! The Colonel broke in, not angry, not sorry, just clear: "Four remain." He said he was repairing the bridge at Lick Creek, but he had business with the rest of the men who had burned it and spoiled the railroad line. They were being kept for him in Knoxville.

Listening, Joshua felt the ridges of the wainscoting against his back, like the grooves in Mam's washboard. It seemed to him a terrible thing to keep the boxes on wheels from gliding along the rails, for *he* knew how wonderful it was, that grinding chug, chug, and then the pictures flying past the window. But he felt something else, too. A stab of pain passed through him cleanly as a needle, just as it did when Mam told him to wait in the cabin till Old Joe had time to whip him for the oranges, when he'd only stolen the fruit because his stomach said *do it*.

When he swept the hearth that night, he found some of the loose pages, black and thin as a beetle's wing, spoiled drawings for later messages. He traced the letters with his eyes.

HEADQUARTERS,
Greeneville, November 30, 1861

Hon. J. P. BENJAMIN, Secretary of War:

Two insurgents have to-day been tried for bridge-burning,

~~judged~~ *found guilty and hanged.*

D. LEADBETTER,
Colonel

There were other pages, already powdering into soot. The next day, there was a crowd of workmen in the yard, and someone reading aloud:

HEADQUARTERS,
Greeneville, East Tenn., November 30, 1861.

TO THE CITIZENS OF EAST TENNESSEE:

So long as the question of Union or disunion was debatable so long you did well to debate it and vote on it. You had a clear right to vote for the Union but when secession was established by the voice of the people you did ill to distract the county by angry words and insurrectionary tumult.

He knew it was the Colonel, but it sounded like the Bible. . . .

I proclaim that every man who comes in promptly and delivers up his arms will be pardoned on taking the oath of allegiance. All men taken in arms against the Government will be transported to the military prison at Tuscaloosa and be confined there during the war.

Bridge-burners and destroyers of railroad tracks are excepted from among those pardonable. They will be tried by drum-head court-martial and be hung on the spot.

D. LEADBETTER,
Colonel, Commanding.

By the eleventh day of the twelfth month, within weeks of the Lord's birthday, Joshua was living in the attic of a two-story wooden house not far from the Knoxville prison. The Massa and Missus who owned the house had left it to the Army of the Confederate States of America. So it belonged to the Colonel now. It was pushed right up to the street, with hardly room for the three steps up from the track where horses and carts went clattering by, in a cloud of dust that settled on everything. Mary, the cook, and Sam, the houseboy, had been waiting for them just inside the door. These two came with the building, and something about their shiny black faces was as surprising as the house. They looked at the Colonel and said "Welcome," without waiting for him to speak.

Mary reminded him of Mam. The top halves of her apron folded across her chest like the wings of a swan, and she had a turban on her head so white it made him blink. Sam was tall and thin, with a head like a knob on a walking stick. Round cheeks, round nose, and round forehead under a fuzz of ginger wool. He was maybe as old as Peter, but he stood easily, a little back on his heels, regarding every person at chin level. *That* look, Joshua'd seen before. It was the way Old Joe put visitors in their place when the outdoor folks came to the back door in Mobile. *Scrape yo' feet, nigga. You in* my *house.* Joshua tried a little smile and then sighed. It was always the cook who mattered anyway, so he beamed up at Mary.

The Colonel put things in order, and every day was the same. Mary lit the fire in the outbuilding while the sky was still dark, and brought the coffee to the pantry, where Joshua put it on a silver tray and took it up to the Colonel's sleeping room. Sam washed the floors and opened the door for visitors and carried messages around town, but it was Joshua who attended to the Colonel's personal belongings and sat by his door all day long. Mary called this room the "parlor," but it was the place where people came to see Mas', and where he read messages and wrote answers.

On the twelfth night of the twelfth month, the Colonel told him to put more wood on the fire. "I'd forgotten how cold . . . ," and then his voice died away. He was alone, except for Joshua. He'd been thinking of Miss Delphine, most likely. Maybe he was writing to her, while he sat with a blanket around his shoulder, in the circle of candlelight. He'd given Joshua his coat, telling him to polish up the two rows of buttons. As always, Joshua wore his red cap, and pulled it cozily around his ears as he sat at a small table in the corner. You needed two candles for a letter, but only one for a button.

"Joshua." Had he been dozing! He opened his eyes wide. The Colonel was leaning back in his chair, gazing at him, asking how many buttons he had polished. Before thinking, Joshua began counting . . .

two . . . five . . . eight . . . "Nine, Mas'."

"And how many are on that coat?"

"Foh-teen!" It was just about the highest number he knew.

"So, how many are left to polish? No. Don't count. Look up here. Tell me." Joshua's mouth dropped open. Where was Peter! He knew how important it was to answer the Colonel smartly. How else could he see Mam again, and Obie and Bushrod . . . but he knew, too, that there were worse dangers in the world than never going home again. There were limits to what a slave should know. Letters were forbidden. But Old Joe could count, and that was all right, because he always had to know "how many" of this, and "how many" of that was stored in the cellar. Desperately, Joshua closed his eyes and said the numbers in his head, tapping his fingers on the coat until all were used up. "F-five?"

"Come here, Joshua." That was almost the way he spoke to Miss Delphine, a warm, paying-attention kind of voice. Joshua stood up and brought the coat with him, instinctively hiding behind its heavy gray bulk. "That was a very good answer," said the Colonel. Oh, Lord be praised, though it was Peter who had taught him. "You know how to count, then. What about letters?" Joshua sensed a keenness in the Colonel eyes, that sharpening of the light that made you duck behind trees. "Nuh-uh, Mas'. Don't know 'em."

The hand was at his head before he could jump back. The Colonel stroked the red cap with a slow, gentle movement, cupping Joshua's cheek before taking his hand away. "Our own lil' Zouave," said the Colonel slowly, as if from memory. Then his hand came back, and his thumb touched the dent in Joshua's chin. Startled, afraid, curious, Joshua looked into the pale human eyes and understood that they were sad. Mas' was thinking of home, too. Then the Colonel sat back and Joshua breathed again.

"And what about the days of the month, Joshua? Did Sophie teach you those?"

"Peter . . ." flew out of his mouth, and the Colonel gave a half smile, as if agreeing *of course, Peter.* "Finish the buttons in the morning, Joshua. Do it early. I need that jacket after breakfast." Only after he was nestled into his pallet, drawing the coat snugly over himself in the wintry air that poured through the cracked roof, did he realize what he'd seen on the Colonel's desk. It was a small sketch of an upright beam and a crossbar with a loop hanging down from it. It reminded him of the combination ruler, opened to form a corner.

His head jerked up. The snoring sound had stopped. The Colonel was awake! Getting to his feet again, Joshua wrapped his arms around the coat and held it to the side, so he could see to go down the stairs. Down, down all the way to the back room, where he left the pile on the table for Mary to press with her flatiron, as she did every morning. Out the back door, running to the stables, where he ducked close to the horses and relieved himself on the straw. There was a skin on the water in the rain barrel, and in spite of the cold, he dashed his hand on the surface to make it shatter. Dabbing some drops on his face and arms, he rubbed himself vigorously with the towel left on a nail for him, and hop-skipped for the house again.

Mary was doing her slow bending back and forth, and he lifted his spoon, double-time, from the corn mush to his mouth. Bend, raise-lower; bend, raise-lower. It must be a special day. There was milk in the bowl, too. With the coat folded over his left arm, and the tray in his right, he balanced carefully up the stairs and then stopped. He couldn't knock on the Colonel's door. He needed a third hand. As if by magic, it opened in front of him, and his burdens were taken from him.

In the parlor that morning, the Colonel seemed unable to stop moving. "Joshua! Sit in the corner today. I don't want to shout for you." He was wearing his sword, walking slowly back and forth in front of his desk, his hands gripped behind him. Every time he turned by the window, his buttons caught fire. At last, he stopped in front of the glass on the wall and bent toward it, pulling back his lips and turning his head from side to side. "Fiddlesticks," he said, and sat down.

In a little while, Sam went to the front of the house and spoke to someone there. Then he appeared: "Colonel, suh. Mistah Rams'y at the do'."

"Send him in—and tell Mary to step lively."

A man came strolling into the room, with a rolled-up newspaper tucked under his armpit. At first, he didn't seem to notice the Colonel, who had risen behind the desk. The man wasn't large, but he swelled to fill the room. Joshua was very glad indeed that this wasn't *his* white man. Mr. Ramsey had long black eyebrows flaring up at the outer end. To everything he saw, his eyebrows said *oh, really!* His bunched-up lips made a ridge beneath his nostrils.

Joshua jumped. Mr. Ramsey had swept up his arm—"Ha!"—and marched across the room, reaching out a hand as if beckoning for a package. "Thought we should meet, Colonel Leadbetter. I'm John Crozier Ramsey, District Attorney, at your service—well, we serve the laws of our new country, do we not, and we're here at the pleasure of Mr. Davis. You and I both. You've met him, of course, decent fellow."

"Yes, I've met the president. Sit down, Mr. Ramsey. I believe I've seen your father's book, a rather large history of the region, if I'm not mistaken."

"You are not." Mr. Ramsey lowered himself carefully over the chair's glossy cushion, flipping out his coat tails without dropping the tube of newspaper. "It's a book more often *seen* than *read*, particularly by his enemies. My father is a man, if you'll excuse my saying so, who made the history he writes about. If these were easier times, he'd invite you to Ramsey House." Even Joshua could tell nothing real had been said yet.

The visitor leaned forward, glancing over his shoulder at Joshua. "Even the little ones are spies these days."

"Things are different where he comes from. Please go on."

"Let me tell you then, sir, that I speak for the old families, the men of honor and courage who put everything at risk for Secession. They—we—understand why it is necessary to—do—what you—hmmm—*do*. You cannot put down a rebellion without stretching a few necks."

"We can't tolerate wire cutters and bridge burners. They reverse human progress."

"There speaks the New Englander!"

"Not at all." Something moved in his cheek. "I am speaking as a Southerner, not by birth but by—"

"Marriage?"

"By conviction, Mr. Ramsey. I am in a position to compare the chilly North and the balmy South—I refer to temperament as well as climate—and my choice is well considered. It is stronger than mere habit or association. But I am speaking also as an engineer. If there is a stress point, it must be relieved, and it must be done so that everyone knows that the structure is sound again."

"God save us! Another man of metaphor . . . !"

The Colonel cleared his throat. "We have disposed of two saboteurs in Greeneville, as you know, and Haun two days ago. The Harmons will be next. There is a sixth, a farmer from the Greeneville area, named Harrison Self, about whom there may be some question, although not enough to save him."

He looked sorrowful now, like the time Mam's brother left. "I am disappointed by how many of these firebrands escaped. They have friends, of course, locally. No doubt we meet some of them in the street without knowing it. We must treat the ones we have as examples for the rest of them. From what I hear, you've charged hundreds of these Lincolnites, who think the Federal Army is coming any day now to rescue them."

Mr. Ramsey twisted in his seat, and slapped his hand on the armrest. "I bring a charge, yes? Yes! I swear out a warrant, true? True. The fool is marched into court. Judge Humphreys, fine old Southern gentleman, well known to my father, sees the poor simple countryman, deluded by that—that *carpenter*—Brownlow, and says . . ." Mr. Ramsey's voice became high and shaky: "My good fellow, you don't *really* want to cause trouble, do you? No, of course not. Here's your writ of *habeas corpus*: 'Swear allegiance to the Confederacy, and go home and feed your cow.'" Ramsey shook his head, "It is the judicial version of *noblesse oblige*. We are foiled by our heritage."

"The civil courts—"

"*Please*, yes, I know. They aren't the right venue. But you must see it from my side. These men are ordinary citizens, not soldiers in uniform. They are *my* responsibility, yet they're taken away from me. Martial law is declared. What can *I* do? I wrote to Richmond, some weeks ago, asking for instruction. Here"—he reached into a pocket and pulled out a slip of paper—"is the reply:

> I am very glad to hear of action of the military authorities and hope to hear they have hung every bridge-burner at the end of the burned bridge. J. P. Benjamin, Secretary of War.

So it would seem"—Mr. Ramsey heaved his shoulders—"you have the handling of this affair. Thank God, there's testimony against the Harmons, father and son, and against the farmer, Harrison Self. But it's that rascal Brownlow who belongs on the gallows. Silence his newspaper, and you quiet the Lincolnites."

"In my limited experience," said the Colonel, "hangings make more converts than editorials."

"I'm not so sure," smiled Mr. Ramsey. "I am pleased to say that I have had Mr. Brownlow—or, 'The Parson,' as he's humorously called—in prison for a week, living in the filth he loves to write about, side by side with your saboteurs and, if you ask me, more guilty than any one of them. He first suggested it, you know. Targeting the railroads."

"You've brought charges, then?"

"I'm trying to. Of course, he's making a fuss, claims he was tricked into surrendering. If he's released, you'll find it hard to convict those who were duped by him. The day after his capture, the *Register*— you were in Greeneville—printed a letter to Davis, begging him not to pardon this *true* arsonist. And just today"—suddenly, the rolled newspaper was whipped into the air, landing flat on Mr. Ramsey's knee.

"Listen to this! 'Why is this ringleader of all the Toryism and devilment in East Tennessee dealt with so leniently and others not half so guilty punished extremely?' In short, Colonel, he *must* be restrained. There are stories of letters getting out, drunken guards at the jail, what a melodrama! Believe me, he is interested in behalf of the Harmons and the other one, Mr. Self. You can't hang the Parson—a pleasure *I* hope to have—but you can, and you must, tie his hands"—the air shook—"or *your* criminals will slip the noose."

The Colonel raised his fingers up to his mouth in a little tent, and spoke from behind it very quietly, tapping his mouth very gently. "We are moving people daily, some to the prison in Tuscaloosa, as you know. It is a messy business. Soldiers are not clerks, and they do some pushing and shoving, and, yes, a little more drinking than they should, but Mr. Brownlow is in jail, and he's staying there. That much I can do. It's up to you to bring charges."

It seemed to Joshua that both men took a rest now. Mr. Ramsey rolled up his paper and returned it to his armpit. Just then, Mary knocked on the side of the open door. Yellow biscuits had arrived. There was some talk about the hour, and then the Colonel filled a small glass for Mr. Ramsey, and another for himself.

"So! You brought this one with you, then?" Mr. Ramsey said,

waving a thumb at Joshua.

"Yes. He's a pet of my wife's. It's useful to keep the same routines from one posting to another."

"We've heard they're less teachable in the lower states. Alabama. Mississippi. Closer to the jungle, eh?"

"That's a fallacy. He's quite bright. Let me show you." Joshua didn't realize what was happening until the Colonel raised his voice. "Stand up, Joshua. Tell this gentleman how many days there are in November. Speak up."

Months swam together in his head, just now, when he tried to think hard. He raised his hands and spread all ten fingers three times. "Th-th-" He couldn't get the word out, but Mas' nodded his head once.

Mr. Ramsey pursed his lips again. "Well, boy, let's see what you do with this one. Feb-u-ary."

"He's only a child." The Colonel turned away, as if he expected no answer, and Mr. Ramsey bent to free his coattails. Joshua, bursting with knowledge, could hardly wait to surprise the Colonel.

"Twenty-eight, Mas'! 'Cep' when it catch up. Then it twenty-nine."

Both men swung around and stared at him. The visitor narrowed his eyes, first at Joshua, then at Mas'. "What in blazes . . . ," Mr. Ramsey said, his face very red, as if the Colonel had played a trick on him. Mas' face was even whiter than usual, which meant that something bad must have happened. *Watch dere faces,* Mam had said. Mas' was looking at him like the green before thunderstorms, as if Joshua had left dirt on the Colonel's boot on parade day, where everybody could see it. Had the answer been wrong? Maybe the days of the month were different here, and he waited for Mas' to explain the mistake and teach him what to say.

Gradually, the weather in Mas' face changed. He looked at Joshua with a raised eyebrow, cocking his head to one side. "They can learn anything by rote," he said, "but there's no understanding." Then he winked at Mr. Ramsey. "I let him look through my telescope one day, out that window there, and he sings out *Massa, I sees Alabama!*"

Mr. Ramsey stopped frowning then, and began to laugh in big rolling waves. The Colonel made laughing sounds, too. After a while, Mr. Ramsey said he had to leave, and the Colonel walked with him to the door, and when he came back into the parlor, he said "Fool!" under his breath, but who he meant, he didn't say.

Joshua heard only the words of a few moments ago, still echoing in his head. Why had Mas' lied? Joshua had never said he could see Alabama through the tube that made things big. Only a baby or an idiot would say anything so stupid, and Joshua was neither of those things, and Mas' knew he was not. Joshua's eyes filled with burning water.

When Mary asked for his help in the kitchen, he was glad, for the first time, to leave his post in the Colonel's room. *Stupid, stupid days of the months.* He was going to forget all about them. He scraped the tan coating off the potatoes and cut them, as Mary showed him, into pieces. Behind the outbuildings, some trees, all their leaves gone, scratched the sky. He'd never see Mam again, he felt sure now. All that belonged to him in the world he carried inside his skin, growing pebbly in the cold. Up above him winked a star, and in the distance, he heard the quiet rumble of the street. He opened and closed his eyes. He was here. He was gone. He opened them again, and felt the cold, slippery object in his hand. A potato. Mary would scold him if he didn't hurry. Of that, he was sure, too. And he knew one more thing: not once, not ever, had he looked through the Colonel's telescope. Maybe he should have, when the Colonel wasn't there. Maybe he *would.*

His last chore for the day was taking the leftover potatoes back down the few steps to the root cellar. In the past, the dark had frightened him, with its rotten, earthy smell. He nudged the sack into its place, pushing the rolling balls inside the cloth.

"PSSSSt."

"What you want?" He knew it was Sam.

"You ain't skeered?"

"Nuh-uh."

Sam took a seat on the stairs, so Joshua couldn't pass him.

"Lemme up." He pushed the older boy's knee.

"Who you pray fuh ev' night?"

"Mam and Obie and Bushrod an'—"

"Oh, shush, boy. Who goin' set you free?"

He hesitated. "Massa?"

"Lissen him!" The round head shook back and forth, a black circle against the starlight.

"Who den?" Was Sam laughing at him, too?

"Mistah Abraham. He d' one we prayin' fuh."

"You 'n' Mary?"

"Us—and some the coloreds 'round town."

Joshua's mouth dropped. "How you do it?"

"Cain't tell—'less you come 'long, too. We gon' pray fuh Mistah Hahmon and his son over t' the jail. They gon' meet Jesus soon. An Mistah Self, he next. Tell Jesus, we ain't responsible. We cain't he'p what *he* do." Sam nodded up the stairs in the direction of the parlor.

"You gon' come?" It was Mary, peering into the cellar, her eyes two white flashes.

He'd never before had a choice, but he made one now.

CHAPTER 6
CASTLE FOX

THE CAGE (DECEMBER 6)

MORNING WAS HARD TO RECOGNIZE IN THE PRISON. No chorus of birds, no brightening of the sky, no bellow of a cow with an udderful of milk. In this place, the windows looked like squares of bleached wall. Every joint pained Harry as, with a sheepish nod, he accepted a hand up from a fellow prisoner. "First night?" "Mmmm." "You'll get used to it." "I hope not." "We're better off than that feller over there." "Mmmm."

He'd answered mechanically, but after he'd been on his feet for a few moments, after he'd straightened the shirt that had twisted around his torso in the night, and just before he realized how badly he needed to piss, he saw it. Or at least the top of it. An iron lattice rose above the field of shaggy heads near one side of the room. Some primitive instinct told Harry he should explore his new home, find its threats and its vantage points. He might learn something of use to his bladder. And so he made his way, slowly, with mumbled apologies, toward what looked like the top of an oversized birdcage.

Which is what it was, in effect. The large, open-work metal box, nearly ten feet high, and about six feet square, was a miniature room within the prison. There was a small door, about four feet high, near one corner. Inside, on the only stool Harry had seen since his arrival, sat a man with his head half-turned away.

As Harry watched, a hand rose and stroked the chin. Something about the gesture, the narrow crown of fine hair . . . the man looked around, and Harry started. Beneath the bony forehead two milky-blue eyes, pushed out to the plane of the face, glimmered above the high cheekbones. His hand dropped, and Harry saw the tufted beard that lengthened the face of his old friend, Christopher Alexander Haun, the master craftsman from Pottertown. Haun, who'd been so nervous that night, who'd clung to the belief that the raiders were "soldiers now."

"Alex!" he half whispered, close enough now to grasp the metal lattice. It was horrible to see a man caged like a beast, but why Haun, of all people? Then he understood. Alex wasn't just a prisoner anymore; he was a convicted bridge burner awaiting execution. Shaken, Harry struggled with his old protective feeling toward the man, knowing in his heart how puny and irrelevant it was now. The caged man's eyes gradually focused on Harry. A shudder passed over the potter's face and he turned away. Shame, perhaps. Or maybe he was afraid of compromising Harry by acknowledging him? More loudly, Harry said, "Alex. I wasn't sure you were here. When . . . ?"

After a moment, as if answering a stranger's question out of politeness, Haun cleared his throat and said, in a rusty voice: "They came to the house the day after." Harry nodded. Yes, he'd heard of the arrest. "And you've been here ever since!" He'd known only that his friend had escaped the hangings in Greeneville. Would Alex have preferred to die there, if he could choose? No—Harry thought of himself, of Lizzie—no, better to have—*that*—done out of sight, far from the people who loved you.

Harry pressed against the iron bars. There was nothing he could say, nothing he could do, except to be that tie to home. For the next few seconds, while Haun seemed to have forgotten him, Harry pored over the sight before him, engraving it on his memory. There was something chilling as well as humbling about a person whose days were numbered, whose thoughts and quirks and habits would soon be erased from the world in which others still breathed. Harry felt driven to study him, to hold back the passing of these last irretrievable moments. In their intense light, Haun seemed burnished with importance.

A rheumy, all-too-ordinary cough wracked Alex, snapping Harry back to practicalities. "Elizabeth has friends," he said, referring to the other man's wife. "They'll look after her and the children." There were several small ones, much younger than his own. "Until you get back," he added lamely, wincing at his cowardice. Haun looked like a man detaching himself from life and getting good at it. False hope was unkind to him. Harry felt his own measure being taken, then cursed himself for that self-regard. He'd faced dying men before, but they were old or sick or mortally injured, not calmly sitting a few feet away, idly flexing their fingers, as if reminding themselves they still could. What did Haun need, now, that Harry could supply. Attention. That was all.

Suddenly, Haun took in a deep breath, discovering Harry again and addressing him. "I've asked for paper to write to them. Some of the neighbors"—decent as he was, he wouldn't name them—"can finish the clay I left, two or three pieces of ware, I think, on order. That'll bring in some money. And then Elizabeth should sell the tools. . . ." He was talking like an old man on his deathbed. Wasn't he about forty? "Jacob—that's my eldest, he's thirteen—he'll have to see to the young'uns. Keep 'em in line." Haun smiled wanly.

"And Jake?" asked Harry. "Malinda said he was taken around the same time."

"He's here. And Henry. And Tom."

"And . . . Hugh? Have you heard anything, seen anything?" The possibility that his son might be in this very prison had sent shock waves through Harry during those first few hours, but by now he felt sure the boy was somewhere else. Relief and despair tumbled over each other, taking turns being uppermost. He could not tell them apart.

Alex shook his drooping head. "I am sorry, Harry. No news."

A shout rose up in the street, and Harry's head jerked around. Haun's did not. Nor did he take much interest in the gathering of Greeneville men near the cage that morning. One by one, they sifted out of the prison population to gather around Haun. Jake and his sons were among the first to appear, having heard by then about Harry. For several moments, the shock of the meeting left them speechless, grasping each other's arms, shaking their heads in pained disbelief. Then, without being asked, Harry gave what news he could of Malinda and the family. He learned of the "Greene" corner of the prison, where he'd find other men from the county, and heard, too, that Jake expected his own trial very soon. That stout fellow, the one who gave speeches, the lawyer who'd been a Unionist and still defended them in court, had Harry heard of him, John Baxter? Yes, he'd defended Alex. No, well, he was still the best chance any of them had.

All too quickly, horror faded into normalcy. It was an ache and a relief, a sorrow and a comfort to see these familiar faces, to hear voices from home, not in dreams but in reality. Tom and Henry seemed often one person, sitting with shoulders touching. Every so often, they whispered with bowed heads. Perhaps they were still hoping for a Federal invasion. Did they think a torrent of blue would burst through the door? Up close, though, Harry saw that the light had gone from their eyes.

Sometimes Harry thought of that night in Jake's house. When it came, he fought against the memory, telling himself that, if it had not been Jake, it would have been someone else who helped Fry. But would Hugh have gone adventuring, if he hadn't felt safe in his uncle's home? Harry had only to close his eyes to see his son looking back over his shoulder as he trudged off into oblivion.

His nephews brought Hugh so vividly to mind, that Harry winced inwardly when he looked at them. Unfair, yes, he knew it was, and it even occurred to him that he might be wounding them with his awkwardness around them, so he would turn away, unable to trust himself. Tom's presence was almost unbearable. His pale, dismayed face seemed always to be saying, *Why can't everything be all right again?*

The appeal was so direct—as if Harry could fix whatever had gone wrong, as he had so often done in their childhood—that he had wanted to shake Tom. Had he done so, he knew he would have ended by crushing his nephew in his arms and comforting him like a child. Only by clenching his own hands and turning away could he withstand the force of this emotion. It would be indecent to vent his feelings on the boy. It would undermine the courage they were all going to need. Not until much later, when it became clear that Jake would follow Alex to the gallows, would it occur to Harry that he had, in effect, set Tom adrift without an anchor.

The midday meal came and went. Only once did Haun respond to the world outside his cage. There was the sudden, piercing call of a red-feathered cardinal: a short dying fall, followed by a series of quick notes. Haun's head shot up, and Harry looked around. *OOOooo . . . chirp! chirp! chirp! chirp!* Someone nearby laughed, "It's only Andy."

That afternoon, the shouting in the street seemed to get closer, and suddenly there was a commotion near the door. Harry, who was bracing a raised leg against the cage and bending over it to stretch out a cramp, lowered his foot and turned toward the sound. The tide of men was lapping toward the street door. Haun showed no interest, and Harry dutifully sat down again. It was evident, however, that something remarkable was happening at the center of a growing ring of men. Tom and Henry had shaken themselves from their apathy and were peering over heads.

"Go," said Alex.

"What?"

"Go ahead."

"I suppose we should see what's going on."

"*Go*. I don't want you here."

A little stung at first, then touched by the hidden kindness, Harry stood, tossing back "We'll let you know." Jake, who barely stirred now, remained near the cage, and the jostling crowd soon separated Harry from his nephews. Briefly, he was among strangers again, men he did not have to love or pity, and something eased in him. What was happening up there? The sea was parting before someone who moved slowly across the room. Who was this Moses? "Hurrrrr-ah!" came a cheer. Many people were talking at once, but soon Harry distinguished a voice, rich and resonant, as if rising from a pump organ.

He was surprised to find that it issued from a tallish and gentlemanly person in a frock coat, with a thick and wavy crest of dark hair, swarthy skin, and large dark eyes. Their melancholy roundness, the loose folds beneath the chin, and the broad and flexible lips gave him a monkey-ish look, but at the same time there was a soulful energy, a preternatural intelligence that twinkled in the eyes. A hint of humor peeked from the corners of the deeply cut mouth. He was instantly recognizable.

It was William Gannaway Brownlow, better known as the "Fighting Parson."

Seeing Brownlow in the flesh, sensing the crowd's respect for him, Harry had pursed his lips and tucked his chin, not knowing what his face betrayed. With all his being, he had wanted to blame this man for Hugh's fate, and he longed to do so now, to tell Brownlow, to his face, that he led children into danger. Yet he hesitated, as he had done that night at Jake's house, in the presence of forces beyond his ken. Like Fry, Brownlow was the tip of a very long spear, and Harry had only a boot knife.

But it was something else that held him back. He bit his lip in silence as he watched the Parson nodding and shaking hands left and right. The truth, when Harry could bear it, was that he himself had been at fault. He'd been so angry at the time—not because Hugh had joined the bridge burners, but because he had listened to the schoolmaster, the newspaper editor, the Army captain—to everyone except his father—and in doing so, had brought the war to Harry's doorstep.

Whatever had been said about safety and prudence, Harry had banished his son because he'd been resentful and annoyed. He'd wanted his old life back, the one he had earned and deserved. Of course, he hadn't thought in those terms, but that didn't matter. Some stringency in his nature, some rude theology of his own, told him that actions leave marks on eternity. They spell your name in God's eyes. He half believed he was in prison not for burning a bridge, which he hadn't done in any case, but for losing Corniah's child.

He was a fair-minded man, and he couldn't, and wouldn't, shift that guilt to the Parson. Yet the man's presence was salt in an open wound, and with that ache came the old prejudice against the wordmonger. As men squeezed past him to see and hear what was happening, Harry stood his ground. He could, at least, refuse to be impressed.

The Parson had doffed a large hat, with a few turkey feathers in the brim—a cavalier flourish that mocked his captivity. As he made a progress through the room, he was greeted by outstretched hands. "Sorry to see you here, Parson." "You sure did put the fire under them Secesh." "Never expected to come to this!" "I once saw you in Maryville, Parson." "Yer among friends here, Sir. We thankee for speakin' up fer the mountain folk."

Harry grunted. He doubted that Brownlow spoke for *him*, although he had to admit, the level gaze of the sad brown eyes nailed your feet to the ground. Harry saw looks of relief and pride on the faces of the men in Brownlow's wake. Maybe he raised their self-estimation—"*I* was in jail with the Parson!" Or maybe they thought his presence would protect them. Without question, he was the most famous man in the prison, and the Confederates must be celebrating. Having caught such a big fish, perhaps they'd throw back the little ones. If such a swap could save Alex . . .

"Hmmmph!" It was a scornful sound, waking Harry from his thoughts. He turned, but the face beside him was stony, except for a curled lip.

As if some internal bell had rung, the editor stopped at the exact center of the room, stroked his lapels, and lifted up a voice that could be heard in the farthest corner. "Gentlemen, don't take your confinement so much to heart. Rather glory in it, as patriots, devoted to your country and to your principles. What are you here for? Not for stealing; not for counterfeiting; not for murder; but for your devotion to the Stars and Stripes, the glorious old banner under which Washington conquered, lived, and died."

Brownlow's voice rose a notch: "The Federal government will crush out this wicked rebellion and liberate us, if we are not brutally murdered; and IF we are, we die in a good cause. I am here with you to share your sorrows and sufferings, and here I intend to stay until the Rebels release me or execute me, or until the Federal Army shall come to my rescue. YOU may take a different view of the subject, but I—*I*—regard this as the proudest day of my life."

The huzzahs and cries of "Good man!" and whistles of approval were deafening. They rose in short bursts and long waves, and were so loud that Harry could barely hear the low voice at his shoulder: "Pompous showman! He'll get us all killed."

Again, Harry turned his head. Again, he couldn't be sure who had spoken. "Did you say something?" he asked. Suddenly the man with the curled lip turned small burning eyes on him and growled, "Do you think that peacock really believes he'll be hanged like the rest of us? He's enjoying hisself." The man grunted in disgust and slipped away through the crowd. Harry looked back at Brownlow. The editor was bowing slightly to the left and right, accepting the applause.

THE MOURNING DOVE (DECEMBER 9–17)

By the time Harry had been in jail for four days, he was used to the routine, but not yet, not ever, to the nearness of his fellow prisoners. His legs ached to walk over his fields in long strides, with not another soul in sight. He longed for the quiet of early mornings and late evenings, when a robin's chirp, or the ping of an acorn striking the ground, were clear and distinct. Sometimes, even in the prison, he thought he heard a mourning dove's *hoo-WHOO-hoo-hoo-o-o*. He missed Corniah's singsong voice, her eyes creased with small worries that vanished when she smiled, as she always did, when she looked at her children or at him. He missed her warmth at night, the round solidity that turned to quicksilver. . . .

And Lizzie—how he missed her energy, her delight in teasing him, her tentative contrariness that, until very recently, he'd taken as a favor she paid him. Even in this place, he felt a surge of tenderness, or was it sadness, for her girlish air of competence. She'd put his pipe in his pocket! Better a razor, perhaps, but no, it would have been taken by the guards. Or a comb! He had little enough vanity, but was neat in his habits. Most of the men were shaggy, like bears. Having shaved all his life, he hardly knew himself now. But she had wanted to give him something he loved to handle, a piece of home that would comfort him.

At first, he was grateful. As his thumb caressed the bowl, his gaze would turn inward. He was in a sanctuary then, a private world where his fields, his family, his animals, resided. But he couldn't find peace there. His home would be ravaged by grief now. His wife abandoned. And Lizzie! What would happen to her without a father to protect her? This was the way the war had come to Greeneville, not with slaughter on a battlefield but with doubts and betrayals and compromises that drained your lifeblood. Waking at night, hearing the restless stirring, the grinding teeth of dreaming men, he shuddered, for he lay among the wounded in this fight.

Alex had been given permission to write to his wife, and materials were supplied. That had been five days ago. Today, on the ninth day of December, Alex had two visitors whose manner and appearance said "official." One was a stout man who kept brushing his well-tailored frockcoat with stiff fingers. The other—tall, lean, commanding—cleared a space around the cage with a mere wave of his hand. Behind them, a slave carried what appeared to be a portable writing desk. Benches were brought, and Mr. Stout entered into a low-voiced conversation with the prisoner. No words were overheard, but in the end, Alex was handed a series of pages. Without reading them, he signed each immediately, returning it to Mr. Lean, who affixed something to each page as he received it. When he had collected the lot of them, he folded the stack and handed it to Mr. Stout, who tucked it under the long fold of his collar.

Later, Harry learned that the two men were associates of John Baxter, the lawyer defending Alex, but when he made his way back to his place on the floor by the cage, he found Alex dull eyed and unresponsive. It was as if the meeting had done more than shatter all hope; it had cored out the soul of him. The same hair was there, the old nose, the familiar chin—but not Alex, the man himself. Addressing one of the bars to the side of Harry's head, a barely audible voice said that arrangements had been made for the body to be sent to the Midway Depot in Greene County. "And I signed . . . ," but with a contortion that sent a quiver of life over his gray face, Alex caught his breath in a sob, turned away, and would not speak again. The next day, the two men came again, and this time the name they called was "Jacob Harmon."

On the eleventh day of December, 1861, Christopher Alexander Haun was taken from the cage, his hands bound behind him, and led away, amid cries of outrage from the East Tennesseans. Later, the guards took pleasure in describing the testing of the rope, the taut rebound of dead weight falling, and the twitching spin of the body. But the men grumbled about other things as they wandered about with lowered heads and clenched hands. Haun had asked for a Methodist minister to attend him. He'd been refused. The Confederates had made him a proposition: if he swore he'd been misled by Union leaders— which is to say, by Brownlow—he could save himself from the noose. The eloquence of his reply lay in the fact of his death.

When the rumor reached him, Harry's eyes had filled with water that burned like acid. At the very end, Alex had known himself again. Tears were common in that prison, and Harry's fell unnoticed. Until that moment, he'd believed the atrocities were more or less evenly divided between the Confederates and the Unionists. He'd believed that if you cut through the political dogma, you'd find ordinary folks who simply wanted a government that understood them. Now he had to ask himself what kind of government would kill a man like Haun after urging him to lie.

It was a bitter thought, and it seeped into his brain, contaminating that private space. What would he have done, if he'd been offered that devil's bargain? These days, oaths were as common as cow pies. Swear allegiance to the Confederacy and you're free to go home. Why not take the pledge, if it's only "from the teeth out"? Was he any better than Hugh? He cringed at his fellow prisoners, and at himself. No man knew what he'd do if temptation had his name on it. But Alex had found out. He'd tested his words for purity and strength, with the same truthful eye that guided the potter's hand.

The mountain man

Every day, one of the inmates was allowed to go outside to refill the water bucket from a hogshead beneath the window. The larger barrel was replenished, throughout the day, by a boy who drove a cart like a cistern on wheels. On one occasion, Harry had seen the water boy, and he was not alone. A black male child was with him, a slave no doubt, who sat on the cart with his chin in his hand, gazing at a building where freemen were treated worse than animals.

Although Tennessee grew chilly in December, an active man could sweat through his clothes, and the guards would often wash their faces and hands in the water reserved for drinking. On behalf of the prisoners, the doughty editor announced his objection to such behavior. Within minutes, the reply was bruited among the prisoners: "Did you hear what that carrion-faced devil said to Parson Brownlow? 'By God, sir, we will have you know that where a Jeff Davis man washes his face and hands is good enough for any damned Lincolnite to drink!' The swine! Let him just say that to me, face to face, on open ground!" Harry heard about the exchange, several times, in fact, as it made the rounds of the prison, but it hardly registered on him. He was like a man being stung by a mosquito while being eaten by a dragon.

Evening closed in. "I can-not be-lieve it!" said Harry to himself, but aloud.

"And what's that, friend?" The speaker was taller than anyone in sight, and so thin his hands resembled talons as they cradled his upper arms. He had the look of old mountain men, whose skin was annealed to their bones, but you couldn't tell his age. He might have been in his thirties, weathered by the elements. "Andy Slocum," he said, unhooking one of his claws and extending it.

Harry shook it reluctantly. Like an amused bird, the man was cocking a beady eye at him. Harry gave his name, and then nodded toward the corner of the room where Brownlow had ensconced himself. "Just as if nothing's happened." Ever since his arrival, the editor had taken his meals apart. They were supplied by his wife, and brought on a covered tray.

"What's happened, then?" asked Andy Slocum.

Such a feeling of despair swept through Harry that his throat seized up and he shook his head. Was the man demented? Some who had been imprisoned for weeks lost touch with reality. They were treated with sad kindness, or impatience, depending. "Nothing," said Harry. "Just that a good man was murdered the other day."

"Ah!" The knob in his throat bounced. "You knew him."

Harry grimaced his reply, not interested in conversation.

"Who's next, d'you suppose?" Andy was scraping his chin with a ribbed thumbnail as thick and yellow as quartz. He might as well have been asking about the weather.

"Guess you're not afraid it's you," said Harry dryly.

"Well, nuthin' would surprise me," replied Andy, as if enjoying a new thought. "There I was, sittin' on my porch, and a few of them fellers with cotton balls in their hair ride up and one of 'em says, 'Hear'd you been spreading some hellfired Union talk.' 'Who, me?' I says. ''Less Bill Bailey's got two nephews name o' Slocum.' Never did like my Ma's kin. Guess they ain't too fond o' me, either, else I wouldn't have the pleasure of yer comp'ny." There was a sound like strangulation. From the expression of his eyes, it was clear that he was chuckling.

Harry turned away. He didn't know if this cheerful highlander was bravely indifferent, morally deficient, or mentally unhinged. He had neither the interest nor the will to care one way or another. Solitude was impossible, and the frustration of the caged animal seethed inside him. He wanted to strike the wall, or someone's face, and they were the same to him. Self-preservation kept him far from Brownlow, whose masticating jaw, slowly absorbing real bread and beans, was too tempting a target. He understood, of course, that his rage was the other side of fear. How long before he, too, was dragged out to a fake trial, hurled into that iron cage, and hung by the neck until dead.

He was weak from some havoc in his bowels, and tired from the alternate squatting and standing he practiced from necessity, but also by choice. He needed to keep moving. He had to kill time. When his turn came that night, he fell, bone by bone, joint by joint, to the unforgiving floor. For several hours, he was free.

"Alex!" He must have cried out the name in his sleep, then wakened to the memory of it, like an echo.

"Ay," said an elderly voice in the dark. "He were a fine fellow. I won't forget 'im. Nor will ye." That must have been what had pricked Harry, the fear that Alex would fall through some trapdoor to oblivion. Without knowing whom to thank, not even fully awake, he refolded himself on the floor and fell truly asleep this time.

THE BONNET (THAT NIGHT)

One eyelid opened.

Then closed.

A splinter of sunshine had entered.

In the distance, he thought he heard someone playing a banjo.

No, it wasn't a banjo.

It was the plangent call of a bird cleaning its feathers on a treetop.

Were there trees in this town?

There were trees in the valley of the Nolichucky, sun-shot, soughing branches, dappled shade, a dimpled face.

Her bonnet was lined in sky blue.

There were mockingbirds in the summer, wings with white edging, sharp, throaty calls so loud, so loud, so l-loud, so l-l-l-loud. . . . "AH-H-H!"

THE SPOON (SOMETIME BEFORE THE SEVENTEENTH)

Harry awoke with a start. Dazed, furtive, damp, he coughed and bent his knees with an innocent groan. No one was paying any attention. For such a motley group of men, drawn from all walks of life, there was a surprising habit of courtesy, a pretense of ignoring the odors and sounds of the body's private life. Or perhaps it was just that any reaction, of humor or disgust, would soon lose its point from repetition.

A dab of air cooled his cheek. The windows had been opened, as they were occasionally, to let in some fresh air. Then memory seized his gut, and he would have retched, had there been anything inside

him except despair. After Alex's death, the guards moved Jake and Henry into the cage, and Harry's first sight of them in that death trap brought a cry so sudden, so stricken, that even in a place so clotted with misery, heads had turned. "Who's that?" "Self, I think." "What's the matter?" "He knows them." "Who?" "The Harmons." "Who be they?" "Bridge burners." "Where they from?" "East of here. Greeneville." "Like the other ones, then?" "Aye." "Lord ha' mercy."

Jake's trial had been, like Alex's, a mere formality. Harry had known, as they all did, that the Rebels hungered for bridge burners. Jake would be meat to them, and yet, couldn't they see, didn't they realize, that he just happened to have a big dining room? An agreeable fellow like Jake, a man who loved tobacco but chewed mint leaves because his wife forbade smoking, and a man must have something between his teeth. . . .

Of course, there were other men on the brink of death, sentenced not by the court but by age or disease. One of them, Madison Cate, had been dying for days, shaking with a fever that made his heels tap like drumsticks. He was a farmer from Sevier County, with many small children. His only crime, Harry had heard, was that he'd paraded with some Union guards with a rifle on his shoulder. In his present condition, he couldn't lift a spoon.

Harry knew he belonged by the cage, but while he still had the freedom of the prison, shouldn't he keep his eyes and ears open? Soon enough, he would have to look through those bars. So Harry chose the closer and easier destination. He would see how Cate was doing. The old man was stretched on a ragged piece of carpet that muffled the tapping heels. Was this another kindness from Dr. Gray? The brigade surgeon was, you had to admit, a decent man. He visited the prison almost every day and had recently brought with him a few benches. Harry, only a few yards away now, could see how wasted Cate looked. His lips could no longer close, so he appeared to be grinning. Harry was about to turn away, when Parson Brownlow pushed his way into the small clearing around the sick man.

Ignoring the damage to his trousers, the editor knelt beside the pallet, supporting the man's neck and lifting up his head. Brownlow had been carrying a small dish that someone now held steady for him, as he spooned what looked like stew between the dying man's lips. The savory smell made Harry's mouth tingle painfully. This was clearly not prison food, but a share of Brownlow's imported dinner. Harry almost gagged at the scent of fresh food. He could barely watch Brownlow on his knees, prying that spoon between those teeth with the gentle force of a parent.

"I reckon it's harder for you folks," said a pleasant voice at his shoulder. Andy Slocum had materialized. His gangly figure could pass through a crowd like mist between trees, and suddenly he was there. Harry drew a deep breath, glad of the distraction. He doubted that any creature of the forest—deer, squirrel, or bird—could escape from this hunter.

"You folks?" he asked.

Andy pointed a bony talon first at him and then at Parson Brownlow, as if they were a pair. "Them as gets used to good food," he explained.

"Oh! Well, yes. But nobody in this prison should have to eat what they give us."

"It's not so bad," said Andy, with his irritating cheerfulness. "There's been times I've eaten slugs and berries for a fortnight, and not by choice."

"Maybe not, but you were free at the time. Makes a difference."

Andy scraped his chin, as he had before. It seemed his habit whenever a thought was taking shape. "Right you are, friend. Better to starve in freedom than feast in prison."

Harry looked at him curiously. Aphorisms were more in Brownlow's line, but then again, he'd known mountain men who could whittle a phrase like any minister. "Come over here to the Parson," said Andy. Brownlow had finished his ministrations and was briskly slapping his dusty knees and the edges of his coat. Harry's elbow was gripped by a pincer, and before he could hang back, he was face to face with the man Hugh had idolized.

"Parson," said Andy, with the same easy address he apparently used for everyone. "This here is Harrison Self, of Greene County. Taken up for bridge burning."

Harry braced for a gush of patriotism, but the melancholy eyes creased with sadness. "I'm sorry for your friends," said Brownlow, from the deep drum of his chest. "You must have known Hensie and Fry?"

"*Hinshawe*," said Harry. "And Haun, too. Alex—Christopher

Alexander Haun."

"Yes, yes. Haun's a potter of some note," Brownlow informed Andy.

Harry tasted the rising bile in his throat. "And others before long"—he nodded toward the cage—"and for what, Mr. Brownlow? I had no part in it, but my son . . ." He shook his head.

"Your son?" Brownlow moved forward, with a pastoral expression, and Harry stepped back. He'd never found much comfort in the ready-made sentiments of the churchly. He took a breath and remembered who he used to be. Harrison Self, owner of a fertile strip of land, possessor of good steeds and fat cows, earning his keep and paying his debts, living in peace until other men, in other places, turned the world upside down.

"My son is no concern of yours, sir," he said, lifting his chin. "I am for the Union, Mr. Brownlow, but I was never for the burning of the bridges. It's done little good and a great deal of harm, if you'll pardon me. And not just to those"—he nodded again toward the cage—"who will die for it."

"As I've said myself," chimed in Brownlow.

Harry stared at him. "You deny . . . !"

"I've been misrepresented, friend," said the other man, with the deeper resonance of public speech. "Yes, I warned that the railroads would be destroyed, but I was never a party to that ill-fated plot. That drunken scoundrel Ramsey has manufactured the case just to get even with me."

So the victim, now, was Brownlow! Harry felt he was standing at the end of a very long line, and that he could never understand, or influence, what was happening at the head of it. He nodded to the other two men and turned away. Behind him, he heard them speaking in quiet tones. Perhaps they pitied him, or mocked him.

The light was fading when a susurration began in the crowd, and Harry gradually distinguished the sound of his name: "Selllll. Sel-f, Harrrrr. Ison. Where's Self?" He was elbowed toward the door, where a guard with an upswept moustache and a piratical beard handed him a small slip of paper, with a dark smudge where his thumb had been. Opening it, Harry found that the world had changed again. It was the notice of his trial to begin the next day.

"Oh," said the guard. "*You're* Harrison Self?"

Harry nodded without looking up.

"Girl was asking about you. Said her name was Elizabeth. Choice bit of a thing."

It happened in a flash. Harry sprang forward, and the side of his head exploded where the gun barrel landed.

THE BLANKET

With the blood still closing his right eye, weaving unsteadily on his legs, Harry aimed himself toward Brownlow. His mind reeled dizzily, and spots danced in the corner of his one open eye. He couldn't form a thought, but he felt an overwhelming imperative to humble himself, to apologize, to beg, to plead, to say, swear, or do whatever was necessary. Other prisoners were looking at him with concern and curiosity, bunching behind him and following him across the room, but for some reason, no one dared touch him.

And there was Brownlow, now, watching him approach. Harry felt he was walking through water as high as his chin, each step a lazy, heavy motion that advanced him an inch. The Parson, moving quickly, took him by both arms and seated him on the end of a hastily found bench. Harry gaped like a fish tossed on land. Bending nearly double, Brownlow peered upwards into Harry's drooping eyes. "What is it, man?"

He tried again. "Lizzie."

Brownlow looked around at the bystanders, as if asking what the word meant, and then he bent down again, this time taking Harry's head roughly between his hands, shaking it side to side. Harry's one eye focused. He freed himself, and got the words out. "I think my daughter"—he swallowed—"is here. In Knoxville. Lll-Elizabeth. She's alone. She can't . . . she won't . . . can you help me? Your friends outside?"

Brownlow whipped up to his full height, as if a spring had been released. From his pocket, he drew a sheaf of small papers and ripped one from the stack. From another pocket, he drew a pencil, daggerlike, with a flourish. Motioning to another man to lean over, he used the sloping back as a desk and wrote furiously for a moment or two. He barked questions: Where would she stay? *Didn't know; wait—a cousin. Forrester.* Where? *Union Street—I think.* Who else would she know in town? *No one: just me; well, her uncle and cousins, the Harmons, but they're here in jail, too.* Brownlow nodded as he wrote. Then he folded the note, and strode away.

Straining to see, Harry watched him go to the nearest window, say something to the man guarding it (who stood aside), and call out into the street. When he returned, he straightened a few of his own blankets on the floor and nodded to another man to help him lift and deposit Harry on the ground.

He did not sleep, but he was conscious of nothing except an occasional coolness and wetness on his face, and the tightening of something around his forehead. A bandage? He did not sleep, but he was aware of time passing. He did not sleep, but he dreamed that Lizzie was standing on the gallows, and he screamed so loud he couldn't believe no one heard him.

The Pipe

In spite of himself, he must have fallen asleep, for how else could he have this feeling of rising up through layers of consciousness? It was dark, except for faint patches of light from the windows. Men were whispering. Brownlow was nowhere in sight. Andy was gone. Harry noticed that something covered him. He fingered it curiously. A blanket. Then all came rushing back and he tossed his head in agony, which he then regretted, as his injury pulsed. Brownlow appeared. "Rest easy, my good man. If your daughter is in town, we will find her." Harry was too weak to ask who "we" might be.

When he had recovered sufficiently to move about, he thanked the Parson and forced himself to think of Jake. From then on, he spent every hour beside the cage. Jake, of course, had noticed Harry's wounded head and the makeshift bandage, but Harry kept his trouble over Lizzie to himself. It was Jake who filled his heart now.

The Harmons' trial had been brief. It was widely known that Jake had hosted the saboteurs. Many had heard those words about "Henry Harmon's gun." Tom, though, had been spared, or so it seemed for now. Jake pleaded with Harry to watch for the boy, and Harry, of course, agreed. He did not think it likely Tom had been released, and he'd heard of an auxiliary jail somewhere nearby. Perhaps some guard, out of charity or cruelty, was keeping the son away from his father and brother in their final hours. Harry remained close, willing himself to be Malinda and Tom and the other children, as well as friend and neighbor. He said little, mostly murmuring promises to convey the messages he was given, if God granted him the chance to see home again.

Once, though, an idea came to him. He passed the word that he would like to see Andy, and the hunter appeared magically, as was his habit. "Have ye a morsel of tobacco, or know ye anyone who does?" Harry asked. About ten minutes later, Harry whispered softly to Jake, handing over his own beloved pipe, full and fragrant, though unlit. Nobody would admit to owning matches.

Night fell too soon. It was during the deathwatch—while Harry sat beside the cage, wondering where Tom might be, but asking nothing, saying nothing—that a space was carved out of time. He did not know if God was present, but he and the caged men were in the valley of the shadow, and the foul air was sacred.

It had been wrong to burn the bridges. He'd said so himself. He'd even guessed that men would hang for it—some distant cousin, maybe, or a neighbor's friend. Never Jake. But prison had instructed him. Most of the inmates, he'd come to realize, were guilty of the same crime, some rowdy allegiance to that freely constrained Union they thought of as their homeland. It came to him gradually that Jake was dying of an experiment—something new on God's earth, not certain to survive without crisis and renewal.

If living meant betraying better men who'd come before, then dying put you right, with them and with yourself, and with your children most of all. It was a painful kind of reasoning. It was an old man's way of thinking, not for Henry or Lizzie, or for children like Hugh. Would their trial come later? He reckoned that was so—or later still, for their children's children. Reasons fade over time, if there's no one to remember.

Had he spoken? Jake stirred in response, and Harry, printing the bars on his face, reached in for him.

THE COFFIN (DECEMBER 17)

Just before dawn, they heard it. Someone said, "There's a cart by the door." Then, in a lower voice: "With two coffins." The soldiers and the

sun arrived together, and it was Jake and Henry they were after. Dazed and stumbling from lack of sleep, the two men from Greeneville were prodded out the door. But not Thomas Harmon. No, not Thomas. He'd not been seen for many hours.

Harry had expected the crowd to shout and stamp their feet, as they had when Haun was led away, but most of them just bowed their heads. When the rumbling of the cart had died away, Harry felt he had stepped through a wall of fire. All surfaces were burned away, leaving only stubble in his heart, the toughest roots of his being.

With Jake gone, he thought it likely that he himself would be next in line for the gallows. First, of course, there would be the trial today, but he knew the outcome had been decided at Lick Creek. No quibble about motive would make a difference. Hundreds of men had struck matches that night, but look who had been hanged. Alex, Jake, soon Harry himself—men of substance, men whose deaths would be noticed, whose confessions would matter. Apparently, the Confederacy had a role for him, but, like Alex, he reckoned he'd decline. Killing him was one thing. Using him, another.

As he waited in line for breakfast, he noticed the stitches mending a tear in the shirt of the man ahead of him. How small they were; how precise. He counted them. He knew, too, how many paces to the trough, to the ditch for relieving oneself, to the corner where Brownlow lived, to the cage with its door swinging open now. The jail had become a place to him, a scene of daily life, of routines and adjustments. He knew how far you could stretch your leg, and how long it took the sun to reach that stain on the floor—the one shaped like a hand. He knew where and when you drew a line you would not cross.

Adrift in contemplation, he felt a hand on his arm, and saw Brownlow, unaccountably smiling. "Put your mind at rest, my friend," intoned the Parson. "Your daughter is found." Had he Lizzie in his pocket? Harry stared at the man, wondering if Brownlow, or he himself, or the whole prison, had gone mad.

Looking very pleased with himself, Brownlow added, confidingly, "Tonight, she will be under my roof, Mr. Self. I have a daughter, Susan, a brave girl, too. Susan discovered your Lizzie at the . . . well, she found her! Imagine that, can you! What a pair they make, true daughters of the Union. . . ." Brownlow gazed on a distant scene.

Harry, grasping only the word "safe," broke into a choked laugh and shook Brownlow's hand like a pump handle. "How can I thank you," he said. Andy, who was nearby, looked on in calm dismay. Even as Harry's heart warmed toward the Parson, he knew Brownlow would get something for his trouble. How many future audiences would hear about the "daughters of the Union"?

Suddenly, relief died. In Knoxville, in the Brownlow circle, Lizzie could not fail to hear about the trials. He had hoped she would not know what happened to him until some time had passed. She should be at home, with friends to comfort her. But she was here. She might see.

"What is it, man?" asked Brownlow, with a hint of impatience. "I told you. The girl is safe." Andy stepped close to Brownlow, facing away, and said a few words that Harry, dazed by the new agony, did not hear. He did see the Parson shrug, did hear the words "shame" and "but." Then Brownlow tossed up a hand with a little twirl of finality and moved away toward somebody who needed him.

Andy turned to Harry. "Susan's a rare bird, I've hear'd tell. I reckon she'll keep your daughter outta crowds and the like." Despite his worry, Harry understood. He nodded, grateful for the reassurance, and then found that a bench had been vacated for him. No thanks were required. With the Harmons gone, Harry was the man with the most to lose that day. In honored isolation he sat, and began to gnaw what he'd been clutching in his left hand all this time, throughout joy, throughout terror.

As he ate, and scratched his scalp, and watched the light grow, he got his bearings once again. During the following hour, several men passed by without speaking, but a few more chunks of bread appeared on the bench beside him. It was the language of the prison. Most of the men ignored him, having troubles of their own, but some still had charity in their hearts, or perhaps they were just glad not to be Harry. What they were offering was the only gift they had to give—not bread but awareness.

The day bloomed. In Greeneville, the morning sky would be smiling at itself in the river. There'd be a whisper of pink on the underside of clouds, a splash of gold on the tops. He had wakened there, in his mind, every day. But now he pushed the dream away for good. Did anyone have a comb? For a piece of bread, could he borrow it, just this once?

They came for him shortly before nine o'clock.

CHAPTER 7

ON TRIAL

I. The Law

JOHN BAXTER MOUNTED THE SIX STEPS TO THE PROMENADE in front of the courthouse and, deciding against the stairway sweeping up between the white columns to the main entrance, slipped into the building at ground level. This choice had nothing to do with the rude behavior he'd just experienced. Someone riding by in the street below had shouted "Which door is it today, Bax'? Tory or Secesh?" Lifting his chin with dignity, he'd turned toward the street, but all he'd seen was a stout man's back and two bouncy rumps, one human, one equine. He shouldn't have looked back. What you gained by defying, you lost by acknowledging.

Inside, Baxter was helped out of his heavy winter coat by gnarled, coal-black hands. Tennessee might be a Southern state, but these eastern valleys were frigid in December. His cotton gloves had been useless, and so, shifting his papers from arm to arm, he blew on the fingers of alternating hands to warm them as he made his way to the antechamber he'd reserved for meeting his client.

He'd done what he could for Haun and the Harmons. "Why?" his associates, Haynes and Fleming, had asked. They couldn't understand why he'd put himself in that position. "You do realize," they had said, "that we'll lose." They didn't have to say "the case." They meant, too, that the firm would lose money. And that's not all, their eyes added. In their experience, no one with roughened hands had deep pockets, but

115

that wasn't what troubled them. They didn't like the looks they were getting on the street these days, or even at home.

"We must think ahead," Baxter had told them. "We'll be known as the firm that defended . . . wait, wait, hear me out. Even now, in Richmond, we're men of principle. Justice is blind, and so forth. Integrity above politics. But in Washington, we're heroes in disguise. Patriots." Seeing that they had caught up with him, he dropped back. It was Haynes who forged ahead. "The war won't last forever. The point is, we're just pursuing our livelihood." Fleming nodded: "procedure; routine." They would armor themselves in paperwork.

And so they had drawn up deeds of trust for parcels of land owned by Haun and the Harmons. The documents had been signed in the prison and duly witnessed by the county clerk. If the clients could not pay, well, then, their land would be forfeit. Nothing unusual about that. Good soil, over in Greene County. There might even be a few dollars in it someday. Meanwhile, just business as usual. He must finish it today when he talked to Harrison Self.

Haun had died, and the Harmons would hang today, but they'd been seen at the bridge, and there'd never been any hope for them. The Unionists he'd helped in the past had been guilty, at most, of carrying a banned rifle, or cheering the wrong flag. It was just local noise. But to organize hundreds of men across several counties, to destroy a supply line during wartime—that was a page in history. Now there was martial law in East Tennessee. Now there was a military court, which was nothing more than a gateway to the gallows. *A gateway to the gallows.* He liked the phrase.

"They's got Mistuh Se'f in the hall, suh," said Lucas, hanging Baxter's coat on a peg behind the whitewashed door and moving toward the fireplace.

"All right," said Baxter, looking at Lucas in surprise. But then again, everyone, from the governor to the bootblack, knew the names of the bridge burners. Watching the old man poke the embers, he wondered if there was any truth in the rumor that the traitors gave ideas to Rebel slaves. You couldn't reason with anxiety. It was immune to legal argument. And yet he must deal with it, as a lawyer for the arsonists. If, by some chance, he could put the matter in a certain light, convince the judges that Self had merely bumbled his way into trouble, hadn't known what he was doing. . . .

There was something Baxter hadn't said when arguing for the firm's involvement. He hadn't confessed the attraction of these cases, the feeling they gave him of being associated with valor, if only at secondhand. He hadn't the courage—or the cowardice—to walk away from men like Self. They could be the future, if the North won the war. They could make it safe, once again, to love the Constitution. He felt a pleasant twinge of nostalgia.

"Stir up that fire, Lucas, and bring him in. Oh—and watch for Major Campbell. Let me know the minute he arrives."

"Yessuh," came the reply, so automatic that Baxter hardly heard it. He didn't know for sure—he'd once joked that Lucas had been loaned out years ago by a city alderman and then abandoned in the courthouse, too old to be reclaimed—but Baxter sometimes thought of the stooped figure as belonging to the building itself, like the heavy cloth drapery at the windows, or the rough-hewn desk and hard bench where he was settling himself now. Never mind the lawyers and the judges. Without Lucas, everybody would be standing around shivering, not knowing where to go. Baxter smiled to himself. In certain Knoxville homes, he could float this genial fantasy and be considered proslavery; in others, he'd be welcomed as a secret abolitionist. That was the era, and the town, in which he lived.

"That will do," he said, as the orange flames took hold of a stubborn log. Lucas slipped out into the hall.

A moment later, the door opened and Harrison Self was pushed into the room by a guard who then squared his arms and leaned against the doorjamb. The smell entered with them. Baxter wrinkled his nose, although he was familiar by now with the odor of prison life. He noticed that Self, a tallish, straight-backed man in his fifties, had closed his jacket to the top, despite two missing buttons. There were ridges in his greasy hair, as if he'd battled it with a comb.

"Please step outside," Baxter said to the scruffy man with the up-ended rifle.

"I've orders to keep 'im in sight," said the guard, nudging Self with the flat of his bayonet.

"He'll do me no harm," said Baxter, pointing to the wooden chair opposite him, and nodding toward Self, who bowed his head slightly and took the seat. "What we need," went on Baxter, "is a guard on the outside, so no one can disturb us."

"'Tain't likely. Most folks're at the hangin' today."

Damn fool, thought Baxter, though he imagined the Harmons were already on Self's mind. Coldly, he addressed the guard: "Can you manage by yourself, or shall I call for reinforcements?"

The man made a snorting sound, banged his gun on the floor, and reestablished himself outside. While the guard was taking his noisy leave, Baxter thought he saw a rictus of pain, or was it humor, on the prisoner's lips. When he turned to face him, however, he saw no trace of it.

Baxter took up a sheaf of papers and tapped them into alignment, first one side, then the other. It was his way of taking a moment to regard his client. Harrison Self had undoubtedly lost weight in the prison, but his frame was sturdy, with strong shoulders and large hands. His face had the open, fair, squared-off look of the Scots-Irish immigrants who had peopled the Carolinas before Tennessee was sectioned off. Yet there was a narrowness to the eyes, a prominence in the nose, and a firmness in the chin that gave him the look of someone to be reckoned with. Baxter put down his papers and rubbed his hand over them.

"The time is out of joint, Mr. Self," he sighed with professional wisdom. "You are, by all accounts, a man of substance, a farmer—am I right?—with property in Greeneville. You are the sort of person against whom crimes are committed by the lazy and the lawless. Yet here you are, here you are." He shook his head. "I will do what I can, of course. I am accredited in these courts, but I'm not a stranger to Union sentiments. Parson Brownlow was—and still is—a friend of mine."

"I've heard of ye," said the other man civilly, but with finality, as if to close the topic. "And as for these present times, I reckon there's somebody born to set 'em right, but he an't in Tennessee. I reckon he has bigger troubles than you or me."

Heat rose in Baxter's neck. There was nothing in the man's tone to suggest sarcasm, no hint of a challenge in the parried quote from *Hamlet*, and yet the lawyer bristled. He prided himself on gauging his clients' mental as well as economic resources, and he hated to be surprised. Clearing his throat, he said, as if reaching a decision: "I can be frank with you, I see."

Self eyed him steadily. "I should hope so, Mr. Baxter. And I'll be the same. Ye will be paid for your trouble—I or my family will see to that, so far as we can—but I'll not put my land on the block, not for you or Dan'l Webster or Saint Gabriel."

Baxter quelled his first response, which was to suggest that Self hire the archangel as his attorney. But he knew better than to let the other man set the tone. So, instead, he said drily, "Such flattering company for a Knoxville lawyer! Right now, however, the only property you should be worried about is a railroad bridge."

Noting that his client looked a little shamefaced, Baxter settled more comfortably into his chair. Self might be of consequence in Greeneville, but Baxter had his measure now. These small-town farmers wanted value for their dollar. They had to be convinced that they needed to feel indebted.

Pulling out the second sheet from his pile and laying it on top, he fingered it as he talked, "Let me tell you a little about the proceedings. I doubt"—he smiled affably—"you've been on trial for your life before. First, you will be asked if you object to any members of the court. You do not."

"How can I? I don't know 'em."

"They're the officers General Carroll assigned to this duty. The ones he can spare. You'll do yourself no good by objecting to any of them." Self nodded.

"Major Campbell is the judge advocate. That means—"

"He'll bring the case against me."

"Yes. Next, you'll be asked to name your lawyers. Messrs. Haynes and Baxter." Seeing his client's raised eyebrow, he went on, "I, John Baxter, and my partner Landon Haynes, although he's not involved in this case. Those are the formalities. Before the charges are read, I'll interveeeene." Baxter drew out the last syllable. He'd entered the realm of strategy, of legal action. "I'll challenge the venue—that is, the right of the military court to try you at all. You are a civilian, not a soldier."

"True, sir."

"You are a citizen of Tennessee—"

"'Deed I am."

"—and of the Confederate States of America."

Self blew out his lips and shook his head. "There ye be wrong, sir. I am no bridge burner, although, yes, I was on the scene, I admit that.

I was trying—well, I was there for other reasons. I never wanted any part of it. But I am a citizen of the United States. Can't say otherwise."

"You've been listening to the good Parson," said Baxter, with a wry smile. "He can afford to wave the flag, but hear me out."

"I cannot say—"

Baxter tapped the table impatiently. "Listen to me! Lincoln doesn't need your loyalty now, and the Confederacy doesn't want it anymore. It wants your neck."

He had hoped to shock Self into accepting reality, which is to say, into accepting better legal advice than he'd any right to expect as a Greene County farmer. But Self hadn't flinched. During his office-seeking days, Baxter had canvassed enough of the mountain counties to know what the small-town gentry were like. For the most part, they were honest and stubborn, but saw only a yard in front of them.

"Look—" he began.

"Mr. Baxter," cut in Self. "I've left my wife alone in my house. My son, no more than a boy, is lost to me. I don't know where he is, or if he lives. My daughter is out there"—he gestured toward the window but his eyes looked through and beyond Baxter—"in this godforsaken town. Afraid for me, as I am for her. And I am accused of burning bridges, when all I tried to do was keep me and mine out of mischief."

"I understand," said Baxter, holding up a finger. Time was passing.

Self rocked forward. "My friends have been hanged for . . . well, for grabbing the tail instead of the head of this business, and the horse ran away with 'em, but they knew which road they were on. Same one they've always been on, since the Union was made. I don't hold with burning bridges. I went there because my son, a mere sixteen-year-old boy, was drawn into it, and I wanted to get him out. But there's worse things happening in Tennessee these days, and if ye're a man of the law, ye ought to know it."

To hell with the fellow. Then, disdaining to be annoyed, Baxter remembered something he'd often observed about these people. They thought insolence was country candor. Besides, in spite of himself, he was curious. That business about the son could be useful. "Worse?" he prompted.

"Aye. You folks are burning up the Articles."

Not sure what his client meant, Baxter resorted to wounded gravity. "I'm here because I want to help you, Mr. Self. Please grasp that fact and keep it firmly in mind. And if you mean we're—they—are attacking the Constitution, well . . ."

"That, too. It an't healthy right now, but I'm the same feller I was before Tennessee voted out, and so are most o' the folks in the eastern counties. We're an embarrassment to the gov'nor." Self had the look of a man remembering something, or realizing something for the first time. "I reckon that's why *I'm* here," he said, almost companionably, and Baxter suddenly understood. This was a man who was used to being listened to. "Sir, I'm a Greene County man, and so was my family before me. We fought for our country once already, but I reckon the king comes back every century or so, to drive a wedge into the Union."

"King! Don't be ridiculous. Times change. Conditions change." How much easier his task would be, if Self were either a great deal less, or a good deal more, intelligent. It was this backwoods simplicity, masquerading as wisdom, that Baxter could not reason with. Brownlow, in his pro-Union harangues, had drawn upon that native resource, turning it to his purpose without losing its coarse appeal. But even the Parson, and certainly this farmer—lord of a few acres and incapable of seeing further—could hardly appreciate the arguments that had persuaded Baxter himself to accept, at least provisionally, the Confederacy's claim to a soul, and a mission, of its own.

His chest rose and fell with a sigh. "Look," he said, as if conceding a point. He hoped the man could understand what a difficult problem his rural stubbornness posed for a well-intentioned lawyer who wanted nothing more than to mitigate the excesses of either side in the present fraternal conflict. He, Baxter, once an outspoken Unionist, had taken the oath of allegiance to the Confederacy in order to continue practicing law after Tennessee seceded. After the first Battle of Manassas, Union sympathies were a luxury. What good could he do if he were barred from the courtroom? How could he make Self realize . . . ?

"Now look, Harrison. May I use your Christian name?" Not waiting for an answer, he pressed on, telling his client to show no anger or surprise in the courtroom, and, above all, to keep silent, lest he unwittingly sabotage his only chance of survival. Baxter would, of course, introduce Self as a citizen of the CSA, *not* the USA, and

121

he wanted no interference from this Revolutionary recidivist, this . . .
RE-cessionist. Oh, he must tell that one to Brownlow—then he caught
himself.

For a moment, when he revealed the list of witnesses for the
prosecution, his client's face darkened and twisted with pain or
disbelief, but then it hardened into a shell that hid the man's feelings.
When Baxter had finished, he tapped his papers again, gathering his
thoughts on how to proceed, but it was Self who spoke next. "And
now," said the farmer, "I have a question for *you*, sir. If I'm found
guilty, do ye lose by it—or gain?"

Baxter opened his mouth for a quick reply, and then closed it.
He considered the man in front of him. After the weeks in prison,
this once-reputable citizen looked worse than a beggar, yet there was
no servility, no self-pity, in his weathered face. Something latent, or
long suppressed, stirred in Baxter, and he answered genuinely, "That
depends on the outcome of the war."

Self nodded. "Now I think ye're being honest with me, Mr. Baxter"
he said. "We must take our chances then, the two of us."

Insolent familiarity, surely, and yet Baxter heard it as acceptance,
and was unexpectedly gratified by what sounded like trust. To ask,
in addition, for a lien on Self's farm would be chilling now, and
undoubtedly futile. If some small understanding had been reached
between them, it was tentative and unspoken, and had nothing to do
with fees.

As he met his client's eyes, Baxter smiled grudgingly at first, but
then ruefully, in agreement. Self was right. The next hours would
test them both, and, for the first time, Baxter wondered if there might
really be a chance he could save this man's life.

II. The Evidence

Here. Or there. To the end of his days, Tom would wonder if he'd
ever really had a choice, ever stood on the threshold between this
course and that. He was here, on a bench outside the room where Mr.
Self was on trial. He was not *there*, with his father and his brother.
He hadn't been near them for days now. Never in the cage with them.
Why? Such a commotion this morning. A guard had pulled him
roughly aside, and then pushed him through the door. When he'd

seen Pa and Henry taken out, too, it had been all he could do not to spring forward, but they were being pushed away from him toward a cart with—

"Paaaa!" he'd screamed, his arms yanked behind him until they could go no further, and then hitched higher against his back. A purple haze of pain and grief had blinded him, and so many people had crowded between him and his family that he couldn't have sworn he'd seen them. All around him, the world had roared outside his head, like a tornado that had lifted and carried him against his will.

Somewhere along the way, his knees had gone loose and he'd folded to the ground. Two men had hauled him up and swung him between their arms. It was simply ridiculous that anyone should want to harm his father, in public, with so many people watching. And silly old Henry, to whom he'd once said, "I'll kill you if you tell on me," thinking he meant it but knowing he didn't.

Someone would interfere. Someone always did. His father had told him not to talk that way to Henry, and sent him to feed the pigs. The worst things, the things you scared yourself thinking about, almost never happened. Did they? Behind him he'd heard the clamor of the crowd, but the sound had moved away, too, in the other direction, as the wagon and all those people headed *there*. He'd stumbled along in a daze, his brain in shock. Across the street, up the stairs, and over to this bench.

So here he was now, and he would never know if it had been in his power to be anywhere else. In later years, no one would say he should have died with his father and his brother on the gallows that day, but perhaps they would think it. The unfairness of it would clot inside him, like phlegm. What had he to do with all these angry people shouting at each other and at him? What had the Harmons ever done to them, except cause some delays on the railroad? He would not, could not, imagine such things as steps, as ropes, as trapdoors. Father and Henry would be waiting for him when he got back.

Tom hunched over still more on the hard bench. It was cold in the hallway. His teeth were chattering and his nose was running. Suddenly, his head jerked up: "Hennnnryyyyy!" keened out of him, a call or a moan. Someone came close, not in uniform this time, carrying something folded. A coat it was, and the person draped it over his shoulders. The warmth fooled him into thinking he'd been dreaming, so he looked up eagerly, gratefully, but what he saw was a horrible black mask, white eyes and grinning teeth, and he cried out again, this time in fear, and shrank back.

"Lucas! Leave the boy alone." It was the uniformed man again. "They're just about ready for him. Take that coat away. Oh, all right, let's put it on him properly." They stood him up and pulled his arms through the coat, the way he and his father had dressed the straw man in the field to keep the crows away, the crows as black as these claws that fussed over him. Then the one in gray sat down on the bench, too. Tom looked down at the man's knee, the size of a melon, next to the knob of his own. The man said, "This is a hard day for you, lad, but if you do your duty, you can tell your grandchildren you decided to help your country."

The wide plank flooring creaked in the distance where shadows passed back and forth. There was wainscoting on the wall, with the dry smell of old sawdust. Tom looked up, and the pieces came together—nose, chin, forehead. The small eyes were nested in wrinkles, but they looked kind. Suddenly, Tom felt himself coming to life, swimming up to the surface of his fear, wanting to explain something to this nearby gentleman whose attention he now had. "W-we just thought—we thought we were doing what we were supposed to do."

"I'm sure ye did. But the right or the wrong of it is not in the action, Thomas." At the sound of his name, Tom's eyes filled. The man went on, "It's in the way it looks to those who have right on their side."

Amazed, Tom straightened. "My father said that, too!"

"I'm sure he did," sighed the man. "You folks in East Tennessee are under a spell. The Devil's busy there, believe me. Your father and brother, and Mr. Self in there, were all led astray. You're no help to them, or to yourself, if you aid their delusion. Don't you see, it's up to you to redeem the good in them? Before he lost his way, didn't your father teach you to tell the truth?"

"Yes," said Tom, confused, but hopeful. They couldn't hang a man who had good in him.

"Well, then! Be a witness for the man your father used to be. Just tell us the truth." A guard had approached them, and nods were exchanged. "Stand up, Tom" went on the man, adding to the guard, "Show Mr. Harmon the way. He knows what to do."

Tom was helped up, and the coat was straightened on his

shoulders. Its rough wool lining pricked him through his shirt, but it was warm and holding up its weight made his body feel stronger. The high, furled collar helped him lift up his chin. The man in gray surveyed him and squeezed his shoulder.

The heavy wooden door with its brass handle twanged open and the courtroom lay before him. Tom blinked. Ahead of him was a long table under a row of windows. Against the white glare, the judges were featureless. There were, he would later realize, only seven of them, but at first they seemed to stretch in number across the room, tilting this way and that, like guests at a banquet. He was directed to a seat on one side, and found to his surprise that the man in gray was once again beside him. Then he looked across the room. A stout man with a very white collar was leaning to speak to someone behind a railing, and when he pulled back, there was no one between Tom and the tall, familiar figure of Uncle Harry. Tom's throat ran dry, as if he'd been tricked, as if all along he'd expected to see an impersonator, not the man he'd known from childhood.

Inside the borrowed coat, his stomach clenched and shivers ran up and down his arms. Every bone and muscle urged him to run across the room to Harry, to stand with him in this room of strangers. Afterwards, he thought he would have done it, too, no matter what the consequences, if Harry's face had invited him. But after glancing at him when he entered, Harry had turned toward the judges and never looked his way again. Tom had not thought it was possible to feel more alone than he had when his father was torn from him, but what he experienced now—standing some few yards from the averted eyes of his mother's brother—was a rejection, a dislocation from all he'd known and all he'd been, so complete that it yawned like a chasm. Was there no way the world could make sense again? *Harry,* he begged silently, *what should I do!*

"Thomas Harmon, do you swear that you will well and truly perform your duty to the court and tell the truth in this matter between the Confederate States and the prisoner to be tried, so help you God?"

The man beside him, who'd been addressed as Major Campbell, bent to his ear. "Say 'I do.' "

"I do," echoed Tom. He was then led to a small table to the side.

"Tell us," said Major Campbell, in a reasonable and encouraging voice, "what transpired on the day preceding the night on which the

Lick Creek bridge was burned."

"D-daniel Smith came to my father's house."

"Was your father present?"

"No, not then."

"Go on."

"S-smith said that he had particular business with my father, Jacob Harmon." Saying the name, Tom flinched, but then stiffened. He'd always been able to imagine his father's voice inside his head, telling him to hang up a bridle or clean off a plowshare, and now he closed his eyes, conjuring up that presence. "He—Smith—said that Fry—Captain Fry—was to be there that night at my father's and he was going to tear up the railroad." There, he'd said it. Everyone knew it anyway.

Tom squinted toward the judges. One of them had a round face that seemed amiable, so Tom explained to him: "He—Daniel—said Fry wanted Father to come over to his house. When Father came back, I told him what Daniel Smith had said. Father went in the direction of Smith's house."

"But—"

Tom jumped.

Campbell went on: "But there was no meeting at Daniel Smith's house. It was at your *father's* house later that night, was it not?"

An eyeglass caught the flicker of a candle and glinted. One of the judges was wearing a gold-rimmed pince-nez that he removed now. He took a square of white cloth from his pocket and wiped the glass in methodical circles between middle finger and thumb. The gesture was reassuring. Such a man would never put a rope around a soft human neck. Never let a body drop its horrible weight from its lassoed head.

Swallowing the bile that burned in his throat, Tom tried to sound more adult. "That night at about eight o'clock a crowd commenced assembling at my father's house." "We know who was there, but you must tell us now again, for that man over there." The major indicated a small person with a ragged beard who held a feather pen in his hand. The feather bobbed rapidly, then stopped.

Tom looked at Harry, but still found no help. So it must have been his father who gave him the courage to say the names of the dead: "Alex Haun, Matthew Henshawe, Henry Fry—"

Major Campbell silenced him quickly with a raised hand. "These names we know. Give us the others." And so Tom did as he was ordered. Some of these men, he'd heard, had escaped into the hills, and if they hadn't, well, then they were in jail, and couldn't be helped. Nobody had helped his father and Henry.

"What happened next?" asked Major Campbell. Then, bending his head, as if to remind Tom of something, he added more softly. "Remember, lad, only *you* can set things right."

"Fry made them swear to do everything he told them to do and not to tell anybody." Then he lifted his head suddenly. There *was* something he could do. "I did not see my uncle swear." That was true. He hadn't seen Harry lift his hand. Didn't that prove . . . ? He looked at Round Face, then Eyeglass, but their expressions were unchanged.

"But you saw him in the company on the way to the bridge?"

"We were all together." He wanted to talk about the time Harry had helped put out a fire in the Harmons' barn, wearing a shirt around his head like a turban, looking so—

"Did the defendant have a gun?" demanded the major quickly. A gun? Did that matter? Tom glanced at Harry again. Again, he was ignored. How could he make Harry turn his head, recognize him, *know* him again? He took a deep breath and said more slowly and loudly than before: "I DID NOT SEE THE DEFENDANT HAVE ANY GUN."

In fact, he couldn't remember what he'd seen. Harry might well have had a gun. Clearly, that was what the court wanted to hear. If they could put a gun in his hand, they could do—that—to him. *Harry, please look at me. I understand it now. People are the truth, not any of those things that happened.*

"Thank you, Mr. Harmon," said a voice from the table up front. "Does the defendant wish to cross examine the witness?"

Tom watched eagerly, as the lawyer in the white collar bent to speak to Harry. His uncle shook his head. "No," said the lawyer.

"Then you are excused, Mr. Harmon." Tom's first impulse was to say no, he hadn't finished. He'd never seen Harry hold a match. Come to think of it, he'd never seen Harry near the bridge.

The guard pulled on his arm. Once again, Tom was forced away, craning his head over his shoulder. Once again, he felt abandoned. *Didn't I help after all?*

III. THE SENTENCE

Lieutenant Colonel T. P. Bateman guessed the windows were acting as a burning glass. Concentrated and overheated, the pale winter sun speared him in the back of the neck as he presided at the long table. Damned uncomfortable, his dress uniform in a room like this, but the occasion demanded it.

By now, he'd expected to be back in the field with his men, but the trial had been adjourned four days ago, and was now in session again. It was ten o'clock in the morning, Friday, December 20. Late on Tuesday, Baxter had discovered a witness for the defense. It would take several days to get him to Knoxville. Reluctantly, Bateman had granted the postponement. He couldn't imagine what difference it would make.

Campbell had presented plenty of evidence—from the guard at the bridge, from those neighbors who'd spoken with Self and been with him at the scene, and from that miserable boy, Tom Harmon. They all agreed that Self had gone to the bridge and done nothing to stop the burning. When pressed, McDaniels had said, "I heard someone of the crowd say that the defendant was going to fetch his gun." Hearsay, but telling.

Still, Bateman hoped to be surprised. You didn't know, when you went into a skirmish, what shift in the weather, what flanking movement, what unforeseen bravery or cowardice would tip the balance one way or the other. Five men had been hanged for that one bridge in Greeneville. Leadbetter had made his point. Wasn't it just possible that this Harrison Self, this fellow who held himself rather well for a farmer, who looked you in the eye, deserved a milder fate? Why not be seen to be judicious, or maybe even generous? Sending back a man like Self might change some minds where it counted, in East Tennessee. Hanging the farmer would just stir up more treason. But that was a question for generals to debate.

He called the session to order and asked Baxter, "Is your witness here, sir?"

A mild-looking blond man stepped forward, announced that he was Alexander Lowe, a private in Colonel Powell's regiment, in the Confederate States Army. The oath was administered. Accustomed to watching the interaction of men in groups, Bateman noticed that

Self's manner had changed. On Tuesday, he'd barely looked at the witnesses. Now, he turned toward Lowe not, it seemed, with any particular excitement or gratitude, but curiously. Baxter had swelled a few inches in the chest, as he nodded and smiled at Lowe, encouraging him with a slight shooing motion of his hand.

"I resided on the defendant's farm at the time the Lick Creek bridge was burned," said Lowe, settling into a storyteller's rhythm. "Before the burning of the bridge on the evening previous to its being burned defendant said it was a bad thing to burn the bridge." Here was a man you couldn't hurry. "On the evening before the burning of the bridge Jacob Harmon came by the field where I was pulling corn with John McDaniels and told us to come down to his house that night; that the bridge was to be burned that night. In the evening in question . . ."

Country loquacity—or planned simplemindedness? Bateman couldn't tell, and Baxter gave no sign. "I asked the defendant if he was going. He said he didn't know . . . said he thought it was a bad thing. Don't know that he said it ought or ought not to be done. . . . Harry—I mean, the defendant—had been a strong Union man, but he wasn't a fool about it. He never acted harshly or made any threats to my knowledge. He wasn't hostile to soldiers of the Confederate States."

Lowe paused, and then his eyes brightened. "Why, he sold them supplies once! Some salt. *I* never heard of his refusing to sell supplies. He lives a little over one mile from Jacob Harmon's. He said it was a bad thing. Those are the only words of condemnation of the bridge burning that I recollect of his using, but I wasn't giving the conversation particular attention. I did not think the thing would be done at all." Lowe looked around confidentially, sharing his incredulity.

Baxter coughed, and Lowe went on in the same vein for a time, and when he had finished, Campbell stood up. "Did you see the defendant after the events of that night?"

"I saw him next morning early at home. He said nothing concerning the bridge. I did not know then that the bridge had been burned"—Lowe hesitated, his eyes darting around the room. Then, more aggressively, he said, "I have been a Southern man and openly said that when I fought I would fight for the South."

"And did the defendant know of these sentiments?"

"I have talked with the defendant about another army coming in here. He said it would make things worse here; that it would make the matter worse for the Federal Army to come in here but I do not recollect that he ever said that if by volunteering he could prevent another army coming in here he would volunteer himself—"

Baxter had sprung up, and Lowe, unsettled, had trailed off with some words about Self's age and his children and grandchildren. Bateman noticed that he smiled at Self as he was being led away, but got no sign in return. Self, most likely, was intelligent enough to know that Lowe, while meaning to help, had done little good. Baxter then asked for time to prepare his final statement, and Bateman, running a finger around his collar, adjourned the session until the following morning.

Chilled, the same small group, familiar enough by now to roll their eyes at the weather and exchange tired greetings, gathered again on December 21. The room was dimmed by clouds on this, the shortest day of the year. Before Bateman could call for them, candles appeared. A shuffling black man gripped them under his arm, and carried also a dozen tin holders strung by their handles on a ring like a turnkey's. Without asking anyone's permission, he deposited the holders around the room, screwed in the tapers, and lighted them with a match. As the flame leapt in front of him, Bateman saw it reflected in the veined marble eyes in the black face.

Baxter stood leaning with fisted hands on the table. Then he rose to his full height, folded his arms, and finally let them drop. He furrowed his brow, and began his speech haltingly, as if finding his way, searching through the debris of reality for the golden thread of truth.

"Distinguished members of this court-martial. Honorable judge advocate. Let me begin by—shall we start with what we know? I always find that helpful when I'm faced with a big decision. As we— as *you* are today. Some things we've known from the beginning." Momentarily, he appeared to have lost the thread, and then to seize it. "We've known that Mr. Self went to a meeting at the home of Jacob Harmon, where Captain Fry organized a raiding party on the night of November 8. We've known that Mr. Self was present at the Lick Creek bridge that night, and that he saw it destroyed. He knew many of the men who were also there that night, some of whom set fire to the bridge. The bridge was burned. *Ergo*, there were bridge burners.

Mr. Self would be the first to admit that undeniable fact."

Strengthened by logic, he rolled on. "But it is only one fact among many. There are some things we know now because we heard about them at this trial. We learned that Captain Fry demanded an oath of obedience to his false authority, *but that Harrison Self did not take that oath.* No one saw his hand raised in that devil's bargain. Very well. We have heard, too, that he rode with the company that night, and was seen by the guards at the bridge, *but it was Captain Fry who threatened those guards, not Harrison Self.* Pine knots were lit and matches were struck, *but none were in the hands of this man.* So what have we so far? We have a man who was in the neighborhood."

Bateman noticed a few smiles, but the candlelight was deceptive. Baxter lowered his chin all the way to his chest, and then looked up seriously, the very picture of a man with something to confide. "And now I am going to reveal to you some things you didn't know, although the wiser among you will have sensed them. Mr. Self had a reason for going to Harmon's house. *He was looking for his son Hugh, a boy of sixteen, who was easily led by men like Captain Fry.*

"Not finding Hugh there, he was faced with a choice. If you are a parent, you know the agony he suffered. As a citizen, he ought to've turned back. As a father, well—is there anyone here who'd admire him for doing so? No. He had some hope still of finding his son and bringing him away. Far from wanting to burn bridges, he had said— you heard the testimony—that it was 'a bad thing.'

"Hear this, distinguished members of the court: *It was never his intention to prepare the way for invaders.* You heard the testimony. He knew, as well as you and I do, that the coming of Federal troops would be the ruin of Tennessee. He did nothing to invite them, nothing to aid their cause. On the contrary. *He sold salt to our men.*"

Pain creased Baxter's face, and he spoke now as if communing with himself, rehearsing the obvious. "This, *this* is a man who took under his roof, who served at his table, many young men who learned their trade on his farm. This is a man whose kindness and fairness were legendary. A man of gentleness and steadfastness, beloved by his wife and children, respected by his friends. This is, by all accounts, a *good* man. A man of Unionist sympathies, yes—I admit it. He admits it. But a man who has never been a traitor to the Confederacy."

He leaned forward again, his hands striking the table with each sentence. "You must be equal to the challenge of this case. Please God, you will be as brave and as broad-minded as this father. Do not let this court become *a mere gateway to the gallows.* Let it be seen by all the world for what it is—the noblest expression of Southern justice and civility."

When he had finished, Baxter wiped his forehead and subsided into his chair. If he expected Mr. Self to ply him with thanks, he was disappointed, thought Bateman. The defendant continued to look calmly in front of him and said nothing. Bateman, as president of the court, gave the order to clear the room of everyone but his fellow judges. By now, the heat of bodies and rhetoric had warmed the room like the winking coals in the fireplace. When he rang a small bell and asked for some water, the slave who had earlier brought the candles returned with a pewter jug hazed with a sweat that beaded and ran in drops down the side. The seven men adjusted their chairs into a half circle facing their leader.

Bateman withdrew some slips of paper from his pocket, and distributed them to his seven companions, along with the pencil stubs he'd found in a drawer of the table. He asked for a nonbinding vote of "C" for "Convict" and "A" for "Acquit." The results were evenly divided, with three C's, three A's, and a question mark on the seventh.

Those who were in favor of conviction pointed to the order of the secretary of war to try all bridge burners by drumhead court and hang them near the bridges they'd destroyed.

"Ay," said the ginger-haired captain, "but this man didn't actually burn a bridge."

"What the order *means,*" said another, whisking the ends of his moustache through his fingers, "is we're to punish anyone who was on the scene."

"So," said the round-faced captain, leaning forward and looking confidentially around the group, "If yer daghter is kidnapped to a brothel, and ye knock in some heads to get 'er out, ye're guilty of . . . fornication?"

Nervous laughter broke out, and Bateman tapped his knuckle on the table. The captain with the golden pince-nez cleared his throat. "Yes?" encouraged Bateman. The man said earnestly, "What we're missing is the bigger picture. Five men have been hanged, and as far as I know, the evidence was no stronger in those cases. If we treat

Harrison Self differently, if we acquit him, all those hangings may be questioned. Not now, perhaps, but when this . . . fracas . . . is over."

"And are we to hang this one man, to keep ourselves in countenance for hanging the other five?" The man who spoke was lean and quiet, with a corrugated brow. Bateman suspected him of coming from the eastern counties.

And so the discussion went on, returning again and again to the same points, in slightly different form. Eyes turned to Bateman in frustration. It was time for him to put into words what he had spent a dreary night pondering, wrapped in a thick quilt before a cold hearth.

"There is no doubt that we *all*"—he sent a meaningful glance toward the round-faced captain—"understand the gravity of the situation. It is no light thing to cut off a man's life by signing a piece of paper, when he has offered you no harm personally. We must think like men, weighing all the factors involved—the evidence of witnesses who may not be reliable, the orders of those in authority—but we must act like a court, which is something more than a group of men in a room. *And,* we must act like a military court, which is something different from a civilian one."

"All well and good," said the ginger-haired captain, impatiently. "But is Self a Lincolnite or isn't he?"

Bateman ran his finger inside his collar. "I, for one, believe that Harrison Self is a credit to his community, a solid man, a man who would not cheat me or lie to me. I am prepared to make a statement to that effect. But my opinion of his character is irrelevant to the decision I have to make now, and that you, too, must make."

He saw the puzzled arch of an eyebrow, the squirm, the uneasiness, all of which translated into a silent demand for guidance. He'd seen that look on the faces of his staff before battle. To get a soldier to live in a ditch or kill a good man, you had to make him see an intolerable necessity as a reasonable decision. You absorbed the guilt yourself. That was leadership. And so Bateman unveiled what had come to him late at night, as the worms of disquiet gnawed his heart.

"We are a country—or so we claim to be, and must prove to be. We are a nation at war with another nation. Our armies are in the field. When those conditions prevail, the actions of noncombatants must be judged as helpful, neutral, or harmful. By swelling the group of men who made a show of force at the bridge, by failing to warn the guards or oppose the saboteurs in any way, by colluding in the clandestine nature of the raid, Mr. Self undermined the Army of the Confederacy, whose interests we are charged with protecting. When he did so, he made our choice for us."

As the concerned parties reentered the room, Bateman noticed that most of the tapers were guttering into hardened pools at their base. Yet there was light enough to see the straight form and steady eyes of the prisoner. Bateman looked away, speaking to a point where a man's face might be if he were standing between Major Campbell and John Baxter. "Having maturely considered the evidence, the court do find, more than two-thirds of the members of the court concurring in the finding, the defendant Harrison Self:

"Of the first charge, that of bridge burning, Guilty.

"Of the second charge, that of being in arms against the Confederate States, Guilty.

"And for such his offense the court doth sentence the defendant to be hanged by the neck until he is dead."

He did then meet the eyes of the man he had condemned, and saw there, as he would see whenever he awoke in the small hours of the night, the verdict of history.

CHAPTER 8
THE HANGINGS

I**N THE STORAGE ROOM OF A SMALL HOUSE ON UNION STREET
IN KNOXVILLE**, surrounded by tattered brooms and boxes of
old clothes and broken hardware, Lizzie pulled a musty blanket
around her shoulders and stared into the darkness. She had been given
a candle, but a draft had blown it out. That was all right. She wasn't
trying to read the few pages, covered in her own spidery script, that
lay on the quilt below her drawn-up feet. Her diary was her umbilicus,
her connection to home, but it didn't matter now.

It was the sixteenth of December, and all was lost. If she had been
capable of speech at this moment, she would have said she would
never take up her pencil again. Eventually, of course, she would look
back on what she had written about her last week in Greeneville.

MONDAY, DEC'R. 9. Pa has been gone for five days. This morning the
barn was hidden by a swarm of snowflakes. I do not think I will
ever be warm again. Since those two men were hung in town a
week ago last Saturday, we are like cattle stunned by a blow to
the head. No one born in Tennessee could have done such a thing.
They say it was that man from Alabama, whose heart is an icicle.
Ma made a batch of cornbread before breakfast, and then another this
afternoon, forgetting she had made the first. Andrew, Biddy, Jane,
and the others come to visit, but they have chores and worries of
their own. Now that the bridge has been repaired (so little did
those vandals accomplish!) the news is coming through again

137

from Knoxville. Friends from town bring us word, but there have been days when we have heard nothing and we do not know if that is because there is no news or because no one has the courage to ride out to the farm. We have heard that Pa is in a prison in Knoxville, but that is all.

TUESDAY, DEC'R. 10. I could not sleep last night, and the prospects for tonight are no better. I cannot bear to know and I cannot bear not knowing. My mind is already in that city, and I must follow it, or I will burst at the seams. Ma says it is impossible for me to travel so far. I am not a soldier or a man of business or even a woman with an escort.

FRIDAY, DEC'R. 13. With what joy, this morning, I discovered that Pete was in Greeneville again, and would soon return to Knoxville. I whipped poor Castor, although he is still somewhat lame, because I feared I would not find Pete still at home. When I got there, he was instructing his mother on the proper way to fold a soldier's blanket. He was very glad to see me, but I soon realized it was just his vanity that was pleased to see me so eager and pleading on his doorstep. As soon as I told him my errand, that I wished him to take me by train to Knoxville, his pleasure diminished.

—You are upset, he said, as if closing the subject.

—I have reason to be, I answered, trying to look all of my twenty-five years. Pa has no friends in Knoxville. He needs someone to help him. What about that lawyer you spoke of? (I could not remember the name.)

He shook his head, as if I had said something very foolish. The best thing you can do for your Pa, he said, is to stay out of harm's way. Knoxville is not the place for a country girl like you. Besides, no one can change the course of events. The only actions that matter now are on the battlefield.

I grasped his hand, as I had when we were children together and before we were this awkward thing of man and woman. I saw that he was affected, and I pressed my advantage. Once we are in Knoxville, I said, you can leave me in the depot and go straight to the fighting.

—But where will you stay? he asked and my heart soared.

Chapter 8: The Hangings

SATURDAY, DEC'R. 14. How can I fit this day into words! I have watched trains panting and belching in the railway next to the ticket office in Greeneville, but to be inside those corridors on wheels, to see the world begin to slide by the window and then to fly behind you in a roar of speed! I am ashamed to say I almost forgot my sorrow in the excitement of the journey.

I had never seen so many people in one place as awaited us when the train reached Knoxville. My shoulder was bumped I do not know how many times, and with all the noise from the dray carts and hostlers calling out the names of their establishments, I could not hear Pete unless he lowered his head and spoke into my ear. He gripped my elbow and steered me away from the crowd and out into a street with buildings lined up like cliffs. I tried to find the sun to get my bearings, but it was nowhere in sight. Pete had taken the address I gave him and inquired of a soldier in a strangely mixed uniform of blue and gray. He then grasped my sore elbow again and told me to make haste.

I had not seen my distantly related cousin Barbara since her marriage in Greeneville and her departure to Knoxville nearly fifteen years before. I did not know if Mistress Forrester would remember me, or be willing to give me shelter, but I did not mention my fears to Pete. When we arrived at a badly weathered house with nailed shutters, my courage nearly failed me, and did leave me entirely when a man with ragged hair and a loose shirt stared at us from behind a crack in the door. When I explained who I was, he called behind him and my cousin replaced him in the narrow slot, with a hesitant look that made me fear I would be abandoned on the street.

Barbara offered many reasons why I could not stay, but there was really only one. She was afraid of harboring a Lincolnite. When I said that Pa was in the city jail, she held her head in her fists and said Oh Lord Oh Lord many times, while I told her over and over that Pa had committed no crime and that it was a terrible mistake for him to be in prison.

Pete now said that he could stay no longer, and that he would take me back to the depot, where I must stay until the next train to Greeneville. I whispered to him to go around the corner and leave me alone with my cousin. When he had done so, I waved after him. Then, turning to Barbara, I declared that I would take my satchel and find a doorway or a stable to sleep in and that God would surely forgive her for turning away her mother's husband's sister's child to suffer a terrible fate. I kept talking, allowing my voice to grow louder and more plaintive, until fearing the neighbors would hear she pulled me quickly through the door. Once I was inside, she began to ask me about people she knew in Greeneville, and I thought she became rather sad as if she missed her earlier life there or maybe just the younger self she had been before her marriage. While her husband snored before the fire, she gave me a supper of boiled onions and potatoes and a corn-husk pallet and old quilt in a storeroom behind the kitchen. Tomorrow I will go to the Knoxville Jail.

The next day, crude map in hand, Lizzie ventured into the streets of Knoxville, knowing she looked like a country girl in her plain woolen cloak. She was glad of the heavy material, although the bottom edge was soon stained and weighted with muddy snow. Overhead, the grim sky pressed down on the buildings. They stretched before her with unending sameness, without a stream or a hillock in sight.

At the corner of Union and Prince, she turned south, walking the four blocks to Main. There she turned left toward Gay Street, entering the busier thoroughfare with her heart flipping in her chest like a fish on dry land. She recognized "Castle Fox" immediately. Like the dungeon of an evil king, it pulled her gaze and repelled it. She could not look away, but her feet dragged, as if great weights were attached to them.

Two guards, squeezed on the stoop that climbed two steps above the street, exchanged something she was still too far away to see. As she neared, a stream of tobacco juice hit the walkway, carefully aimed to miss the boots of the man in front of her. She was in the city now, but she had grown up knowing that you do not enter a thicket before circling it. So she kept on walking until she came to an alley beside the prison, down which she could see carts moving and a window above street level. A large barrel stood beneath it.

Out of sight of the guards, she felt a sudden weakness and put her hand on the side of the building to brace herself. The contact seared

her flesh. Was it really possible that her father was on the other side of that wall? If she called out, would he answer? Almost the urge conquered her, but a natural caution and the strangeness of the place kept her silent.

In her quandary, she'd been standing in one place longer than was prudent. A grin suddenly blocked her view. It would have been a coarse face, whiskery, loose-lipped, bleary-eyed—the face of many a conscript rousted from his home, ordered to enforce martial law, then forgotten in the backwash of occupation. Lizzie saw only a frightening mask, inches from her nose.

The words "Air ye lost, Missie?" blew over her with a sharp odor she recognized as whiskey breath. She stepped to the left, and, as if partnering her in a dance, he copied her move. Dodging to the right, she was faced with him again. Pure annoyance gave her courage. "Get out of my way!" she demanded. Losing interest, he bowed in mock courtesy, staggered down the alley, and joined the men who were crowding around a large wagon driven by a black boy. It was filled with barrels knocking against each other like drunken soldiers.

Pressing herself back against the wall of the building, she watched as the cart progressed down the alley and stopped by the barrel beneath the window. A bare-armed soldier leapt upon the spokes of the wheel, unfastened a chute that swung out over the side and soon gushed water into the container on the ground. After the cart had moved on, she saw her rude cavalier plunge his filthy head into the clean water and lift it again with a shout and a shake, spraying drops in all directions and rubbing his face with his arm. At the time, she had no way of knowing that this was the drinking water for the men inside, or that this pollution of the barrel was deliberate. Her thoughts had already moved on. Taking several deep breaths, she retraced her steps toward the front of the jail.

The two guards at the door had barely changed their position. One was tall, with hair so pale it seemed to merge into his white skin; the other, short, had a crown of dark curls, an upturned moustache, and a sharply pointed beard. She chose the younger and fairer of the two, and stationed herself just below him, looking up with all the earnestness and innocence she could muster. "May I trouble you, sir, with a question?" He looked uncertainly at his companion, who answered, "You may trouble us all you like, but take your questions somewhere else."

Seeing her mistake, Lizzie turned to the dark-haired man and tried again. "If you please, I would like to speak to my father, Harrison Self."

"Harrison Hisself? Now who would that be?"

"Harrison *Self*," she repeated, anxiously. "S. E. L. F."

"Bob," said the man, addressing the other guard. "This young woman here, walking these streets as brazen as can be, she thinks we need schoolin'. I'm inclined to take offense. Air you, Bob? Air you inclined to take offense?"

The world began to spin for Lizzie. "Please," she begged. If only Pete had come with her, but he would not have stood here, in full view of the passersby, who were looking at her curiously. She felt, rather than saw, that two or three had lingered, watching her humiliation. "Please. May I just see my father for a moment?" Helplessness, beyond any she had ever felt, made her weak with frustration. She was frightened of her unimportance. A voice behind her called out, "Oh, what's the harm! Give her a glimpse. An't they hanging a few on Monday? Maybe her Pa's one of 'em." She whirled, wide-eyed. A woman caught her arm and whispered, "Keep your feet, girl."

She turned back toward the stoop, collecting herself for a question, but the dark-haired man had tilted his scabbard, poking it indecently in her direction, to the amusement of the bystanders. "Come back on Monday," he offered. "We'll have somethin' for y' to see then. You and the likes of you." He let fly, again, with the tobacco juice, this time striking her squarely on the chest.

Worse than the indignity was the fact that it was allowed. The stinging in her eyes came from tears of dismay. How could this be happening to *her?* She stumbled back into the woman who had spoken to her, who now pushed her upright, marched her a few paces, and gave her a brisk shove to send her on her way. Shocked and bedraggled, Lizzie returned to her cousin's house, without any memory of the intervening streets. When her cousin questioned her timidly, she stammered that she had taken a wrong turn and lost her way. It was true.

The scene of her failed mission played and replayed in her head as she sat in the storeroom that night, unable to write a word. She had not lived so long without knowing that people can be cruel, or that power makes the weakest men bullies. She knew what it was like to be overlooked when her elders or her betters were in charge. But she had never before been nullified so completely. It was as if her existence, without any will or intention of her own, was an affront that deserved punishment. A caustic bubble of shame trickled up into her throat, and burned there. At long last, exhaustion brought relief.

On the morning of the seventeenth, she awoke early, with aching head and dry throat. Her cousin had placed a bucket of water within reach, and she now poured the liquid over a strip of cloth torn from her petticoat and wiped away the films and stains of the past twenty-four hours. She undid her hair and smoothed it with the small brush from home. Gradually, she began to look, and feel, more like herself. With each stroke of the bristles against her scalp, her shame receded and her situation became clearer. Looking back on this moment, she would say it was the first time she knew her father could no longer mediate the world for her. She was alone, but she carried him inside. She must be the person he would recognize.

Barbara, frightened by her cousin's strange behavior the day before, and by some news her husband had whispered to her, begged her lodger to stay out of sight on that day of all days. Lizzie, whose cloak had a linty, rubbed area on the chest, said she had an errand in the city. The Forresters watched her leave, then glanced at each other, and then dropped their eyes. Neither of them had offered to go with her. Had she noticed? She had, but she would have refused their company.

At first, the crowdedness of the streets seemed just the hustle of a Monday morning, as business and politics resumed after a day of rest. Soon, however, Lizzie noticed that the traffic was all flowing toward her. Workmen in dusty clothes, bonneted women with children firmly grasped by the hand (were there no schools here?), gentlemen in beaver hats and ruffled shirts, all seemed headed toward some destination behind her. Consulting her map, she guessed they were moving northward.

After a time, a strange milling occurred, and she could feel an excitement in the air. People were stopping each other and asking questions about which street and when and how many and then a portly man with a huge fuzz of whiskers halted nearby, looked back down the street behind him, and remarked companionably, "It's a father and son, they say. We should hang every one of those bridge-burning devils!"

Chest heaving, Lizzie stepped aside, leaning against a brick wall to catch her breath. Was he talking about Pa and Hugh? She stood there, an island of sickness and dread, while the crowd paused to crane its collective neck. Shouts of "I see 'em!" and "Git out o' the road, you!" were quickly drowned in a larger sea of noise, from which cries of "Traitor!" and "Bridge burner!" jostled to the surface. Suddenly energized, Lizzie pushed her way to the curb in time to see an open cart moving up the street. It was very much like the wagon she had seen the previous day, but instead of water barrels it conveyed several men dressed like the guards at the prison, and lower down, either kneeling or seated, two figures with bowed heads.

Her scream was lost in the general outcry. She had recognized her uncle Jacob and her cousin Henry. Horror and relief and horror whipped through her. She must get to them! Even more than the day before, she felt herself in a dream, where feet moved without touching the ground, and the light had a phosphorescent glow. "Hennn-ry!" she screamed again. All that mattered to her was that he should look up from this horrid journey and see one person who loved him.

Gallows Hill was on the north side of Knoxville. Lizzie, eyes red with weeping, pushed her way through the moving crowd, barely noticing the surprised looks on the faces of people who gave way for her, as if she were wearing a mask that disturbed them. Once, when the wagon turned a corner, she could see that her uncle and cousin were seated on coffins, and the bilge rose in her throat again. She wanted to scream that it was all a mistake, that her uncle was a kindly Greeneville farmer and potter who had never harmed a person in his life. That her cousin was a foolish boy who still played with toy swords.

When she could bear to look ahead, she saw a platform about twenty feet wide and six feet from front to back. On either end rose a square post twice the height of a man. They supported a horizontal beam. At each end, a slanting brace formed a triangle with the vertical posts. Two ropes hung from the crossbeam. Closest to the platform, a line of soldiers, some with bayonets aloft, some with swords raised in menace or salute, kept the crowd back from the parked wagon. A child, standing on an upturned hogshead with a drum hanging from a strap over his shoulder, sent a fusillade of beats over the heads of the crowd. Another child, bending to the ground, rose and hurled a stone toward the gallows.

It flew through the air and hit Jake's knee. He paid no attention. Henry was all he must have seen in the whole wide world. A soldier placed the rope around the boy's neck and another moved to do the same for Jake, but the third official on the platform signed for him to stand back. Words were spoken that couldn't be heard, but then the crowd fell silent, as if frozen in time. Henry's trussed body suddenly dropped from sight, while the frayed end of the rope swung free in a sickening arc. Evidently, the cord had broken, and Henry had fallen through the trapdoor to the ground below.

Jake had collapsed, and now swayed on his knees. Cheers erupted as the staggering Henry was guided up the stairs, for the second time, onto the platform. A new rope, ending in a noose, had been produced and attached to the crossbeam. "Hang the bridge burners twice!" sang out someone to loud applause. Jake lifted his eyes then and lived his worst moment all over again. He must have wished for oblivion. There were no further delays. Henry's form dropped, jerked upward, twisted with the torque of his flailing legs, vibrated once or twice, then hung straight as the weight on a plumb line.

Lizzie had sunk to the ground and did not see her uncle likewise transformed from a living person—a man who used to give her mint leaves from his pocket—into a thing tied to a cord. Someone did help her to her feet—"Did you faint, dear? Is it your first hanging?"—and when she began to think again, she looked toward the scaffold and saw that the bodies had already been cut down. Taking deep breaths, she steadied herself and looked around, not expecting to find any help, and then suddenly, there he was, some twenty yards away, looking directly at her as other faces intervened. When they were gone, he was gone, too. It was not the last time she would ever see Peter, but she hated him now for everything he could have been for her and was not.

Lizzie steeled herself and walked over to the men who were nailing down the coffin lids. This time, she knew better than to ask prettily. Her voice was cold, as if her demands were her right, and this time, she got answers. That was how she learned the name of the person responsible for these deaths, and where she must go to ask that the bodies be sent to Greeneville, and whom she must speak to about her father, who was still alive somewhere in that Confederate hellhole guarded by a two-headed Cerberus—no, she corrected herself, by a pair of stupid and ill-bred men who would be in jail themselves if the Federals ever came.

Terrible as the place was, Lizzie could not leave before the wagon did. It would have seemed like turning her back on those dear ones. And so she was standing nearby when she was approached by a black woman with an aureole of crinkly white hair. "You be Miz 'Lizbeth Se'f?" she asked, adding, with a glance at the wagon, "You be a relation o' these po' folks?"

Lizzie's eyes filled again, this time with gratitude. It wasn't that the words were kind, although they seemed to be. It was simply that they weren't cruel. But then she had to wonder: "How do you know my name?"

"I'se just askin' for Miz Susan, over dere." She pointed to a small pony cart that had stopped on the side of the hill. A tall, dark-haired young woman was trying, very energetically, to quiet a horse that kept jerking its head toward the animals harnessed to the wagon. "She Miz Susan Brownlow. If you be Miz Se'f . . . ?" Lizzie nodded. "Then she say she got some news from de jail."

And that is how Lizzie met the Parson's daughter, and that is how she learned that her own father was alive and aware of her proximity. Susan, with the brisk easiness of a local resident, soon had Lizzie seated beside her, with the black woman folded into the rear of the cart. They went first to Union Street, where Susan had stopped that morning.

Her father, Parson Brownlow, had smuggled out a note from the prison, as he often did, when their servant brought his food. He had given Susan the name and street of Lizzie's cousin, and questions had led to the right house. Authoritative knocking had brought the frightened Betty to the door, and Susan quickly learned of the relation between the Selfs and the Harmons. Armed with a full description of Lizzie's appearance, including the clothing she was wearing that day, Susan had set out to find her. Still, it would have been a fruitless search, if Lizzie hadn't gone to Gallows Hill, or hadn't lingered by the coffins. Both young women thanked God for this providence.

In Union Street, Lizzie collected her belongings and gave her daunted and embarrassed cousin a chilly kiss. From there, they trotted into a wider lane and eventually into the open court before the Brownlows' door. On a tall pole hung a Union flag. When Lizzie pointed to it in surprise, Susan tapped her own jacket, where another flag, in miniature, had been embroidered. "My father wasn't pleased," she said, and after an exchange of knowing looks, the two daughters smiled, even on this tragic day, even in this warring town.

Susan's father, the notorious editor of the *Whig,* was also in jail. But this was his town and his daughter's, and she still had many sources of information. As a child, she had sat on the knee of Mr. John Baxter, the erstwhile Unionist and now moderate Confederate defending the conspirators. Lizzie recognized the name, but her heart sank, for by now she knew that he had also defended the Harmons and Alex Haun, all of whom had died on the gallows. What chance was there for her father?

"There is one hope," said Susan meditatively. It was the evening of the twentieth, and the crushing news had arrived: Harrison Self, after a postponed conclusion to his trial, had been sentenced to death. At first, Lizzie had been numb with despair. The Rebels were a runaway engine tearing through her homeland, her family, her pride, her very heart. It did no good to tell her, as Susan tried to do, that the verdict had been decided long ago.

"Justice has nothing to do with it," Susan remarked, patting her new friend's head, which rested on her shoulder as they sat together in a parlor tactfully vacated by the other Brownlows. Perhaps it was a mercy that Lizzie did not know, until much later, that petitions for clemency had been submitted and denied.

Susan continued to muse. "My father says that the Rebels are terrified of a counterrevolution on their very doorstep. They're afraid to show mercy, but they're also afraid to look uncivilized. They don't want to give the North an excuse to invade. They wouldn't dare hang the editor of the *Whig.*"

The proud complacency of that remark quickly yielded to embarrassment, as she realized her tactlessness. She stroked Lizzie's hair and spoke more gently, but with growing determination. "Nor, I am sure, would they want the world to know they hang innocent men like your father. So. There *is* something you can do—if you are brave enough."

That night, Lizzie lay in a real bed with linen sheets, but she slept very little. Pictures raced each other through her exhausted brain, but the one that kept recurring, that horrified her more than all the others, more than the insulting stream of tobacco juice, more even than those twisting deadweights in the air, was the swaying end of the broken cord. It should have been an image of reprieve, but instead it was a ghoulish taunt that raised the hairs on her forearm. What her mind absolutely refused to imagine was her father standing on that platform.

On the morning of the twenty-first, Lizzie knocked on the door of a two-story house not far from the Knoxville Jail. Susan had offered to come all the way with her, but both had realized that Lizzie's chance of success, if it existed at all, would be lost if a Brownlow accompanied her. But she'd been helped in other ways. Mrs. Brownlow, sizing her up with a glance, had lent her a clean, respectable dress, answering every protest with an airy "for the Union." Lizzie wasn't sure that the older woman understood the mission for which she was preparing her guest; nevertheless, after a full-twirl inspection, Mrs. Brownlow pronounced her "ready."

In place of the stained, spat-upon cloak, Lizzie wore a neat serge coat that suited her trim figure. Before parting with her a few blocks away in the pony cart, Susan had declared that no one would suspect Miss Self came from a small town like Greeneville. Lizzie had smiled wryly, but said nothing. She was facing a worse threat than big-city prejudice.

Ripples of anxiety swept through her now, and she was about to turn and flee when the door was opened by an ebony-skinned woman in a dazzling white turban. As planned, Lizzie gave a short answer to the inquiring look: "I have a message for Colonel Leadbetter." Because the woman held out her hand, expecting a letter, Lizzie added "—to be delivered in person."

"What you come 'bout, Missie? De Cuhnel awful busy. He don't see peoples less dey come on bizniss he know 'bout."

"My business concerns what history will think of him."

The housemaid, for so she appeared to be, looked doubtful, but hesitated. Tilting her head, she scanned the visitor closely. Maybe it was the drape of the coat or the immovable stance, or maybe it was simply a slave's reluctance to offend a respectable white woman. It didn't occur to Lizzie that her "message" might pique the interest of a black woman. After a second, the maid bent her head in consent, and Lizzie grasped her skirts and stepped over the threshold.

She was ushered to a lyre-backed chair in a dim, quiet hallway that seemed miles from the street outside. As Susan had advised, she called herself Elizabeth Cobble, using her mother's maiden name. "Whatever you do, you must get through the door. You must see him face to face," her strategist had reminded her. In truth, she waited only ten minutes, but it was time enough for a hundred second thoughts.

The house was plain, but still far grander than any she had been inside before. She was about to meet a person whose position in the world was far higher than her own. It took a great effort of will, but she fixed her mind on something her father had taught her: we're descended from people who thought the highest rank was "farmer." When the maid came for her, she felt her legs turn to water, but she was in the tide now, and it carried her forward.

The room was pleasantly bright from the sun streaming in the tall windows. The light washed out the features of the man standing behind a desk at the far end. Instead of the monster who had hanged Hinshawe, Fry, Haun, and her two relatives, there was only a sandy-haired, wey-faced man with a small ruff of beard below his chin, very pale eyes, a delicate mouth, and a disengaged air. So this was "the Colonel." The most definite thing about him was the double row of shiny brass buttons on his chest.

He pointed to one of two chairs with horsehair cushions, and Lizzie, having no faith in her legs, took the seat. Continuing to stand himself, he said, almost distractedly, "Why do you wish to see me, Miss Cobble?"

In a faltering voice that became stronger as she went along, she told him that she spoke for a group of citizens in Greeneville County. It was a half-truth, like the name she had given. "They understand that you must punish the men who burned the railroad bridge." At the word "bridge," the man stopped rifling through papers on his desk and looked at her keenly.

"I cannot discuss this matter with you," he said coldly. "Go home and tell your neighbors to stop behaving like children playing with matches. They have burned themselves, and must take the consequences."

"That is what my father said." The admission was disorienting, because it was true. Her father had always thought the conspiracy was child's play.

"Then I commend him. Who is Mr. Cobble? The name is not familiar to me."

"My father is Harrison Self."

The Colonel slapped down the papers he was holding and walked to a window that overlooked the street. Before he could decide what to do with her, she spoke rapidly to his averted shoulder. "I do not know what was said in court, but the truth is that he went to that place only to get my brother . . . who is only sixteen . . . who thought it was all a game—"

"You behaved very badly yourself," interrupted the Colonel without turning around. "You lied about your name."

Surprised, she said, "My mother was a Cobble before she married. I was afraid you wouldn't see me if I used my father's name."

"Deceit runs in your family, then?"

His priggishness goaded her. "Here is the truth, sir. My father is loyal to the government—the old government—but he has no grievance against you, if you will let him alone. He would never lift a hand against a fellow citizen because of a difference of opinion. He is not like that. He is not. He is a good man."

"Difference of opinion?" The Colonel, turning, cocked an eyebrow at her. "Is that what you think this war is?" Clearly, he didn't expect an answer, because he returned to his desk, sat down, reached for a small handbell, then stopped and said, "Joshua." A sound behind her made Lizzie aware that someone had been in the corner of the room all the time. He came forward now, a slender black boy with intelligent eyes, wearing a sort of stocking cap of bright-red cloth.

"Call Mary from the kitchen, and tell her to give our visitor some tea—real tea"—he confided to Lizzie—"from Montgomery. And Joshua—tell Sam that he, not Mary, is to answer the door at all times, and remind him that he is not to admit anyone without asking me first. Good day, Miss Self."

The floor seemed to heave as Lizzie stood, and she blurted without thinking: "You've hanged two of my family. Isn't that enough?"

"I understand your feelings," replied the Colonel, with forced patience, although the words made her heart jump. "And I am sorry for you. But, you see, I cannot know your father's motives. I deal only in facts, and now I must ask you again—"

"No," she said with sudden bitterness. "You do *not* know his motives. You do not know him at all. He meant no harm to the Confederacy. If you kill him, everybody who knew and respected him will think you are a murderer"—no, that wasn't strong enough—"a worse tyrant than anybody in Europe . . . in Asia . . . in . . ."

"What vandals think is irrelevant," said the Colonel, drily, "although I doubt I shall be compared to Genghis Khan."

She barely heard his second remark, for she was seized by an idea. "Oh, but just think! If you were to save him, if you were to inquire into the case yourself, you could prove that the Confederacy really does have a noble spirit. Wouldn't that be worth doing? Then nobody would listen to the radicals like"—she hoped Susan would forgive her—"like Mr. Brownlow." She was borrowing Peter's rhetoric.

He did grant her a twitch of the lip, but she could not tell if it was amusement or anger. What else could she say? What else did he want? "Killing my father won't gain you anything—not now, not anymore. But don't you see? Saving him would make you . . . ," she could not say "a hero" or "a saint." Her thoughts were all pejorative: "less of a devil"; "less of a monster." The words that finally came were "a good person." But, of course, he thought himself one already. She heard the plaintiveness in her voice, how close it was to a sob. The sting of failure was so sharp that she no longer cared that her eyes had brimmed over.

The Colonel walked around his desk and, with a light touch, guided her down into the chair again. The door opened behind her, but he held up his other hand in a staying motion, turned the vacant chair to face her, and sat down. "What you must try to understand," he said, primly but not unkindly, "is that I cannot change the course of these events any more than I can make water flow uphill." Lizzie heard the finality in his voice, and all her hope, all her joy in the world as she had known it, died.

He went on talking about the bigger "family" of the South, about a "sisterhood" of states bringing forth a second New World that would extend into the Caribbean, a new beginning that she would one day understand. . . . When she gave no sign of listening, he rose from his chair and replaced it exactly where it had been. "Well," he said, crisply, "I have nothing more to say to you. The only person who could possibly intervene now is President Davis himself, and he has made his wishes clear through Secretary Benjamin, whose orders I have followed to the letter."

At his signal, the turbaned woman slid into the room. "But," he concluded, as if unwilling to send a lady away in tears, "I will do you this favor. I will grant you permission to visit your father in the jail next Friday. Would you like that?"

Just before she died, half a century later, Lizzie pointed to a shadowy corner of the room and said, "Take the cage away." Everything else had faded from memory decades before: the peppery scent of urine, the oniony smell of unwashed clothes hanging on skeletons, even the haggard eyes, gleaming from thickets of hair, not with lust or curiosity, but with a marveling regret, as if the woman who passed through the crowded room must be an optical illusion.

No one, however, who had seen the inside of the Knoxville jail in the beginning months of the Civil War, ever forgot the crosshatched enclosure, an oversized iron birdcage, where condemned men were put on display in the midst of their fellow inmates, as a warning and a safeguard. Once a hanging was announced, the jailors wanted no disappointments, no quiet departures to the next world on the prisoner's own terms, in some dark corner shielded by friends.

The young woman who entered the jail on December 27, the daughter who knew her father was to hang at four o'clock that same afternoon, was not the person who had left Greeneville twelve days before, aglow with love, hope, and high spirits. Nor was she the person who had staggered away in shock after being spat upon. There was something in her of the grittier self that had waited by her uncle's coffin, and a good deal of the determined citizen who had braved the Confederacy in its den. But most of all, she was the emerging partisan who, turning at the door, had thrown a challenge at Colonel Leadbetter: "What kind of 'family' destroys its parents?"

She had feared he might withdraw permission for her to enter the jail, but he did not. The lesson was not lost on her. Growing up, she had liked giving tit for tat. She had taken pride in never backing down from an argument. What she was learning now, in the world beyond

Greeneville, was the power of her own conviction. When she turned Leadbetter's homily against him, she'd been crying out for the fathers she knew—for Harry and Jake and Alex—but later, she realized she might have meant Father Abraham, and before him, the parents of the Revolution, George and Martha and Thomas and John and Abigail and before them, John Sevier and James Robertson in the mountains of East Tennessee. She meant those who had a vision of equity, even if they failed to live up to it. She meant the lineage of the Union, even if she did not say as much to herself. Not yet.

Her head was buzzing with half-formed ideas, and one in particular—something Leadbetter had said—circled just out of reach. But when she presented herself at the prison door, she put aside the tumult of the last few days, promising herself not to cause her father any more grief than he was already suffering. It was nine thirty in the morning, but she would be allowed only a short time in the jail. She was determined to be his staff and his comfort on his last day on earth. What she had not counted on was the sight of him. His thin figure, hollow eyes, and shaggy hair undid her completely, and when he pressed himself against the metal grid and stretched his arms through the apertures, she doubled over, as if her soul had cramped in pain. Then she ran to him, and it was some time before the guard, a black man with a white sash across his chest, could pry them apart in order to unlock and open the cage door.

She had no way of knowing that a few things had changed, in honor of her visit, or in pity for the condemned man. A small bench had been placed in the cage, and Harry wore a clean shirt, provided, she would later learn, by Parson Brownlow, from the fresh laundry his wife supplied. Lizzie and her father could just fit on the bench, leaning against each other for support.

"How did you get to Knoxville?" Harry asked, stroking her head with a cupped hand, as he had done when she was a child. She told him about the train ride, but said only that a neighbor had accompanied her. Hugh? He didn't know, hadn't heard. Must still be alive somewhere. Surprisingly, he did know that she had been found by Susan Brownlow. "The Parson is a good man," he said, and then fell silent, simply taking her in with his eyes, as if memorizing what he already knew better than his own body.

"I—I tried to . . ."

"To what, dear?"

"To convince that awful man, that Leadbetter . . ."

"You saw him?" Harry smiled encouragingly, as if listening to a dream she was retelling.

Weighed down with emotion, she did not try to explain. Better he should not know. He asked her about Ma and the farm. He wanted to know if Castor's shin splints had healed.

In a spasm of regret, she whimpered, "I'm sorry I called you a . . . a . . . Tory!" His chuckle, his dismissive "Oh, that!" was even harder to bear. "I'm even more of a Unionist now," he admitted. His eyes, so familiar, so warm in their love for her, scanned her face over and over, as if it were his map of heaven.

Suddenly, he gripped her shoulder firmly and said in a low voice, "I want you to go to the depot right now, and take the next train back to Greeneville. Do you have the fare?"

"No. No. No." She shook her head. "I won't leave."

"Do as I say, Lizzie," he said, with all the authority she had ever heard in his voice. "There is no reason for you to stay, and I don't want you to be here when . . . Think of all the men who are going to be . . . who are not going to survive this war. I just know about it in advance, that's all. It will help me, if I can think of you riding that train back to Greeneville. I will keep that thought in my head every single minute. You must do that for me. Please."

He helped her to stand, and as they embraced, he whispered in her ear, "Do you remember giving me my old pipe? Well, Jake and I, we just held it to our noses like a bunch o' violets, and the smell did us good." There was a sound like a strangled laugh. He gripped her so tightly that she would have finger marks on her skin for days to come.

"Parson," he croaked. "Help me, will you?"

At the door of the cage, a tall, swarthy man with a shock of dark hair took over from Harry, and drew her away from the cage. She was aware of a circle of men, most of them with heads bowed. Each passing moment was like a dripping away of her own blood. And then she remembered what it was that Leadbetter had said: *The only person who could possibly intervene now is President Davis himself.*

Turning to the Parson, who regarded her with moist eyes, she seized his arm and said, "Do you have something to write with? I want to send a telegram to Jefferson Davis."

Instantly his eyes focused and he reached into his pocket, withdrawing a small tablet of paper and a pencil. He extended them to her, but she cried in desperation: "What shall I say? He is innocent. He doesn't deserve to hang. He . . . is my father."

Brownlow quickly began to scribble on the page, tore it off, folded it, and handed it to Lizzie. "The telegraph office is just half a block away. Go quickly!"

She turned back to her father, but Brownlow urged her forward, saying to someone behind her, "Take her other arm, Andy." A strong hand gripped her other elbow and she was steered away from the cage. Suddenly twisting her whole body violently, she broke free, ran to the cage, and raising her arms, grasped the rods above her head, crying, "Pa?" with a rising intonation, as if asking him why God allowed such agony. He came to her, and placed his raised hands over hers. With tremendous effort, he spoke quietly to her. "Lizzie, be a good girl. Let me see you walk out of here without help. Give me that to remember." As he stepped back, she heard Brownlow's urgent reminder: "The telegraph office!"

Lizzie did walk through the jail without the aid of her supporters, whom she thanked tearfully when she begged them to step aside. Although it was she who had asked for Brownlow's help, news spread of the Parson's intervention, and she was greeted by a curious crowd at the door. She did not know if they were jeering or cheering, and she did not care. Several of them ran ahead, directing her to the office, where she handed over Brownlow's note. When it was read back to her for confirmation, she could not believe what she was hearing. Not a word about her father's innocence! The editor had betrayed her by highlighting her own plight, which had never occurred to her. The telegram merely said:

Knoxville, December 27, 1861

Honorable JEFFERSON DAVIS:

My father, Harrison Self, is sentenced to be hung this evening at 4 o'clock on a charge of bridge-burning. As he is my only earthly stay I beg you to pardon him.

Elizabeth Self

Susan had by now made a path to Lizzie, and, placing an arm around her shoulders, guided her back to the pony cart, pulled up across from the jail. It was known that Lizzie had permission to be in the vicinity, and the sight of the two women huddled together beneath a blanket for warmth and disguise—useless, of course—seemed to touch some chord of sympathy. Occasionally, people would pass close by, scowling or nodding, depending upon their politics. For the most part, though, the two women were left alone to watch the prison that held their fathers. They were part of the scenery on the day of another bridge burner's execution.

Around eleven o'clock, there was a stir. A bandy-legged man, whom Susan thought was Fox, the marshal of the prison, strode officiously to the door and disappeared within. After perhaps twenty minutes, he reappeared, spoke to some of the people in the street, and looked directly across at Lizzie and Susan. To their dismay, he approached rapidly, with a grim and angry expression on his ratlike face. "Well!" he said, accusingly. "Which of you is Self's daughter?"

When Lizzie raised a finger, the man glared at her. It was obvious that he felt badly treated. "Why your father insists on hanging, I can't imagine. I made him an offer any sane man would accept." The words brought dark spots to Lizzie's eyes. He went on, "All he had to do was say that Brownlow put him up to it and gave him the money to burn the bridges, and he'd have had his reprieve." Fox leaned uncomfortably close. "You wouldn't want to go back in there and convince him, would you? Come on. I'll take you back."

All her life, Lizzie would wonder how she found the strength to say, "I will go nowhere with you." Was it because Susan sat beside her, in shock at the proposition? Was it because she knew her father would never save himself with a lie? Maybe she was just too crazed and too drained to move, or maybe it was simply that Fox, in his coarseness, repelled her so completely. He barked in frustration, "Let him die, then," and stormed away like a gust of dirty wind, kicking up litter as he went. Lizzie crumpled over until her head touched her knees.

In some distant corner of her mind, she wondered if she *could* have persuaded her father—never for his own sake, but for Ma's sake, for her own sake. Shouldn't she have tried? Or borne witness herself? What kind of daughter was she! How could she miss any chance to save Pa, right or wrong? Brownlow was guiltier of sedition than any bridge burner they had hanged. Perhaps Susan guessed her thoughts and shrank away from her. Each woman sat in isolated anguish, and neither could look at the other.

Just before two o'clock, Lizzie heard shouts from the direction of the telegraph office. Wiping her face, she thought of leaping from the cart and running far away. But she couldn't move, could only whimper below her breath. What was coming seemed worse than all she had endured so far. The noisy crowd was flowing across the street toward her, crying "Hurrah for Jeff Davis!"

The President of the Confederacy had replied.

Susan Brownlow

CHAPTER 9

FATHERS AND DAUGHTERS

PHILADELPHIA, PENNSYLVANIA, JUNE 13–14, 1862
KNOXVILLE, TENNESSEE, NOVEMBER 8, 1876

1.

T HE ROAR WAS LIKE THE PARTING OF THE RED SEA, as if God, too, were present, opening the way for him. Sound crashed against the pillared balconies, washing back over the lighted faces, rising to the spray of diamonds that hung, like an inverted hoop skirt, from the carved ceiling. Bigger, that chandelier, than the house he was born in.

For just a moment, it seemed to Brownlow as if the audience fell silent, and all the noise was in his head. Perhaps he was dreaming, as men did when half asleep on the prison floor, trapped in a vision of gilt and velvet. Then the clamor was outside him again, rolling in waves toward his feet. He started to raise his hand, but wait. The cheering was not for him.

The Ladies of Philadelphia had commandeered the stage of the Academy of Music. All around him gowns swayed and fans tapped as women milled about. Then, at a sign he failed to catch, they drifted into line, elbowing each other into place with much rustling of taffeta. From the bevy of matrons came muffled girlish laughs, urgent whispers, and the dusty scent of powdered sweat. Or was that simply the aroma of the place itself on this hot June night. Hundreds of naked bodies trussed in finery.

Why, why, why had he agreed, this one time, to bring his wife? Everyone, she'd said, had heard of the Academy, just five years old and already the grandest opera house in the nation. Up there in her

159

gilded box, she'd be looking down her nose at the stage, half envious of the ladies' dresses, half glorying in her perch. Susan, though, devil take his smiling daughter, would be laughing at the sight of him, outmaneuvered by ceremony. She'd know he itched to begin.

Not that he hadn't suffered it before, this onslaught of crinoline. After his release from Knoxville, while stalled in Shelbyville on his way to the Federal lines, he'd been captured by flower-laden, soup-bearing, cake-wielding gentlewomen. City after city, he'd met with similar attentions, and though he still enjoyed them, he could slip, now, into a ready-made warmth, ah, ladies, you do me too much . . . , the times have forced me . . . , your valiant hearts . . . , and so on, while inwardly, after hours on the train, he pleaded with his bowels.

His gratitude might be practiced, but it was no less real, no less heartfelt, for being eloquent. Of course, it was *they* who should thank *him*. The news he brought was music to Northern ears, he merely the instrument, the trumpet rousing the army, no, the soldiers of Armageddon. If every one of them bought his book, here in the city of its publication, how much newsprint could he buy, when at last the *Whig* reopened? As always, his thoughts raced ahead. Some days, he turned a corner and had to wait for himself to catch up.

What now? Heads were turning and cheers were mounting. They'd discovered his wife in the first balcony, and Susan, well, he would have to bow now and thank them on behalf of, but there was a commotion, and Susan rose, and was being led away and then the matrons on stage regrouped, almost blocking his view, as his daughter was brought forward to the proscenium.

All eyes were upon her. It was as if he'd put on a pair of spectacles, seeing her as she looked to others. Tall, yes. They'd see the shiny wings of her parted hair, dark as his. The wide, full mouth—they'd recognize that, too. "Like father, like daughter." There were pictures of her in circulation, but none did justice to those large brown eyes. Somehow, the story had got out, that she had challenged some Rebel louts while he himself was away from home. She'd put a Union flag in the front yard (actually, *he*'d done so) and then defended it, sighting down the barrel of a rifle, but scaring them even more, so went the tale, with the flash of her eye. The efficacy of that orb was the part he believed.

Nevertheless, far from her hometown, with no experience as a public speaker . . . her exposure struck him physically, like a stab in the chest. He took a step forward, but the matrons had the field. A path opened from the rear. With solemn faces, two older women, doughty in feathered headgear, walked slowly forward, arms thrown out, carrying between them a suspended flag. It seemed to hang from an advancing battlement. Fringed in gold on three sides, its starry corner emblazoned with an eagle and union globe, it bore an inscription he finally saw as the banner took center stage. The sentiment was his, if not the spelling: "Liberty & Union, Now & Forever, One and Inseperable."

Wheeling left, the flag bearers faced Susan, and again he was cut off. The presentation began, led by a dowager who stepped forward from the ranks. She referred to the swinish Rebels, the lifted rifle, and, of course, to the flashing eye. What a victory, she said, for the Union cause, which put such steel in the tender flesh of woman! Here, before them, was that heroine of Tennessee, who, as they all knew by now, had saved her flag and her virtue at one and the same time.

It was the dearest wish of the Ladies of Philadelphia to present this token of their respect to so brave a member of their sex. Then the flag bearers engaged in a slow *pas de deux*, folding the cloth into a square the size of a swaddled infant. This they held out to Susan. He cleared his throat, but it was her voice he heard, as, flag in arms, she turned to face the crowd that had come to hear him.

"There is nothing I can say to you," she began, in surprisingly clear and ringing tones, "that would adequately express my humble thanks for the great honor the ladies of this city have paid me." My God, the girl had been listening to him. She went on: "But it is an honor undeserved." A chorus of pleased denials. "I can accept it only if you will do me the further honor, of allowing me to stand before you, as the representative of my sisters, in Eastern Tennessee." The rhythm! It was his, too.

"I am fortunate to be here in this beautiful building, but they are living, so many of them, in fear every day, of starvation—or worse." Knowing and appreciative groans followed. "Their farms have been ravaged, their husbands shot in the field, just for raising this"—she held her gift aloft—"flag. If you could see—"

"My friends!" He'd had, finally, to push his way through, with less courtesy than force. "You see before you a proud father." He was

161

gratified to hear whistles in this jewel box of a hall. "Yet—were this rare girl *not* the daughter of Parson Brownlow, as I am known"—he bowed slightly to the cheers—"were she *not* the Pride of Knoxville, as she is called, I have no doubt you would pay her the same tribute. In the hollows and in the hills, there are many who deserve it. There is one—shall I name her? She came, like a visitation, to the prison where I was—illegally!—kept for a time." Shushed now, they waited.

He hadn't planned it, but how could he resist. Some transitions are a gift. With Susan by his side, he began the story of that day in Castle Fox. He drew for them a picture of the cage, its flat iron bars trapping a doomed soul like an eagle in a sack. Imagine, he urged them, a gray-haired man, a once-proud farmer, awaiting the executioner. And why? What had this simple fellow done? He had dared to love his country. Oh, he had been accused of burning bridges. So had the Parson himself been defamed—"I am," he confided, "their favorite target of slander"—but Harrison Self was as innocent as he was.

Feeling Susan about to withdraw, he found her wrist. His theme was fathers and daughters. Into that hellhole had come a country lass. Think what it must have been like, rough men on every side, bearded and hungry from long imprisonment. Foul water, rotten food, and the stink of abandonment. It had been his care and his duty to lift their spirits when he could, but what a horror for a girl to witness!

"No older than Susan here"—he squeezed—"she was allowed, after days of pleading at the gates, to enter a scene no woman should ever see, much less a daughter. I tell you, a hush fell on that evil place, and with a common instinct, the most hardened of my fellow prisoners bowed their heads. And when she passed through the door of that cage, and that father clasped that daughter in his arms! Oh, my friends, you would have wept at the pity of it. Never have I seen a more tender meeting in a more gruesome place."

He could have been now in some rural church. Lowering the pitch of his voice, he swept the crowd with his eyes, searching, making contact. "The guards themselves were moved, but they knew what was expected of them by their hell-bound superiors. They tore her from his arms, and would have pulled her from the room, but she twisted away and threw herself upon my bosom. Yes, friends, I was standing nearby, a witness to it all." He squeezed again, meeting some resistance. Only a moment more.

"Tears streaming down her face, she begged me to save her father, her sole support, the very center of life. What could I do, a prisoner myself! Then came to me the staff that is always at hand while there is breath in this body. While I live, I can speak, and while I *can*, I *will*. And so I offered to write a telegram on her behalf to Jeff Davis. What think you? Is there a trace of humanity beneath that scrofulous hide?"

Wrong time for a smile. He let sorrow crease his face, but grimness had come already. Outrage had never left. "That such a man, that such a daughter, should be ripped apart, as our very nation is pulled asunder. It is unnatural. Here, I give you word for word, what I wrote on that occasion: *My father, Harrison Self, is sentenced to be hung this evening at 4 o'clock on a charge of bridge burning. As he is my only earthly stay I beg you to pardon him.*"

The words spilled into the room, upon the ruffled shirts of the men, the glowing breasts of the women, and soaked in. He waited, as if he, too, needed time to absorb them, familiar though they were. That was the way of it. Each time a story was told, it grew in power if only one more heart was touched. Several hundreds lay before him. He waited.

Somewhere from the depths of the hall, a voice hallooed him, as if calling across a moat. "What happened?"

He'd bowed his head prayerfully, and only when he raised it, only when he heard that clarion call to the storyteller, did he realize that Susan had slipped away. "Friends," he said, unable to keep his voice from shaking, "HE WAS REPRIEVED."

The roar that billowed forward drowned his voice, but there were cries of "Quiet!" "Let him speak!" and at last he had the floor again. "Not two hours before he was to hang, the man was saved. Word came from Richmond, commuting the sentence. Oh, he was not set free. He remained in the prison, and may be there still, for all I know, though likely he was thrown into some vile pit in Alabama. A terrible fate that is, to be sure. Yet I believe it has advantages over hanging."

Now the smile, now the laugh, shared by speaker and audience. All effort, all fatigue, dropped away. "No doubt the girl returned home," he mused, "comforted by the knowledge that these iniquities cannot last. It is in the hope of shortening our national trial that I bring you news of your fellow citizens, of their sufferings under the brutal thumb of the Confederacy." He continued speaking for two hours.

On the way back to the hotel, Susan was oddly quiet, looking, he thought, rather pointedly away from him. Eliza, making up for her daughter's silence, had much to say about the orange rosettes in the hair of some woman who might herself have been a flagpole. Two rooms had been taken for them at the Continental, where he had lodged on that first visit in April. Susan lost no time disappearing through one door, saying she was tired and would see them in the morning. In the second chamber, he told the servant where to place the candle and the luggage, and then lowered himself, joint by joint, into the nearest chair. Eliza was still standing. Closing his eyes, he took a deep breath, and then looked again. She had not removed her hat. He sighed. "Have you errands to run, my dear?"

"Yes. One. I am needed next door, husband."

"Is she ill? Well, the excitement."

"You might have mentioned that it was Susie who found that girl wandering alone in the city, and brought her home, and fed and clothed her. Gave her counsel, too."

He started to say, *but that would have been a digression.* Instead, he threw wide his hands and let them fall in his lap. "She has the flag. Tell her it will outlast me and my failings."

"Will you not tell her yourself?"

"Not now. I have some work to do on the book. I'm meeting with Childs tomorrow morning, so you and"—he tossed a glance at the neighboring room—"will be rid of me for a few hours."

He'd welcomed the chance to speak at the Academy, but his real mission this time was to see his publisher. Weeks before, in retreat in New Jersey, he had worked steadily on the compilation of his writings—letters, editorials, diaries—that would spread his influence far beyond the reach of his former newspaper. The North would weep. Lincoln had been too busy to see him in Washington—ashamed to face him, no doubt, after failing the Loyalists of East Tennessee! Well, the truth would reach the President behind closed doors. These burning pages would light a fire under that skinny rump.

His wife turned away, then looked back. "So will your book. Outlast you, I mean." He met her eyes, saw no witticism, no special kindness, but no uncharity, either, in the *memento mori.* Maybe Susan needed her, or perhaps Eliza guessed that, after such an evening, he wanted to be alone. It was true. After a great success, he would often sit for an hour or two in a forgotten body, his mind retracing the event. He would murmur of the Union to an audience of mice.

Tonight, it was the peroration he recalled. Not a finger stirred, but his arms waved in memory. He mouthed a few words as the shadows, cast by the dancing flame, waved back at him. "Had I the power, I would arm and uniform in Federal habiliments every wolf, and panther, and tiger, and catamount, and bear, in the mountains of America; every crocodile in the swamps of Florida and South Carolina; every devil in Hell and Pandemonium; . . ."

His pulse quickened. "And we will crowd the Rebels and crowd and crowd them, till I trust in God we will rush them into the Gulf of Mexico, and drive the entire race, as the Devil did the hogs into the Sea of Galilee." He felt the dirt beneath his bare feet. "We can whip the Southern Confederacy; we can take in England and France; we can whip out all Creation."

At moments like this, he sometimes wished he had not forsworn alcohol. Wine he could abjure, but a sip of mountain fire would have tempted him. No one would know, if he paid the servant for a dram to help him sleep. No, not true. Eliza would know, as surely as if she were in the room with him, and she would never mention it, never betray her knowledge, until one day, in two or three years, she might say, *you cannot afford this bonnet, but you could bribe that servant in Philadelphia.*

Smiling, refreshed, as he always was, by the liquor of imagination, he rose from the chair and pulled a leather case from its nest among his clothes. Taking it to the small table on which the candle flickered, he opened it. A stack of pages lay within, through which he now shuffled, taking care to preserve their order. Then he pulled one out, pushing the case and its contents to the side. The sheet before him was covered in his angular handwriting, but he found the place at once in the diary of his imprisonment—"her short limit to remain with her father expired, and she came out weeping bitterly, and shedding burning tears."

Very well, Elizabeth Self had not thrown herself upon his bosom. He had retold the story many times, and at some point, that detail had crept in. He'd excused himself for the decoration, for it only highlighted the truth. She had thrown herself upon his fame. "Requesting me to write a dispatch for her"—all right, it had been *she* who had asked *him*—"and sign her name to it." But surely he'd been more than the amanuensis. "I took out my pencil and a slip of paper, and wrote the following: . . ."

He looked up, his eyes narrowing but seeing nothing. He'd been about to read the words he had quoted in his speech this very night. They were printed on his memory. "My father, Harrison Self, is sentenced to be hung this evening at 4 o'clock." Feeling in his pocket, he brought forth the pencil he always carried. As if moved by a will of its own, the leaden point scratched through some words and wrote above them: "to hang at four o'clock this evening." Better that the "sentence" itself should "hang" the man, than that he should "be hung" by the mere course of events.

Self is his daughter's "only earthly stay." Well, what father isn't. He was Susan's, until she married. It was an economic fact, but it must wrench the heart. "As he remains my earthly all," yes, that was better, "and all my hopes of happiness centre in him." For a moment, the room swam. There'd been a time when he, and only he, could wipe the tears from Susan's face and make her smile. He looked again—"my earthly all / all my hopes." Chiasmus. Words, at least, still jumped at his call.

Moving quickly, he changed "I beg you to pardon him" to "I implore you to pardon him," savoring the alliteration. Something else had worked, too. Women beg, but imploring is for ladies. Harrison Self's daughter deserved just as much respect as any blue blood on that stage tonight. He looked at the revised wording and found it good.

His book was a 400-page telegram to the North, ending with his own letter to the editor of the *Philadelphia Press*. This time, he wasn't pleading for one farmer's life: "In God's name, I call upon President Lincoln, and upon his Cabinet and army-officers, to say how long they will suffer a loyal people, true to the Union and to the Government of their fathers, to suffer in this way." Tapping the page, he returned it to the sheaf, put the case away, crawled into bed, and fell instantly asleep.

2.

Susan awoke to a warm stickiness. Her eyes itched and strands of hair were caught in her mouth. She pawed at the web, felt her elbow strike something dense, heard a grunting whine, and sighed. The bedding had caught beneath her mother's leaden weight, and it was a moment before Susan could free her legs and swing her feet to the floor.

Last evening came back to her, the three of them in the carriage, exhausted with triumph. Then Mother sidling into her room, pattering on about "I am here, my dear," and "the public man" who "belongs to the country, not to us." Father had wanted to be alone, apparently. She stood now, raising her arms and arching her back. MMMMphphphhh. Pushing all her sinews to their limit, she reveled in the stretch.

He had said he would be meeting with his publisher this morning, and so they should breakfast without him. By the time Susan was fully clothed, Mother, in her quilted silk dressing gown, had opened the door for a young woman in a starched apron, who was setting down a small gilt tray of buttered bread and tea. The maid was retreating when Mother called after her, "Oh, do wait, if you please. Move the tray to that table over there by the window." She waved in the general direction of Chestnut Street. "We desire to enjoy the view." Out of loyalty, Susan refused to meet the girl's look. Let Mother play the *grande dame*. At home, she'd lift a sack of corn or roll a barrel right along with Bo or Milly.

Two or three times that morning, Susan repacked the flag from the Ladies of Philadelphia. While her companion wrote letters to family and friends at home—no doubt describing the finery at the Academy— Susan wandered restlessly about the room. Private letters would often get through the lines, though it amused her to think of Rebel soldiers probing for codes in "low spoon" bonnets and "chimney pot" hats. She'd brought a novel with her, but after a few pages of *Alonzo and Melissa*, she was at the window again. Would Father remember? He had promised to take her to Independence Hall today.

Nothing gave Susan greater pleasure than accompanying him in public. It was an altogether different feeling from the trill in the veins when a suitor doffed his hat and crooked his elbow. Still, she spent the extra moment before the looking glass. She did not fully understand it herself, the safe and complete knowledge that she was pleasing in his eyes, and yet the flutter of excitement in discovering it afresh. The air was softer, the trees greener, the bricks more distinct when she walked by his side. Perhaps it was just the rarity of having him solely to herself. She knew that others felt it too, the urge to be noticed by him, and perhaps what thrilled her was the absolute possession of his attention. Like all heightened experiences, it was always short-lived.

Close to eleven, he was at their door, giving Mother a silver-wrapped box with a pink bow that must have earned him a knowing smile as he crossed the lobby. He looked at Susan from the corner of his eye, saying, "Are you ready, then, my girl?" And so they departed, leaving Mother to arrange the packing for the evening train.

Once outside, they paused for a moment at the corner of Ninth and Chestnut. She thought his meeting must have gone well, for there was no thundercloud on his brow, but the sun was in abeyance. He was familiar by now with many great cities. His mind could be elsewhere even here, where the buildings towered above them and the streets were like rivers glutted with barges. Her eyes were drenched in moving color, her nose filled with warring scents—the acid tang of horse urine, the muzzy odor of old garbage—but it was the sounds, the cawing of drovers, the cracking of whips, the tinkling of laugher, that made her grip her father's arm in a spasm of excitement.

He cupped his hand over her fingers and urged her into the stream of pedestrians. Not all of them were on holiday. Just visible to her left, moving with the whole-body jerk of the lame, was a young but haggard man in a leather jerkin that must be stifling in the summer warmth. A soldier whose war was over? Startled, she realized he was looking back at her, and quickly turned her head.

"Your mother is displeased with me," were Father's first words. She smiled at his transparency. Clearly, he wanted her sympathy, her allegiance in some matter.

Knowing what was expected of her, she replied liltingly, "Oh? And, pray, what is troubling Mama this fine day?" Sweet collusion. It troubled her not at all to sacrifice Mother to this arm-in-arm solidarity with her favorite parent.

"She thinks I . . . did you less than justice."

"When?" That the trouble involved *her* was a surprise. "How?" She felt taller, aware of readying herself internally. It was going to be in her power to ease his mind.

"Last night. She thinks I ought to have told more of the story, how you hunted for Self's daughter, how you followed her to Gallows Hill. Mother is right, you know. That girl might never have found her way to me, had it not been for you." How warm those large brown eyes could be. Then he stopped, raised a finger, and said oratorically, "The Athena of Knoxville! Guardian of the flag and savior of lost daughters!"

Susan had to laugh, though she tingled with embarrassment. Several heads had turned. Even *sotto voce*, his words had a ring to them. As a child, she'd put her ear to his chest as if an echo had been trapped there. Many years of public speaking had put a bellows beneath his shirtfront, but he often suffered now from bronchitis. His voice was raspy at times, but still carried.

With some discomfort, she realized that the man with the crutch was still nearby. When she noticed him, he seemed to eye her with intelligence, as if aware of her identity. Had he been eavesdropping? She nudged her father into a gap on the crowded pavement and hurried him along. To distract him, she said, "There is even more to the story."

"More?"

"More than my search for Lizzie." Seeing it just in time, she swept up her skirt with her free hand and skipped lightly around a wet coil of dung. "More than bringing her home. Did you perhaps recognize her coat?"

"You supplied it!" The one thing her father loved more than his own stories was a tale he could borrow.

Her smile said *who else,* but her narrative lay elsewhere. "While that telegram was on its way to Richmond, where do you suppose Lizzie waited?" A surreptitious glance told her she had not yet lost their follower—for so she now thought of him. "Why, with me, of course!" she announced softly, keeping her voice intimate in this public throng. "She came to sit with me in the pony cart a little way off from the prison. It was cold then—December—but there was a blanket and we huddled together. That terrible man found us there."

"Who?" Father looked around at her, his wide forehead creased above his nose.

"Someone connected with the prison. The marshal, I think."

"Fox?"

"If I ever knew his name, I am glad to have forgotten it. He made Lizzie a vile proposition." Father's eyes narrowed. "Worse than that even." Susan brushed past the ordinary sins of mankind to approach the extraordinary: "He wanted her to persuade her father to give false testimony against, well, against *you* most of all."

"Ah!" Father nodded. "I know about that. About the temptation placed in Self's way. I wrote about it. Let me see. I said that men who would stoop so low as to make such an offer 'deserve the lowest and hottest apartments in the infernal regions.' "

That was Father's way, to pluck condemnations from old sermons. There was something so familiar, so automatic about the reference that she pursed her lips. Yet his anger was real, as fresh as the razor's nick on his cleft chin. With what fierce honesty he hated betrayal, whether of the Union or of himself, though he might confuse the two victims. All her life, his sincerity had been as palpable as a battering ram that pulverized its target. Never mind what else was crushed. Did he even realize . . . ?

"Father," she said tentatively. "Think how Lizzie must have felt. She was tempted, I know she was."

"By Satan, yes, in the body of that flea-bitten, hell-favored, dung-livered—"

Impatiently, she broke in. "By love."

He stopped in midstride, turning to face her, dividing the flow of passersby. Surprise would have been natural, maybe even dismissal, but this was much harder to bear, this questioning look from those deep-set eyes. She looked away—and met another stare. Quickly she pulled Father's arm and whispered, "That man has been following us. The one with the crutch." He glanced over her shoulder and then, walking on, drew her back into step with him. Conversation ceased. All that mattered was reaching the corner of Chestnut and Sixth.

Soon they saw ahead of them the brick mass of Independence Hall. As they were crossing the plaza, he turned toward a bench that had just been vacated. She knew he had given a speech at this very spot on his first visit to the city, addressing a huge crowd before the nation's birthplace. She expected him to refer to that occasion, but all he said was, "Such a fine day. Let us take the air for a moment." Seeing no one who appeared to notice them, she did not object, though she was thinking of something else. Had she really said *by love?* How could she explain or defend herself? In the center of each palm, anxiety burned a hole.

He sat beside her, his long legs extended and his arms akimbo, draped on the wooden backrest. Eyes closed, chin uplifted, he seemed to be collecting the rays of the warm June sun. She was, after all, his daughter, and like him, she hated uncertainty. "Father."

"Hhmmm?"

"What I meant was," she began, hoping that the sound of her own voice would dislodge some meaning she hadn't seen yet. "She—Lizzie—had to choose. Of course it would be wrong to urge her father to lie about you. But I do not think she knew what the truth was, except that her father was innocent. You have said so many things. Now this person was telling her she could do something more, try harder to save her father. If I had not been there . . . I sometimes wonder. Or if I had been in her place . . ."

A shadow fell across them. She did not have to look up to know who it was. The one human foot, the two wooden ones—the peg leg and the crutch. As her eyes traveled upward, she saw that he was dressed untidily, but not poorly. There was nothing of the beggar about him. The breeches were good broadcloth, the open shirt fine linen. But the clothes were stale and wrinkled, the body rank, as if he had not seen water in days. Her nose twitched.

The man stared down at them intently, his expression far from friendly, but not simply hostile. Father said, "Have you business with me, sir? If not, kindly move on."

"Aye, I have business with ye." Some strong emotion passed over the man's face, rippling its surface. He was broad featured, with eyes, cheeks, and chin nearly all on the same plane. He carried no weapon, so far as Susan could tell, except his crutch. Having taken his stand, he seemed in no hurry to proceed. "Unless ye are not Parson Brownlow," he finished at last.

Father drew his arms down and folded them on his chest. She felt the change. He was alert now. It was not unusual for him to be recognized on the street, but Susan, too, sensed a challenge in the air. She glanced about the plaza to see that witnesses were present. What could the fellow do in such a place? It was the middle of the day. He was . . . a cripple. Perhaps even she, with a sudden push, could topple him.

"Well, sir, you know who I am. State your business and be off." She heard the deeper note in his voice and something wilted in her soul. A drama was emerging, and Father loved a stage.

To her surprise, a wry smile twisted the man's face. "Be off, ye say? Aye, 'be off' and chase the Rebels to their lair. 'Be off' and *drive the Rebels to perdition.*"

Father, too, realized he was being quoted. "You are . . . were . . . a soldier, then? You blame me for . . . this?" he gestured at the crutch.

"This?" The man snorted. "This is nothing."

"Oh, you are wrong, sir. It is something. It is a badge of honor. It is—"

"A stump where a leg used to be. Joe heard you, too. How many others. Joe was fifteen. He thought he could 'whip out all Creation.' You told him so. I was there. I *heard* you." The fierce intensity of his voice charged the air, and several people turned their heads, slowing to listen.

"What happened to him?" asked Father, going, with his instinct for verbal mayhem, to the bloody root of the matter. He must have known, as Susan had instantly, that the man in front of them was grieving for a death, an absence where a person used to be.

"The same as what happens to hundreds who listen to you and think war is a shouting match. Bullets are just words to you. If you had any decency . . . ," he trailed off, unable, apparently, to name what a decent man would know, or say, or do, when his country split apart. "What happened to my brother?" he resumed in a thickened voice. "His head was blown off by a cannonball."

There was a ladylike gasp somewhere, not from Susan, although she, too, had quailed at the image. Surely, the war was not Father's fault. It would have happened if he had never been born, never published his newspaper, never given his speeches. But what if this Joe, what if only one person, had lost his life not because he believed in the Union, but because he believed in the Parson? For the second time this morning, she was frightened by her thoughts.

People were gathering. She did not have to see them. Their presence was in the tensing of Father's body. Slowly, carefully, he rose to his feet. Unwillingly perhaps, his accuser stepped back to give him room. Then Father turned, mounted the bench, and again faced his audience, this time from a height of several feet.

"You are drawn here," he said to them, in slow and somber tones, "by a human tragedy." There was a murmur of agreement. The man with the crutch shook his head, and looked, almost pleadingly, at Susan. He was beginning to realize what was happening, what Susan could have told him would happen. She met his eyes. *Go home*, she wanted to tell him. *Take your sorrow, while it is still yours.*

"I have met this man for the first time today, although he tells me he has heard me speak in the past. I do not doubt it. Since March, when I was hounded from the Confederacy, I have been welcomed in most of the great cities of the North."

The man's mouth worked, as if he would interrupt, but he made no sound. He moved the crutch, in small increments, in a reverse circle, as if preparing to turn away. The voice above him said, "Yet I know him. I know his brother Joe." The man's head spun back, and he gave a wounded cry. What was Father doing!

"He is a messenger, my friends. He comes to us from the field of Armageddon, far from this sunlit square, this"—he waved his hand toward it—"this monument to our independence. What a price was paid for it! Boys died terrible deaths then, too, or you"—he pointed first to the man on crutches, and then his hand encompassed them all—"you would not be standing in this hallowed place."

To Susan, the quick transition from one war to another was not surprising, but it seemed to bewilder the one-legged man. He shook his head again, as if to clear it. Father continued quickly. "We are all the sons and daughters of Washington, of Jefferson, of Madison. Joe was their child, too, and so he is not just *your* brother"—Susan sighed—"but their brother, and mine, too, and my daughter's."

"You never knew him!" cried out the real sibling.

"Not as you did, no. Unfortunately, I did not. But I am sure he was a decent lad, this hero of the War for Re-Union. These good people should hear of him."

Susan felt herself shrinking beside her father's sturdy shoes. He was responding, as always, to opportunity, picking up words and deploying them. What, after all, *did* "decency" mean, in times like these, when all that mattered was survival? One thing she did know. Her visit to the prior century had become a trope in her father's arsenal. She doubted she would ever see the inside of the buildings behind them.

Suddenly, the bench quivered. He had jumped to the ground. In an instant, he moved to the one-legged man's side and placed a hand on the turned shoulder. It was no gentle grasp, as Susan could see, for it stopped the man's retreat, as it was meant to do. Almost in his ear, Father whispered, "I think that is why you followed me this morning."

Then he raised his voice again, addressing the crowd, still with a hand on the man's shoulder. "I beg you to listen to him. Here is someone who has seen all, sacrificed all, for the sake of"—again a wave across the mall—"the nation that was born here. He has fought for you, and deserves your kindness." Looking around at the growing crowd, he said, as if offering a benediction, "I leave this noble soul in your care."

Quickly, he reached for Susan, pulling rather than raising her from the bench. From the feel of his hand, she knew his intention was to march her away, but the people would not have it. She knew what they were thinking: *who will believe us—here is Brownlow in the flesh.* There were cries of "speech!" and "Parson!" and "Tell us about the bridges!" Her father stopped.

3.

The summer of 1862 was a series of hotels linked by railroads. Susan often accompanied her father on his speaking tours, and acquired something like fame in her own right. She was known as the Heroine of Tennessee, and learned to speak graciously for a moment or two about her reverence for the flag, at which point—her father's idea— she would unfurl the banner given to her in Philadelphia.

In their time together, neither of them referred to the man with the crutch, although Brownlow did not hesitate to draw upon the memory indirectly. One day, the relevance just came to him. The one-legged man was Gideon, purging the land of the Midianites, those Baal-worshipping Secessionists. Joe's was the blood that glued the Union together. The Parson felt quite justified in the appropriation, for he believed that God, the Author of all Creation, approved a good metaphor.

The men and women who had gathered around them that day in June had been calling for a performance. When had Brownlow ever refused an audience, even when his voice was little more than a croak? Later, he would not know himself whether it was the presence of the wounded man that affected him, or whether, in the communal face of the jostling crowd, he saw a glint of amusement that gave him pause. Were they mocking him? It was as if he had seen the worm in the apple.

He raised both arms with hands spread and appeared to be tamping down the sound, calling for silence. When it came, suddenly, expectantly, he filled his chest with air and expelled it. "You must excuse me. If you will not attend to this man, then shall I. Good day." And so saying, Brownlow grasped the man's arm again and drew him out onto Chestnut Street.

"Will you accompany me, sir?" said Brownlow. Though a stranger in the city, he knew one location, the offices of his publisher, George W. Childs. At that time, the businessman leased premises hardly a block from Independence Hall. Brownlow had visited there earlier in the day, and could return now to ask a favor—a quiet corner, a few chairs, privacy, a glass of water. "If we are to speak, I must know your name," he added, and then, with a lopsided smile, "I cannot be calling ye 'Joe's brother' all the time."

The one-legged man had allowed himself to be guided. To Susan, he seemed like all the others who, friend or foe, were drawn to her father like iron filings to a magnet, but to Brownlow himself, there was something curious in the man's reluctant yet undeterred presence. Even hampered by a crutch, he had kept pace with them earlier, following his quarry down the busiest street in the city. Whatever the reason, he had wanted to be near them. "Evans," came the answer. "William Evans."

It was just as Brownlow had foreseen, and it was not long before he and Susan and Evans were seated in a small room lined with bookshelves and stacks of bound volumes rising from the floor like stalagmites. There was a window, but it was closed and painted shut. Brownlow hardly noticed the gritty feel of the place, having breathed the inky dust of the *Whig* offices for many years. Susan, too, found the mustiness familiar, though the heat of the day and the lack of ventilation made her wrinkle her nose again at the odor of despair and soiled linen. Evans appeared ill at ease, trying many locations for his crutch before finally standing it between the one good leg and what remained of the other.

"Where were ye born, Mr. Evans?" asked Brownlow, intertwining his fingers and resting them on his belly.

"Why does that matter?" parried the younger man, as if trying for belligerence. In his discomfort, he sounded only querulous.

"We carry that soil with us," said Brownlow. "I, myself, was born in a small town in Virginia."

"That has nothing to do . . ." Evans stopped, as if the end of his sentence were lost in the thick atmosphere. Waiting for it to materialize, he gripped and regripped his staff.

"Do your parents yet live?" continued Brownlow, so companionably that the next few words, spoken just as mildly, stunned his daughter and his guest. "For, if I am accused of Joe's murder, I would know who brings the charge. Is it just you, Mr. Evans, or your parents, or your town, or the Union I assume Joe must have loved, for certainly I did not bind and gag the boy and force him to enlist, and surely if I was in his ear, you, his older brother, were in his heart, and I would be surprised if your example had not the stronger voice. In this matter. At that time."

Brownlow had spoken conversationally, for not only would it be futile to meet anger with anger, but he did not really want to deny that his words had consequences in other people's lives. He hoped and believed they did. Susan, sitting a little apart to free the men from a female presence, was, for the third time that day, unsettled. There had been a slight buzzing in her brain, a wave of darkness before her eyes, when she had caught the righteous gleam in the stranger's eye. He was driven, she knew, by love. Was he justified?

Her father's rhetoric had saved Harry Self, but killed Joseph Evans . . . was that possible? Of course it was Jeff Davis who had saved Harry and a cannonball that had killed Joe, but for a moment she could not tell cause from effect, villain from savior. Was it the war that confused her so? Then, as she realized what her father had just done, how he had lanced the guilt in the man's anguish, her fear drained away. What was left was impatience. Must he always be vindicated?

A mighty groan startled her, but it was not her own, nor did it come from Brownlow. Evans had slumped forward against the up-ended crutch. "Susan," said her father, quietly, "will ye leave us now? You know the way back to the hotel. Tell Mrs. Brownlow I am coming."

Dismissed, glad of it, but also resenting the exclusion, Susan gathered herself together, straightened her bonnet on her head, and stood up to depart. She made a process of it, as if to claim the timing as her own, but no one noticed. At the door, she turned her head.

Brownlow had leaned forward and was removing the crutch from the man's hold, replacing it with his arm and then his shoulder as he put a hand behind the grieving man's neck. Quickly, she left the room.

Susan would never know whether Evans forgave her father—or if the Parson brought any comfort to the wounded man. She thought that perhaps he had, for she had seen, as neither his many enemies nor his public friends ever would, the great tenderness of which he was capable toward a fellow mortal in need. Even the citizens of East Tennessee would hardly have recognized the man who embraced Evans, unless—the realization came swiftly—they had known his pastoral care, too.

4.

In the summer of 1863, General Ambrose Everett Burnside at last fulfilled the promise Lincoln had made to East Tennessee nearly two years before. In early September, Knoxville was retaken by Union forces, and on November 11, readers held in their hands the crisp white sheets of the *Knoxville Whig and Rebel Ventilator*. Brownlow had returned. Longstreet had been driven from Knoxville, and, to Lincoln's great relief, Tennessee was now Federal territory. When the president declared, on December 7, a national day of thanksgiving for "this great advancement of the national cause," the editor of the new *Whig* snagged the tribute for himself. He appreciated the honor, he said, although, as a servant of the truth, he was forced to point out that it was long overdue.

Despite failing health, Brownlow continued to scour his enemies. After he returned from exile—and a very lucrative speaking tour— he was appointed the United States Treasury agent for the eastern counties. With Old Testament vigor, he went about his business, refusing a permit here, exacting a fine there, dispensing penalties and rewards according to his lights. When Andrew Johnson was promoted from military governor of the state to the national candidate for vice president, the East Tennessee Central Committee nominated Brownlow for governor, along with a brand-new state legislature. On March 4, 1865, the Parson was elected by a vote of 23,352 to 35, and Tennessee was restored to the Union.

Whoever those thirty-five naysayers may have been, they were prescient. Given a bigger platform and a greater power, all the demons of Brownlow's nature broke loose. Reconstruction was his weapon. Even his daughter Susan, whose entire life had been lived at the loyal center of a firestorm, could not entirely ignore the charges that her father, out of pure vindictiveness, left the state in ruins.

Nor did his subsequent years in the United States Senate do much to change people's minds, although he caused little damage, and even did some good, while in charge of war reparations for widows and orphans of American battles, from the Revolution onward. It was at his behest that Congress, in 1870, paid out funds to Malinda Harmon, widow of Jacob and mother of Henry, two of the Greeneville bridge burners who had been hanged in the fall of 1861.

He had known these men in prison. As his public life atrophied, as illness sapped his strength, that interlude in his life seemed to grow in importance. He had, of course, described it in the diary at the heart of the great, messy volume known as *Parson Brownlow's Book*. At dinner tables, too, he was fond of retelling—if only in a raw whisper— his experiences in the Knoxville jail. In these tales he was, as always, the hero of the hour. Next to Lincoln, he had been at one point the most touted of all Unionists. Yet he gave the impression sometimes that he was nostalgic for the weeks of his imprisonment. It was as if he had never known better men, never been closer to the sons of Adam, never been truer to his finer self, than in that hellhole of a jail.

It happened that Susan was spending the afternoon with him on a cool fall day in 1876, about five months before his death. By then, he was suffering from a palsy so severe he could barely cross a street under his own power. His fingers could not sign his name. His voice was all but gone. Yet his face brightened when she crossed the room and bent to kiss his corrugated cheek. The eyes, those famously huge and deep-set orbs, now followed her like a spaniel's.

Susan was used to his frail appearance, yet there were times when it sucked the breath out of her. The most ordinary remark, a casual word on the price of pork, could bring a distant, yearning look to his face, as if his soul were in trouble, though he could not think why. More than his health even, what she wanted back was his fierceness, right or wrong.

"Do you know what day it is?" she prompted him, having taken her seat close enough to hear him when he whispered. As usual, she had brought a piece of sewing to occupy her eyes and hands. A rough blanket, the sort he might have carried in his travels on horseback, covered his bony legs, its trailing edge just meeting her housewifely dress of unadorned serge.

"Day?" he repeated hoarsely. She was getting like her mother.

"No-vem-ber EIGHT," she said slowly, with emphasis.

"Why is she shouting?" he wondered aloud. "I know the day's date."

"I cannot believe it was fifteen years ago," she sighed, her needle poised in midair.

Some capacities he had lost, but not this one. "1861!" he said smartly, and then, "Oh-h-h-h." This he did not have to say aloud. The day of the bridge burnings.

Glad of a topic safely in the past, she chattered on. "Do you remember that Lizzie Self wrote to me—I think it was whilst you were governor—to say that her father had come home? She had not the courage to write to you directly, and I daresay her letter would never have reached you. But I am sure I told you at the time. I remember now! She said I should tell you, if I thought 'the gratitude of a good man would be a comfort to you.' Well . . . ," she poked her needle too roughly through the cloth. A mistake, she saw now. There had been a scarcity of gratitude in recent years. Why remind him?

But his thoughts had gone elsewhere. All his life, he had feared insignificance, had battled and blustered his way into notice. God had left him unfinished, a negligible child, and he had taken up the job of creation, making himself unavoidable, unforgettable. In that prison, he had been a force to be reckoned with, and yet he had known, at the bottom of his soul, that men like Harry and Andy were God's favorites, already whole in His eyes.

The old man chewed his lip thoughtfully. "I've often thought of that fellow Self, you know, Susie, and the others who shared that purgatory with me. There was"—a short bark of a laugh—"that hunter who nearly killed me in the Smokies."

Susan had dropped her hands into her lap. There had not been this much animation in her father for many days. Caught in the flow of memory, he went on. "Somehow, the Rebs found him, and jailed him, but I would not be surprised if he escaped. A tall, gangly fellow. You thought you heard a jaybird or a cuckoo behind you, there in that filthy room, and, bless me, it was only Andy." Brownlow paused, listening to those sounds again.

When he resumed, he was talking to himself, as he often did when piecing out an argument. "He was someone who knew exactly what he was. A mountain man. Pure iron ore." His hand reached absently for the pen that was not there. "But Harrison. He only knew what he was *not*. There may have been many like him, but not among my acquaintance. He was not the kind of person who would tell a lie or steal a penny. He was not the sort of man who burned a bridge. He was . . ."

Distressed by the spasm in his throat, Susan leaned close. For the first time in her life, she dared to brush the hair back from that war-bitten face, listening for the words that nearly strangled him: "most decent man in . . ." Knoxville prison? Tennessee? He hovered for a time over the hole in his mind and then forgot about it.

She was never to learn how wide was the world in which Harry stood alone.

Andy Slocum

Chapter 10

Over the Mountain:
A Tale of the Mountain Empire

East Tennessee
Spring 1862

Spring plays hide-and-seek with winter in East Tennessee. When you are least expecting it, a soft breeze will touch your face. Lifting your head, you will scent a moistness in the ground, a hint of sap rising. The very next day, the harsh winds of March will funnel through the mountains, whipping branches into chaos and chilling you to the bone. Yet, there it comes again. A milkier blue in the sky. A row of furled buds on a twig. When spring finally sashays into the open, all warmth and color and renewal, it will ruffle your hair and blow you a kiss, as if it had never left.

It is May 1862, and Greeneville is wary, secretive, and stoic as bands of roving Confederates pillage the countryside. Yet those who have lived here all their lives still pause a moment to watch the dawn skim the mountaintops. They hide their chickens at night, but in the daytime, they milk their cows and plant their fields and pick their berries as usual.

Andy Slocum has spent the night in far less comfortable quarters than the barn on Harrison Self's farm. No one knows he is there yet, and he doesn't want to frighten the young woman who is coming down the hill with a pail swinging at the end of her left arm. There's something in her other hand that makes Andy consider his situation. It's a Remington 1858 pistol, as long as her forearm, with a kick that might send any lass head over heels backwards. But perhaps not Lizzie Self.

He remembers her, although he only saw her once. She is tall and fair-haired, with a set to her jaw even though she thinks she's alone. When she is about twenty yards away, approaching the clearing in front of the barn door, he grabs the three-legged milking stool and throws it against the opposite wall. At the cracking sound—he hadn't meant to break it—she drops the pail and swings up the pistol.

"Who's there!" she calls. "Is that you, Alex?"

Guessing that the walls of the barn won't stop a bullet, he steps behind a post before he sings out, "No, Miss. It's Andy Slocum. I was with your Pa." Then he thinks to add, "In the Knoxville jail."

He can't see her now, but he imagines she's weighing her options. Then he hears, "Come outside, Mr. Slocum." He leans his rifle against the wall and obeys, taking care to hold his hands out to the sides, away from his body. The soft early light is behind her head, but he takes her in appreciatively, despite that third metal eye aimed at his chest. She has set down the pail and holds the pistol grip with one hand and the barrel with the other. That won't work, but she could still do some damage. Her gray eyes are steady, and he remembers the sculptured mouth. Its corners are pulled into her cheek as she squints at him.

"I'm sorry I frightened you, miss," he says, tossing her his best smile.

"Poachers don't frighten me," she throws back.

The words sting. Is it because she's called him a thief, or because she doesn't remember him?

"Your Pa taught you to be careful," he says approvingly. "That's good. The truth is, miss, I didn't come to take—whatever you got hereabouts. I came to bring you something. From your Pa."

"Is he . . . ?" She hasn't lowered the gun, but there's something pleading in her eyes now. Quickly, he says, "Oh, he's all right. Not in the best o' spirits, but he's a strong feller. He'll last. He told me to tell ye that."

Still, the gun. He doesn't usually meet resistance from country girls. But she's a rare one, he can see that. Doubt, sorrow, trust, hope, doubt—they pass over her face like the shadows of clouds without changing the landscape. Her chin is still squared. Then he remembers his mission.

"I an't in the habit of sleeping in barns, Miss Lizzie, but your Pa told me you do the milkin' at sunup. I had a hankering to stretch my legs, y' see, and I told your Pa I might be comin' over t' Greeneville, so he took the opportunity"—he reaches into his shirt—"to write you—this."

She doesn't jump for it, as he'd expected, but screws up her eyes suspiciously. "They let you go?" she asks.

He settles to the story. "In a manner o' speakin'. They let me join the folks being shipped to Tuscaloosa. On the way t' the depot, they let me edge over to the side, you know, along the street. There were wagons lined up there, and I guess they let me roll under the wheels when nobody was lookin'."

There! He's done it. The corner of her mouth is trying not to lift, but it can't stop, and there it is, a flicker of a smile worth a crick in his back and some straw in his hair. But she's no bird in the net.

Her next words are, "Put the letter on that stump there, Mr. Slocum, and step back, if you please."

He does as she asks, saying, "It's rubbed a bit from bein' in my pocket the last week, but you can make out the words."

"You've read it?"

Hearing the reproof, he's chagrined, then annoyed. Carrying messages to Unionists is a shooting offense, especially if the Rebs want you dead for other reasons. He has risked his life to bring her that letter. "I figured, if I was stopped, I should know what to lie about."

She nods slowly, "Oh, I see." Without lowering the gun, she opens the page against her hand and reads what he knows by heart:

> Lizzie, I hope you are safe at home. I am still in the jail, and must thank you and the Parson and the Lord that I am not in my grave. Your cousin Tom was very sick and was sent home but I do not know if he is alive. Andy Slowkum will bring this letter if he is able. I want you to give him my heavy shirt with the lacings and any food you can spare. I think of you every day. My own Cordelia, try to be happy after this War is over. Your loving father.

Had he wished, he could have knocked the pistol from her hand as she stared at her father's writing, but he has faith in the letter. Although it is unsigned to protect the carrier, Lizzie will know that only Harry could have written it, and when she looks up, her eyes will be kinder.

They are not. "You came all this way for a shirt and a pone?"

"What? No-o-o-o!" Damn fool girl. "Y'have the horse by the fetlock. I came—"

But he hears something more threatening than her contempt. He grabs her elbow with his birdlike talons, vaguely aware that he has done so before, and pulls her toward the barn. She resists but then she doesn't. She's heard them, too. Hoofbeats. The two of them run for the barn.

Just as the door is about to slide shut, he sees it.

"The pail!" she moans.

"I know," he sighs.

He cannot remember a day when he has made so many mistakes in a row. Pointing to the low wall that forms an enclosure around the cow, he indicates that she should hide behind it. He retrieves his rifle and springs up from hay bale to rafters like an oversized monkey. In the haymow, as he already knows, the latched covering of the chute is braced open, just enough to give him a bead on the clearing. Satisfied, he looks back down into the barn, only to see Lizzie taking hold of the milking stool and looking from its broken leg up at him and back again, accusingly. He's no Audubon, but he knows one bird from another. No dove, this one. Pure jay.

The horses are slowing and he hears a voice calling, "Circle the barn," and then one man rides into the clearing below. He is wearing a gray jerkin, with crossed swords on the cuffs. Andy hears the other two men spreading out, one to the left and one the right. The newcomer is experienced. Checking to see that Lizzie is hidden, he is amazed to see her leaning the stool upright against the wall, placing the pistol on top of it, and sliding the door open. He cannot stop her without betraying his position. The next thing he knows, she is standing by the horseman.

"What are you doing here, Pete?" he hears her ask. She doesn't sound welcoming, but she obviously knows the man.

"Hello, Miss Lizzie," says the Reb, swinging down from his mount. Arm raised, he leans back on the saddle, as relaxed as you please. "Done your milking yet?"

"Are you offering to help?" Andy cringes, but she seems to know the fellow won't oblige. Her tone, he realizes, was sarcastic.

"I'm here on military business," says the soldier, straightening up.

"Where's the battle?"

This time, there's no missing the bitterness.

"Why do you still blame me, Lizzie?" The man she calls "Pete" steps closer to her and speaks in a quieter, almost wheedling voice. "You *know* there was nothing I could do. It was a ruling of the court. It was the *law*."

Her voice is low, too, but fierce. "The law! To put Pa in prison! To hang a boy like Henry! And Uncle Jake. You *left* me there. *I* had to go to the depot and . . ." She breaks off, steps back, and says, in cool dismissal, "Just go away, Pete."

"This isn't a visit, Lizzie. We"—meaning more than the three horsemen, that's clear—"we're looking for someone. We had him in jail in Knoxville, but he pulled some vile trick and escaped. We think he may be looking for work around here. He's a pilot, we know that much. He's been guiding stampeders through the mountains at night. Seen anybody you don't recognize?"

"Your two friends there," she nods back at the outlying cavalry, whom Andy can't see. "And you," she adds pointedly. "I don't recognize *you* anymore."

"That's because you don't really look at me, Lizzie. You think I'm still ten years old." Then Pete lowers his voice again. "I can bring a few chickens by the house tonight."

"The ones you stole from us yesterday?" She is giving him no quarter, and Andy appreciates her gumption, but he is tired of aiming his rifle at Pete's left eye. With the girl in the way, it's the only shot he has.

"What were you doing in the barn," asks Pete suddenly. "That's your pail over there, on the ground." He's walking over to pick it up.

Andy stiffens, but her answer comes readily. "How could I know it was you? I was tying my shoe and heard someone coming, so I hid . . . and forgot the pail. Now give it to me"—she holds out her hand imperiously—"and skedaddle. Miss Sadie can't wait."

When Pete surrenders the pail, she turns brusquely and reenters the barn. Andy holds his breath, for the man stands irresolute, as if wanting to follow her. Just then one of the others rounds the corner and says, "No sign of 'im, Captain." *Of course, there isn't*, thinks Andy, but he is still glad to hear it. Pete lifts his foot into the stirrup and jacks himself up into the saddle, pulling his horse's head around.

He looks back at the barn door, and then canters off, followed by his two shadows.

Andy watches for another minute, flexing his bent fingers. When he lands on the floor again, he looks inquiringly at Lizzie, who has turned her face away. "Who's Miss Sadie?"

Lizzie makes a gargling sound and points at the cow. He's not sure whether she's laughing or crying, so he just says, "Thank you." He means, *for sending Pete away.* She nods and enters the stall, but then realizes she doesn't have the stool. Her voice is thicker than before when she says "I'll get the shirt and some food." She tries to slide past him.

"Wait," he warns. "They may be watching. Don't leave without the milk."

"But I can't . . ."

He sees a bench against the far wall and nods toward it. She sits. Then he takes hold of the stool, laying the pistol on the ground. The leg is snapped but not separated. At the fracture point, each side ends in a fan of splinters, and when he pushes the parts together, they knit like the fingers of two hands. She says, "But . . ." and again he silences her with a look. He moves purposefully toward the center stall, where his satchel is half buried in the straw. The old roan who lives there neighs softly. Andy finds some lengths of rawhide. He douses the slender ropes in the water bucket, then wraps the strands around the wounded section of chair leg. "It will hold you," he says. "And tomorrow it will be stronger than before."

She has been watching him with interest, an experience he rather likes, and finally she says, "I think I understand why you threw it across the barn."

"Do ye?"

"You thought I'd shoot at the first sound I heard."

"Yes, that's right," he admits. "I knew you were brave—comin' to the prison the way you did—but you mightta been a jumpy sort o' gal."

"I never used to be," she says, sounding more puzzled than defensive. "But since the bridges were burned, and Pa's gone . . . I couldn't hit a wagon, you know, but people steer clear of me when they see—*that*." She nods at the gun. "Strangers are always passing by. Not you, I don't mean you. I remember you now. You were kind." It's a strange series of confessions, but where it winds up both startles and pleases him. He searches for a compliment, but all he finds is, "I can see now—*you* an't the jumpy sort."

When she returns that evening, the trees are black fingerprints on the rim of the horizon. It is past nine o'clock. He can't make out her face until she enters the clearing, but he knows her shape and her movements by now. Without his having to suggest it, she has changed her dress to one that is dark and absorbs light. Like a peasant woman, she carries a cloth bag over her shoulder, and he admires her straight back and long stride.

When she is close, he opens the door a crack and she wedges in sideways. She deposits her sack next to his, and watches as he quickly transfers the folded shirt, wrapped bread, and something that might be dried beef or pork into his own kit. He tells her he can't leave just yet, it isn't dark enough, and asks her if she can stay for a while, holding out the promise of more news from the jail.

They can sit outside, he says, if they stay in the shadows. He takes his pack and his rifle and slips out the door. She follows without comment. Against the most sheltered wall of the barn, he has already placed the milking stool, toward which he now gestures grandly, and then seats himself on the ground nearby, leaning back against a stump and crossing his long legs at the ankle.

"Are you sure there's no one watching?" she asks, primly or anxiously, he doesn't know which. As she sits down, he tells her that he has made a circuit of the property, and that they are safe for the time being. He will hear anyone approaching. What he does not tell her is that he found a stream, that he washed his lean face, with its beetle brows and beady eyes and beaky nose, but also, as a lovestruck girl once told him, his handsome mouth and dimpled chin. He has run his fingers through his uncut hair and scraped his chin unmercifully, leaving, he suspects, a trail of tiny scabs. His shirt has been torn at the wrist and flaps open. Still, this is, for now, his Sunday best. He is amused at himself, but alert, all his senses alive. He feels a prickle of ants on his skin, but it is only the breeze lifting the hair on his forearm.

He has assured her that Harry was taken out of the cage as soon as the reprieve arrived. She wants to know if he is eating anything, if he still has his pipe, if he can sleep, if . . . "Whoa, there," says Andy, but gently, and tells her as much as he can remember, editing out the details like dysentery and lice. Then she asks about his own escape, about what happened after he rolled under the wagon.

"I rolled straight out on t'other side, smack into a crowd o' darkies." As if they'd been waiting for him, he says, they stuck a cap on his head and a broom in his hands, and hustled him away into a side street. That night, he slept in an empty cellar. The next day, they darkened his face and gave him food and directions. Andy stops and smiles. One of the children, he recalls—a boy with a red stocking cap—asked him if he was going to see Uncle Abe.

"And the Parson?" Lizzie asks. "Is he . . . ?"

Andy reports that Brownlow became ill soon after Lizzie talked with him in the jail. After being kept under house arrest for two months, he was finally given safe-conduct to leave Knoxville. As far as Andy knows, he's traveling through the Northern states now, telling everybody about the awful goings-on in East Tennessee. Lizzie says, as if to herself, "Pete used to say Brownlow would burn in hell for writing against the South."

"If he does, he'll teach the Devil a trick or two."

Lizzie laughs—a full-throated chuckle he's rarely heard in a woman.

"You've known Pete a long time?" he remarks, with studied casualness.

"Since we were children," she answers. "He and Tom . . . my cousin, Tom Harmon . . ." She runs aground. Even before he read Harry's letter, Andy knew that Tom Harmon had been sent home without a trial. The boy had wasted away. Conditions in the jail have that effect on the less inured, but Andy knows about the rumors. He's heard that Tom testified against his uncle, Lizzie's father. Does she know that story, too? He hopes not.

"He died almost as soon as he got home," she adds, still speaking of Tom. "He was very sick—and very sad."

Andy nods. War is the making of men like Brownlow, but the undoing of boys like Tom. All their guideposts are gone. These days, loyalty is relative. Still, having met her father, and having seen what she did for him, Andy knows Lizzie would be shocked by Tom's betrayal. Andy himself is Union through and through. His loyalty is bone-deep, to his region and his friends. He loves the principle of self-government. But he doesn't hate the enemy. For mountain men like him, a Rebel is just another critter to be tracked and dispatched for trampling on the wheat and gnawing on the Constitution. If they'd quit being nuisances, he'd stop trying to foil them.

"Do you think the Federals will really come?" she breaks into his thoughts. It's the question that has been asked every day since the bridge burnings. The raids were supposed to prepare for the liberating invasion. Rumor has it that General Thomas got as far as the Kentucky line and then turned back, on orders from Sherman. So the Confederate rampage continues under the guise of martial law. Arrests, conscriptions, bushwhackings—there's no safety for the Lincolnites.

Betrayed and abandoned, more and more of them are hiding in the mountains, more and more are escaping to Kentucky to join the Federal Army. Andy has been bringing small groups up from the Smokies, and now he is on his way to another meeting ground, north of Greeneville. In a few weeks, if he lives, he'll reach the Cumberland Gap. He's made the trip before, and he'll make it again and again, until he is caught or killed, or until the Federals arrive.

"I don't know," he answers ruefully. "Maybe Abe wants us to turn the other cheek."

"But you're not doing that, are you." It's a statement, and the closest she has come to asking why he is being personally hunted by an officer like Pete.

"No" is all he says. She won't betray him, he is sure of that, but he won't involve her. He owes that to Harry, who entrusted him with the letter. He knows by now that he was wrong about her. She's no cawing jay. There's a burnish to her, like the female cardinal, muted in color but drawn to bright red—territorial, monogamous.

"Is Pete right, that you're a pilot?"

"Hmmm? Oh. I'm a hunter, Miss Lizzie. I an't lookin' for trouble. Just bear and possum." Reluctantly, he draws his knees up and prepares to stand. This conversation has pitfalls he can't see.

"But they're looking for *you*."

He's on his feet now, and she is, too. Her pale hair catches a thread of light, like the filament of spider's web. She adds, "Don't let the bears catch you—or your friends."

"I an't worried," he says. "Not if they shoot like you."

He'd meant to lighten the moment, but her eyes fill with tears.

To his astonishment, she leans forward, fingertips on his biceps, and brushes her lips against the right side of his face. Recoiling, she says hurriedly, "Thank you. For bringing Pa's letter. I don't mind—that you read it."

Her touch is like the breath of spring, a delicate shower of maidenly goodwill. "Maybe it an't so bad, turnin' the other cheek," he says, as he pivots his head invitingly. Smiling when nothing happens, he swings his pack to his shoulder and hoists his rifle in his left hand.

"Next time," she promises, but he hears what's underneath. She is shocked at herself, but she isn't sorry.

Because he thinks he'll never see her again, because he fears the men he leads might never see their destination, he finds her mouth in the dark. The kiss he bestows is no gentle rain but a cloudburst of regret, of longing postponed. He hears her low cry as he slips into the trees. Men all over the eastern counties are saying good-bye tonight to the lives they might have had.

On the evening of the second day, Andy reaches his first checkpoint. He hears the river before he sees it. Moving from tree to tree, he heads toward the sound. Up ahead, he sees thin slats of light and knows he is approaching the wide shoals of the Watauga River. It is before the appointed time, and he doesn't want to be seen. There is a thicket of ferns on the bank, and he squats down against the smooth trunk of a sycamore with a vine the size of a man's arm running up its side. The river broadens here into a shallow ford littered with stones. The light is draining from the sky and collecting in the flood. The air vibrates with a steady roar.

An hour later, Andy sees a tree move further down the path, and then another, and another. The men are gathering. When he joins them, he sees there are about fifteen. They are careful to stay close to the riverbank. Nearby is a wide clearing, the famous mustering ground of the Overmountain Men who left from here to defeat the British. Tonight's gathering is very different, though. This is not a bold, preemptive strike against an enemy in red coats. This is a quiet exodus, an escape from neighbors in gray. These men are "stampeders," encouraging each other with oaths and intentions. They will return with the troops and kick the Rebs to kingdom come.

Andy greets the men quietly, then tells them the rules. They will travel at night and sleep in the day. They will avoid the roads and follow the hedgerows and tree lines. They will light no fires that can be seen. When they are lucky, they will find a boat to cross rivers, but they will wade or swim across the creeks in their path. There is a safe house along the route where food is available, but most of the time they will improvise. If one of them is injured or killed, he will be left where he falls. Is that understood? Oh, yes, they say. We understand. But they don't, he knows that. There is no way to prepare for this journey except to take it.

Only one of the men is known to Andy. It's Bill Edmondson, a farrier from Jonesborough. He is a tall and burly man, with forearms like ham hocks, and his wife is almost as large as he is. The men tease him, calling this trip a vacation from the "anvil," winking as they say it, and he grins, until suddenly he stops and cuffs the speaker on the ear, sending him sprawling. Andy thinks of telling them to save their high spirits, but he knows they will settle down once they've waded a few streams and belly-crawled through brambles.

They begin their journey, treading softly on fallen leaves, feeling rather than seeing the roots they must avoid, the sudden depressions that can twist a man's ankle. Their breathing is low at first, then quicker, more stentorian, and then slower and deeper. By the time they reach the Holston River, their feet ache with the strain of adjusting to the unevenness of the ground. Where the toes rub, there are burning points of heat. Andy explains that they will remove their clothes, fold them into their shirts and use the arms to tie the bundle around their necks, so they can carry their rifles above their heads. They wear their shoes for protection against the stones, but the cold water quickly seeps in, numbing all feeling. When at last they fling themselves on the other bank, they pull off the sodden leather and wipe their feet with the cold water. Before they sleep, they stuff coals wrapped in green leaves into the toes of their boots and coat their blisters with grease.

They are following a beeline to their destination, but they are traveling at right angles to the ridges and valleys that score the terrain from northeast to southwest. Occasionally, they find themselves nose-to-nose with cliffs they must scale by hand-over-hand progress up overhanging grapevines or ladders of exposed roots. Other times, they must crawl, like salamanders, beneath thickets of laurel, one elbow then the other, one hip bone then the other, hitching their way forward.

One of the men, perhaps chilled in the river crossing, has developed a cough. Andy sprinkles a small amount of quinine powder on the man's tongue, where it's left to dissolve. He looks into the man's eyes and says, "If it doesn't help . . ." He doesn't have to explain the alternatives. After a second's delay, the man nods. No one has the right to endanger the rest.

The next morning, they are on a ridge overlooking a valley they must cross the following night. For now, they will eat some of the dried corn they have brought, pull their hats over their eyes, and stretch out on the pine-needled floor, untroubled by the stink of the shoes they have removed to give their toes a little air. Andy is the last to fall asleep. His eyes follow a drifting hawk overhead, wheeling through the sky in slow motion. The wings are frayed at the outer end. As the bird carves another circle, he can see the wing tips comb the air like spread fingers. He envies that apparent ease of movement, although he knows the hawk stays aloft by unceasing adjustment to every tremor of air. Maybe what he longs for is the scope of the bird's vision, its indifference to obstacles.

They are lucky. In a few days, they have crossed the Clinch River, making several trips in a small skiff Andy has used before and left hidden. Ahead of them, ranging across the horizon, they can see the scalloped top of Powell's Mountain. In the last valley before the climb, there is a house that Andy knows. It belongs to the Widow Rafferty. Not so long ago, her boys were ambushed on their way to the Cumberland Gap. They, too, were stampeders. She hates you for being alive when they are not, but in the end, she'll help you, to spite the enemy. So Andy and his companions have fresh bread today. They have smoked pork and fresh water and crocheted mittens they use to line their shoes.

By morning they have reached a ledge more than halfway up the mountainside. Like a team of sleepwalkers, they go about the business of clearing out niches below fallen logs. They gather stones for a small firepit, scoop leaves into mattresses. Andy leans into the fork of a tree that bends out over the gorge. In the valley below, he can see the Rafferty farmhouse, no bigger than a toy he could crush with his foot. The day is just starting for the woman who comes out into the yard. He shades his eyes. She's no taller than his little finger, but he can see that she is cradling something in her arms.

Andy knows it is old Mrs. Rafferty with a bowl of chicken feed, but from this distance, it could just as well be a young woman with a sack of laundry . . . or a child. It could just as well be someone tall and straight, with fair hair and full lips. In the pale, slanting light, the miniature scene looks crafted by hand. The logs are tiny twigs and the meadow is green velvet shot with gold. Andy cannot take his eyes from the mock image of tranquility. Then he scowls and shakes his head. He has heard of sailors at sea who dream at the mast and fall headlong to their deaths. It isn't a tumble down the mountain that Andy fears—he can walk up and down precipices in his sleep—nor is he afraid of being tethered to a cottage. He's thinking he might die before he can teach that Pete a lesson.

At first it was hard for them to close their eyes in daylight, but by now they are so exhausted, they fall asleep instantly. Their trousers hang in ragged strips below their knees, their skin is crusty with dirt and blood. The man with the cough turns his head into his arm to smother the sound, as if hoping he won't be heard. There is this peak, and then Walling's Ridge, and from there they will see the Gap.

The air is cooler when they awaken toward dusk. A breeze sets the branches swaying. "Up, boys!" says Andy. "We'll take the top before the light goes." They are careful to skirt the bare rocks, where they might be spotted from below. The foliage at this height is younger than in the valley. On a slender maple at Andy's elbow, some of the leaves are a pale, translucent jade. The newest ones, though, the ones in a larval state, are tenderly crinkled and curled like a baby's fist. They are reddish in hue, as if flushed with a dream of their crimson death in fall.

It happens on Walling's Ridge, shortly before sunset. As they are toiling up this last of the major barriers to the Gap, there is a cracking sound like a tree struck by lightning. Everyone dives for the underbrush with amazing speed, considering how tired they are. Everyone, that is, except Andy. He is sitting in plain view, braced against his knapsack with his rifle across his knees. There is a sweet hush on the landscape, but even stillness makes a sound. The faint tintinnabulation of existence.

Is that a branch snapping? The men wait almost a half hour. Perhaps they were careless as they crossed the intervening hollow, or maybe it was the coughing fit that betrayed them, or nothing more meaningful than the falling of an acorn, a Rebel scout who got lucky. Or maybe it was only a passing hunter, inexperienced, looking for his kill, unaware, moving on.

Bill Edmondson is the first to break cover. Andy speaks to him. With the help of another, anxious-faced man—"Just a scratch," says Andy—he is hoisted from the ground and swung between them. He wants to gain the ridge. From there, he can point them in the right direction.

An hour later, wheezing, bent over with hands on knees, calves burning with the climb, they stand where only God can see them. They are in a small clearing. Andy is placed at the foot of an oak tree, where the view is unobstructed. With his feet splayed at the end of his long legs, he reminds them of the rules. They can make it on their own now. Finally, Bill says to the wavering group, "Are ye for Kentuck, or an't ye? I'll be along directly." Some reach down to squeeze Andy's shoulder. Some offer only a long look, a promise to remember. In minutes, there is nothing left of them except the twitch of a branch down the hill or the skittering of a loosened pebble.

Not just yet, but later, Andy will wonder what will happen to all the men he has guided along this route. Some are shirkers, some are leaders, but they are all of his clay: shy before infants, unembarrassed before kings. They were born for this trial. He, at least, has done his part, in the manner of his choice, and that contents him. He will see the brown of his leggings blur with the leaf meal on the ground. His blood will drain into the earth, and what will be left of him will look not so different from the leavings of life he has spied everywhere in the forest. The question of a soul will not trouble him.

If the aim is true and the word is good, the passing leaves a trace, like the trail sign on a tree trunk. With time it blends in, but it is there, engrained forever. Andy won't think of the war as worth his life. He will think of the signs he has followed, left by men and women who loved nothing more than freedom, except the laws of their God and the wisdom of their forebears. He will think of his compatriots, and of Harry, and the Parson—and long before them, the settlers and framers of a new country. To have been on the same path with them will be grace enough.

Yet he has a regret he hadn't counted on. He should have told her about the letter, how he'd asked Harry to write it, because he wanted the excuse to visit her, to be her connection to what she'd lost. Thinking of her makes him fretful. How ridiculous that he cannot move, when he knows at last where he wants to be! Then her image flickers in the breeze and disappears, leaving the hunter with his wound.

Bill makes a paste of leaves to dam the red stream. Andy lets him. Bill is the sort of person who must do something with his hands, even when the task is useless. To the northwest, the Cumberland Mountains stretch along the fading horizon. Andy dreams he can make out the notch, with its rounded hump on the left and its steep incline on the right, the gateway to the future. From here, of course, he cannot see it, but he knows there is an outcropping of rock on the upper reaches of the pinnacle, a gray tablet on the mountainside. He closes one eye and draws a bead on it.

CHAPTER 11
INTO THE BREACH

GREENEVILLE, TENNESSEE
JUNE 1867

LIZZIE WAS THROWING WORDS AT HIM. "You were almost hanged in Knoxville. You almost died in that *horrible* place in Alabama. You are fifty-four years old. Haven't you done enough?"

In that pause before "done," he heard what she meant to say. *Haven't you suffered enough for sending Hugh away?* His back to her, eyes on the loose shingle he could barely see in the barn's roof down the hill, he made an observation, as if on the scene before him. "I'm behindhand in the doing of things, Lizzie. I fell into the war by accident. It wasn't my choice, going to it. Not like Jake and the others. Here is my chance—"

"Why would you . . . ! The war's *over*, Pa."

"Is it?" Turning to face her, he noticed the height of her forehead. Had she always pulled her hair back so fiercely? Those few loose strands at the edge, fine as down on a baby's scalp, moved something in his chest, but his eye was drawn away to the set of her jaw, the lift of her chin. They were the same as in childhood, when she had cocked her elbows and argued for home rule. But the lines around her mouth had been carved by a real war. If he hadn't followed Hugh to the bridge, if he hadn't been dragged off to Knoxville, she'd never have seen Jake and Henry on the gallows—or *him* in that cage. "Well," she had said, when he had tried to tell her how sorry he was, "then I'd never have met Andy." The forced smile, the bitter edge to her lightness, those had been new at first. Four years later, he still looked at her, occasionally, with uncertainty. Sometimes, there she was, the girl he remembered. Other times, like now, he drew his toes back, gauging her expression, as he might do with another man. He remarked carefully, "Governor Brownlow doesn't think so."

"Brownlow!" Anyone else would have heard only disgust in her voice. There were no halfway feelings about the governor. You either hated him, as the old Rebels and ex-Confederates did, for whipping them with Reconstruction, or you loved him for his story, his devotion to the Union cause. Harry studied his daughter's face.

It had been one of his mistakes to think she would have a fondness for the Parson, their savior in Knoxville. To Harry, it was simple: Brownlow had been a fellow prisoner; he had offered a helping hand. To Lizzie, though . . . what thoughts were crowding behind that high, polished brow? It was only a flitting impression, but he thought he heard stifled grievance. Brownlow, she'd be thinking, had written the editorials that had sent Hugh to the bridge. Women never let a good deed erase a bad one.

Feeling obscurely goaded, Harry raised his hand in mock solemnity. "*Brownlow* says we're on the brink of a 'second civil war.' "

"The brink of his second term, you mean," sniffed Lizzie, pressing down the folds of her skirt, as her mother used to do. "The only way he can win this time is by taking the franchise from ex-Rebels and giving it to the Negroes.'

"To the freedmen," he corrected. "But it was Lincoln who ended slavery, not Brownlow. Though he probably takes credit for it." He smiled, watching her lips for an answering twitch, but she tossed her head and said, illogically, "There's Mr. Ogilvy, for one."

For one what? He'd known the old lawyer for decades. Sarah— "Miss Ogilvy"—was still Lizzie's friend, though she'd married that worthless fellow. The one Harry remembered as a boy. Used to come to the house before the war. Might have been courting Lizzie once, but keen to join the Rebels. A promising young lawyer now. Pete.

"What about Mr. Ogilvy?" he asked, hoping to divert her from Brownlow.

"There's no one in Greeneville more respected. A deacon of the church. Most of the farmers around here have hired him for legal business at one time or another. Including you."

"Yes, well?"

"According to the latest 'proclamation' from Nashville, he no

longer has the right to vote." She let him digest this news before adding, "But his houseboy does."

"Hiram! An't he the husband of the girl they sold down south?" Memories floated from dusty corners, merging into shapes and then faces. Ella, the first black person Lizzie had ever seen. Hiram, with a long, thin scar that lifted his eyebrow in a permanent question mark. Ella had died in the cotton fields, hadn't she?

"Yes, but he's not the houseboy anymore. He works in the livery stable. It's his nephew Jake who replaced him at the Ogilvy's." Having settled that point, she returned to the main argument. "Of course I'm glad they can vote. But if the war is really over, and all men are citizens, then all of them should vote. Not just the ones who support Brownlow."

He could see that she had walked into a trap. Not one that he had set, though. He hadn't the wit for that, nor the will. She would have to admit that the freedmen must be protected when they brought their tickets to the polls. There were plenty of white men—and not just bushwhackers and Klansmen, but diehard Confederates—who would try to prevent any black man from voting. That was precisely why Brownlow had issued his call for volunteers. "Brownlow's Army," it was already being called, but its name was the Tennessee State Guard, and it was mustering in a few days.

About ten minutes ago, Harry had told Lizzie that he intended to join.

"You!"

"Well, my dear, yes, I know I am old for this sort of thing, and there is work to be done here, on the farm, the barn needs repairing, but it will only be for a while—"

"Three years they say!"

"—most likely we will be disbanded after the election, and that is August 1st, so ye see, it will really only be for the summer—"

"But you said . . . ! There's an auction next week. Pollox is too old for the plow, you know that. We have to replace Castor." It pained Harry, that she could mention the death of his old horse in that manner. But she was levelheaded, was Lizzie. He went on. "And there's your mother's cousin to help with the harrowing." Seeing her purse her lips, he added hastily, "Though ye can manage very well by yourself, I know ye can, ye *did* so, when I was . . ." To end the discussion, he had turned to the window.

"You were almost hanged in Knoxville!" she reminded him, but it was her own anguish she remembered.

He had expected resistance, and so, like any prisoner, he made himself endure it by sending his mind elsewhere. He knew he was not saying what mattered, not telling her why he felt this surge of relief, this feeling almost of thanksgiving for what, in the darkest days of his captivity, he had believed was lost to him forever, along with Hugh and Jake and Henry and Alex and the other men whose deaths he carried like hidden weights.

All his life, he had put one foot before the other, in the steps of his forebears, and not once had his path forked, until that jailor in Knoxville had offered him life for betraying Brownlow and he had said "no" instead of "yes." Yet he had been granted life anyway, and to what end. He had failed, a second time, to save Hugh. In the four years since his return home, no recovery from wasting illness, no hours in the fields he loved, no welcome from the townsfolk—nothing had released his spirit from its cage.

When those inner walls closed in, he needed to feel their pressure, to be held by it. So now, laying his hand briefly on her shoulder as he passed, he walked around her to the door. "We'll speak of this later," he said. "I'll be down in the barn."

A peppery, dandelion smell bloomed from the oily rag, so familiar it collapsed the years. Harry breathed deeply. In the warm shadow of the barn's interior, he was sitting on the old three-legged stool, the same one, Lizzie had said, that Andy had mended with that famous string of rawhide. There it was, he could feel it with his fingers. The stall that had been Castor's was empty now, but he could imagine the soft, lipping sound of the animal grooming the hay basket, pulling at loose strands. The fragrant cloth moved slowly over the long strip of leather, leaving his fingers warm and tacky. He had been sitting in the very same place, doing the very same thing, when they had come to arrest him in November of '61. Even now, six and a half years later, he could drop a shutter behind his open eyes and relive any moment of his two years in jail.

After the reprieve in Knoxville that day, cheers rattled the cage as its door scraped open. There were bearlike embraces. He was fondly pummeled by the other men from Greeneville. Yet he noticed the ones who hung back, who looked at him with sidelong glances. Why should they be pleased for him? He happened to have a lovely daughter who brought tears to the Parson's eyes. Jeff Davis, personally, had commuted the death sentence.

Not that Harry deserved the gallows—of course he did not—but in the eyes of their friends, neither had Jake or Alex or Henry, or the ones killed earlier in Greeneville. How petty, how craven, it would have been to say *but I am not a bridge burner like them!* What Harry wanted, in his heart, was to be worthy of the men who had paid so dear a price for being wrong in the right cause. And so, in the weeks that followed his release from the cage, it wasn't only the air of January that chilled him.

Another scene rose up . . . the day they were marched into the street and down to the train station. A March wind blew into their upturned faces. Soon, however, heads were bowed and arms raised, for the crowd was throwing more than curses from the sidelines. A bottle struck his forearm, and something dark and wet grazed his ear. Andy was striding beside him, giving his long legs a kick in the air every few steps—to get the kinks out, he said. They had had only a few hours' notice of the transfer: "Tuscaloosa an't no fun, boys. Ye'll be cryin' to come back to Knoxville."

Andy, whose gimlet eyes had been scanning the roadside, turned to Harry at a point where the crowd was thickest. "Friend," he said, "keep yer head low." Then, laying a significant finger on the pocket of his jacket, the hunter suddenly dropped out of sight. Ears ringing, Harry could hardly breathe. Any moment, there would be a hue and cry, a volley of shots. But the prisoners marched on, accompanied by the guards, and no one sensed a change. His muscles gradually relaxed. His chest rose and fell again.

He should never have doubted Andy's offer to get a message to Lizzie. The man could appear and disappear like a bird in a laurel bush. Later Harry would find out that the hunter had rolled under a wagon and been spirited away by a slave, but at the time he could only raise his eyes to heaven and pray. The God he believed in did not always protect the good or the innocent, but He did seem to favor the brash.

Tuscaloosa. Where they wound up was, after all, not so different from the housing they had left. Harry's contingent was herded into a two-story enclosure a few blocks from the river. It was brick, one of a pair of buildings squatting across the street from one another. As he had done at Knoxville, Harry spent the first few days hoping for news of Hugh. He made the rounds of everyone from Greene County, asking questions of the older men and scanning the food lines for anyone of Hugh's age and height.

A few weeks after his arrival, a new batch of transfers arrived. They were from Salisbury Prison in North Carolina. One glance told the older residents that the newcomers had been lucky. Their clothes were, for the most part, intact. They lacked the gaunt stare of the underfed. It was pointless to be envious, though, because they were here now, and would soon lose their bloom. But it wasn't their condition that caught Harry's attention. It was an overheard reference to the early days at Salisbury.

"That fellow over there"—a grizzled speaker pointed at a smooth-faced boy of about twenty—"he was one of the first, when they set up the place last November. For spies and deserters, it was supposed to be. Johnny says—"

"Pardon me," Harry said, elbowing himself into the little group that surrounded the speaker. "Spies, you say? Was there a lad among them, brown hair, no more than sixteen?"

The older man—for his entire face was netted in a web of lines—bent his eyes on the intruder. Harry knew he was being uncivil, but he couldn't help himself. The word "spies" had seared through his mind, leaving his throat so dry his words were little more than a whisper. The other man's gaze became searching.

"And your interest, sir, is . . . ?"

"My son." Mastering himself with great effort, Harry found a steadier voice and went on. "I believe my son was taken to one of the Southern prisons last November, but which one, I do not know."

"There were . . . of course . . . several youths . . . among the company."

"Hugh. His name was Hugh. Hugh Self. Brown hair. Brown eyes. From East Tennessee. About this tall"—Harry raised his hand to the level of his nose. He had become the center of attention. A red-haired giant of a man on his left began to shift impatiently. "We all have a sad story. If every father or son or brother—"

The grizzled man raised a hand pontifically. "I am quite prepared to help, if I can. Let me think." He raised his chin and pursed his lips, the very picture of a man searching his memory. "There was one . . ."

Harry's stomach turned over. "One . . . ?"

"But no, he was a fair-haired boy. I *think* he was from East Tennessee. Perhaps you knew him? He was called Montgomery. I remember that because his name was too big for him. A slender, pimple-faced lad."

With every word, the blind, buzzing hope drained away, leaving Harry spent, more disheartened than before, with a need, all at once, to crawl away. "Thankee," he mumbled, stepping back into the isolation of the swarming room. It was the first of many times he would go through this cycle of reaching and retreating. Every time new prisoners arrived, he listened and inquired. With the passing months, the asking became more painful, not because he dreaded disappointment, but because he feared that any answer, at this point, might be worse than not knowing. His heart clenched when he thought of Hugh—so eager, so incautious, so impressionable, so young. How could he survive? And if he lived, how must he be suffering! In the night, Harry gritted his teeth and drove his fists into his thighs.

Once, he dreamed that Hugh had been home for months. It was possible. Although letters sometimes reached the prisoners, Harry heard no word from his family. Nor, he was sure, did they know where he was.

Summer in Alabama, in a brick building with few windows, was unintended torture. Food that was already half-rotten, soon spoiled even further, crumbling with inner life. Stomachs revolted, and the stench of liquid feces bored into nostrils. Harry, dreaming of the honeyed air of June at home, grew so thin that he used his belt as a sash, knotting it in front. It was said that packages from the North did sometimes arrive, and were "stored" by the guards.

One day, there was a cry across the room. Some Reb, wearing a rumpled civilian suit, had sauntered by the window where a few of the prisoners were stretching their necks for air. "Hey!" cried one of them. "That's my suit!" The Reb had laughed, cutting a slight caper to show off his attire.

"And how do you know that?" he called mockingly. "You cain't prove it."

"Yes I can. My name's in the watch pocket," came the reply. "Hooray for Jack!" his comrades shouted, but their applause was all he gained. In full view of the prisoners, the suit waltzed down the street.

By August, there was so little space, and the stench was so vile, that a few of the sicker men, including Harry, were moved to a warehouse by the river. Union prisoners had been held here since the beginning of the war. The quarters were less cramped, the windows slightly bigger. Harry, too weak to do his usual canvassing of new faces, lay with his back against a wall, his insides collapsing. A doctor visited the prison-turned-infirmary, arranging, indignantly, for the daily gruel and crust of bread to be brought close to the supine men. As he ministered to them, he touched their arms kindly, as a mother might do. Or so it seemed. Most of the time, Harry did not know if he was awake or asleep.

He had once been hale and vigorous, so his body fought hard against the insult of disease. Strength did return slowly, and one day he pulled himself to his feet. Bracing himself with a hand against the wall, he shuffled toward one of the barred windows. He knew a line would be forming there, as men waited for a breath of air, a sight of trees. There was a rough sense of fairness that kept the line moving. No man clung to the sill for more than a long minute.

As Harry waited, a pair of eyes caught his vacant gaze, held it, focused it, and then veered away. He looked again, seeing only a retreating back. There was nothing familiar about it. The thin shoulders drooped, the head was a mass of filthy hair, grayed with dust. Yet it was as if a drop of silver mercury traveled through every vein in Harry's body. He left his place in the line and followed the slight figure.

It dodged ahead, stooped, dragging its right foot. Once, the head turned slightly, and the wasted profile, one eye peering back, stunned Harry with fear and joy. "Hugh!" he whispered, thinking he was shouting. Was he dreaming again? Often, in his fevered head, the boy would be within reach, and then fade away. "Stop!" he wailed, and some of the men idling nearby were roused by the call to action. "We've got 'im!" they crowed, pinning the drooping figure that hung from their arms like a broken marionette. They turned his head around. "What'd he steal, eh?"

Harry's knees had given way, but a bodiless hand found his elbow and helped him stagger to his feet. Greedily, he devoured the boy's face. With a long, shuddering breath, he shook off the kind grip and walked forward. "Hugh-gh-gh," he sighed, as he had a hundred times in the summer evenings at home, "where have you *been*?" And then he tore his son away from them.

They had exactly eight days. There was not much talking at first. Hugh was ill with more than dysentery. A gash on his right side had grown black and foul smelling, and a red seam reached his groin. Even in the heat, he shivered, and the doctor gave Harry a blanket for a pallet and loose covering. There was no going anywhere for Harry. He would have given all of his food to his son, but was told, *You are no good to him if you die first.* Often he touched the pale damp skin of Hugh's face as tenderly as if he were an infant again. He was as helpless as a newborn. The eyes, almost unrecognizable in their dark hollows, followed Harry's now with an expression they both remembered. Once upon a time, Harry would have said, *What have you done now?*

"I told them ye were there," Hugh whispered on the second night.

"Who?"

"The men who found me."

"That's all right, Hugh. Many people saw me."

"And Uncle Jake."

"Have ye been thinking, all this time, that it was your fault?"

"They talked about it where I was, Pa. I know I killed Henry, too."

"Oh, no-o-o-o-o-o."

Something almost like a grin appeared on Hugh's wasted face. "Now Henry's killing me."

"NO-O-O-O-o-o-o!" Harry shook his head so fiercely, the tears flew from his eyes. Hugh's mind was crazed, but how, at the best of times, could Harry have explained the sequence of decisions and mistakes and coincidences that had resulted in the death of a sweet boy like Henry. It had not started with Colonel Leadbetter or Secretary Benjamin or President Davis, or even, for that matter, Abe Lincoln. It had started with Adam. Trouble landed at your feet and you picked it up. You said, or did, or thought something, and by the choices you made, you formed your own lineage. Hugh had joined the long line of the well-intentioned, those who bend to pressure without meaning any harm. He had been an informer, but he was also something else now,

207

too—a boy who was not intimidated by what frightened courageous men.

It was Harry who could not face what was happening. For a while, he pretended. "Lizzie will be glad to see you. She missed you in spite of herself."

Then he simply hovered, stroking Hugh's hair, listening to him breathe. Sometimes he dozed upright, waking with a start. There was that moment of agony until he saw the chest move. Sometimes he waked to see Hugh's eyes glowing in the dark, still fixed on him.

"It doesn't hurt anymore," the boy noted once, and Harry thought, *He's trying to spare me.* It was a gesture so unlike the old Hugh that it *must* imply a future. A time for starting over. *Let him but live, and I will never . . . I will always . . .*

"Brave boy," he said, patting Hugh's arm, though he had seen that same, unearthly detachment, that same musing calm, in others near the end. He did not even know if Hugh could see him. Leaning down, he brought his mouth close to the hidden ear. "Did ye hear what I said? Listen. Ye are braver than any Union soldier." He was not speaking of truth now, but of love.

The night it happened, Harry woke to a changed quality of sound. The head turned toward him looked suddenly different, more skeletal, more dried out and birdlike. He knew at once that Hugh had left him. They tried to move Harry in the morning, and, in the end, it took two guards to separate him from the body.

It was to be expected that, for the longest time, he did not care about living. Perhaps, if the walls around him had been those of his own home, if the people nearby had been his family and friends, the rage and guilt would have welled up in him, bloating his soul and poisoning his life forever. In the prison, there was no one to whom any of it mattered, though there were some gruff condolences. He did not speak for a month, but no one urged, or needed, a word from him. His might have been the cruelest fate, a parent who had watched his child die, but the loss of a son was common enough in wartime. He might even have been called fortunate. He knew the how and the when, though the why kept eluding him.

The doctor had explained the course of the infection, but so simple, so mean a series of events beneath the skin, could not account for what had happened. For that reckoning, Harry knew he must look elsewhere, and to do that, he must survive. Intuitively he understood that if he surrendered any part of himself—his body, his sanity, his moment in time—he would fail in his duty to the lost ones, though what that duty was, or what it would demand of him, he had no idea. And then, one day in the spring of 1863, the Confederacy at last noticed that he had never been a soldier, nor even a real spy. He was useless for exchange, and so they let him go.

Lizzie found him, a month later, curled up in Castor's stall, asleep and undisturbed by the animal's prodding nose. That summer, Harry watched the harvest from a chair, but the following year, he walked behind the plow. It was not an easy readjustment. When he had quavered, "Corniah?" he had learned what two years in captivity had hidden from him. She had not waited for him, but had died soon after Lizzie's return from Knoxville. It was another reprieve, in a way. He would not have to tell her about Hugh. Then, as he began to recover, to walk about the house and the fields again, he felt her accusing spirit in the landscape of their life together. Would he ever be free of it?

To Malinda, he was the brother who was not the husband, not the son, whose coffins had been shipped to her. But it was Lizzie who surprised him, who caused him most days to stop suddenly and hold her in his eyes as if fearing to lose sight of her. It was she who brought him into the living world again, day by day, choice by choice.

She had welcomed him home with a joy that was almost pain, like warmth on frozen skin. Often, he stroked her hair as if she were five again. His wounded heart ached with all he'd lost, but in his absence she had bought seed, hired men, and hauled the harvest to market. Soon, on the basis of her stint as farm manager, she began questioning the way he had always done things—his decisions, his priorities. Didn't it make sense to plant soybeans for forage? Others were doing it. And what about getting one of those new plows? His caution she dismissed as "pre-war." More and more often, he caught himself thinking, *She would be happier now if I had never come home.*

It was as if Brownlow had appeared, once again, when Harry needed him.

Some twenty yards or so from the recruiting office on Main Street, Harry leaned comfortably against an elm tree that was older than he was. Through his thin shirt, he felt the roughness of the bark anchoring him to the spot. The sun was still low in the morning sky, but already the sweat was gathering at his hairline. It was June 5, 1867, the day before the mustering of the Tennessee State Guard.

He was early. The office would not open for another hour. A slight tingle of excitement caused him to breathe in the warm air as if drawing it all the way to his toes. Others were waiting, too. *I'm joining the infant brigade*, thought Harry, for many of them were in their teens. Younger than Hugh would be now. They would have been children when Sumter fell, schoolboys when the slaves were freed.

Alerted by that thought, he noticed something that was still a novelty to him. Two black men, one older and somewhat familiar, one younger, squatted at some distance from the other future Guards, but they were here for the same purpose. One company had already formed from Greeneville, and this second one, under Captain John Kirk, would make up its quota, said the newspaper, with both white men and black.

When the older man turned his head a few degrees, Harry saw the question-mark scar. It was Hiram, the very person he and Lizzie had remembered. His face still had its shiny roundness, but his hair was saltier now, a crinkly halo around his head. He was dressed rather well, and Harry noticed with surprise the pistol in his belt. The younger man Harry did not know, but thought he was probably Hiram's nephew, what was his name—Jed?—who was now houseboy at the Ogilvy's. Something—the presence of a gun at a black man's hip?—made him tense slightly, but when the tremor in his veins became a conscious thought—*why is a houseboy dawdling at this time in this place?*—he dismissed it as prison nerves.

Whatever he was feeling, though, was infectious. Hiram slowly rose to his feet, pushing down on his knees to bring himself upright. Lightly touching his companion's shoulder, he leaned his head in the direction of the stable down the street. Harry took the hint, too, and saw that several men were gradually approaching. They were taking up all the space on the wooden sidewalk.

In the lead, walking with the springy step of a man parading his delight in the summer morning, was Lizzie's childhood friend, Pete. There was little Harry knew about him these days, beyond what Lizzie let fall. He was not her favorite topic. After the war, Pete had finished his legal studies, married Sarah Ogilvy, and taken his place in her father's law firm. He might be heading toward his office now. Perhaps he had just ridden in from his home outside of town. The lanky boy at his elbow was likely some junior clerk sent to meet him, for he carried over his shoulder a fat pair of saddlebags.

The puzzlement was the third man, who walked with a rolling gait just slightly behind Pete. Harry had never seen so tall a figure, not even when he had lived among hundreds of male bodies. The close-cropped head, towering above Pete's jaunty Stetson, often dipped to avoid low-hanging boughs. The man's shoulders were those of a draft horse, and his arms hung by his side like tree trunks. To Harry, he looked half Hiram's age and twice the nephew's size.

There was some shifting among the men waiting by the recruiting office. Before there was any need for it, they cleared a wide path for the approaching group. Hiram and Jed stepped into the margin of the street, backs to the newcomers, appearing to confer.

"Lovely day, Mr. Self," said Pete, coming to a stop.

Without stirring from his backrest, Harry nodded gravely. He was polite to ex-Confederates, though it was an effort in Pete's case. Harry recognized his ilk. Like some of the cannier folks who had fought for the South and lost, this young man was making the most of Reconstruction. He'd been a captain in the Rebel army, but he was the son of a Union mother, and he played either card when it suited him. In his sleek gray weskit and highly polished shoes, he was the picture of a man reconciled to prosperity.

"Morning, Hiram." Pete had turned away from Harry and was eyeing the two black men by the curb.

Hiram waited only an instant before turning. "Mawnin', Mistah Pete."

"Morning, Jed," pursued the lawyer.

"Mawnin', suh," replied the younger man nervously.

Pete gazed for some time at Jed, with an expression both puzzled and sorrowful. "I am surprised to find you here, Jed. Are you visiting your uncle?"

"N-aw-aw. I mean, yassuh, tha's what I be doin'."

"I was talking to Mr. Ogilvy this morning, and he knew nothing about this visit. He said you were supposed to be cleaning the andirons."

Jed looked pleadingly at Hiram.

Pete continued, in a colder tone, "*He* thought you had run off—taking the clothes he gave you for the job he pays you for. The ones you are wearing, if I am not mistaken?"

By now, a few more men had collected, waiting for the recruiting officer. The tension in the air had drawn them like a primal scent, and they were beginning to form an audience. Hiram took a step forward, blocking Pete's view of Jed. "Mistah Pete, suh, Jed don' want no trubble. He lef' his job. He tole Mistah O. he was gwine t' jine the Gua'ds."

"Mr. Ogilvy has no memory of receiving any such notice of Jed's intent to leave his service."

"Suh?"

"What I am saying, Hiram, is that Jed here is not only a delinquent employee, but a thief of Mr. Ogilvy's property, amounting to one long-sleeved shirt, one pair of black pantaloons, two . . ."

More than anything at that moment, Harry wanted to be free to enjoy the warmth of the sun, the blueness of the sky, but he peeled himself from the tree. "Look, Pete," he said reasonably, for old times' sake, "Are ye sure ye have the right end o' the stick here? Mr. Ogilvy would not care about a shirt and a pair o' pants."

Pete turned pointedly to the boy who was wearing the saddlebags like an ox yoke. "Jerry, you go on to the office. I'll be along shortly." After watching the boy hurry away, Pete vouchsafed a look at Harry. "I think, Mr. Self, that you should keep your own counsel. This is a matter between Mr. Ogilvy and his servant, one who left his post without a by-your-leave, a runaway who has now been discovered with property belonging to his master—*former* master."

"Aye, maybe so, I don't know, but *he* doesn't 'belong' to Mr. Ogilvy. He has the right to join the Guard, if he wishes."

Some jovial grunts could be heard, and a flush began to mount in Pete's face. "Not if he is a felon. Now, I am asking you again not to interfere, Mr. Self." His tone changed for a moment. "Why a man of your age and respectability would want to join Brownlow's hooligans, I cannot imagine! I can't think Lizzie approves. But. Well." He became lawyerly again. "I am acting here on Mr. Ogilvy's behalf. He wishes the return of his servant, or his property, or both. And"—Pete widened his stance—"I am here to collect."

As Pete finished, the giant at his shoulder edged forward. There was no mystery about what was happening. Some men who had been sympathetic to the Confederacy still thought of a former slave as a mule that had somehow escaped the paddock. Such wanderers needed coaxing to return, and if they occasionally died of it, they had only themselves to blame. In the world of such men, Jed's decision to join the Guard was more than an annoyance to the Ogilvy family. It was a public insult and a very bad precedent.

There were still about twenty minutes before any officials would arrive at the recruiting office. Harry cast an eye over the soon-to-be Guards, wondering why they had come. Didn't they know their mission was to keep order in the streets? Well, of course, as Harry later realized, most of them were there for the money. Or they thought— many of the younger ones did—that they had missed the "real" war; they wanted some adventure before it was all gone. Perhaps there were a few recruits, like Harry, with private reasons for joining. But for now, the men at his back had no call, and no wish, to restrain Pete.

So he said, "I daresay Mr. Ogilvy would accept payment for the stolen clothes?" Jed was vigorously shaking his head, repeating over and over, "Ah ain' no thief. Lawdy, no!"

As Harry had hoped, Pete seemed to take the word "stolen" as a concession to his claim. He would have guessed, too, that Hiram and Jed had little money on their persons. So, in answer to Harry, Pete said, "He might consider a settlement, if the whole sum were offered."

"How much?" asked Harry shortly.

Pete hesitated only a moment before naming a price that was obviously out of reach: "I might persuade him to take twenty dollars."

Jed threw back his head, clasped his chest with his arms, and began turning in a circle. Hiram put out a hand to steady him. To Pete he said, "I reckon those clos' is part o' Jed's pay, fo' de work he do 'roun' de house. Ain' dat yo' undastanndin' Jed?"

"Ah ain' no thief," was all Jed could say.

"Perhaps you have that understanding in writing? Charley here will escort you home, so you can show us." At this point, the giant stepped around Pete and took Jed's arm in a grip so tight that the boy cried out, "Aiiighhhh!" He was twisting in pain.

Hiram tried to wedge himself between his nephew and Charley, looking up into the giant's face. "Le' go, le' go." To Pete, he said, pleadingly, "Mistah Pete, you know this ain' right. Jed been a good boy."

The world has not changed, thought Harry, and aloud he said, "I have a proposal."

"Stay out of this affair, Mr. Self," came the warning, but Harry tugged as hard as he could on Charley's arm. Maybe it was the surprise, or maybe there was some reluctance to knock down a white man known to everybody in Greeneville. While looking to Pete for guidance, Charley eased his hold on Jed's arm and the young man writhed free.

"Good," said Harry, covering his relief with a smile. "I have business of my own with Hiram. I was simply going to ask him if he would sell me that pistol in his belt. I may need it more than he does. By the way, it would not surprise me if today was Jed's birthday and he got a present from his uncle." As he was speaking, Harry brought some currency from his pocket. Now he counted out twenty dollars and handed them to Hiram.

The man looked dazed at first, but then drew out his weapon cautiously. For a moment, he stood with both hands full, as if uncertain what to do. Then he gave the pistol to Harry and the money to Jed, while the bystanders began to hoot.

Pete stepped close to Harry, and hissed at him under his breath. "This is outrageous, sir. You have mocked me in the course of my duties, and I will not stand for it."

In the mottled red face of the angry man before him, Harry saw an echo of the boy who had played with Hugh as a child and gone swimming with Tom and Henry. The image did not soften him. Of those four children, only Pete, the least deserving, was still alive. In a colder voice, he said, "This is not a legal matter, and ye know it. There are men in town who want to discourage the freedmen from joining Brownlow's Guard. That's why you're here."

Before he could answer, Pete saw Jed moving toward him, holding out the twenty dollars. It might as well have been a knife, for Charley sprang between the two men. Swinging his arm in a wide arc, he sent the money flying and knocked Jed off his feet. Grabbing him again, the giant laid his arm across the black man's shoulders and began marching him away.

If this could happen, the war had not been won. If he did nothing now, thought Harry, he might as well have stayed home. "Stop where you are," he said, raising Hiram's pistol.

Hearing gasps, Charley stopped. Then, however, he spun around, still holding Jed tightly and now using him as a shield. "Don' shoot!" begged Jed, squirming, a minnow on a hook.

"Mistah Self . . . !" began Hiram.

"Harry," said Pete, and it was the surprise of that address—for Pete had always called him Mr. Self—that made Harry turn his head. The smallest of derringers eyed him from Pete's hand. Slowly, levelly, Harry brought his arm around until his own gun returned the gaze. Nothing and no one moved, and not a sound came from any of the men watching. Even Jed, who had been dropped by the giant, ceased his moaning and did not stir.

"Oh, put that down," said Pete irritably. "Think of Lizzie, for God's sake. You don't even know if that gun is loaded. I assure you, mine is, but the last thing in the world I want to do is shoot you. But I will, if you make me. These witnesses will bear me out."

"Take the money, and I'll put it down," said Harry. "That was the bargain, Pete. Ye set the terms—so, honor them." He could not have been more reasonable, but he could see that Pete had gone too far to retreat before an audience, and he probably was not a coward. He had always been self-important, and, in some men, that was as good as bravery. But very soon, Pete was going to wonder if he looked ridiculous, and then he might just pull the trigger from embarrassment.

The skin over Harry's heart itched. A bullet from such a small gun—could it do much damage? Could the light of life be instantly extinguished? He had seen it happen, and Pete could hardly miss, unless . . . Harry raised the pistol quickly and fired it in the air.

The derringer blinked and Harry's shirt ripped open at his side. The next few seconds were a blur. Several men seized Pete and forced the weapon from his hand. Jed gave a sympathetic "Aiiighhhh!," and Hiram tore off his own shirt and wadded it against Harry's side.

The cloth turned bright red and the raw flesh burned. "It ain' deep," assured Hiram. "Jus' a piece o' yo' side gone missin'."

Harry thanked him, and, over vehement objections, gave back the pistol, saying he had never intended to buy it, but only to rent it for a little while.

"What in God's name is going on here?" bellowed someone. As

voices clamored to inform him, the recruiting officer raised a hand for silence. "The Governor wants you to put down riots, not *start* them. What happened?" The talking continued for a few more minutes, and then the officer pointed to Harry and called, "You! Forward march."

The pain was turning the sky dark. All sensation, all meaning, had rushed into the wound. He thought about lying down, but his feet were moving ahead, as ordered. When he finally reached the officer, the man looked him over curiously.

"Well, well," he said. "I see you've already enlisted."

The cloth was part of him, growing from his side like a wad of crumpled skin. When a hand tugged at the edges, pulling the line of brown crust away from the bright-red gash, Harry drew in his breath so sharply it whistled. He was sitting on the edge of a thin mattress, disliking its height. His feet couldn't quite reach the floor.

"Move your arm, Harry," said Doc Mason, tilting his head to get a better look at his work. A searing bolt of pain shot through Harry as the cloth came away in one sticky, ripping, sucking pull. When the blinding light faded and he could swallow again, he took a breath. "Glad it wasn't a Minie ball."

Steps were rapidly approaching. Voices rose, and Harry guessed that the two men who had helped him down the street to the doctor's office were still waiting outside. Someone had joined them and was arguing for admission. A moment later, the door opened and Pete sidestepped through, saying over his shoulder, "Now, now, boys, stand easy. I'm here to help."

"Who . . . !? Oh, Mr. Pete." Doc had twisted around at the interruption, seeming annoyed at first. But now, forceps halted in midair, he looked back and forth between his two visitors.

Harry waited, too, but not because he did not ache to be rid of Pete's company. He knew all about those days in Knoxville, when Pete abandoned his old playmate Lizzie. He hadn't wanted to be seen with a bridge-burner's daughter. That hadn't surprised Harry. A boy who let his mother do his chores for him. There was that time, too, when Pete's men almost caught Andy in the barn, and would have shot him like a dog.

These days, the clothes were finer, but the same old Pete was inside. He was in league now with men like Ogilvy, men who were trying, by every means left to them, to hold on to the lives they had led before the war. Harry knew what it felt like to yearn for the past—all he had ever wanted was the quiet tenure of a freehold—but for him, there was no going back. There was no way to shrink the world back to the size of his old life, to unsee what he had seen. Still, Harry held his peace. It was Doc's house, his right to say "Go." But no such word was forthcoming.

"Har-r-r-ry, *Har*-r-r-ry" sighed Pete regretfully, as if scolding an incorrigible child. "How is he, Doc? I tried to do as little damage as possible."

Harry barked a small laugh, but apparently Doc had heard what he had been waiting for—permission to see the shooting as no crime. "Fortunately for Harry, he isn't so lean as he once was." He motioned Harry into a reclining position. "No bone or muscle was in the way, just fatty tissue. The bullet tore away some flesh and—*turn a bit more on your side*—there will be a scar to mark its passage." He placed some toweling under the edge of Harry's back. "But, as you say, not *too* much harm done."

"I'm so relieved," said Pete, heartily, and then more expansively. "You really gave me no choice, you know, Harry, old fellow."

Suddenly, cold water sluiced over the wound, burning like the touch of a firebrand. Only a glimpse of Pete's hovering smile kept Harry from crying out. Instead, he bit down on his lower lip until he could taste blood.

As Doc padded the wound with lint, Harry's vision began to clear. Pete was still there. He was talking, saying things like "cannot ride in that condition" and "buggy" and "Sarah would never forgive me." Somehow, a plaster had appeared over the wound, and Doc was helping Harry to sit up. His joints felt rusty, as if he hadn't used them in years. Now Doc was reaching behind him, winding a long strip of gauze around his chest to secure the dressing.

"If I may—" Pete signaled his intention to be heard. Doc stepped back, and Pete leaned in with his news. "Hiram will drive you home, Harry. I told him to bring around a buggy from the livery. At my expense, of course."

Sliding off the table, Harry felt his toes, then his heels, hit the floor. He thanked Doc, saying he would drop in with payment on his next trip to town. Then he started toward the door, forcing Pete to turn slightly to avoid him. How tempting to keep on going, to ignore Pete and walk all the way down Main Street to the tree where he had tied his horse. But no. It had never been in Harry's nature—not in the old days, and not now—to leave a furrow half-plowed.

"I could have forgiven ye, Pete, for leaving my girl unprotected in Knoxville."

"Oh, but—"

"We are all cowards one time or another. No more do I hold it against ye that ye rode your soldiers over my land chasing a man who is worth ten of ye."

Pete's face had darkened. "Now look here—"

"There are plenty like ye in this county, not really caring who won the war, building your fine new houses out of the wreckage on both sides. Oh, hold your horses, Pete. I do not even blame ye for that. Better men have done the same. Baxter and his kind."

"I will not stay to be insulted—"

"But in my book, there an't much to be said"—Harry was almost out the door—"for a son whose Ma digs the 'taters while he chases 'round town. Good day to ye, Doc."

Harry had never wasted much time wondering about Providence. He wasn't the sort to find God's hand in the fall of a single sparrow, though he did marvel at the way a flock of birds could pivot as one, the way the seasons never varied in their sequence. There was an order to things, and if God sent a storm to uproot a sapling, a man had only himself to blame for not staking out the guylines. Harry did not curse the Deity for Hugh's death.

Maybe the war itself was at fault, but he might as well hate the fire that renews the forest or the flood that loams the fields. His country had been sick, was the way he thought about it. The war was the bitter antidote, the countermeasure that had not yet, but would eventually, restore a balance that would, inevitably, be lost again. That was nature's way, and the mass of men were bound to it, but not any one individual. It was not the war that had hanged his friends or killed his son. It was Secretary Benjamin, who had called for executions. It was the man behind the knife that caused the wound that let infection reach Hugh's heart.

By that logic, though, he, too, was guilty. Even Leadbetter, though wrong about the facts, had stumbled on the truth: the father had failed the son. Harry had not known that Hugh would join the raiders, but he could have kept the boy at home afterwards and defended him on his own ground. Instead, he had sent him away. For that choice, Harry raked his soul daily. In his darkest moments, he envied the men who had chosen their own deaths, going to the gallows because they would not betray other men or foreswear their Union faith. There was a cleanness to their bargain, a resonance to their fate, that Harry yearned for, and had not found in the sufferings of imprisonment.

Such thoughts, however, were far from his mind when the sky turned a pinkish gray on the morning of August 1. Election Day. Supporters of Etheridge, the other candidate for governor, had made trouble in Robertson County, so thirty of Kirk's company had been sent here to keep order. By far the oldest of these men, Harry was as new to soldiering as the youngest. As he pulled on his knee-length jacket, its brass buttons already tarnished by sweaty fingers, his palms tingled. He swung his arms crosswise in front of him, as if to shake off a night spent on a thin pallet, but he knew very well that what he felt was excitement.

The town clock chimed seven. Two hours before the polls opened, Lieutenant Burchfield's detachment of militiamen lined up outside their encampment. In their ill-fitting uniforms, most of the men looked the worse for a fortnight of sleeping on damp ground, washing in a scummy pond, and dodging rotten eggs and ripe tomatoes. "Brownlow M'lish OUT! Brownlow M'lish OUT!" had been the usual morning greeting, mixed with "Damn Yankee-lovers, we'll thrash ye this time."

A short man with a thick curtain of beard adding length to his round face, Burchfield was addressing the men from his perch on a tree stump. He had information, he said, that about ten to fifteen locals, all armed with rifles, had gathered in front of the courthouse. "They want to scare away the Negroes, prevent 'em from voting. We are to stand aside, we are not to engage these men, unless they actively intervene."

"What does that mean?" whispered a red-haired boy next to Harry.

From behind came a growling answer. "It means, if they actively kill a nigra."

"Oh."

"Stay behind me," said Harry, "and ye'll be all right."

The Guard formed a loose column and began the brief march from their encampment into town. Already the sun glared at them through a break in the treetops, spying indifferently on the scene below. As the men entered the grassy square, marching down the center of the road that bordered the open space, Harry's skin prickled and his muscles tightened. It was as if the locusts, whose rising and falling buzz rasped the air, were trapped inside his skin.

A few children were trying to keep pace with them, laughing and mocking them with exaggerated strides. "Brownlow's Bummers!" "Brownlow's Bummers!" they shouted, until one of the Guards swung his rifle in their direction and they screamed and scattered. The bravest of them, about five years old, stood his ground, howling, "My Pa'll get you!"

All eyes, however, were drawn toward the courthouse. A few people seemed to have paused in whatever business they had, and were watching the approaching Guards. Up ahead, along the side of the street for about twenty or thirty yards, was a group of men forming a sketchy line. It seemed they had been waiting there for some time, because some were squatting on their haunches, arms locked around their knees.

Harry could see that some were gathered into groups of three or four talking, and a few were sitting by themselves on the ground, crossing their ankles and leaning back on their elbows, chins dropped on their chests. They might have been taking a noonday break in the fields, except that it was almost nine o'clock in the morning in the very center of town. Even before his eyes told him so, Harry knew their faces were black.

The freedmen were here to vote for the first time, and they had had the foresight—some were going to call it effrontery—to stick together. Ahead of them, stretching across the front porch of the courthouse, was another line of men, all white, all standing with squared shoulders and spread legs, all with rifles gripped and ready. They might have been bracing for a cavalry charge.

A few more citizens had stopped to watch as Burchfield's men came alongside the waiting freedmen. In no particular hurry, the Negroes reshuffled themselves, all on their feet now, facing the same way, rolling their eyes from one group of white men to the other. Harry could see that many of them held their tickets openly in their hands, while others had a fist jammed into a pocket, as if afraid their precious ballots might blow away.

One of the courthouse monitors stepped forward. He was middle-aged, sleeves rolled up over knotted forearms, belly pushing his shirt tight. On his head was a battered Confederate cap. He might have been a shopkeeper, or a tenant farmer, or a sheriff's deputy, but there was something in his air that Harry recognized. This was a man with something at his back—a building, a piece of land, a way of life—that he craved a chance to save.

"All right now," he said in a throaty but loud voice. "Here it is. We didn't ask for any help. We can keep the peace just fine by airselves. We shure-z-hell don't need Brownlow's Army gettin' under foot. So if you fellers"—he swept a hand toward the Guard—"will just turn around now and git movin', there won't be any trouble."

Burchfield tilted his cap forward as he scratched the back of his round head. "Must be eighty degrees already. Might reach a hundred, so let's not exert ourselves. You allow these folks to vote, as they have a right to do, and we'll just sit over there in the shade."

The townsman's rifle, which had been cradled in his left arm, now moved to his right shoulder. "Sit where ye like, if ye've come for a show. None of these nigras is goin' inside. Ye call this voting? They don't even know what their tickets say."

The speaker glanced over at the handful of people who were stopping to watch. As if on the hustings himself, he raised his voice even higher. "They the *gov'nor's* slaves now. *He* sent 'em to stuff the ballot box. And we an't havin' no such shenanigans in *this* town." There was a chorus of assent from his companions, though no response from the onlookers.

A wagon crossed the far end of the square, and a man who was sweeping the sidewalk some thirty yards away stopped and leaned on his broom handle. Harry heard again the buzzing of the locusts, or was it just the thrumming of his nerves. At this rate, everybody in the square would stand roasting in the heat all day, and the futility of it made Harry restless. Then he noticed a movement among the freedmen. Some of them were whispering, and those who were standing at the rear of the group began widening their distance from the others. A decision was rippling through the line, and more men turned away. Departure was in the air, in the shaking of heads, the hoisting of satchels. They were going to go home.

Not now, thought Harry, and he placed his rifle on the ground. Stepping away from his fellow Guards, he walked up to the nearest man among the would-be voters. At his approach, the Negro shrank back, but Harry's look said *don't move.* What came from his mouth surprised even him. "I don't aim to waste my time, so one of us is going to vote—and I an't the one registered." The other man's teeth gleamed.

The other Guards had been watching Harry in stunned silence, but now he nodded to them, then tilted his head toward the freedmen. His fellow Guards might have hesitated, had he not been old enough to be their father. They were used to trusting him. Another militiaman laid his rifle down and walked up to another baffled Negro. Soon the freedmen were surrounded by unarmed Guards who were only slightly less mystified by what was happening.

A warning shot rang out over the heads of the advancing men, but they treated it as a salute. With hesitant and irregular steps, the crowd flowed rather than marched toward the courthouse steps. Burchfield, who had scampered to the front, still had his rifle, but he waved it aloft, asserting his command again. As he approached the leveled guns, he cried out, "Will you shoot unarmed men in front of these good citizens?"

Harry did not know what the answer was going to be. He did not know if it would come in words or in bullets. What he felt now was like the wonder of that first glimpse of the ex-slaves foregathering. They must have known they would be threatened with injury or death. Surely many of them had been told that going to the polls meant losing their employment. Harry did not think they even believed they were enfranchised, could not even see themselves voting. And yet they had come.

With each step that Harry took, he saw more clearly what had brought them. It was not so much hope or revenge; it was knowing that the path was theirs to choose. Traveling it made them free. Something of that feeling must have come, in the end, to the bridge burners who had died on their own terms. In this strange town, in this odd company, on this blazing summer day, Harry understood where his feet had led him. The war had seized him against his will, but he had fought no battle that was not his own to win or lose.

EPILOGUE

THE HISSING OF THE LOGS ROSE SLOWLY INTO SONG. In the breeze that blew in with her, the flames dipped and fluttered. "Are ye proud of yourself," he asked.

Lizzie touched his cheek as she passed, removing her heavy woolen coat and tossing it over the back of the chair into which she settled herself with folded hands. "I am," she stated. "And you will be too, once you've seen it. It's in the barn."

He, himself, had no yearning for an Oliver Chilled plow. Yes, it held an edge better. It was easier to clean. "But the old one does the work—if ye have the muscle for it," he had said. They both knew that his carping was for show. He trusted her judgment, and had done so for years. The farm had prospered in her hands, and she had learned, in midlife, how to manage him. He saw her every tactic, and she knew that he did. And so, over time, the struggle between them became a ritual. Not really a tussle of wills anymore, it was a fabric of behaviors that sustained them day by day.

He would have said he was content, though sadness often caught him unawares. In his side was the dent where Pete's bullet had struck him, but he had served in "Brownlow's Army" without further injury, except, occasionally, to his dignity. Pete—running now for a second term in Congress—had been partly right to call the Guards "hooligans." Some of them were. Their real purpose, as everybody knew, was to secure Brownlow's reelection.

The Parson had won, and would be governor again, and then, one day, senator. A driven man, but a cursed one, too. They said he had lost his voice in the end, and could no longer speak to crowds. *What a pity*, mused Harry, for the Parson without a voice was like Andy without a rifle. Harry had already outlived Brownlow by three years. But he had not joined the Guard for its leader's sake. Others had beckoned him, those ghosts who were always near.

Pulling the frayed quilt higher over his knees, Harry settled further back into his chair by the fire. It had taken him a long time, but in the end, he had come to understand what he shared with his country. Their histories were not bequeathed to them, preserved forever in stone. What was best in the past would be forgotten, if not searched for, not chosen, every day. Or so he dreamed, as the room melted away into the heart of the yellow flame.

Author Notes

We allow—even require—the historical novelist to bend facts for the sake of art. In telling Harry's story, I've taken liberties. I've invented minor characters, conjured up scenes that never happened, and imagined dialogue and interior lives that exist only on these pages. This is a novel, not a biography. Yet I've done my best to honor what is known, so far as I could determine it.

And so, for those of you interested in the period, and for anyone curious about the interplay of research and imagination, I've included the author notes below. I know this is an unusual choice for a fiction writer. Call it a mild experiment in form, if you like: the story and the record, two sides of the same coin. You are welcome to ignore these notes, to dip into them here and there, or to treat the whole section as one long, disjointed essay in tandem with the novel.

The following material includes paraphrases and composites of information drawn or remembered from a variety of sources, many of which are noted in the Acknowledgments section, where you will also find complete citations for any abbreviated references below. Any errors or omissions are of course my own, as are any opinions not attributed to others.

CHAPTER 1: THE CONSPIRACY

p. 5: **Greeneville, Tennessee:** Both Greene County, and the county seat, Greeneville, were named for the Revolutionary War hero, Nathanael Greene. The town is located in Eastern Tennessee, in the "ridge-and-valley" portion of Appalachia, between Bays Mountain and the Bald Mountains. Prior to the Revolution, the area had a complicated relationship with North Carolina, sharing many geographical and political features with that neighboring state. In the late eighteenth century, during a period when North Carolina relinquished some of its western territories to the United States government in payment of debts, there was a local movement to establish a separate "State of Franklin" with Greeneville as its capital. That project failed, and eventually Greene County became part of Tennessee. Greeneville's history, especially in the light of earlier settlements on the Watauga and Holston Rivers (see later note on the Wataugans), establishes a pattern of independent thought in the mountain counties of East Tennessee. In the days leading into the Civil War, these counties voted two to one to remain loyal to the Union. When the state as a whole joined the Confederacy, these counties engaged in a civil war within the Civil War. This is the setting for the story of Harrison Self, who farmed land near the Nolichucky River outside of Greeneville.

p. 5: **Harry [Harrison Self]:** The main character in this narrative, Harrison Self is an historical figure, mostly unknown today outside of Eastern Tennessee. Information about him comes from several sources, but mostly from the articles published by Donahue Bible, and from testimony given at Self's trial in Knoxville in 1861. In the transcript, **Alexander Lowe (see note to p. 16)** describes him as "about fifty years of age . . . [with] children grown and . . . grandchildren" (*The War of the Rebellion: A Compilation of the Official Records of the Union and Confederate Armies [hereafter referred to as "OR"],* Series 2, vol. 1, Part 1, p. 864). Family records archived in the Greeneville Genealogical Library give his birthdate as July 15, 1813. Thus, he was forty-eight at the time of the bridge burnings. A year before his birth, the British burned the US capital; in the year of his death, 1907, Picasso painted *Les Demoiselles d'Avignon.* From the War of 1812 to the beginnings of cubism, that was his lifespan. I do not know if he was ever called "Harry," but given his frequent appearance in these pages, I needed a shorter name than "Harrison."

p. 5: **Corniah:** The first name and the age of Harrison Self's wife are listed in the 1860 federal census records. Her maiden name of Cobble was given in a copy of handwritten family records archived in the Greeneville-Greene County Library, Greeneville, Tennessee. There, her death is listed as "[b]etween 1860–61," so I am technically within historical limits when imagining her alive during the crucial days of November and December, 1861. It is not hard to imagine that the terrible events of those days hastened her death. I have no further information about her, and so have taken the liberty of inventing her personal characteristics.

p. 5: **their son:** As noted above, Harry had a number of children, some of whom had married and produced children of their own. I do not know which if any of the older children lived with Harry at the time of the events in this story, but for dramatic clarity and focus, I have placed these other persons offstage. History does record that two sons were present at the burning of the Lick Creek bridge. Hugh A. Self was sixteen years old (confirmed by several sources), and Andrew Self was eighteen (*OR,* Series 2, vol. 1, Part 1, p. 867). However, Andrew is not listed as living in his father's household at the time of the 1860 federal census. For this reason, and because

Hugh was the younger and more vulnerable of the two, and because he was later specifically identified by Colonel Danville Leadbetter, I have elided Andrew and focused on Hugh as the son Harrison Self was trying to save from what he saw as the danger and folly of the bridge-burning conspiracy.

p. 5: **brother-in-law's house:** The meeting described in this chapter took place in the new brick house built by Jacob Harmon in 1858, three years before the raid. See Bible(2), p. 130. Jake was married to Harry's sister, Malinda. The two families lived only about a mile apart, and undoubtedly knew each other very well and spent a great deal of time together. Having no information about Malinda, I have imagined her personality and invented her speech and actions. There is documentation for Jake's visit to Harry's farm on the day of the raid, for his hosting of Fry's meeting, his presence at the bridge burning, and his later capture, etc.

p. 6: **Malinda:** Malinda Harmon, wife of Jacob Harmon, was Harrison Self's sister.

p. 7: **light cast by a single candle:** A famous drawing of the gathering in the Harmon house appears on the cover of *Harper's Weekly*, vol. VI, no. 274 (March 29, 1862). The image shows a crowd of excited men in a dark room, right hands lifted in the air, left hands touching a flag draped over a table. It is a theatrical scene, with sharply defined contrasts of light and dark. Ecstatic faces are lit by a central candle as Captain Fry swears his followers to secrecy and to the commission of the planned raid. Several shirts can be seen hanging from a rope in the rafters.

p. 7: **Haun:** Christopher Alexander Haun was one of the craftsmen for whom **Pottertown (see note to p. 46)** was named. The railroad marked the division between Haun's land and Jacob Harmon's. Donahue Bible speculates that the clay deposits on Jake's land were used by the many potters in the area, suggesting that Jake and/or members of his family sometimes tended or used the kilns themselves, and very likely also leased these facilities (or the use of them) to local craftsmen such as Haun. Later discoveries of some of Haun's handiwork show that he was a rather gifted ceramic artist (Bible(2), p. 131).

p. 7: **Matt and Henry:** Jacob Madison ("Matt") Hinshaw (often mistakenly called "Hensie") and Henry Fry were two residents of Pottertown who participated in the raid. For a note on their later fate, see below.

p. 7: **Seth Gordon:** The schoolteacher is an invented character.

p. 7: **Captain Fry:** Captain David Fry was one of the two serving officers who were among the group of men chosen to recruit and lead the saboteurs in the bridge-burning conspiracy. I have invented the specific words in which he addressed the volunteers at Jake's home, but the oath he administered is based on testimony at Harry's trial. **See note to p. 9, the oath**. I am concerned only about Fry's part in this raid, but his later adventures, including captures and bold escapes, are the stuff of dime novels. Harry is correct when he later tells Hugh that Fry served in the Mexican War. It is important to note that, at a later time in his life, Fry made public efforts to redeem the character of the bridge burners by asserting their legitimacy as soldiers of the Federal Army.

p. 7: **Reverend Carter:** This particular Carter was one of three sons in the prominent Carter family in Elizabethton, Carter County, Tennessee. His older brother, Samuel Perry ["Powhatan"] Carter, a lieutenant in the United States Navy, was recalled and reassigned to the Army, while retaining his naval rank—a unique occurrence in American military history. Eventually, he became a brigadier general active in several campaigns. Early on, S. P. Carter established Camp Andy Johnson, near Barbourville in Kentucky, to organize regiments of "stampeders" (as the fleeing Unionists were called). The younger brother, James, helped enlist East Tennesseans in the Union regiments, and also smuggled arms into the eastern counties to aid the Unionists. William Blount Carter, formerly a Presbyterian minister, became an advocate for the Union. He attended the Greeneville Convention in June of 1861 and soon became convinced that something needed to be done to help the Union cause in East Tennessee. He came up with the plan to burn a number of railroad bridges on one night, and sold the idea to Abraham Lincoln in person.

p. 7: **Camp Dicky:** The bridge-burning plot was hatched at Camp Dick Robinson in Kentucky. **See note to p. 22, "Federals are in Kentucky."**

p. 8: **Lick Creek:** This small stream winds through the countryside about fifteen miles from Greeneville. It would have been only a few miles from the homes of many of the men central to this story, including Harrison Self, Jacob Harmon, and Christopher Alexander Haun. The Lick Creek bridge served the East Tennessee and Virginia Railroad line, and was one of nine railroad bridges targeted for destruction on the night of November 8, 1861. Only five were successfully burned. Physical descriptions of the creek are based on present-day visits to the scene.

p. 8: **supplies that come by rail:** From very early on, Lincoln and his generals understood the importance of East Tennessee's railroads as a supply line for the Confederate Army in Virginia. Troops from the cotton states were also brought into and through Tennessee by rail.

p. 9: **the oath:** In his court testimony, Alexander Lowe said that Harrison Self "came late" to the meeting at Jacob Harmon's house, and that he, Lowe, did not see Harry take the oath. The crucial question was the status of the oath itself. Was it merely a rousing call to the night's adventure and a promise to keep it secret? Fry would later claim that it was a formal swearing-in ceremony, attaching the men to the military unit he commanded: Company F, Second Tennessee Volunteer Army. Therefore, any bridge burner caught by the Confederate authorities should be considered a prisoner of war, not a traitorous spy, and if killed, his widow would be eligible for compensation. See Bible(2), pp. 131ff.

A more formal and public, if retroactive, swearing in did occur two years later. Bible notes that "All of the dead [executed] men [were] posthumously sworn into the service of the United States by a special act of Congress in 1863." (p. 136). In 1871, then-Senator Brownlow urged the Senate to affirm a bill passed by the House of Representatives on June 21, 1870 (H.R. #2252), granting relief to Jacob Harmon's widow, whose husband's land had been deeded over to the defense lawyers for payment of services. On November 9, 2002, a ceremony was held at the Harmon Cemetery in Greeneville, honoring all of the men who were executed for the raid, declaring them heroes with the words "In the Hour of Their Country's Peril, They were Loyal and True" (p. 136).

p. 11: **Lizzie:** The only historical information I found about Elizabeth Self comes from two sources. Her name and age are confirmed by the federal census of 1860, which lists Harrison's eldest daughter as "Elizabeth A. Self, 24." She was thus 25 at the time of these events. Her visit to her father in prison, and its consequences, are documented in Parson Brownlow's diary, as later notes will indicate. For the most part, however, I have imagined Lizzie into life, often inspired by diaries written by women in this part of the country during the Civil War. Other helpful books include 1861 and 1862 almanacs, and Juanita Leisch's study of female clothing during the period.

p. 12: **Mr. Brownlow's editorial:** William Gannaway Brownlow, editor of the Knoxville *Whig*, is a very important figure in Tennessee's history, and he will appear in person in several later chapters.

p. 12: **"gassy Union-destroyers" [etc.]:** Brownlow was well known for his colorful invective, especially his enthusiastic lambasting of Secessionists, or, indeed, anyone who didn't agree with him, whatever the topic. The phrases cited here do come from his writings, although not specifically from editorials that Hugh would have seen. The labels can be found in Brownlow, pp. 23, 128, and

137. Later examples of Brownlow's rhetoric also come from his writings.

p. 13: **"Jersey coast in August"**: In a brief online article about Oliver Spencer Halstead, a Civil War businessman, the following note appears: "He wormed his way into the White House by befriending Mary Todd Lincoln on her August 1861 vacation on the New Jersey shore." http://www.mrlincolnswhitehouse.org/inside. asp?ID=180&subjectID=2

Accessed: December 15, 2014

p. 13: **that cockscomb Peter:** Lizzie's friend Peter is an invented character. Although the eastern counties were mostly loyal to the United States, some of the residents, and in particular, some of the young people, were captivated by the romance of Secession. Peter's language echoes phrases from contemporary accounts. Harry's antipathy toward him has many obvious sources, including generational tension and a farmer's suspicion of a college-bred lawyer.

p. 16: **Alex Lowe and John McDaniels:** Both of these men testified at Self's trial, recounting what happened in the hours leading up to the bridge burning. In his testimony, Lowe mentions that he was residing on Self's farm at the time, and according to Donahue Bible, "Low or Lowe lived on Harrison Self's farm as a tenant farmer" (Bible(3)). McDaniels mentions that he was pulling corn in a field by the road when Jacob Harmon and Jonathan Morgan came by with news of the planned raid and the meeting to be held at Harmon's house that night. Lowe, in his own testimony, says that he was with McDaniels when Harmon stopped by, but does not mention Morgan. Lowe adds that he spoke with Harry at the hogpen that evening, that they discussed Harmon's news, and that Harry said the raid "was a bad thing."

Lowe also mentions his visit to Harry early the next morning, when neither of the men made any reference to the bridge burning. I have followed the court testimony quite closely, but taken liberties in fleshing out Lowe's character. He was, indeed, a Confederate at heart, and later joined the Rebel army, but in portraying him as self-serving, I may be doing the real-life person an injustice. Like the invented character Pete, Lowe reminds us that there were many Rebel sympathizers throughout the mostly Union counties.

p. 16: **Cordelia:** The reference, of course, is to *King Lear*. It may seem surprising that a man like Harry would have a copy of Shakespeare's plays in his parlor. However, there was a literate tradition in the eastern counties, and several institutions of higher learning (most notably Tusculum College, still in existence today). Harry likely did not have more than a rudimentary education, but it is quite plausible that his family would have passed down through the generations such staple volumes as the Bible, *Pilgrim's Progress*, and the plays of William Shakespeare. The colorful mountain "pilot" Daniel Ellis, a wagoner by trade, salts his autobiography with quotations from several English authors, including Shakespeare.

p. 17: **King's Mountain:** In Tennessee's Revolutionary War history, this is the most famous battle. Settlers on the Watauga and nearby rivers countered an ultimatum from the British by mustering an entirely voluntary company of citizens at Sycamore Shoals in Elizabethton. Their numbers grew as they made the long march to King's Mountain, where they surprised and defeated the British. These citizen-soldiers became known as The Overmountain Men. Stories of their heroism were (and still are) part of the folk culture of the Tennessee mountains, and it is almost certain that a Greeneville man like Harrison Self would have told his children the tale many times.

p. 18: **Governor Harris [and following]:** This very brief and simplified review of historical events is drawn mostly from Oliver P. Temple. Isham G. Harris was the governor of Tennessee during this crucial period. He wished to align Tennessee with the South, and took some dubious steps toward that end—such as getting the legislature to approve a military alliance with the Confederacy that effectively committed the state to the Southern cause, *before* the citizens of the state had voted on the issue. Early indications were that most people wanted to remain in the Union, but the definitive vote came in the June 8th referendum. As noted, the state as a whole did vote to secede, but the eastern counties voted, two to one, to remain in the Union. The geographical, historical, and cultural divide between the western two thirds of the state and the eastern counties is the subtext of the present story.

p. 18: **Temple:** Oliver P. Temple was an important figure in the political, commercial, and legal life of Knoxville from 1848 until his death in 1907, at age eighty-seven. In the early days of the Civil War, his office on Gay Street was a meeting place for Union sympathizers, including the radical editor William Gannaway "the Parson" Brownlow. Early in 1861, Temple helped to canvass the eastern counties in support of the Union cause, and he played an important role in the reconvened Union Convention in Greeneville in June of that year. Harrison Self might very well have heard him speak on that occasion. For my purposes, Temple is most important—indeed, invaluable—for his comprehensive history of the period, *East Tennessee and the Civil War* (1899). The book reflects his partisanship, and may at times seem defensive or self-justifying, but it has undoubted authority as a firsthand account by a man who had a prominent role in the history he is describing and was personally acquainted with nearly all of the other major players. While Temple vindicates the bridge burners as brave and committed men, he makes absolutely clear that he believes the raids were ill-judged and counterproductive, leading to a reign of terror in the eastern counties.

p. 18: **General Felix Zollicoffer:** Zollicoffer's early tolerance for the Unionists in the Eastern District would have been well received by people like Harry, but it was doomed. As Harry had foreseen, it was the bridge burnings that ended the "live and let live" policy. Zollicoffer felt deeply betrayed by the sabotage and by the subsequent uprisings near Elizabethton and Sevierville. He supported the harsh crackdown by the Confederacy.

p. 19: **banks of the Watauga River:** The Wataugans were the first white homesteaders along the Watauga and Holston Rivers, who, in 1772, formed an association for the regulation of local affairs, in communities whose existence violated the Royal Proclamation of 1763 reserving this land solely to the native inhabitants. From these few undisputed facts spread two main branches of opinion about who the Wataugans were.

According to Oliver P. Temple, they were "strong, earnest, educated, law-loving men, mostly of the Covenanter race, who had not braved the dangers and the hardships of the wilderness in a spirit of reckless adventure, but had come to build up for themselves and their posterity a free state and a Christian civilization" (p. 7). He quotes selectively from Theodore Roosevelt, who had praised the Wataugans in *The Winning of the West*. Much more than Temple, Roosevelt acknowledges the moral as well as physical challenges of the westward expansion, by which the white farmers, whose God frowned on "idle" land, displaced the red hunters, whose ownership of that land was a function of tribal memory, communal burial grounds, and shifting boundaries with rival tribes. Roosevelt believed that the Wataugans "outlined in advance the nation's work. They tamed the rugged and shaggy mountains, they bid defiance to outside foes, and they successfully solved the difficult problem of self-government" (Roosevelt, quoted in Dixon, p. iii).

Of course, if you tune out Teddy and listen to the revisionists, you hear a different story. For some later historians, Roosevelt's message is littered with code words: "winning" means imposing your cultural imperatives; "taming" means deforesting old hunting grounds; "foes" are people whose rights you ignore; "self-government" is the allocation of dubiously acquired farmland. I was going to say that the truth lies somewhere between Roosevelt's red-blooded chauvinism and the revisionists' multicultural sensitivity. But I am not sure there is anything close to a "truth" here. What does seem undeniable, however, is that the descendants of the Wataugans thought they had a special relationship to the Declaration of Independence.

As they saw it, there could never be a need, or an excuse, for another Revolution, such as the Confederacy now desired. In one of the strange recalibrations of history, the stubborn rebelliousness of the Revolutionary-era Wataugans had morphed into the stubborn loyalty of the Civil War–era East Tennesseans. What the two groups had in common, obviously, was a fierce attachment to their point of view, a tough instinct for survival, and a possessive love for the "lofty grandeur and venerable majesty" of Appalachia.

p. 19: **debtors flayed alive:** I have invented this treatment of debtors, but there is evidence that crimes were summarily and harshly punished in this fragile outpost of civilization. Dixon, pp. 23–24.

p. 21: **"I think it is a bad thing":** These are Self's actual words, according to Lowe's later testimony. I will repeat them (and italicize them) further on in the conversation, because they are the strongest evidence that Harry did not approve of the bridge burnings, and would not have gone to the bridge that night for any reason except to save his son from what he regarded as dangerous and useless folly. For my own purposes, I have also imagined Harry's strong aversion to anything like criminal behavior, especially involving the destruction of property and civic order, and the likelihood that he would have been very upset over unfair damage to his standing as a good citizen.

p. 22: **"Federals are in Kentucky":** The conspirators believed they were preparing the way for the Federal Army to invade East Tennessee and liberate the beleaguered Unionists in this mountainous territory. Their isolated plight was well known to Lincoln, who several times urged his generals to relieve their suffering, and capture this vital ground in the contested area between North and South. **William Blount Carter (see note to p. 7)** and Greene County ex-tailor and politician Andrew Johnson had written to Lincoln on August 6, 1861, telling him that "our brave men are daily organizing, and are only waiting for you to place arms in their hands with which they may strike in defence [sic] of themselves & their Country" (Current, p. 34).

The bridge-burning raid was planned at Camp Dick Robinson in Kentucky, on September 30 (Current, p. 34), where W. B. Carter met with his brother, Samual P. Carter, as well as Andrew Johnson, Congressman Horace Maynard, and US Army generals George

H. Thomas and William Tecumseh Sherman (Judd(1), pp. 31ff.). Carter then met in person with President Lincoln, General George B. McClellan, and Secretary of State William F. Seward. At that meeting the sabotage of the bridges was approved by Lincoln, and Carter was given $2,500 to finance the raid.

On his return to Camp Dick Robinson, Carter received assurances from General Thomas that his troops would move south to be ready for the supporting invasion after the attack on the bridges. General Sherman had been reluctantly persuaded to agree to this plan. Subsequently, two officers—Captain David Fry and Captain William Cross—were assigned to the mission. They would organize and carry out some of the attacks, along with local leaders to be chosen later. On October 18, the band of conspirators entered Tennessee and began the work of recruiting and planning the assault on nine key railroad bridges in Tennessee and Alabama.

Tragically, support from the North never came. After a brief skirmish with General Zollicoffer, Thomas got ready for his push toward Knoxville. However, Sherman had changed his mind, or, rather, he had reverted to his earlier opinion. Thomas got as far as London, Kentucky, when Sherman ordered him to stop and return, fearing that the mountain passage was too difficult and convinced that military targets in the middle and western parts of the state were more important. News of the canceled invasion did not reach Tennessee in time to matter. The bridges had already been burned. There were many urgent appeals, from W. B. Carter and from Lincoln himself, for General Thomas and General Sherman's replacement, General Don Carlos Buell, to invade and rescue East Tennessee. However, by then, the focus of the war had shifted elsewhere.

CHAPTER 2: LICK CREEK BRIDGE

p. 26: **Isaac Hacker:** A corporal in the cavalry company under Captain M. Live, C. S. Army, Isaac N. Hacker was the first witness for the prosecution in the trial of Harrison Self. Having suffered at the hands of Captain Fry, who captured and intimidated him, Hacker cannot be considered an impartial observer. *OR,* Series 2, vol. 1, Part 1, p. 862.

p. 27: **prisoners were already inside:** Trial testimony states that the guards at the bridge were surprised by the saboteurs, and then kept inside the tent throughout the raid, perhaps to prevent them from recognizing any of the conspirators. However, stories about the various attacks reveal occasional lapses in foresight, and Captain

Fry was known to be flamboyant, bold, and aggressive, rather than cautious or circumspect. Isaac Hacker also testified that "in less than five minutes the bridge was in flames." Either this observation is hearsay, or it is speculation, or he witnessed the conflagration, in which case it is likely that he and possibly the other six guards were outside of the tent for at least some portion of the time. In any case, I have taken the liberty of placing them outside the tent for a brief period. Hacker quoted Fry as bullying and taunting the guards in a childish and mean-spirited way. As mentioned earlier, Hacker is hardly an impartial witness. Whether or not his report is accurate, I felt justified in omitting this behavior from my own portrait of David Fry, as there is evidence from other sources that he was a colorful but decent man. Bible(2), pp. 121–123.

p. 28: **"Where is Henry Harmon's gun?":** This exchange is quoted from Isaac Hacker's testimony at Harry's trial, and would have been damning evidence against both Henry and his father, Jacob, both of whom were captured and imprisoned by the Confederates. Another son, Thomas, who says a few invented words in the present chapter, was also captured, and gave testimony at Self's trial.

p. 29: **gave their parole:** Hacker testified as follows: "After the bridge was burned the band or a large part of them came to the tent, gave us of the guard our choice either to take an oath not to take up arms against the Government or to die right then and there, to be killed immediately. We took the oath" (*OR,* Series 2, vol. 1, Part 1, p. 862). Dorothy Kelly's account of the bridge burnings notes that, at the Holston River bridge at Union Depot (now Bluff City), the conspirators "decided to take a chance on the word of the guards and, after securing a promise not to reveal the names of the bridge burners, they released the guards unharmed. . . . As had been feared, however, the guards immediately reported the burning . . . and the identities of all the men they had recognized" (Kelly, pp. 127–128). I am making the small leap to assume that a similar oath was demanded of the Lick Creek guards, and that it was similarly betrayed.

p. 31: **"headed into the mountains":** After the bridge burnings, when the Confederacy declared martial law, hundreds of men went into hiding or fled to Kentucky. They were by no means the first "stampeders." From *East Tennessee and the Civil War,* by Oliver Temple: "On the first Thursday of August, 1861, the real flight of Union men from East Tennessee commenced. . . . [T]here came to be a constant stream of refugees silently working their way by night, through the wide expanse of mountains separating East Tennessee from the thickly settled parts of Kentucky. Many of these left without any settled purpose as to what they were to do when they reached their destination. They fled from what they regarded as a present and terrible danger. Anything that could befall them was better than their condition at home. In Kentucky there would be at least freedom of opinion. . . . Before autumn had passed away the First Tennessee Infantry, with Robert K. Byrd as Colonel, was organized and equipped. And then followed in rapid succession, the Second, Third, Fourth, Fifth and Sixth Regiments, and still others from time to time till the close of the war.

"The condition of the Union men remaining in East Tennessee was day by day becoming more disagreeable. Arrests and imprisonments had commenced. . . .

"It was now becoming evident that a reign of terror if not one of persecution had been inaugurated, and there was no safety for loyal men living in the country, except in flight" (pp. 368–69).

p. 32: **martial law was declared:** News of the bridge burnings caused a panic among the Confederates in charge of the Eastern District of Tennessee, headquartered in Knoxville. General W. B. Wood immediately declared martial law, thereby authorizing roving parties of soldiers and militia to interrogate citizens and arrest suspected bridge burners. Most of them were brought before Colonel Danville Leadbetter, who was stationed in Greeneville at the time (later, he would relocate to Knoxville). He had been sent by the Confederate government in Richmond, via the infamous "Special Orders #216," to repair the bridges and restore order. Those suspected of armed resistance to the Confederacy were to be sent to the prison in Tuscaloosa, Alabama. Those identified as saboteurs were to be tried by drumhead court and executed immediately. If possible, their bodies should be left to swing near the bridges they had burned.

Both Parson Brownlow and Oliver P. Temple would later acknowledge that the bridge burnings were counterproductive. The preeminence of the Carter brothers was resented by some who blamed them for the backlash against Unionists. Even Andrew Johnson later undermined their reputation. Not knowing that Lincoln had given W. B. Carter $2,500 for the raid, Johnson wrote to the President: "This W B Carter procured some $20,000 from the War Dept. to aid in burning bridges in East Tenn. Many of the men employed lost their lives and sacrificed large amts. of property. Their families have rec'd not one cent from this fund. This matter should be looked into. I wish we were clear of the whole 'Carter Concern' " (Current, p. 45). Descendants of the bridge burners justifiably honor their memory, but it is difficult to see this episode in terms of heroes and villains. It is a story of mixed motives, rash judgments, good intentions, and human fallibility.

p. 33: **Colonel Danville Leadbetter:** This Maine-born Confederate officer is important to the story this book tells, and will be central to Chapter 5. He also appears in Chapter 8. There is a fuller account of him in the note to p. 75.

p. 33: **named their coconspirators:** Leadbetter had executed Fry and Hinshaw on November 30, but he had spared Harry's son Hugh, considering him too young, too simpleminded, and too impressionable to be treated as a responsible adult. I have altered that assessment slightly for dramatic purposes, letting Hugh stand for the boys on either side who were infatuated with the *idea* of glory, while having no understanding of the realities of life and death in East Tennessee.

Note that Leadbetter assumes that Hugh was drawn into the plot by his father, but that would have been the generic assumption. All the other evidence (which Leadbetter would not have had or would have discounted) suggests just the opposite: that Harry was *not* in favor of the raid, and wanted to prevent Hugh from participating in it. Did Hugh betray his father to the Confederates? Given what Leadbetter says, there is a high likelihood that he did, though perhaps unwittingly. Here is the rest of the first paragraph of Leadbetter's December 8 letter:

> All confessed their own and testified to the others' guilt, and also gave as correctly as they could remember the names of the whole party engaged in that crime. Fry and Hensie [Hinshaw] were tried by drumhead court-martial on the 30th ultimo and executed the same day by hanging. I have thought it my duty to ask of the Department that the punishment of Hugh A. Self be commuted to imprisonment. He is only sixteen years old not very intelligent and was led away on that occasion by his father and elder brother both of whom I learn have now been captured by General Carroll's troops. [*OR*, Series 2, vol. 1, Part 1, p. 852.]

p. 33: **marched up Depot Street:** At one time, based on an engraving that appears in Brownlow's *Sketches* (between pp. 300 and 301), it was believed that the corpses of the two men hung so close to the railroad tracks that passengers on the rear platform could poke the bodies with their canes. That account was indignantly denied in 1932 by George F. Robertson, in *A Small Boy's Recollections of the Civil War* (Clover, SC: George F. Robertson, 1932). According to his putative eyewitness account, the tree was located "not less than three hundred or four hundred yards from the railroad" (p. 37). I have followed his version, despite his obvious Rebel sympathies. I've also drawn from his description of the scene leading up to the hangings: "Two men were taken in the act [not exactly: they were not captured at the scene of the burning]. At their trial they were defiant and said they had burned bridges and would do so again if ever they could get away. The sentence of death was passed upon them and at the appointed time, the two hapless victims of their own folly were led out with hands bound behind them. Placed in a hollow square of soldiers they marched up Depot Street. There was a considerable company of people along the sidewalks . . ." (pp. 35–36).

p. 34: **In the first days of December:** As far as I could determine, it is not known exactly where or how Self was captured, although it happened shortly after Colonel Wood was replaced by General William H. Carroll as commander of the Eastern District (Judd(1), p. 98). Therefore, the scenes at Self's house are pure invention. However, they are within the parameters of possibility. In the first part of a letter dated December 8, Colonel Danville Leadbetter—who was still in Greeneville at the time—refers to the capture of several of the Lick Creek bridge burners, including Self's younger son, Hugh.

> Greeneville, Tenn., December 8, 1861.
>
> General S. Cooper, Adjutant and Inspector General.
>
> SIR: At the date of my last letter a part of the force under my command was engaged in the pursuit of a party of insurgents moving from their camp in the northern part of Greene toward Cocke County. As usual their force was dispersed and only some stragglers could be picked up. Among these prisoners were three who had been of the party that burned the Lick Creek bridge. They were Henry Fry [not to be confused with David Fry, the leader of the raid], Jacob M. Hensie [Hinshaw] and Hugh A. Self. [*OR*, Series 2, vol. 1, Part 1, p. 852.]

CHAPTER 3: ON THE FARM

p. 37: **Diary of Elizabeth A. Self:** More than any other chapter, this one departs from the documentary evidence. Frankly, it is doubtful that Harrison Self's daughter kept a diary, although it is not impossible. Diary keeping was a common practice at the time, and many of the authors were young women. We have today in book form several diaries by Confederate women of East Tennessee, including those by Ellen House of Knoxville and Myra Inman of Cleveland (a small rural town in East Tennessee). Neither woman is a model for Lizzie, but both diaries provide some useful details of daily life in the period, and Ellen's has some of the introspective commentary and lively display of personality that I have given, in a different way, to the invented diary. I've also drawn some details from advertisements in *The Farmers' Almanac for 1861* (New York: Griffing, Brother & Co.).

The crucial question is Lizzie's level of education. W. G. Brownlow, whose interaction with Elizabeth Self is based on his own account, mentions her twice in his famous book, *Sketches of the Rise, Progress, and Decline of Secession, With a Narrative of Personal Adventures Among the Rebels* (1862). The first reference is in the section reproducing the diary of his imprisonment in the Knoxville jail, where he records her visit to the jail to see her father. Here he refers to her as "a noble girl, modest, and neatly attired" (p. 326).

Toward the end of the volume, in the transcript of a lengthy speech delivered in the Cincinnati Opera House after his exile from Tennessee (dramatized in Chapter 9), Brownlow revisits the event. His memory may have faded, but it is worth noting that he now describes her as "an intelligent and well-educated lady" (p. 418). It is highly likely that he was embellishing for effect; perhaps unconsciously, he transformed a farm girl into a "lady" to appeal to the romantic sympathies of his audience. At the very least, I think it is fair to assume, given the absence of contradictory evidence, that Self's daughter could read and write fluently, although she may have been ignorant of the subjects studied by girls in more affluent or urban families and may not have written "compositions" for school, as did Ellen House.

There is also the question of orthography in the invented diary. Neither House nor Inman uses contractions, although I found "didn't" and "I've" in the contemporary diary of John Guilford Earnest, a Confederate soldier from East Tennessee. Conventions for representing speech varied in the contemporary novels I examined, including *Alonzo and Melissa* and *Ellen Bracken*. Therefore, I allowed Lizzie some idiosyncrasy in these matters.

p. 38: **ALONZO AND MELISSA:** Sarah Ogilvie, her lawyer father, and her slave Ella are all invented characters. However, the book she lends Lizzie is a real novel popular at the time: *Alonzo and Melissa,* by Daniel Jackson, Jr. (Middlesex, England: The Echo Library, 2009; based on the 1851 Boston edition). I do not know which, if any, books the historical Elizabeth might have read or heard about; however, it is at least possible that she read this one, or ones similar to it.

p. 41: **hickory stick:** After Manassas, the Confederacy was strengthened in its view that a Southerner, intrinsically and by virtue of his way of life, was superior in character to a Northerner, who lacked the same heritage and code of honor. Pete's boast is typical of some of the rhetoric that was common on the Confederate side.

p. 41: **Tusculum:** Tusculum College, so named in 1844, dates back to a series of educational institutions in Greeneville, Tennessee. During the days leading up to the Civil War, the campus was the scene of lively debates, drawing large crowds of local citizens, including Andrew Johnson. Many of the students were attracted by romantic notions of the Southern cause, becoming the "antiestablishment" demonstrators of their day. Pete, an invented character, is molded in that image.

p. 42: **Knoxville WHIG:** This was the last Northern-sympathizing newspaper in the South. Founded in 1839 by its editor, William Gannaway Brownlow, it was famous for the anti-Secessionist rhetoric of his editorials, and the often vitriolic, *ad hominem* attacks on anyone he perceived as disagreeing with him or challenging him in any way. His colorful writing was widely influential, and a constant irritant to the Confederate authorities. Not surprisingly, they accused Brownlow of having instigated the bridge-burning conspiracy. It is quite certain that he had nothing to do with the actual events, and, indeed, thought them ill-judged; however, it seems equally certain that his rhetoric did much to heat the atmosphere in which the plan was devised and carried out. The printing press was finally closed down in 1861, and Brownlow himself was exiled from Tennessee soon after (further information about his life is provided in the notes to later chapters). Upon his return in 1863, he resumed the editorship until he was elected governor of the state in 1865, at which time his son took over the job.

p. 43: **Constitution of Tennessee:** Pete, a law student, is referring to, and then quoting from, the 1834 constitution of the state of Tennessee (McKenzie, 48). The text as represented in the "diary" is subject to Lizzie's orthographic vagaries. She is recalling from memory what Pete said aloud earlier in the day.

p. 43: **John Baxter:** John Baxter (1819–86) is the Knoxville lawyer who defended several of the bridge burners. He enters in Chapter 6 and is central to Chapter 7, where more information about him will be provided.

p. 46: **Pottertown:** Pottertown is the name given to this area near Greeneville, today in the neighborhood of Pottertown Road, which briefly parallels one section of Lick Creek. A short lane leads from this road to the Harmon family cemetery, where, among others, Jacob Harmon, his wife Malinda, and two sons Thomas and Henry are buried. Gravel Woods Road branches off from Pottertown Road and heads south across the railroad tracks before ending in McDonald Road. According to Donahue Bible, the Harmons owned the land between Lick Creek and the railroad tracks, while Haun owned the land south of the tracks. Bible believes that the rich clay deposits on Harmon land supplied various potters in the area, including C. A. Haun. Bible(2), p. 131.

p. 49: **This issue of the *Whig*:** In *Sketches*, pp. 250–51, William Gannaway Brownlow reprints his own editorial from the Knoxville *Whig*, dated Oct. 24, 1861—less than a month before the bridge burnings. The words Hugh reads are quoted from this source.

p. 50: **take some bread and cheese to the men:** I have added Lizzie to the scenes involving Lowe in this chapter. There is no evidence that she interacted with him, although they undoubtedly knew each other. In other respects, these scenes are closely based on Lowe's later testimony at Self's trial.

p. 51: **Fremont [Frémont] Proclamation:** Without permission from Lincoln, General John C. Frémont, in command of the Department of the West and headquartered in St. Louis, issued a proclamation declaring martial law in Missouri and ruling that any property belonging to Rebel combatants would be confiscated, and that any slaves belonging to these persons would immediately be freed. These orders went further than the Confiscation Act passed by Congress, which affected only the slaves that were actively serving the Rebel troops in the field, and said nothing about freeing them. Doris Kearns Goodwin, *Team of Rivals: The Political Genius of Abraham Lincoln* (New York: Simon & Shuster, 2006), pp. 389–90. Lincoln believed this unilateral proclamation not only usurped his own authority but also undermined his efforts to keep the Border States in the Union. Lowe's testimony that the proclamation hardened his support for the Confederacy shows that Lincoln was right in fearing a backlash against Frémont's action in states like Kentucky and Tennessee.

CHAPTER 4: IN THE WILDERNESS

p. 55: **neither gilded nor carved:** The facts of Brownlow's early life are taken from the biographical section of his *Sketches*, pp. 15ff. I've relied heavily on Brownlow's own writings for the words and events attributed to him, but kept in mind his habit of exaggeration and self-promotion.

p. 56: **shock of dark hair:** Brownlow's swarthy skin, soulful eyes, and thick dark hair were well known from his frequent public appearances. I have based my descriptions of him on photographs from the period.

p. 56: **small replica of the United States flag:** See later note on Susan's association with the flag.

p. 58: **"Parson" Colonel Wood:** Brownlow is being sarcastic here, but Wood did style himself a Methodist preacher and did give sermons on occasion in Knoxville.

p. 58: **"friends who help us on our way":** This scene, and this speech, are invented.

p. 58: **gorges and ravines of the Smokies:** Brownlow's own account of this retreat to the mountains can be found in *Sketches*.

p. 62: **A figure as tall as Brownlow:** The person introduced here is Andy Slocum. He is an invented character, a composite of the rugged men who owned small freeholds in the mountains or lived by hunting and fishing in the wilderness. Somewhat anachronistically, he is a literary relative of James Fenimore Cooper's Leatherstocking, but he also shares characteristics with the real-life Daniel Ellis, who, during the period of this story, piloted escapees through the difficult mountain passages into Kentucky. Like Ellis, Andy has been a guide for many "stampeders" (men evading conscription into the Confederate Army and hoping to enlist in the Federal Army) and many bridge burners trying to escape capture. The characterization of Slocum was also influenced by the autobiography of another mountain man from the period, Captain Sam Massey.

p. 64: **"thinkin' of stampedin' ":** "Stampeders" were Union men who fled through the mountains, by foot and at night, guided by pilots like Daniel Ellis, to escape conscription into the Confederate Army, and in most cases to join the Federal Army in the hope of returning to regain control of their homeland in Eastern Tennessee. See Daniel Ellis's own account of his life in *Thrilling Adventures*.

p. 65: **fingers that met his were coal black:** Although Isaiah is an invented character, he is based on true accounts from that time and place. Massey frequently mentions relying on the slaves of local

Confederates to give him supplies and to pass along overheard conversations and witnessed troop movements, thus helping him to survive in the mountains and evade capture.

p. 66: **go their separate ways:** Brownlow describes the dispersal of the men by twos, and names the Rev. W. T. Dowell as his companion. The return stopover in Wear's Cove is invented, but Brownlow does report going to a place six miles from Knoxville, and receiving the help of his friend, John Williams. In *Sketches,* he provides the text of the various letters reproduced or alluded to here. All of the quotations from the letters are part of the historical record. His state of mind at this period and his opinion of the men responsible for his arrest are clearly indicated in *Sketches.*

p. 70: **arrested at the door of his home:** Most likely, Brownlow was taken from his home to the jail, but these departure scenes, like the scenes with his wife and daughter, are entirely invented.

CHAPTER 5: OUR OWN LIL' ZOUAVE

p. 75: **Headquarters of Colonel Danville Leadbetter:** Danville Leadbetter, who had been directing the Bureau of Engineers in Richmond (see below), was sent to East Tennessee on November 10, the Sunday after the bridge burnings, which occurred on the night of Friday, November 8 [his orders were dated November 11]. He presided over the drumhead conviction and subsequent hanging of Henry Fry (*not* the leader of the group, Captain David Fry) and Jacob Madison Hinshaw in Greeneville on November 30. He later moved to Knoxville, where he probably was at the time of the hanging of Haun on December 11, and certainly was for the hanging of the Harmons on December 17, the trial of Harrison Self on December 17; 20–21, and much of the time Brownlow remained in prison.

Leadbetter was born in Maine, August 26, 1811, graduated from West Point in 1836, and became an Army engineer. In 1853, he was stationed in Mobile, Alabama. When that state seceded from the Union, he resigned his US Army commission and became a lieutenant colonel in the Army of the Confederacy. In 1861, he was called to Richmond, Virginia, where he served in the Engineers Bureau. Almost certainly, his wife, Delphine,* remained in Mobile. However, it is believed that many Confederate officers brought their own slaves (sometimes boys) to serve them while away from home, and that is the basis for the invented character, Joshua. [See http://histclo.com/essay/ war/csw/sold/black/cwb—conf. html]. *Delphine E. Kennedy Hall Leadbetter [Name identified in http://boards.ancestry.com /surnames.leadbetter/97/mb.ashx (accessed 11/30/2011). See Reply #6 to "Brigadier General Danville Leadbetter (1811–1866) m. 1) Elizabeth Waterman 2) Delphine E. Kennedy," posted by Jacqueline Sleeper Russell on 11/17/2009].

p. 75: ***Later, he would tell about it, but first he had to live it***: This chapter, purportedly from the point of view of the young slave, Joshua, is a what-if scenario. Joshua is an invented character, as are the other slaves mentioned in the story. However, all of the other characters in this chapter are historical. Even though I found no evidence that Leadbetter and John Crozier Ramsey actually met face to face as depicted here, such a meeting would have been feasible, and perhaps even likely.

p. 75: **caught him and sent him back**: "The Fugitive Slave" law, requiring nonslaveholding states to capture and return escaped slaves found within their borders, was enacted as part of the Compromise of 1850. The Confiscation Act of 1861 (signed into law August 6, three days after Leadbetter arrived in Richmond to become acting head of the Confederate Civil Engineers Corps), declared that Federal authorities could confiscate, as "contraband," any slaves who were directly or indirectly serving the cause of rebellion. Joshua could have been confiscated, if he or his master had fallen into Federal hands.

p. 77: **"Our own lil' Zouave"**: During the Civil War, a number of regiments—mostly Union, but some Confederate—adopted the exotic costume of the Zouaves, French soldiers in Northern Africa in the 1830s. These uniforms often included baggy pants (sometimes striped) and short, embroidered, cutaway jackets, as well as red caps, sometimes shaped like a fez and sometimes resembling a stocking cap with a tassel.

p. 78: **Nobody changed hands then**: "Hiring Day" was January 1. On that occasion, owners who wished to hire out their slaves brought them to a designated place where these deals were made. After the hiring was concluded, the selling commenced. The days between Christmas (which the slaves were generally allowed to celebrate) and New Years were marred by the dread of Hiring Day, when family members might be separated for a year—or possibly for life. See Harriet Jacobs [pseudonym, Linda Brent], *Incidents in the Life of a Slave Girl*. Ed. Lydia Maria Child. Boston: 1861. Reprinted in *The Classic Slave Narratives*. Ed. Henry Louis Gates, Jr. New York: Signet, 1987 [2002], p. 456.

p. 78: **then out into the wide ocean**: Sometime between August and early November of 1861, Leadbetter was sent to Yorktown to oversee the strengthening of defenses at the entrance to Chesapeake Bay. Two photographs contributed details and inspiration for this scene:

Author Notes

1) "Yorktown, Virginia (vicinity). Group of contrabands at Allen's farm house near Williamsburg Road," http://americancivilwar.com/statepic/va/va009.html (accessed 4/2/2012), and 2) "Yorktown, Virginia," http://www.old-picture.com/civil-war/Embarkation-Yorktown-Virginia-Landing.htm (accessed 4/2/2012).

p. 80: **"We're going to war"**: The following document established Leadbetter's role in the Confederate response to the bridge burnings. It is frequently referred to as the infamous "Special Orders #216."

Richmond, Va., November 11, 1861.

1. Col. Danville Leadbetter, Provisional Army, is hereby assigned to the command of the troops to be stationed for the protection of the railroads between Bristol and Chattanooga, Tenn. He will reconstruct bridges, repair and keep open the line of communication between those points and will call upon railroad companies for such aid as he may require to carry out this order.

By command of the Secretary of War

OR, Series 2, vol. 1, Part 1, p. 841.

p. 80: **"bodies hanging in the vicinity of the burned bridges"**: Reply from Judah P. Benjamin, the Confederate States of America Secretary of War, to Colonel W. B. Wood, the military commander at Knoxville. Colonel Wood had captured six bridge burners and had asked what to do with them. The letter is dated from Richmond, on November 25, 1861. *OR*, Series 2, vol. 1, Part 1, p. 848.

p. 81: *Two insurgents have to-day been tried*: I've imagined Joshua finding a discarded early draft of this message, but except for the crossed-out word, this is the communication sent from Leadbetter to Benjamin, dated from Greeneville, on November 30. *OR*, Series 2, vol. 1, Part 1, p. 851.

p. 82: **TO THE CITIZENS OF EAST TENNESSEE:** The full text of the Proclamation appears in *OR*, Series 2, vol. 1, Part 1, pp. 851–52.

p. 84: **There were limits to what a slave should know:** A number of slave narratives, including the autobiography of Frederick Douglass, point out that it was illegal to teach a slave to read or write.

p. 86: **Mr. Ramsey had long black eyebrows:** Brownlow's *Sketches* are full of invective against John Crozier Ramsey, referring to him as "but a few degrees removed from an idiot" (p. 290), "[t]his corrupt man Ramsey" (p. 298), "influenced by his deepseated malice" toward

247

Brownlow (p. 301), and a thief who was later "detected in drawing rations and clothing" for more men than were under his command, for which he was "drummed out of the service" (p. 302). Personal animus is clearly at work here.

p. 87: **"that *carpenter*"**: Brownlow made a point of his humble origins as a house carpenter. He was later a circuit preacher, which gave him a wide knowledge of the East Tennessee population, and good practice as a speechmaker. It was a short step from hellfire preacher to hellfire editor. He owned and wrote continually for one of the most flamboyant (and last surviving) pro-Union newspapers in the South. As sides were being drawn over the issue of Secession, Brownlow equated the Rebels with the decadent aristocratic slaveholding class and the Unionists with the honorable working class who did not disdain to do their own labor. He deliberately stirred up class warfare in order to make rhetorical points for his political agenda. Ramsey, son of one of Knoxville's oldest and most prominent families, would have thought himself socially superior to Brownlow. The animosity had a very personal edge. Ramsey hated Brownlow for successfully suing his father—the elder Ramsey— when the old man's bank failed and he showed favoritism in paying off his creditors. In turn, Brownlow hated the Confederate district attorney for being, in his view, an unscrupulous and drunken idiot who was out to get him.

p. 87: **"I am very glad to hear of action of the military authorities"**: Communication from J. P. Benjamin to J[ohn]. C[rozier]. Ramsey, dated November 25, 1861, in reply to a peremptory demand by Mr. Ramsey for instruction and (implicitly) support. Ramsey had sworn out warrants for the arrest of Unionists, had brought charges against them, and was trying to get these cases tried. He was thwarted by the leniency of judges like West H. Humphreys, and by the declaration of martial law, which preempted the civil courts. *OR,* Series 2, vol. 1, Part 1, p. 849. There was a recurring debate over jurisdiction between the civil and military courts.

p. 88: **"others not half so guilty"**: In citing this view that Brownlow was much more guilty for the bridge burnings than the men who were hanged, Ramsey is quoting from an article published in the Knoxville *Register* (a Southern-sympathizing newspaper in Knoxville) on December 13, 1861, and now retrievable as an enclosure with a letter J. J. Craig sent to Secretary Benjamin, dated January 3, 186[2?], *OR,* Series 2, vol. 1, Part 1, pp. 924–25.

p. 88: **"It's up to you to bring charges"**: Although I have portrayed Leadbetter as a hard but not vicious man, the Unionists viewed him as a monster. Brownlow is no kinder in his assessment. In his diary entry for Monday, December 9, 1861, he mentions learning about the hanging of Matthew Hinshawe and Henry Fry, along with the story of their bodies being mistreated. He apparently believes all that he is told, and says, "The bloody scoundrel who tied the knot was one Colonel Leadbetter." A few sentences later, he envisions the Federal Army arriving in East Tennessee and capturing "this murderer, *Leadbetter* [sic]," and expresses the wish "that he shall hang on the same limb, and that Fry's widow shall tie the knot around his infernal neck" (Brownlow, p. 311). This is partly the political rhetoric of the day, but it is difficult not to hear some personal outrage behind these words.

p. 91: **"Mistah Abraham. He d'one we prayin' fuh"**: In Knoxville, slaves would sometimes meet secretly to pray for Lincoln and the Union Army. McKenzie, p. 184.

Chapter 6: Castle Fox

p. 93: **Castle Fox:** While the Confederacy was in control of Knoxville, a man named Robert Fox was in charge of the county jail where Unionists were incarcerated. Thus, the facility was nicknamed "Castle Fox." McKenzie, p. 197.

p. 93: **(December 6):** I was not able to determine the exact day on which Harrison Self was arrested, nor the date on which he entered the Knoxville City Jail. He probably was not among those picked up right after the raid, as he is not mentioned in a later account by Jonathan Morgan describing the first arrests on November 9 (see Morgan's letter transcribed by Donahue Bible, January 1997, and used by him with permission from Mr. Cecil Stines, a great-grandson of Jonathan Morgan). On December 8, Colonel Leadbetter, writing to the Confederate secretary of war, mentions the much earlier capture of Fry, Hinshawe, and Hugh. A. Self, and adds that Harrison Self and his son Andrew [elided in my narrative, as explained in the notes to Chapter 1] "have now been captured by General Carroll's troops." Assuming that "now" indicates a fairly recent event, and wishing, for dramatic purposes, to place Self in the jail when Brownlow arrives there on December 6, I am hypothesizing that Self was imprisoned on or about December 5.

p. 93: **in the prison:** My description of conditions in "Castle Fox" is largely based on Brownlow's account of his own incarceration there. Some details are, of course, invented, and others come from other sources, but the following are drawn from Brownlow's overview introducing the diary (Brownlow, pp. 305–306): the number of men present, the sleeping conditions, the absence of furniture, the inside water bucket and outdoor hogshead (along with the taunt from the guards), the poor quality of the food, the identification of the jailor as a local innkeeper, and Brownlow's privilege of receiving his own meals from home. Later details from the diary include the earlier arrival of news about the hanging of Hinshawe and Fry, Haun's refusal to implicate supporters of the bridge burnings, the arrival of the carts carrying coffins on the day of the Harmons' hanging, and other details identified in separate endnotes. I have used other sources that will be identified in later notes, but this chapter owes its greatest debt to Brownlow's diary.

p. 93: **oversized birdcage:** I am basing this description of the cage on an engraving in Brownlow's *Sketches*, representing a later event in the prison. I found no mention of Haun being placed in the cage, but assume he was, as it was reserved for men sentenced to death. Brownlow places the Harmons and later Harrison Self in the cage.

p. 94: **glimmered above the high cheekbones:** This description is based on a photograph of C. A. Haun in Bible(1).

p. 95: **Wasn't he about forty?** Haun was born September 5, 1821 (Bible(1)). We therefore have his exact age on the day of his death, but Harry would probably not have known this detail so precisely. Note: Brownlow says that Haun was "a man about twenty-seven years of age" (p. 312). I cannot reconcile this discrepancy, but believe that Bible is always the more reliable authority.

p. 95: **"Keep 'em in line":** In a letter to his wife four days earlier, on December 10, the day before he was executed, Haun speaks of his neighbors finishing his works in progress and tells his wife to sell his potters' tools. He includes instructions for raising his children as good Christians. Bible(1).

p. 100: **two visitors:** A few years before the publication of his definitive account of the bridge burnings in 2005, Donahue Bible discovered some surprising and shocking documents in the Office of the Greene County Registrar. During the time of the bridge-burner trials, John Baxter's law firm obtained deeds of trust for land owned by certain prisoners. C. A. Haun and the Harmons (Jacob and his sons Henry and Thomas) signed over some portion of their land to pay for their legal defense. Bible suggests that they may have hoped Baxter would appeal their cases before the Confederate government in Richmond. However, there is no proof that the lawyers ever made such a plea. Bible(2), pp. 135–136.

Eventually, Baxter did foreclose on Jacob Harmon's property, selling it for $4,193.50 on July 27, 1868. News of this action reached then-Senator Brownlow, who brought the matter before Congress. With uncharacteristic brevity and restraint, Brownlow summarized the story of the bridge burnings, asserting that the perpetrators had been sworn members of the Federal Army and had "lost their lives in the service of the government." While not naming the lawyers involved, Brownlow referred to "this debt of oppression," and urged Congress to vote "[f]or the relief of Malinda Harmon." On June 21, 1870, the Senate confirmed H. R. 2252 (passed by the House three days earlier), ordering compensation for Malinda Harmon in the amount of $4,696.70.

I do not know if Baxter himself visited the prison to obtain the signatures on the infamous deeds of trust. Bible states only that "[t]he deeds were signed in the jail at Knoxville in the presence of Knox County Court Clerk William Craig on the tenth of December 1861" (Bible(2), pp. 135–36). He goes on to say that the same law firm "had also secured such a deed of trust from Christopher A Haun on the ninth of December 1861, only two days before he was hanged."

Haun's willingness to sign away property that should have gone to his family puts a different light on his instructions to his wife in that final letter. He told her to sell his tools, and to get neighboring potters to complete his unfinished wares to augment her income. This sounds like coolheaded practicality, but maybe it was something else. Surely Alex must have felt guilty about that deed of trust, about robbing his family to pay his attorneys. The fact that he and the Harmons took such a step proves how desperate they were—or maybe how persuasive their lawyers were—as the day of execution approached.

p. 102: **"from the teeth out"**: This was a common phrase at the time. It meant that your words did not come from the heart. It usually referred to the loyalty oath required by whoever was in power at the moment, and was a way of saying that you swore allegiance under duress or out of expediency, and didn't consider yourself bound by the forced concession.

p. 105: **Madison Cate:** Brownlow refers to two different men named Cate. The first reference, in the diary entry for December 25 (Christmas), is to a Baptist minister about seventy years old. He was arrested simply for cheering the Federal flag as it was carried past his house. Brownlow shared his food with this old man (p. 325). The second reference is to Madison Cate, in the diary entry for December 27. This man is a small farmer from Sevier county with six small children. He is described as very ill and likely to die (p. 328). His wife was initially prevented from seeing him, but Brownlow intervened on behalf of the grieving woman and her babe in arms. She is allowed in, and Brownlow describes the scene with typical bathos and self-importance, as well as perhaps genuine sympathy: "[S]he approached with faltering step, and sank down upon his heaving breast, bathed in tears of anguish. I asked her to give me the babe as she ventured up; for I saw that she was unconscious of having it in arms" (p. 329). My portrait of Madison Cate borrows selected details from both of these different men.

p. 105: **Dr. Gray:** Brownlow speaks favorably of Dr. Gray, the Confederate doctor who, at this time, was assigned to the prison. He mentions the almost daily visits and calls Gray "a gentleman and a humane man" (Brownlow, p. 307), and notes that he had some benches made for the prisoners.

p. 106: **"Come over here to the Parson":** This encounter between Harrison Self and Parson Brownlow is, of course, fictional, although it is virtually certain that they "met" each other in the crowded prison at some point, since they were both there at the same time, and Brownlow speaks of Self in his diary. Brownlow mentions Self's good reputation, implying he knew (or had heard) something about the Greeneville farmer's character. The later scenes between Self and Brownlow in the chapter are also fictional.

p. 110: **it was Jake and Henry they were after:** From Brownlow's diary entry for December 17: "Two more carts drove up with coffins in them and a heavy military guard around them. This produced in our circle of prisoners great consternation, for we did not know certainly who were to hang. They, however, came into the jail and marched out Jacob Harmon and his son Henry, and hung them up on the same gallows!" (p. 319).

p. 111: **"Susan, a brave girl, too":** Brownlow mentions flying his Union flag outside his home and defying the Confederates who threatened his peace. Later, a bombastic and melodramatic short novel was published, purportedly about the adventures of Miss *Martha* Brownlow (either an error or an intentional pseudonym for Susan). According to the novel, drunken Rebels with designs on her virtue threaten to remove the flag one day when her father is out of town. She heroically protects flag, home, virtue, and freedom by scaring the scoundrels off with a rifle. In real life, Susan accompanied her father on his speechmaking tours in the North, and she was often treated as a celebrity in her own right, as is dramatized in Chapter 9. See W. D. Reynolds, *Miss Martha Brownlow, Or, the Heroine of Tennessee: A Truthful and Graphic Account of the Many Perils and Privations Endured by Miss Martha Brownlow, the Lovely and Accomplished Daughter of the Celebrated Parson Brownlow, During Her Residence with Her Father in Knoxville* (Philadelphia: Barclay & Co., 1863).

CHAPTER 7: ON TRIAL

p. 115: **Knox County Court House:** The location of this trial is a presumption on my part. Almost immediately after the bridge burnings, martial law was declared in East Tennessee. The two hangings in Greeneville were authorized by drumhead courts created on the spot by Colonel Danville Leadbetter. In Knoxville, the accused bridge burners were tried in a military court convened for that purpose by Brigadier General W. H. Carroll, the Confederate commander of the District of Eastern Tennessee. Very possibly the venue was a military facility in the town, as is suggested by the summary treatment given Alexander Haun and Jacob and Henry Harmon. Harrison Self, however, received a more formal and extended trial by the military authorities, suggesting a more "legal" setting. I have therefore taken the liberty of placing the scene in the Knox County Court House, as the county court was not in session at the time.

A transcript of the trial exists and is the basis for the courtroom scenes in this chapter (*OR,* Series 2, vol. 1, Part 1, pp. 859–869). Both that record and other contemporary sources make clear that there was tension between the civilian and military legal systems. The civilian Federal District Court, then functioning as the Confederate District Court for East Tennessee, was presided over by Judge West H. Humphreys. From the point of view of District Attorney John Crozier Ramsey (see Chapter 5), Judge Humphreys was far too lenient. He often released defendants after they simply swore allegiance to the Confederacy or posted bond for their future good behavior—a successful money-raising activity for the Confederacy (McKenzie).

In contrast, the accused bridge burners—including Haun, the two Harmons, and Self—were tried in a military court made up of officers specifically assigned to that duty and willing (and no doubt expecting) to impose capital punishment. In a frustrated note to Confederate Secretary of War Judah Benjamin, District Attorney Ramsey complained, in effect, of being denied the chance to try the bridge burners in his own bailiwick. However, despite his best efforts, it is far from certain that he could have won death sentences in a civilian court—and Benjamin wanted nothing less.

p. 115: **John Baxter:** Harry's lawyer, John Baxter (1819–86), was a well-known figure—lawyer, banker, politician—in Knoxville at the time. He had moved there from North Carolina, where he had been in the state legislature. He was a friend of Brownlow's, and later, without the Parson's knowledge, interceded for him with the Confederate government. History records him as a Unionist who collaborated with the Confederates at the beginning of the war in the hope of easing tensions. He was a successful man for whom the war was both a problem and an opportunity, as it must have been for many men of stature and ambition. Thanks to original research by Donohue Bible, information has come to light about his manner of levying fees from condemned prisoners. **See note to p. 100, two visitors.**

p. 115: **slipped into the building at ground level:** This description of the courthouse (including the ground-level entrance) is based on a 1961 painting, by Russell Briscoe, of the Knox County Court House as it was in the Civil War era.

p. 115: **Haynes and Fleming:** The trial transcript refers to "Haynes and Baxter" as the lawyers representing Harry, but only Baxter is mentioned as present or active in the defense.

p. 116: **deeds of trust:** As explained in the notes to Chapter 6, Baxter did secure a deed of trust to land owned by Haun and land owned by the Harmons. I have no evidence that these deeds came about through a debate between Baxter and his law partners, such as the one recounted here. That is pure invention for dramatic purposes. It is true, however, that I know of no similar deed signed by Harrison Self. Why was Harry the exception?

I have supplied a possible reason, weaving it into the dramatization of the Harry-Baxter relationship. The nature of that relationship is, of course, my own invention. I have wanted to suggest (1) that Baxter's famous vacillations and compromises might have coexisted with a wishful core of integrity masquerading as practicality (or vice versa?), and (2) that Harry, unlike Haun or the Harmons, had a moral force, a straightforwardness of character, that Baxter clearly didn't have himself, but which he could recognize and respect. The outcome of the trial does seem foreordained, but I believe it is permissible to assume that Baxter might have wanted to do his best for Harry. Whatever one thinks of Baxter as a person or as a lawyer and public figure, he offers another perspective on the complicated loyalties of East Tennesseans.

p. 116: **Lucas:** The slave who appears as the factotum (or unacknowledged *genus loci*) of the Court House is an invented character. However, Knoxville had seven aldermen at this time, and it is quite possible that some of them owned slaves who would have been house servants or attendants in places of business.

p. 117: **Major Campbell:** Major T. J. Campbell was the judge advocate, the person assigned to bring the case against Harrison Self. *OR*, Series 2, vol. 1, Part 1, p. 860.

p. 117: **Harrison Self was pushed into the room:** It is reasonable, although not necessarily probable, that lawyer and client met at least once and at least briefly before the start of the actual trial. However, this meeting between Baxter and Self is invented.

p. 119: **"and of the Confederate States of America.":** In the courtroom, Self was, indeed, introduced as a citizen of the Confederacy. The transcript does not record that he voiced any objection at that time; however, I think it reasonable to assume that he considered himself a citizen of the United States, not the Confederacy.

p. 122: **Tom [Harmon]:** It is true that Thomas Harmon testified against Harrison Self on the same day (December 17, 1861) that his father and brother, Jacob and Henry Harmon, were publicly executed in Knoxville. However, the prior scenes depicted here—of Tom's being kept apart from his father and brother, his departure from the prison at the same time as they were being taken to the gallows, and his meeting with Campbell outside the courtroom—are all invented.

p. 125: **like guests at a banquet:** According to the details of the trial enclosed by General Carroll in his report to Secretary of War Judah Benjamin on December 27, the officers present as members of the court-martial on December 17 were "Lieutenant Colonel Bateman, Major Lucas, Major Thrasher, Captain McReynolds, Captain Thomas, Captain Cotter, and Captain Green." I have invented the seating plan for the room. The spoken words are taken almost verbatim from the transcript, although, like Cameron Judd in his account of the trial (Judd, pp. 98–108), I have sometimes broken up the sentences that occur consecutively in the record, presenting them as answers to invented questions from the judge advocate.

p. 128: **Lieutenant Colonel T. P. Bateman:** Lieutenant Colonel T. P. Bateman, of the 11th Tennessee Regiment, was, indeed, president of the court-martial. However, beyond that fact, I have no information about him. His feelings and opinions are products of my imagination.

p. 128: **Alexander Lowe:** We have already met Lowe as the tenant farmer in Harry's employ, and learned something of his putative character from Harry's and Lizzie's qualified reactions to him. The circumstances of his appearance at the trial are historically accurate. John Baxter learned (or said he learned) of Lowe's existence only toward the close of the first day of the trial, and needed a few days to make the man available. Hence the adjournment from the seventeenth to the twentieth of December. I have shortened Lowe's testimony, but kept very close to the transcript (*OR,* Series 2, vol. 1, Part 1, p. 864). The main change has been to restore some pronouns and articles that were dropped as a kind of shorthand. Thus, "has been strong Union man. Not been a fool about it. Never acted harshly" is reconstituted as "has been a strong Union man, but he wasn't a fool about it. He never acted harshly."

p. 130: **"Distinguished members of this court-martial":** Baxter's closing statement is not recorded in the transcript, so I have supplied him with one, drawing upon the themes that *are* represented in the record.

p. 132: **the order to clear the room:** According to the transcript, "The court was then cleared for deliberation." (*OR,* Series 2, vol. 1, Part 1, pp. 864–5). The private consultation of the judges, is, of course, unavailable, giving me some leeway to imagine the points that might have been discussed.

p. 133: **statement to that effect:** Right after Self was convicted on December 21, the members of the court-martial sent a letter to Brigadier General Carroll requesting commutation of the sentence. See "further historical note" under entry for p. 163.

p. 134: **"Of the first charge . . .":** I inserted a repetition of the specific charges, and deleted some pro forma wording, but in other respects, this is the exact verdict recorded in the transcript. *OR,* Series 2, vol. 1, Part 1, p. 865.

p. 134: **the verdict of history:** I would like to think that Bateman had a bad conscience about condemning a man like Harry to death, even though, as an officer in the Confederate Army, he was duty bound to achieve what he would have considered a military objective. In fact, the verdict of history was pronounced not too many years later, when Captain Fry and Brownlow argued that the bridge burners should have been treated as Union soldiers (i.e., honorable prisoners of war), not hanged as Confederate traitors (i.e., criminals). Later historians and interpreters of the bridge-burning episode have carried on the work of reparation.

My own perspective is slightly different. While I, too, see the hangings as a tragedy, I believe the gathering at Lick Creek Bridge puts the special case of East Tennessee under a spotlight. The confused loyalties of that torn region can be seen in the varying motives of persons as different as, for example, Self and Lowe, or Brownlow and Leadbetter. We no longer need to rehabilitate the Unionists or deplore the Confederates who were part of this story. We can, however, get to know them better.

Chapter 8: The Hangings

p. 137: **a small house on Union Street:** We do know that Elizabeth Self visited her father in prison on December 27, the day on which he was scheduled to hang. How and when she got to Knoxville, where she stayed, and what she did in the intervening days is all invention.

p. 137: **Andrew, Biddy, Jane:** Andrew is one of Lizzie's siblings, but the other names are invented. I believe Self had a number of children, but I do not know their names. As mentioned earlier, I am assuming that most of the other children were older, with homes of their own, so that they would not, at this time, be living with their parents. They would visit, but not be in a position to take over the household in their father's absence.

p. 138: **woman with an escort:** Corniah is referring to the social norms for respectable middle-class women before the war. Her sense of decorum is, however, slightly old-fashioned even for 1861, suggesting her aspirations toward gentility.

p. 139: **cousin Barbara:** Lizzie's cousin is an invented character.

p. 140: **corner of Union and Prince:** The street map I am using here comes from McKenzie, p. 129.

p. 144: **her uncle Jacob and her cousin Henry:** It is unlikely, but not impossible, that Lizzie witnessed the execution of her uncle and cousin.

p. 144: **Two ropes:** The description of the gallows is taken from the engraving included in Brownlow's *Sketches*, between pp. 322 and 323. Purportedly, the drawings in this volume are based on his verbal instructions to the illustrator, but their accuracy is seriously in doubt, and in some cases (e.g., the picture of the Greeneville gibbet within reach from the railroad cars) has been directly challenged. He or his publisher obviously selected scenes for their emotional impact and thematic importance, even though for most of them (the later scene with Lizzie at the prison being a notable exception), he was not an eyewitness.

p. 145: **cord had broken:** Donohue Bible records the breaking of the rope and the cruelty of making the father go through the horror of watching his son "die" twice. Brownlow says that there was only one rope, and so only one person could be hanged at a time. In both versions, the father must watch the execution of the son. Both versions are heartbreaking, but I have chosen the more dramatic incident of the broken rope.

p. 146: **how Lizzie met the Parson's daughter:** The meeting between Susan

Brownlow and Lizzie Self, along with all the scenes between them, is, of course, imaginary. We do know from Brownlow's diary of his imprisonment that he was in contact with his family, who were allowed to send in special food for him, etc. See Chapter 6, "Castle Fox."

p. 148: **"I have a message for Colonel Leadbetter"**: Admittedly, it is unlikely that Lizzie would have met with Danville Leadbetter in person. However, appeals for clemency were not unusual, and this invented meeting prepares the way for her historically documented appeal to Jefferson Davis.

p. 155: **The telegram**: Taken word-for-word from *OR* Series 2, vol. 1, Part 1, p. 866. As will be revealed in Chapter 9, Brownlow's version of this telegram, which he claims to have written (see *Sketches*, p. 327), is significantly different from the official record.

p. 156: **"his reprieve"**: According to Brownlow, Self stated that Fox had offered him a reprieve "if he would confess his guilt as a bridge-burner, under the gallows, and would state that BROWNLOW, TRIGG, BAXTER, and TEMPLE had put him up to it and furnished money to burn the bridges. . . . He replied to the wicked, malicious, and infernal offer that he could not say so, as it would not be true. What an effort to involve innocent men! And what a temptation for the man about to hang! The men who authorized this bribe deserve the lowest and hottest apartments in the infernal regions" (p. 328).

While I have kept closely to the terms of the bribe, I have focused on Brownlow alone as the man Self was asked to betray, and I have invented Fox's attempt to involve Lizzie in this "infernal" machination. Brownlow does not know, or record, who authorized the offer relayed by Fox. It is possible that Leadbetter did, for Brownlow sees him, not entirely accurately, as having control of the military courts in Knoxville. In his diary for January 28, 1862, Brownlow describes how "[t]hat prince of villains, tyrants, and murderers, *Colonel Leadbetter*, has come rushing into my room [during Brownlow's then-house arrest at home], and insultingly demanded to know when I would be ready to *leave the Confederacy*" (p. 353), implying that Leadbetter still had a role in the military governance of the region.

CHAPTER 9: FATHERS AND DAUGHTERS

p. 159: **Ladies of Philadelphia:** This group did present a flag to Brownlow's daughter Susan, in June of 1862, to honor her bravery in defending this symbol of the Union. In dating this event on the thirteenth rather than the fourteenth, I am following Celia Walker on the educational website, *Shades of Gray and Blue*, rather than E. Merton Coulter in his biography of Brownlow. My description of the flag is based on the image reproduced on the *Shades* website.

p. 159: **Academy of Music:** I do not know the exact location of the ceremony at which the Ladies of Philadelphia presented Susan Brownlow with a memorial flag on June 13, 1862 (*Shades* website). Nor do I know whether her father was present, and if so, what, if anything, he might have said. However, for several reasons, I have taken the liberty of placing the flag-bestowal ceremony in the Academy of Music in Philadelphia and allowed Brownlow to give one of his speeches there that same evening. His publisher was located in Philadelphia. The Academy of Music was completed in 1857, five years before the night in question. Earlier that spring, at the start of his northern speaking tour while in exile from Tennessee, Brownlow did give one of his standard speeches at "Pike's Opera-House" in Cincinnati (*Sketches*, p. 400). I have therefore conflated elements from the two closely related events, guided by memories of my own visit to the Academy of Music years ago.

p. 160: **release from Knoxville:** The various references to Brownlow's speaking tour are based on *Sketches* and Coulter's biography. For more on his publisher, George W. **Childs, see note to p. 164.**

p. 160: **pictures of her:** Most notably, Susan's portrait was featured in *Harper's Weekly* (December 21, 1861), p. 805. Her image accompanied a brief laudatory article describing her heroism in defending the flag. As the date indicates, her story received national coverage while her father was still in prison.

p. 161: **"Liberty & Union":** The inscription on the flag can be seen in the image on the *Shades of Gray and Blue* website: http://content.mtsu.edu/u?/shades, p. 38.

p. 163: **the thethe that occasion:** This is a transcript of the telegram as officially recorded in *OR*, Series 2, vol. 1, Part 1, p. 866.

Further historical note: Brownlow's intervention is the one that is generally remembered, but he was not the only one who tried to get Harry's sentence commuted. Several other attempts are documented in *OR,* Series 2, vol. 1, Part 1, pp. 859–865. Composed right after the guilty verdict was announced, the first appeal came, amazingly, from the very men who had just voted to hang Harrison Self. The president of the court-martial and one of the judges, representing them all, signed the following message to General Carroll:

> The members of the court-martial sitting for the trial of persons charged with bridge burning and other offenses beg respectfully to state that they have just concluded the trial of Harrison Self,

charged with having burned the Lick Creek bridge, and from the testimony in the case have found him guilty and under a sense of stern justice have sentenced him, the defendant, to death by hanging. The court is unanimous, however, in the be[lief]—from the testimony in the case, from the character of the prisoner, from what the members of the court know of his previous life and conduct, from his known kindness of heart and his standing in the community as a good citizen, and from many other circumstances occurring in the trial which cannot be transferred to paper—that this is a proper case for commutation of punishment. It is our belief that the public interest will suffer nothing from this course, but that on the contrary every object will be gained that can be attained by the extreme penalty of death.

Carroll was unmoved. On December 26, he wrote to T. J. Campbell, the judge advocate:

The sentence of the court-martial in this case is approved and the prisoner is ordered to be executed in accordance therewith at 4 p.m. tomorrow.

As the appeal was addressed to someone who dismissed it out of hand, very likely Jefferson Davis never realized the court had petitioned for clemency. From today's perspective, the message the court was sending looks confused, if not schizophrenic. If so, it reflects the disorienting effect of the bridge burnings.

The other petitions: As we have seen, the judges' appeal had no effect. A second petition, however, presumably did reach the Confederate capital. It was a letter, signed by two Confederate colonels, James W. Gillespie and R. R. Looney, along with "25 other officers and citizens," addressed to Jefferson Davis apparently on the same day as Elizabeth Self's petition (*OR,* Series 2, vol. 1, Part 1, p. 866). The argument was simple: "Already five persons have expiated upon the gallows for the burning of [the Lick Creek] bridge. The public danger which called for such punishment has in the opinion of the undersigned passed away."

The authors went on to affirm Self's relative innocence. "We have heard and believe the fact to be true that Self who at first assented to the proposal to burn the bridge relented and abandoned the purpose; said it was a bad thing; and we have reason to believe that he tried to dissuade his comrades from the execution of their purpose." They "recommended a milder punishment than that of

death," concluding with "the earnest hope that your excellency yielding to the dictates of mercy will spare this man's life." If Davis did see this petition, he appears to have turned it down. Nevertheless, the wisdom of the argument, or the stature of the cosigners, might have left an impression. The Gillespie-Looney petition might have prepared him to respond favorably to Brownlow's telegram on Lizzie's behalf.

A third appeal came from Lieutenant Colonel R. Arnold of the 29th Regiment of Tennessee Volunteers. Oddly, it was dated ten days *after* the sentence was remanded, so its motive is obscure. The author may have been unaware of recent events, or he may have used the occasion to improve his own standing. Addressed to the Confederate Secretary of War, Judah Benjamin, Arnold's letter claims to be a follow-up and confirmation of the court's initial petition.

Its tone is more informal but its range is more ambitious. Arnold's ultimate goal is to improve the image of the Confederacy. Show mercy, he argues, and you "will make our cause and our Government to be loved and idolized in the little circle of this man's distressed family where before they did not know the principles or appreciate the men who are the head of our Government." Be lenient, he urges, and you will encourage his sons, who have already borne witness against the bridge burners, to volunteer for the Confederate Army. "Would it not be best to let the young men volunteer and hold their father as a hostage for their good behavior? We would lose nothing by this course but we would probably gain much. Let us economize the muscle and sinew of the South and never let an opportunity pass to turn it to our account."

Arnold frequently invokes God, who "has prospered our cause," but he seems less devout than insinuating. He comes across as a salesman currying favor with his boss by suggesting a new marketing ploy. That is why his patronizing and somewhat demeaning view of Harrison Self needs to be seen in context. He confirms that the father trailed his son to Lick Creek in order to call him back, and that he tried to dissuade the other "mad men" from burning the bridge. However, he suggests that Self, too, was deluded. Writing as a "neighbor" who knew Harry well, Arnold calls him "a very good-natured, unsuspecting man, easily to be deceived, imposed upon or misled."

Arnold's letter is the primary evidence for Harry's true motive in going to the bridge that night—to save his sons (conflated into one son, Hugh, in the narrative). However, the father is described as suggestible and naïve, whereas I have portrayed him as intelligent and strong-willed. I chose to do so not only because the events of his life seem to call for such a man, but because I see his story as a window on the special circumstances of East Tennessee in the early years of the Civil War. If asked to justify my departure from Arnold's portrait, I would say that this letter writer had a clear motive for downplaying Self's independence of mind and spirit. It is to Arnold's advantage to show Self as a good-hearted bumbler, someone ignorant of, and not responsible for, his supposedly treasonous actions. Moreover, the tone and language of the letter become fulsome toward the end. Arnold is turning Self into a lost lamb in order to put the Confederate leaders on a par with a merciful God. Perhaps this is a clever ploy for Self's benefit, but I hear self-serving piety. I hear a man ingratiating himself with the authorities. Therefore, I feel no obligation to share Arnold's view of Self where not corroborated by others.

p. 163: **"HE WAS REPRIEVED"**: This is the answer to the question left hanging at the end of the previous chapter: was Harry hanged or saved? Only a couple of hours before he was scheduled to die, instructions came, by return telegram from Richmond, to suspend the sentence. Harry was returned to the Knoxville jail. What happened to him afterwards is unclear, but see the Epilogue for a wrap-up of what is known.

p. 164: **Childs:** George W. Childs, well aware of Brownlow's notoriety and the huge crowds he drew for his speeches, met with him just outside of Philadelphia, at the time of Brownlow's first visit to the city, and offered to publish his writings. At the time, Childs was an ambitious young entrepreneur who had started a growing bookselling business. Later, he would purchase the *Philadelphia Ledger Express* and build it into a major newspaper. The particular meeting posited for the morning of June 14 is speculation, though perfectly feasible. Of course, the use of the premises for the meeting with Evans is fictitious. Childs is credited with having invented the promotional "book tour," but it was Brownlow's notoriety, and in particular his fame as an incendiary speaker, that prompted many cities to invite him as their guest. He was often welcomed by crowds at the train station.

p. 165: **"Had I the power"**: What follows is a selective but only slightly altered quotation from Coulter's representation of the Englishman George Augustus Sala's quotation of a speech by Brownlow. Sala thought Brownlow's rhetoric "inspired by depravity, by delirium tremens, or by the dog days." See Sala's *My Diary in America in the Midst of War*, II (London: Tinsley Brothers, 1865), pp. 403–4. The main source here is E. Merton Coulter's biography of *William G.*

Brownlow: Fighting Parson of the Southern Highlands. Knoxville, TN: U of Tennessee P, 1999 [originally: Chapel Hill, NC: U of North Carolina P, 1937], pp. 228–29.

p. 166: **"to hang at four o'clock"**: The occasion for these revisions to the telegram is invented, but the changes in the wording are factual. As noted above, the telegram as Brownlow supposedly quoted it at the Academy of Music is the version that actually appears in the official record **(see note on what I wrote, p. 163)**. The version he supposedly created in the hotel room is the telegram as it appears in his book (*Sketches,* p. 327). Although I have invented the occasion for the revision, the timing is feasible.

p. 166: **until she married**: Susan Brownlow was, in fact, already married at this time, and there is evidence that she already had a child. Brownlow's immediate family was evicted from Tennessee about six weeks after he himself had left the state. I have taken a number of liberties with the historical Susan, not least of all in portraying her as still a single woman in the spring and summer of 1862.

p. 166: **"I call upon President Lincoln"**: This quotation comes directly from Brownlow's book. Very close to the end, he reproduces a letter he claims to have written to the editor of the *Philadelphia Press. Sketches,* p. 453.

p. 171: **A shadow fell across them**: The man with the crutch, later identified as William Evans, is a total fabrication. Hence, the entire episode of his encounter with Brownlow and his daughter is fictitious.

p. 177: **Brownlow had returned**: The Parson's postwar career is a checkered one, as noted in Chapter 9. He was Tennessee's first governor after the Civil War (April 1865–February 1869), and its senator in Washington immediately after that (March 1869–March 1875). As the face of Reconstruction in Tennessee, Brownlow's visage—with its looming forehead, round, soulful eyes, and many-layered jowls— became history's dartboard. His vituperative and vengeful nature, coupled with the powers of the governorship, had unfortunate consequences. Eager to punish his former enemies, he allied himself with the Radical Republicans in Congress, imposing harsh penalties on ex-Confederates. To begin with, he disenfranchised them. Through his intolerance, he fueled the counter-vengeance of the nascent Ku Klux Klan, founded in Tennessee between 1865 and 1866.

p. 177: **"this great advancement"**: Lincoln's declaration is factual. See *OR,* Series 1, vol. 30, Part 4, p. 25 and vol. 31, Part 3, p. 277. [Coulter, p. 249]. Of course, the response I've attributed to Brownlow is imaginary and, no doubt, unfair, even to the Parson's colossal ego.

p. 177: **United States Treasury agent**: Brownlow's appointment to this

The Reluctant Patriot

government position, no doubt intended as a sop to the barnstorming Unionist, is factual.

p. 179: **"Lizzie Self wrote to me":** While Self's survival can be documented, this letter is, as far as I know, fictitious. Brownlow's failing health is well documented in Coulter's biography. I did not invent the worst irony of his decline—the near-total loss of the power to lift a pen or to speak above a whisper.

p. 179: **"her father had come home":** In the federal census records for 1880, Harrison Self is identified as the head of his household in Greeneville. His birth year is listed as "1814" (though some family records say "1813," the date I've used), his marital status as "widowed," and his occupation as "Farmer." Lizzie, at forty-three, was undoubtedly the mistress of the house. https://www.censusrecords.com/record?id=usc%2f1880%2f1000151337546. Accessed most recently on June 19, 2014.

Chapter 10: Over the Mountain

p. 183: **Andy Slocum has spent the night:** The events of this chapter are fictional.

p. 190: **Brownlow became ill:** As noted elsewhere, my summary of Brownlow's experiences following Self's reprieve conforms closely to Brownlow's own account in *Sketches*.

p. 190: **"He died almost as soon as he got home":** Lizzie's account of Tom's fate is based on the record. According to Donohue Bible, "Thomas Harmon . . . died a few months after his father and brother from exposure and mistreatment in the wretched Confederate jail in Knoxville" (p. 135). A reproduction of Malinda Harmon's letter to Major General George B. Thomas includes these words: "the other [son, Thomas Harmon, was] released and died in a few days after he got home" (p. 138).

p. 191: **Cumberland Gap:** Andy's role as a "pilot"—including many of the details in the later part of this chapter—draw upon the autobiographies of real pilots like Daniel Ellis and Sam Massey. I have also included a few details from a present-day visit to the Cumberland Gap, which has been a National Historical Park since 1940.

p. 193: **Bill Edmondson:** This character is invented, though loosely based on the many men who followed the "pilots" into Kentucky.

264

CHAPTER 11: INTO THE BREACH

p. 200: **"second civil war"**: By 1866, "Governor Brownlow and other Radicals believed a second civil war within the state of Tennessee was inevitable, perhaps imminent." Severance, p. 11.

p. 201: **the right to vote**: In March of 1865, Brownlow became the first postwar governor of Tennessee. In June of that year, the General Assembly passed a franchise law that "temporarily forbade some eighty thousand ex-Confederates from voting. . . . In May 1866, a second, more severe, franchise law was passed. This new act created commissioners of registration for each county under direct executive control and permanently disfranchised all ex-Confederates." Thus, in June of 1867, freedmen were empowered to vote (the state had ratified the 14th Amendment on July 19, 1866) but ex-Confederates like Pete and Mr. Ogilvy were supposedly disenfranchised. Severance, pp. 5–8.

p. 201: **Hiram**: This character, along with his nephew Jed and the two men accompanying Pete in this scene are, like Pete himself, purely fictional, as is the entire episode of the encounter between Harry and Pete.

p. 201: **Klansmen**: The Ku Klux Klan was founded in Giles County, Tennessee, in 1865. By the time Brownlow was standing for reelection in the summer of 1867, Klansmen were a recognized threat to the freedmen's exercise of their newly granted right to vote. Severance, p. 9.

p. 201: **Tennessee State Guard**: "On February 20, 1867, the [A]ssembly passed the Act to Organize and Equip a State Guard." Severance, p. 11. For information about the nature and actions of the Guard, I have relied extensively on Severance's revisionist account of this militia. While this armed force did serve Brownlow's interests, it also provided necessary and often effective protection for the freedmen who were voting for the first time. The Ku Klux Klan is the most infamous of the groups that tried to prevent blacks from voting, but there were many other perpetrators of violence, especially in the middle and western counties. The scenes portrayed in this chapter are fictional, but the atmosphere of intimidation is not.

p. 204: **Salisbury Prison**: This prison in North Carolina, located near what is now Duke University, was established in late 1861, and began receiving prisoners in December of that year. The timing is close, but Hugh *could* have been sent there. http://www.rowancounty.info/salisburyprison/. Accessed September 30, 2016. The prison's early purpose as a jail for spies is mostly my own invention.

p. 205: **"That's my suit!":** This incident is based very closely on a true event that I have relocated from Virginia to Alabama. The prisoner who saw his suit on one of the guards, and who claimed that his own name could be found in the watch pocket, was Lieutenant Maginnis, of the 18th Regiment, Connecticut. The story can be found in a letter from Lieutenant Colonel Farnsworth, 1st Connecticut Cavalry, who was confined in Libby Prison, near Richmond, Virginia, from July 14, 1863 to March 14, 1864. *Report of the Sanitary Committee*, p. 379.

p. 209: **recruiting office on Main Street:** I do not know the exact location of the recruiting office.

p. 210: **Captain John Kirk . . . both white men and black:** Two companies of militia were raised in Greene County, both captained by a man named "Kirk" (their relationship to each other, if any, is unknown to me). "J[ohn] L. Kirk recruited volunteers from Greene and Washington counties, land rich in Radical manpower. On June 6, he mustered his sixty-eight recruits (race ratio unknown)." Severance, p. 49. I have taken a few liberties in dramatizing a scene from the day before the mustering. For example, most of the black members of this mixed company were later recruited from Montgomery County. However, in general, I have tried to honor the historical record.

p. 219: **thirty of Kirk's company:** A small group of men under Lieutenant Burchfield were, in fact, sent into Robertson County to quell disturbances at the polls. However, the details and events of the scene as depicted here are fictional.

p. 221: **their tickets:** Persons registered to vote were given tickets for one candidate or the other, which they then deposited in the ballot box on Election Day. Severance reports an incident in which some illiterate black voters presented tickets marked "Etheridge," but, when asked, said they thought they were voting for Brownlow.

Acknowledgments

I grew up several states north of the events in this story—and almost a hundred years later—so my project necessarily began in libraries and museums. The authors, reference works, and displays I consulted are too numerous to mention, but I owe all of them my first and most heartfelt thanks. They helped to situate me in Harry's world. There were famous works like James M. McPherson's *Battle Cry of Freedom: The Civil War Era* (New York: Oxford UP, 1988) and Allen C. Guelzo's *Fateful Lightning: A New History of the Civil War & Reconstruction* (New York: Oxford UP, 2012). Some were unexpected finds like Juanita Leisch's *Who Wore What? Women's Wear 1861–1865* (Gettysburg, PA: Thomas Publications, 1995). For background information, I turned often to Richard Nelson Current's *Lincoln's Loyalists: Union Soldiers from the Confederacy* (Boston, MA: Northeastern UP, 1992). Contemporary diaries and autobiographies were invaluable, and so were the data retrieved from census records, trial transcripts, and, of course, *The War of the Rebellion: A Compilation of the Official Records of the Union and Confederate Armies*, a mammoth, digitized, searchable "eHistory" maintained by Ohio State University.

If documents are the red meat of research, firsthand testimonies, in all their subjectivity, are the appetizing fruit. I relied heavily on William Gannaway Brownlow's diary of his retreat into the Smoky Mountains and his time in the Knoxville prison, where he met Harry and Lizzie in person: *Sketches of the Rise, Progress, and Decline of Secession, with a Narrative of Personal Adventures Among the Rebels* (Philadelphia: George W. Childes, 1862), referred to as *Sketches* in the notes. Another eyewitness account, more objective yet still personally invested, is Oliver P. Temple's *East Tennessee and the Civil War*, 1899 (rpr. John City TN: The Overmountain Press, 1995). It's an inescapable reference work. Several autobiographies of the colorful mountain men of the region helped me portray Andy Slocum: Daniel Ellis, *Thrilling Adventures of Daniel Ellis, the Great Union Guide of East Tennessee for a Period of Nearly Four Years During the Great Southern Rebellion; Written by Himself* (New York: Harper & Brothers, 1867); Samuel E. Massey, *Captain Sam Massey, Union Scout Living in Enemy Territory*, ed. Chester A. Massey, Jr. (Knoxville,

TN: Chester A. Massey, Jr. Inc., 2002).

If there is a single authority on the events and *dramatis personae* of the bridge burnings, it is Donahue Bible, a descendant of Harry's contemporaries and a regional historian who did me the great kindness of answering some of my questions by email. In the notes, his early account is listed as Bible(1): *Broken Vessels: The Story of the Hanging of the 'Pottertown' Bridge Burners November-December, 1861* (Mohawk, TN: Dodson Creek Publishers, 1996). However, his definitive work, identified as Bible(2), is *The Hanging of the Greene Country Bridge Burners. Tennessee Ancestors: A Tri-Annual Publication of the East Tennessee Historical Society* 21:2 (August 2005), 130–139. An email to me, Bible(3), is dated October 9, 2013. In the same issue of *Tennessee Ancestors*, there is another fine contribution: Dorothy Kelly's "The Bridge Burnings and Union Uprising of 1861" (123–129).

Many books helped me understand the various mindsets of the period. For information about the heritage of independence in the mountain counties, I am grateful to Max Dixon's *The Wataugans* (Johnson City, TN: The Overmountain Press, 1976, rpr. 1989). Robert Tracy McKenzie was my guide for the chapters set in Knoxville, and I owe a large debt to his splendid, authoritative *Lincolnites and Rebels: A Divided Town in the American Civil War* (New York: Oxford UP, 2006). The fictional events of Harry's postwar service in Governor Brownlow's militia-style police force draw heavily upon Ben H. Severance's wonderfully detailed, revisionist portrait of *Tennessee's Radical Army: The State Guard and its Role in Reconstruction, 1867–1869* (Knoxville: U of Tennessee P, 2005). Both books are essential to an understanding of the locale and the period. There was, of course, another side to all these stories of white men fighting for the country's future. I am grateful to William Andrews for his edited collection of *Six Women's Slave Narratives* (The Shoenberg Library of Nineteenth-Century Black Women Writers, New York: Oxford UP, 1988).

As far as I know, only one other modern author has dramatized the events central to this book. In *The Bridge Burners: A True Adventure of East Tennessee's Underground Civil War* (Johnson City, TN: The Overmountain Press, 1995;1996: cited as Judd(1)), Cameron Judd gives a carefully researched account "in a novelized fashion" of the bridge-burning episode, including the incarceration, trial, and reprieve of Harrison Self. In his historical novel, *The Shadow Warriors* (New York: Bantam, 1997: cited as Judd(2)), he further fictionalizes many elements of the same story, retelling the burning of the Lick Creek Bridge. I'm grateful to this author for helping to inspire my own interest in these events, and I am pleased to join him in making fiction out of these public materials, but the characterizations and invented scenes, as well as the form and style of my book, are entirely different. In the house of history are many fictional mansions.

Let me turn now to the people who met with me in person or by letter, giving of their time and perspective with incredible generosity. I found Celia S. Walker on the eighth floor of the Jean and Alexander Heard Library, on the campus of Vanderbilt University in Nashville. As Director of Special Projects, she was the guiding spirit behind *Shades of Gray and Blue*, an educational website (www.civilwarshades.org) that catalogues images from the Civil War period in Tennessee. Celia listened attentively as I talked about my project, and that alone was a gift at that very early stage. She also gave me some crucial referrals, starting with Robert McKenzie's *Lincolnites and Rebels* mentioned above. Finally, she pointed me toward the Center for Historic Preservation at Middle Tennessee State University, and to its then-assistant director, Caneta S. Hankins.

The Center was responsible for several monographs, as well as reams of articles and columns of web prose, anthologized stories and traveling displays. I quickly ordered a large book called *Ploughshares and Swords: Tennessee Farm Families Tell Civil War Stories,* coauthored by Ms. Hankins and Michael Thomas Gavin, a scholar associated with the Tennessee Civil War National Heritage Area. Like *Shades of Gray and Blue,* it links physical heritage with handed-down stories that help us imagine what life was like during the Civil War.

Via email, Ms. Hankins told me about the Tennessee Century Farms Program, which identifies properties that have been in the same family and kept in "continuous agricultural production for at least 100 years." She gave me the names of several people she thought would welcome me as a visitor to their historic freehold, and it was Ann Birdwell, of Still Hollow Farm, who offered me the chance to walk into history. I spent several hours exploring the land and talking with the Birdwells. In my imagination, I was visiting the world of Harrison Self, and I am grateful to Ann for that unique opportunity. Some of my experience that day found its way, directly or indirectly, into the diary of Elizabeth Self.

My notes and photographs were invaluable, but Ann Birdwell gave me something even more useful—an introduction to the executive director of the Nathanael Greene (now the Greeneville Greene County History) Museum in Greeneville, Tennessee, the town where "my" bridge burners had lived. Later that day, I walked into his office.

Earl Fletcher was leaning back in his chair as he spun around to face me. He was a dapper man, with a genial air of old-fashioned courtesy, and he welcomed me to their domain—for his wife, Betty, was smiling at me from her own desk across the room. I would later come to enjoy his gift for retro-formality, a genuine but twinkle-eyed gesture of affection for a bygone style, in, for example, the closing of one of his official letters to supporters of the museum: "Until we are able to converse again, I shall always remain . . . Your Humble Servant, Earl W. Fletcher Jr., Executive Director." It was another revelation, however, that stunned me on that first visit.

I'd wanted to ask, among other things, whether Mr. Fletcher could help me identify the location of the Harrison Self farm. I knew, and on a later occasion would visit, the rural area where many of the Greene County bridge burners had lived. I would visit C. A. Haun's grave in the cemetery behind the Concord Baptist Church, and stand before the tombstones of Joseph Harmon and his son Thomas in the family plot just off Pottertown Road. If possible, I'd wanted to set foot on the ground Harry and Lizzie had walked in their happier days before the war.

Mr. Fletcher could not give me that address, but he named somebody who might be able to, and in the course of talking with me about the period in which I was interested, he mentioned that he was, himself, a descendant of an executed bridge burner. Three feet away from me, in some figurative but also very literal way, sat a living link with a family I had known only as names on a page or on gravestones. This was history as flesh and blood.

Sadly, Earl Fletcher died on August 22, 2014, before I could speak with him again to confirm and enlarge some details that arose during our one conversation. He was a deeply respected and influential member of the Greeneville community, and he is one of the many local historians to whom this book owes a fundamental debt. At the time I met him, my project was only just beginning. I regret that I was never able to tell him how very much his help encouraged me. I left his office with the address of someone who probably knew the most about the bridge burnings.

If anyone had a right to these stories, it was Mr. Donohue Bible, whose work I mentioned above. He is an amateur historian with highly developed skills as a researcher and a very professional code of objectivity, despite his private investment in the truth of what had happened during one of Greeneville's darkest hours. Having diligently searched through family papers, old legal documents, and other local sources, he had published his findings on several occasions. I've mentioned his important article in *Tennessee Ancestors*, but it was his earlier typescript, *Broken Vessels* (1996), that was my urtext. It had been one of my earliest excitements on the trail, as I'd reverently handled the original in the library of the Tennessee Historical Society in Nashville.

In reply to an emailed request, I received a generous reply. It was thorough and businesslike, but with a narrative energy and flow that came from long engagement with the tale and a never-flagging sense of its interest and importance. Mr. Bible explained that he had not paid much attention to Harrison Self, but he went on to give me a telling insight into the testimony of Alexander Lowe (or Low) at Harry's trial. Thanks to him, I gained a better appreciation for the complexities of the so-called "trials" of the saboteurs.

It wasn't until I met the local historians, the custodians of a past still ticking in their DNA, that I realized my obligation to Harry, even as I transmuted him into fiction. I wanted to tell his story, and for the chance to do so, I am thankful to Aubade Publishing. I am forever grateful to Cosette Puckett, who understood Harry at first meeting, and whose literary training, practical wisdom, and artistic talent made her the most wonderful reader and designer an author could have. Joe Puckett, the book's editor, caught every slip of the key, but what I appreciate the most is the care and interest he brought to every aspect of the novel. It was a joy and a privilege to work with the visionaries at Aubade Publishing. I owe them my warmest thanks. In a business too often associated with passing trends and commercial coups, they look for eternal stories and preserve what they care about.

Finally, and dearest to my heart, are the friends and family who believed in my writing before anyone else did. In the old days, I rarely began a story without remembering David Luther Pickles, a Rilkean poet channeling Hemingway, who badgered me to "start with one good sentence." For decades now, I've had the great good fortune to know Michael Trussler, my cherished colleague and correspondent. He's a Canadian writer of tantalizing stories and soul-searching essays, always asking the questions humanity can't answer. He sees the hairline cracks in the quotidian. Poet, scholar, teacher, and memoirist, he has always been remarkable for his learning and compassion. The genial and the abstruse often meet in his emails, which challenge me with their brilliance and warm me with their kindness. His interest and support have been a constant throughout the years, and I am grateful for his friendship.

I owe an immeasurable debt to Martin Roper, an Irish writer, teacher, and reader *par excellence,* whose devotion to literature transcends all the vagaries of fashion. His lean and beautiful art is about the timeless and the real in the valley of the shadow. When I sent the manuscript to him, it was because we are the sort of friends who catch each other's eye, and share the same thought, in any gathering of writers. In many ways that matter, we speak the same language. He found the typo, the overheated word, the slip in point of view, but what I treasured most were the frequent, lovely notes on the characters and their lives. It was like meeting my story all over again in the company of a wise literary soul. Thank you, Martin.

Others who have listened patiently to this Civil War tale, strengthening my resolve to tell it, include my sister, Elizabeth Blackwell, my brother, Will Kuhlmann, and, in spirit, my parents, Ann and Rudolf Kuhlmann. My ultimate gratitude, in this as in all things, is to my husband, Michael. On this project, he was my first and, for a long time, my only reader. A writer himself, and a person of wide experience and deep intelligence, he has an unerring eye for the overblown phrase, the lazy characterization, or the missing link in a narrative. I cannot imagine writing this book, or living my life, without his support and companionship. This book is dedicated to him with all my love.

SUSAN LOHAFER grew up in New Jersey. She is a graduate of Harvard (B.A.), Stanford (M.A.), and New York University (Ph.D.). During her teaching career at the University of Iowa, she specialized in short fiction theory. Her books include *Coming to Terms with the Short Story* and *Reading for Storyness: Preclosure Theory, Empirical Poetics, and Culture in the Short Story*, as well as the co-edited volume *Short Story Theory at a Crossroads*. Shorter works include a personal essay listed as a Notable Essay of 2011 in *The Best American Essays 2012*, and short stories in venues like *The Southern Review* and *The Antioch Review.* She now lives with her husband in Tennessee, where her interests in creative writing and nineteenth-century history come together in her debut novel *The Reluctant Patriot,* a fictional retelling of a true story from the region's past.